I0604402

KYRIE WANG

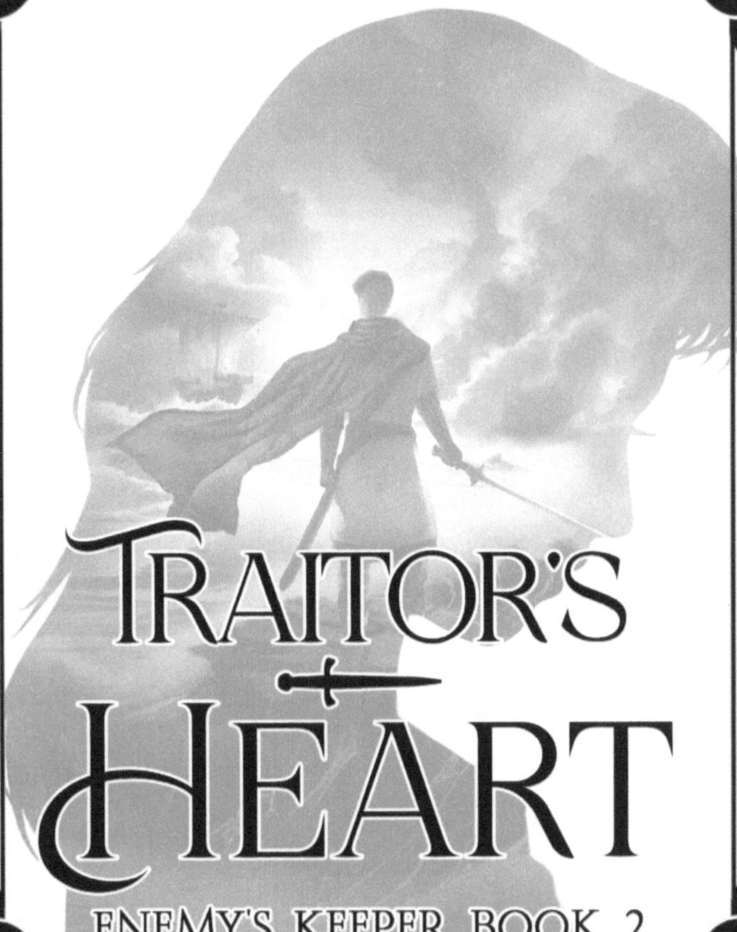

TRAITOR'S HEART

ENEMY'S KEEPER BOOK 2

Traitor's Heart (Enemy's Keeper Book 2)

Copyright © 2025 by Kyrie Wang

All rights reserved. No part of this publication may be reproduced, distributed, or transmitted without the prior written permission of the author, except in the case of brief quotations embodied in critical reviews. Please do not encourage or participate in piracy of copyrighted material. Thank you for respecting the hard work of this author.

For permission requests, write to the author, addressed "Permissions Request," at author@kyriewa ng.com

ISBN: 978-1-0696887-1-2 (Paperback)
ISBN: 978-1-0696887-2-9 (Hardcover)
ISBN: 978-1-0696887-0-5 (Electronic Book)

Any references to historical events, real people, or real places are used fictitiously. Names, characters, and places are products of the author's imagination.

Cover: GetCovers.com
Editor: Allison D. Reid
Map: Kyrie Wang and Sen Li
Back Matter Character Art: Kyrie Wang and Sen Li

Silver Dreams Publishing

For the author's artwork, music, and more, please visit KyrieWang.com

A Note to My Readers

Enemy's Keeper is a **no-magic historical fantasy** series in which the last Vikings, now rebels and mercenaries, discover gunpowder in a world that's almost 11th-century Europe, but not quite.

I've blended in elements from other times and places, including:

- The first hand grenades

- Celtic tribes thriving beyond their historical timeframe

- Advanced shipbuilding (vessels with hulls and hammocks, ahead of their time)

Historical purists may find these liberties challenging, but readers seeking heart-pounding adventure, wholesome romance, and boldly reimagined worlds will find much to love. Welcome to the journey!

Newsletter Subscriber Bonuses

Receive a free ebook of **The Thief's Keeper** *(An Enemy's Keeper Prequel)*
when you <u>subscribe to my newsletter!</u>
KyrieWang.com/EK
Bonus: A free **medieval fantasy coloring book** and a **graphic novel** The
First Dance (An Illustrated Epilogue of The Thief's Keeper).
1-2x a month, I send newsletters with book giveaways, character art, writing
updates, historical tidbits, and more.

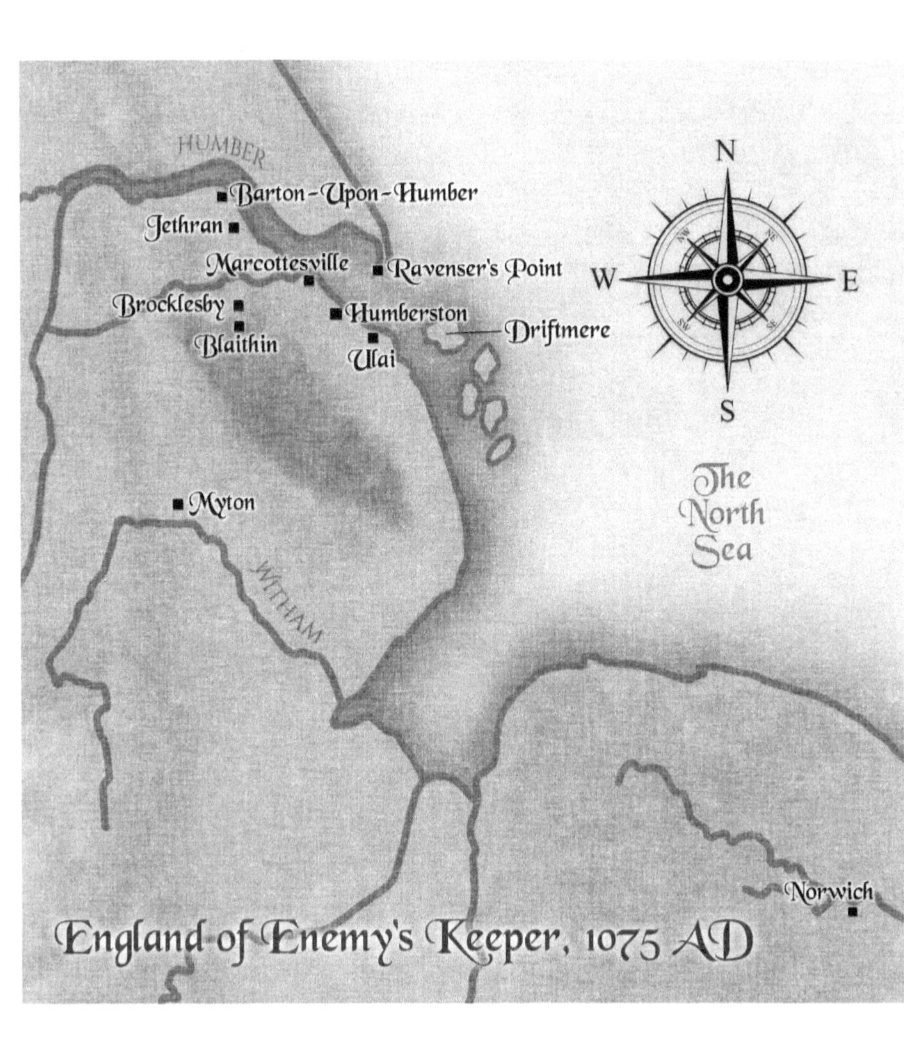

HUMBER
Barton-Upon-Humber
Jethran
Marcottesville
Ravenser's Point
Brocklesby
Humberston
Blaithin
Driftmere
Ulai
N
W E
S
The North Sea
Myton
WITHAM
Norwich
England of Enemy's Keeper, 1075 AD

Characters

	Loyal to King William	Rebels
Bishop	His excellency, Geoffrey de Montbray	
Earl		Lord Ralph de Gael
Baron	Lord Seville	Lord Yeaton
Knight	Jacques Verdun	Ransley Boltan Edward Boltan Toby Boltan
Squire	Matthew Marcotte	
Foot soldier/ Mercenary	Aelfric Norman Rochefort	Axlan Cilebi
Orphan	Evelyn Marcotte Marie Marcotte	Zelrin Emma

UNDETERMINED ALLEGIANCE
Aliwyn
Kato
Miriam (deceased)

VASFIANS
Reiya
Namanti
Abithi
Domilo

Characters List

Loyal to King William

Aelfric – Aliwyn's childhood sweetheart. An English foot soldier serving the Marcotte family and Lord Seville.

Matthew Marcotte – Norman squire. Aelfric's close friend.

Evelyn Marcotte – Matthew's older cousin.

Marie Marcotte – Matthew's younger cousin.

Norman Rochefort – Former Norman knight. Dismissed due to drunken behavior.

Lord Seville – Norman baron training Matthew for knighthood.

Geoffrey de Montbray ("His Excellency") – High-ranking Norman bishop tasked with crushing the rebellion.

Sir Jacques Verdun – Norman knight serving under Bishop Geoffrey de Montbray.

Rebels

Tobias (Toby) Boltan – Young rebel leader with many secrets.

Ransley Boltan – Toby's father; mastermind behind the murder of the Marcotte family.

Edward Boltan – Toby's uncle.

Emma – A girl Toby rescued from the streets.

Zelrin – A teenage boy Toby rescued from the streets.

Lord Ralph de Gael – One of the three earls leading the Revolt of the Earls; resides in Norwich.

Lord Yeaton – English baron who lives in Brocklesby's manor.

Axlan – Former English aristocrat whose land was confiscated by the Normans.

Cilebi – Danish mercenary.

Undetermined Allegiance

Aliwyn – Healer's apprentice living in a watermill.

Miriam – Former healer of Brocklesby and the mentor of Aliwyn and Aelfric.

Kato – English peasant who sells ale for Norman Rochefort. Unwanted by the Vasfian tribes.

Vasfians

Reiya – Chief of the Mehi tribe.

Abithi – Reiya's mother.

CHAPTER 1
THE PROMISE KEEPER

September 30, shortly after Aliwyn and Toby jumped into the Brocklesby Ravine

Matthew

Matthew had no warning that the search for Aliwyn would end with his disappearance.

Night still cloaked the river's shore in shadow. Matthew hardened his jaw to stop his teeth from chattering while he trudged through the mud. The redheaded Vasfians behind him muttered in their guttural tongue as the light of their torches crept over rocks and matted leaves.

Hours had passed since Aliwyn's scream echoed through the ravine. Matthew had searched relentlessly, yet no trace remained of her or of Tobias Boltan, the English rebel whose family had ambushed Matthew's own.

Evelyn and Marie had recounted how the Boltans killed nearly his entire household aboard their family's ship. The girls had only escaped with Aelfric's help. Weeks later, when Matthew was captured, Tobias' father had locked him in a cellar without water. Those murderous beasts! Matthew would've died in that rotten cell if not for Aelfric's desperate raid and rescue. Only Matthew had walked away that night.

Now, Tobias had escaped the bridge where he'd been suspended and kidnapped Aelfric's adopted sister. Matthew clenched his fists. When he saw Tobias again, he'd strangle that imbecile with his bare hands.

But for now, he could only drag his soaking boots.

The air was thick with the scent of damp earth and decay. Every boulder by the dark waters made Matthew stiffen. He would approach each one, half-expecting to find Aliwyn's lifeless body in the torchlight, only to find shadows instead. He'd release a tense breath only to have his chest tighten all over again. Aliwyn had to swim better than the child he'd accidentally knocked into the water. He couldn't lose her, not after losing Aelfric. The memory of his best friend's death clawed at him, but he shoved it aside. Fear would only sabotage him.

Reiya, the chief of the Mehi tribe, marched ahead with her green and red checkered tunic gleaming in the fire's glow. This wandering was getting them nowhere. Suppressing a cough, Matthew caught up to her.

"Tobias and Aliwyn could've left the forest by now," he said. "Did your men find anything? Any clue where they could've gone?"

She didn't look at him. "I have noticed no clues. I thought your commanding knight, Jacques Verdun, was already investigating Myton."

"Tobias could've been lying to us about his men traveling to Myton. It's only a riverside hamlet. They must be sailing elsewhere from there." Matthew struggled to swallow his impatience. "What exactly did your warriors confiscate from the Boltans? Just those reeking crates?"

"Every delectable one," she muttered.

"What were the Boltans hiding? They packed the crates with manure to deter thieves."

Reiya shot him a glare. "My spoils are none of your business. I already spoke to your commander about what to do with them."

She flipped back her cape and bypassed him. Matthew's nostrils flared. Sir Verdun should've kept a few crates for a thorough investigation. Whatever the Boltans had concealed inside, like maps, battle plans, or letters, might hold clues to where they had taken Aliwyn.

His Excellency, a Norman bishop, should never have allied with these Vasfians to defeat the rebels, but no matter. The alliance wouldn't last. Once Reiya's failure to capture Tobias became known, His Excellency could annul the treaty.

Matthew's body ached from exertion. He pulled a glove over his frigid right hand, the one bitten by the girl he'd knocked into the ravine. The pine sap salve Aliwyn had applied stuck to the leather, and he growled. As Matthew leaned against a tree, tugging at his glove, the Vasfians stopped to sip from their drinking horns.

Reiya watched him while fingering the stock of her crossbow. She was hiding something. He could feel it. How to talk her into revealing information?

"We'll search till daybreak," she said. "If we still don't find them, I'll dispatch messenger doves to my sister tribes. They'll help us capture them."

"What will they do to Aliwyn?"

"My people do not keep prisoners." Reiya shrugged. "We kill them."

"Kill her?" Matthew pushed off the trunk. "You'll kill her for being kidnapped?"

Reiya's voice was quiet but seething. "She wasn't kidnapped."

"Yes, she was! I saw Tobias grab her and force her over the edge. I don't know how he got off that bridge, but Aliwyn is innocent!"

"She's at my mercy if I find her within my territory. And even if she didn't free Toby, she invited him inside with her thoughts."

What a pile of pagan hogwash. "Her *thoughts*?"

"Yes. Don't your people practice this thing called prayer?" Reiya flipped back her braid. "You should've seen Aliwyn kneeling by the bridge and talking to Tobias. That look on her face said everything."

Matthew's eyes widened. Aliwyn had done what?

"Aliwyn also attacked my warrior when Toby crawled into her mill," Reiya continued. "Otherwise, my warrior would've shot him in the eye."

"We already talked about this. Aliwyn was scared. She was trying to run!"

"Don't forget she's English, like those rebels."

So what if Aliwyn was English? Not all the English were rebels. Aelfric had been an Englishman, and he'd fought for the Norman crown until the end. Heat flashed down Matthew's chest. This incompetent chief just didn't want to take responsibility for Tobias' escape.

Reiya turned to keep walking, but Matthew rounded on her.

"Once you send those messenger pigeons, I'm leaving for Barton-upon-Humber. I'll report to His Excellency's knights that Tobias escaped under your watch. We'll see what happens to your alliance."

Reiya widened her stance, her upper lip curling. A chill ran down Matthew's back. He'd been desperate to counter her, but maybe he'd gone too far. *Bloody Kraken*. If only he weren't alone with a horde of redheads. He reached for his sword, but the warriors surrounding him made him freeze.

Reiya must know that if he vanished around Brocklesby, her Mehi tribe would be the prime suspect.

"You're too weary to walk to Barton," Reiya said. "My warriors can take you to rest in my hillfort until tomorrow at noon."

"I'm not resting—"

"If I don't find Tobias and Aliwyn by noon, I'll travel with you to Barton and notify your warband."

Matthew scoffed. "That means a whole morning lost. I'm leaving at day-break."

"I deserve more time to recapture Tobias," she said through her teeth. "Don't tell your men just yet. Do we have an understanding?"

Her warriors tightened their circle around him with their crossbows in hand. Matthew stumbled back, his hand twitching toward his sword. Aelfric would've smooth-talked himself into a deal, but Aelfric was dead. A stabbing pain pulsed up Matthew's stomach, and it was all he could do to keep standing.

"Let's search until the next bend," Reiya muttered.

Matthew dragged his boots after her. No signs of Aliwyn. No resolution to her fate if she were found by a Vasfian tribe other than the Mehi. The heavy chainmail covering his body seemed to double in weight.

Reiya's claim that Aliwyn had sided with Tobias gnawed at him. Villagers had been flogged for feeding the rebels' horses far to the west. Any sympathy for the rebels meant torture or death. But why should he believe Reiya? Aliwyn wouldn't talk to a rebel after all Aelfric had been through. She wouldn't betray Matthew, either, after inviting him to sleep upstairs just hours ago.

Regardless of what Reiya said, Aliwyn had been kidnapped. If he didn't find her soon, the rebels would sell her as a thrall or force her into marriage. What could Tobias be doing to her tonight? A sour taste flooded Matthew's tongue, and he coughed again.

Reiya marched ahead of him. Her cape barely hung low enough to hide that she wore a tunic, trousers, and stockings like a man. Utterly indecent. Matthew stiffened when she turned around and said something garbled.

He frowned at her as he stepped past. Turning his head while wearing the cumbersome helmet made his neck muscles spasm. Pain blurred his vision. Reiya sure looked funny with her face split into two. His foot caught against his leg, and he crashed onto his side. The impact knocked the air from his lungs.

Matthew's father had beaten him many times. After the worst episode, Matthew hadn't been able to move for days. This fall felt just as painful. He couldn't react when Reiya squatted, withdrew his sword from its sheath, and flung it aside.

Panic flared as Reiya knelt on his shoulder, holding him down by his neck. "Hold still, Matthew Marcotte. If I wanted to choke you, I would've done so days ago."

Vasfian boots surrounded him. Matthew eyed the crossbow tips and studded clubs hovering close to his shoulders. The stench of rotting leaves clung to his nostrils, and his eyes bulged. He writhed as Reiya's fingers squeezed the length of his sore neck.

For four days following Aelfric's death, he had reluctantly resided with her scouting team as they'd herded Tobias and Edward Boltan toward a dead end. Matthew had locked himself in the tempest in his mind and snapped at everyone who got close. Somehow, Reiya had resisted strangling him then.

"Your glands are very swollen." Reiya's freckled face blurred in and out of focus. "You should've stayed in the mill after all. I didn't know you were sick."

Matthew tried to speak but coughed instead. Reiya muttered something to her warriors with a wave of her hand, and he rolled onto his side. "What did you tell them?"

"To bring you to my hillfort in Blaithin."

"Why? I'm not going! I must find Aliwyn!"

Reiya smiled. "Then try standing again."

Matthew's arms wobbled like eel jelly. He couldn't push himself up as the slick leaves slipped under his hands. What a disaster. He needed a drink, some quality fermented pear poiré from Normandy and not the frothy horse piss the English called ale.

The warriors approached him with a large blanket and spread it on the ground. Matthew coughed and gasped for air. Better comply or enjoy having his head smashed in. Two warriors grabbed him by the arms, and Matthew supported his weight as they pulled him onto the blanket. He landed with his boots in the air.

His heart hammered. He was being pulled from the search team. If the Vasfians found Aliwyn without him, what would they do?

"Aliwyn's innocent," he croaked. "Don't hurt her if you find her."

Reiya eyed him up and down. "With you in this condition, I'm ending the search for tonight. We'll take turns carrying you back to my hillfort. Everyone must rest. Now, take off your chainmail. You weigh as much as a cow."

"But you'll still send messenger pigeons!" he shouted. "You'll tell the other tribes to find Aliwyn and shoot her!"

"I told you…we simply don't keep prisoners." Reiya sighed and rubbed her forehead. "Remove your chainmail and helmet."

"I can't. This is not even my armor; it belongs to Sir Verdun. I borrowed it and I'm responsible. You must know how much it costs."

"We're not stealing your armor. We must carry it separately."

"I'm not taking it off."

Her glare was piercing. Matthew couldn't stop his teeth from chattering. Forget how much armor costs; taking it off meant getting shot through the heart.

Reiya shifted her weight as she squatted, her expression unreadable. She began speaking in Vasfian to those behind Matthew. His vision tunneled, and soon a heavy cloth fell over his head.

"Mmph!" Matthew grabbed what felt like a damp sack clinging to his face.

The drawstrings around his neck tightened, and someone kicked him onto his back. Matthew flailed his limbs in vain. Hands grabbed his arms and pinned them down. Boots pushed on his shoulders to roll him until he was wrapped within the blanket with his arms trapped against his sides.

"What is the meaning of this?" he cried. The sackcloth stank of pungent herbs.

What felt like a foot landed on his chest.

"Calm down," Reiya said, rubbing her boot against his sternum. "This blanket is medicated to calm warriors who have been wounded.

"It's not calming at all! Let me out!"

"I'll unwrap you eventually, but pledge to wait till noon tomorrow before you report Tobias missing. I need time to redeem myself. If I don't find him, I'll go with you to Barton to notify your superiors. Only I should deliver this news."

"I'm not your prisoner! I'll leave whenever I want!"

He thrashed with fire in his veins, but the medicated vapors were taking effect. Each kick felt like treading knee-deep in water. Finally, Reiya's boot lifted, and a sharp blow struck the side of Matthew's knee. He yelped. Her boot stomped back on his chest.

"Listen, Norman squire." Her voice was quiet but charged. "Your warbands are already scouring the forests for the rebels. Your report that Tobias is missing won't increase their efforts. You just want to humiliate me and my Mehi tribe. Am I right?"

How dare she say such a thing, even if she *was* right? Matthew squirmed as the pain in his knee spread over his thigh. *By the Devil's tail.* She sure knew where to strike.

"I'm also taking a risk by bringing you to my hillfort," she muttered. "Behave, and my warriors won't hurt you. Understand?"

Matthew gritted his teeth. She'd regret this. As soon as he arrived in her hillfort, he'd search amongst her spoils of war for clues as to where the Boltans were traveling. Maybe he'd also find evidence of the Vasfians' treachery against His Excellency. Why else was she so secretive?

But he was feeling giddy now. His body floated off the ground toward flashes of non-existent daylight. Holding his breath didn't help. Matthew shivered despite the heat condensing on his face.

"What are you going to do with me?" he gasped.

"I'll discuss that with my village druid and elders. Hopefully, they won't throw you into a pit."

Druids were the pagans' priests and infamous skull collectors. They were sorcerers that the Church abhorred. Matthew's stomach turned. Perhaps submission now was his only chance at *not* being thrown into a pit.

"I yield." He gulped in much-needed air, letting his body go limp. "We'll go to Barton together, but tell the other tribes not to hurt Aliwyn. Not for me, but for Aelfric. Please."

Aelfric had partnered with Reiya to rescue him from the Boltans only days ago, but she already seemed to think highly of him. It was no surprise; Aelfric was charming and knew how to talk.

Reiya's boot remained heavy on Matthew's chest. She didn't respond, and the warriors chuckled and mumbled amongst themselves.

He never dreamed he'd beg a Vasfian for anything, and even begging didn't seem to work. Shame came as a downpour of chills. What could he still do for Aliwyn?

All of him shook with the desperation to breathe. Sucking in the vapors thickened the fog in his mind, and he sank into a dreamless void.

AN ICY CURTAIN RUNNING up the length of Matthew's face awakened him. Metal links slid off his forehead.

He opened his eyes. The night was still dark, and he was still lying on the ground, but breathing was now easy. Neither his armor nor Reiya's boot weighed on his chest.

His arms had been raised over his head, and the shaved sides of his head prickled from the cold. Reiya's warriors had finally stripped off his helmet and chainmail. Matthew twitched his freezing fingers. He otherwise couldn't move.

Reiya crouched before him, but he couldn't focus on her face. The memories of Aelfric's death assaulted him. Matthew had been running on top of Ransley's manor fortifications, desperate to reach the battle below, when he saw Tobias slash Aelfric across the neck. His world had caved in at that moment.

The Vasfians had fired a volley of arrows, but the wind was against them. Tobias and his father had fled into the night in a covered wagon.

Fiery torchlight and yelling still flooded Matthew's memories. Aelfric had lain on the muddy bank, the way Matthew did now. He had cradled his best friend until the end, swearing through gritted teeth he'd find Aliwyn and protect her.

The hot tears welling in his eyes brought Matthew back to the present. Had Aelfric been here, he never would've let Reiya strip him as if he were a dead enemy. She reached down and pulled out Matthew's collar, rubbing the cloth with her fingertips. What was she doing? He wanted to jerk away but couldn't.

"Don't hurt Ali," he sputtered.

Reiya shifted her weight and withdrew her hand.

"I can't deny that Aelfric cared about her," she said. "I'll ask the tribes to spare her. Then you Normans can punish her for treason."

Her voice was emotionless, but it didn't sound like she was lying. A trickle of relief steadied Matthew's breathing. Aliwyn was innocent. No one would punish her. He only hoped she was still alive.

Reiya reached for his arms and lowered them, folding them over his chest. The torchlight caught the golden lining of his sleeves. Embroidered clovers.

Aliwyn had sewn that symbol all over Aelfric's clothes, which Matthew now wore. Reiya must've been fingering the clovers on his collar, and a wrenching pain returned to his chest. Aelfric had loved his younger sister and talked about her every week. She must be suffering tonight, and Matthew couldn't rescue her.

Aliwyn, where are you?

Fire burned down his throat when he coughed. At least he'd be carried to where the Vasfians kept their loot. It would soon be time to do some scouting. As long as the redheads didn't know what Matthew was doing, he was still "behaving."

Reiya raised a slender whistle to her mouth and blew. The warbling bird sound that soon filled the woods sounded warped. His eyes rolled back. Something warm, carrying the fragrance of wild roses, floated over his body.

Was he...hallucinating? His teeth stopped chattering, and everything went dark.

CHAPTER 2

It's Almost Samhain

Matthew

MANY VOICES MUTTERED AROUND him, all incomprehensible. His eyes blinked open to a pillowcase striped in green and red beneath his head. The air hung thick with vinegar and unfamiliar herbs. This wasn't the squire's quarters back home. He held his breath. The walls were made of jagged rock, and he was...lying in a cave?

"Can you help me ride a horse?" asked a boy's voice.

Who just said that? Matthew couldn't see the speaker, but the boy's Vasfian accent sent memories of last night crashing back. He had argued with Reiya over Aliwyn's fate until she threw a bag over his head. Dread flooded him before he could remember anything else.

A small, freckled face lowered itself to the ground before him. "Can you—"

Matthew yelped and jerked upright. At any moment, someone could bag his head again. His vision swam, then steadied. A dozen redheads of all ages had surrounded him. Pigeons were perched on their shoulders.

His fingers dug into the fur blanket covering his chest. Something tickled his skin. He glanced down.

"Where's my tunic?" he cried.

A stout old woman spoke in response, her face unreadable in the hearth's glow. Matthew caught none of her words, but the crossbow and studded club at her waist made everything clear enough. His pulse pounded as he took in the rest of them. The children gripped slings, while the women held staves adorned with small skulls.

His hands shot to his sides, searching for his sword or dagger, but he was unarmed. Panic flared as a flash of heat. He needed a translator. Who had spoken English just now?

Fast footsteps pattered behind him. Before he could turn, something small and solid slammed into his back.

"Afix!" a girl shouted.

Thin arms clamped around his neck. He gagged, pried at the iron grip, and flung his attacker down. But it was only a child.

Her upper body bounced off the mattress while her legs struck the ground. A wail split the air. The perched pigeons took flight in a whirl of wingbeats.

Matthew winced. What in blazes was going on?

The girl sat up, her wavy hair sticking to her tear-streaked face. As an adult scooped her up, her open hand left something behind on his mattress. It was his blue tunic, now clean and dry.

She had only been returning his clothes. Matthew swallowed hard. Did "afix" mean something in English? No. He was trying too hard to make sense of Vasfian words.

The gibberish continued around him. One more misunderstanding between him and the Vasfians, and they'd club him on the head. He raised his hands in a half-surrender. Fully yielding to women and children was unthinkable.

"I need an interpreter," he stammered. "Is Reiya back yet?"

The old woman who had spoken before scowled and adjusted the thick gold torque around her neck. Her wrinkled eyes, framed by wiry gray hair, smoldered as she muttered something and tipped her staff toward a boy beside her.

Matthew frowned. The child wore a checkered red and green scarf tied behind his ears, an odd choice for headwear.

The boy glowered at Matthew and turned on his heel, but the woman pulled him back into place.

Finally, he crossed his arms and said, "I speak English, but I don't want to translate. You made my cousin cry."

Matthew scoffed. This had to be a joke. His gaze swept the room. "Is there an interpreter older than six?"

"I'm almost eleven," the boy snapped. "I'm just small. And you're *mean*."

Matthew rolled his eyes. Surely one of the adults knew English? But they only busied themselves gathering pigeons, eyeing him with varying degrees of suspicion. He resisted the urge to groan. His headache pounded worse than a hammer to the skull. What had he sworn to do once he woke up?

Right. Investigate the crates for clues as to where the rebels had gone.

He turned back to the boy. "I thought your cousin was attacking me. I need to leave with Reiya and speak to my men in Barton-upon-Humber. She was supposed to be back by noon."

Hesitating, Matthew looked up. No daylight reached this cave, and only the firelight glowed from deeper within. It was impossible to tell the time.

The boy shuffled his feet. "Reiya isn't here yet."

"What time is it?"

"It doesn't matter. Our druid and elders want you to wash in the hot spring." He pointed down the dark tunnel. "You're insulting our ancestors with your stink."

Matthew blinked. He was supposed to be scouting Vasfian supplies, yet here they were accusing him of filth. He almost argued but caught himself. If they were inviting him further into their settlement, he'd be a fool to refuse.

He checked the ground for any small bones he could use to pick locks, if it ever came to that. Nothing.

Hiding his disappointment, he looked up and nodded. "I'll go."

With a thin smile, the old woman lifted her staff. "Namanti." She gestured toward the boy. "Domilo."

"She's my grandmother," Domilo said. "And she's our elder druid, so you'd better listen to her."

Matthew clenched his teeth. Practitioners of the dark arts surrounded him, and his interpreter was barely the height of his waist.

Domilo pointed at the tunic embroidered with clovers. "Take the clothes and get up."

Matthew cautiously lifted the blanket. His stockings and boots were gone, but his trousers were still intact. He exhaled in relief, pulled out his legs, and grabbed the tunic.

His head felt like a jug of water as he stood, the low ceiling brushing his hair. He stumbled after Namanti and Domilo, who were flanked by two Vasfians carrying clubs.

Turnip lanterns lined the carved ledges of the limestone walls, each containing a flickering flame behind a sinister face. Matthew shuddered. The road to hell would probably be lit like this.

"Did anyone find a woman named Aliwyn?" he asked. "Or Tobias Boltan?"

Domilo thinned his lips. "No, but Reiya sent messenger doves to our neighbors to look for them. None of the birds are back yet."

Matthew sighed quietly and prayed that Aliwyn was safe. His men were scouring the forests for rebels, but here, among the Boltans' confiscated belongings, he could find maps, letters, or something else that would help the royal army track the rebels. It was all he could do for Aliwyn now.

Yet, the ache in his chest remained.

Domilo's cousin trailed beside him with her eyes still wet. The boy murmured something to her, and she smiled before skipping away. Matthew tracked her small form disappearing deeper into the cave, her oversized tunic billowing behind her. At least she wasn't hurt, unlike the other girl he had accidentally sent flying into a ravine.

Emma.

His bitten hand itched. Last night, while searching for Aliwyn along the shoreline, he'd hoped to find Emma also, to no avail. Clenching his hand beneath his tunic, Matthew tried to smother the guilt gnawing within him.

Focus. Maybe the Boltans' crates are hidden here.

Shafts of sunlight speared through vent holes overhead and turned dust into golden threads. It must be noon. Reiya could return any moment. He had little time to search.

His gaze shifted to Domilo. The boy was the only one he could understand, but how to make him talk?

Matthew forced a casual tone. "Where's the horse you wanted to ride?"

"Forget about the horse." Domilo didn't turn around. "I don't want your help anymore."

Matthew hardened his jaw and tried again. "You speak English very well. Who taught you?"

"Someone much nicer than you. He'll never come back, though."

"Oh, really? What happened to him?"

Silence. Domilo and Namanti turned right into a tunnel. The druid's staff tapped beside her as she walked, and Matthew ducked to avoid hitting his head. He could guess who had taught the boy English. Many English priests visited the Vasfian hillforts to convert the pagans, and many of them ended up dead in a river. When Lord Seville, Matthew's tutor, arrived in England, he kept his vassals away from the redheads.

Domilo glanced behind, his face wrinkled with grief.

Matthew raised an eyebrow. "What? I only asked what happened to your English teacher."

"Go ask Reiya about him."

"Well, I'd love to ask her, but she's supposed to meet me at her hillfort. I'm not even in your hillfort."

"Yes, you are. This is Blaithin, and we're in a special cave. My grandmother wants you to be clean before we let you out."

What did they want him to bathe in, deer entrails? Matthew's skin itched all over.

A gust of warm air from ahead blew past him, carrying a bizarre scent of metal mixed with eggs. Matthew had heard of various hot springs in England, but he'd never visited one until now.

The tunnel opened into a cavernous chamber with a tall, domed ceiling rivaling Lord Seville's Great Hall. Matthew's bare feet met cold stone as a torrent of heated air engulfed him. He steadied himself. He'd better find those crates.

The platform before him featured a crackling bonfire surrounded by a dozen redheads. Some played a flute or sat beating a leather drum, while others chanted as they carved large turnips. Their airy music floated in the room, carried by mists from the hot spring below. Above them, shafts of sunshine streamed from vent holes and reflected off the water like a silvery web upon the chamber's walls.

The effect would've been beautiful had it not been for the countless skulls embedded in the wall. Matthew's stomach had ached from hunger, but now it roiled with dread. Those skulls could only have come from "Outsiders" like himself. Part of him wanted to spin around and bolt, but his scouting had just begun.

Matthew followed Namanti and Domilo past the crackling bonfire. The gathered redheads lifted their gaze toward him. Most were young women crowned with woven yew branches and blood-red berries. Their sleeveless linen dresses were too short and exposed slender calves and ankles.

Matthew averted his eyes. The women back home would never uncover themselves like this.

A pathway carved into the rock spiraled downward to the dark waters below. Matthew glanced over the edge and doubled back. The drop measured twice the height of the wooden ramparts surrounding Lord Seville's manor. Far too high. He bumped sideways into the wall and choked on his spit.

The subsequent coughing set his throat on fire. *Blast it.* He'd forgotten how sick he was, and he hadn't eaten since yesterday afternoon. His hand shot to his missing belt, where his costrel should have hung. No food. No water. How long could he last?

As if sensing his thoughts, Namanti called out to the women around the bonfire. One approached Matthew and presented him with a wooden bowl of porridge and a goblet.

Domilo jutted his chin. "This is porridge and a drink for you. Both have medicine for your cough."

Matthew stared at the porridge's bumpy surface, then at the clear golden liquid within the goblet. The scent of sweet, fermented pear tickled his nose. Poiré? How did they know he had a weakness for this drink?

Nonetheless, he shook his head. "I don't want any."

For all he knew, their offering had been poisoned.

Domilo rolled his eyes. "Just eat and drink already. My grandmother says you'll faint otherwise."

"I'm fine."

Namanti glared at him and dismissed the woman bearing the food and drink. Matthew dared to breathe again.

Domilo narrowed his eyes. "It's rude to say no."

"You said I'm here for a bath."

The boy chewed on his inner cheeks. "Fine. The spring is this way."

He turned to lead the way. Matthew licked his cracked lips and followed. That poiré would've been delightful, but there was another reason he had to refuse. He'd crave ten more goblets after the first, and he'd seen what drunkenness had done to his father.

Domilo led him down the winding path toward the central spring. The sheer drop to Matthew's left made him cringe, and he pressed his bare shoulder against the rock wall. He was shamefully afraid of heights. Back at Brocklesby Ravine, he'd been so dizzy that he'd knocked Emma into the water instead of away from it. He'd searched for the girl downstream after Aliwyn stormed off, but he'd never found a trace of her. How would he ever forgive himself?

A sudden poke to his gut made him jolt.

"Why are you staring at my aunties?" Domilo glared up at him, hands on his hips.

"I'm not," Matthew retorted. "I was wondering about all these skulls."

"They're the most valuable thing an enemy can own. Our gods love them, especially Lenus."

Matthew swallowed. "Wonderful. And the carved turnips?"

"They ward off the dead who want to harm us."

"What do the dead do? Dig themselves out of the ground?"

"No. They come back as evil spirits." Domilo turned and continued walking. "Have you heard of Samhain?"

"Never."

Domilo told Matthew about the dead and living worlds colliding at the end of each harvest season. Their hot spring was the opening to the underworld. During Samhain, the Vasfians kept a fire burning at the entrance to the underworld to prevent evil spirits from returning.

"Our loved ones also come back as spirits," Domilo added. "If we make them happy, they'll ask Lenus to help us do things. Like...make cripples walk again."

The boy's voice softened, but Matthew barely listened. Where were those crates? Figures moved along the rocky banks below, where a bonfire flickered against the jagged cave walls. Vasfians fed the flames while children played by tossing bean bags into baskets. Their hair and skin glowed red in the light.

Finally, the rotten egg smell of the Boltans' pellets accosted his senses. Matthew wrinkled his nose and scanned the scene below, but no crates appeared.

Why couldn't he find them? His legs wobbling, Matthew forced himself toward the walkway's edge. The telltale stench disappeared again with a draft of warm air. Cloaked figures continued to carry planks of firewood to feed the flames. His jaw tightened. He'd have to search the shores later, but if the Vasfians caught him, he'd have only his fists to fight with.

The sight of the rippling water so far below made his vision spin. Staggering back, he bumped into Domilo.

The boy grinned. "Are you fainting?"

"No!"

"I know you're hungry. You should try something I made with my friends."

Domilo pointed at a concavity carved into the wall of the pathway. A few boulders obscured its presence, but light glowed from within the recess and illuminated a table with a red tablecloth.

"Refreshments for everyone are on that table," Domilo said. "You'll feel better if you eat something."

Matthew eyed the smiling child. Was he trying to be friendly? If they spoke long enough, maybe the boy would show Matthew around the cave, and he wouldn't have to risk sneaking around.

"All right," Matthew said. "What did you all make?"

"*Kubozi*. Come see."

Domilo led him past the boulders to where the table stood. Two bowls sat on top, each filled with round objects wrapped in leaves. A carved turnip glowed between the bowls, its slit-like eyes fixated on the closest bowl as though it were a greedy monster.

Such hideous decor. Matthew was about to look away when the rich scent of butter and honey wafted to his nose. Pastries? He used to sit outside

Lord Seville's kitchen, playing chess with Aelfric, as they waited for fresh fruit tarts. Matthew searched the tables for sweets, his stomach turning with hunger. Yet, he found only strange leaf balls filling the bowls.

Domilo stopped beside the table and lifted the red tablecloth. The space underneath erupted in soft giggles as several small children crawled out. Each held a clump of barley dotted with walnut pieces. One youngster was Domilo's cousin, and she looked up at Matthew with gleeful eyes.

Grains of barley stuck to their faces. Matthew had never seen desserts wrapped in leaves, but they smelled good, and they shouldn't be poisoned if the children were eating them.

Domilo stood back up, grabbed a ball from the bowl, and presented it to Matthew.

"Try a *kubozi*. I'm going to talk to my friends. Then I'll take you down to the hot spring."

Matthew held out his hand, his mouth watering against his will. Domilo dropped the dessert onto his palm before sliding under the table. The tablecloth fell to obscure all the children once more.

The dessert felt heavy and dense, probably drenched with butter and honey. He may as well eat it. Matthew peeled off the elongated leaf wrapped around it. Sinking his teeth into the intense sweetness made his scalp tingle. The nuts and grains crumbled in his mouth, moist and with a distinctive aftertaste of pine sap. His stomach burned for more. Matthew took another satisfying bite, but a sudden whiff of the rotten egg stench made him tense.

He sniffed the *kubozi* he held, but it wasn't the culprit. His gaze fell on a small opening along the cave floor. Peeking through it would grant him a view of the level below.

Matthew glanced at the tablecloth. It hadn't moved again. He warily approached the gap until he could look into it.

He stood roughly two stories above the cavern floor. A faint orange light illuminated a hidden corridor that led from the banks of the spring and the bonfire farther to his left. Crates of the same size and sandy pine wood finish as the Boltans' crates lined this passageway, and Matthew almost gagged.

But what was this? All the crates were missing their lids. Their contents were gone. Further along the cavern's wall, redheads sat prying loose the nails holding the crates together. Everyone wore a handkerchief over their noses to ward off the stench. A woman walked past and picked up some fallen nails. Following her shadow, another carried an armful of planks toward the bonfire.

Matthew's jaw dropped. The Vasfians were disassembling the crates to use as firewood and salvaging the nails. They had disposed of the pellets somewhere, along with the rest of the crates' contents. What had happened to the rebels' maps, stolen seals to forge letters, and secret battle plans? They must be elsewhere in the village, above ground.

He needed to finish his bath and exit the cave. Matthew shoved the rest of the barley ball into his mouth. Swallowing hard, he pined for water to wash it down, but no water was in sight. He coughed into his arm and shuffled back to the table, where he lifted the tablecloth.

"Domilo, let's go."

The space underneath was empty save for discarded leaf wrappers. His eyes widened.

"Domilo?"

Matthew called the boy's name again, but no one responded. Squatting on one knee, Matthew noticed a small and silent crevice gaping at him from the shadowy wall. His breath hitched. The children must've gone into hiding, but what were they escaping from?

He stood again and stared straight into Namanti's dark scowl. Before he could speak, she burst into an incomprehensible rant and wrenched the dessert wrapper from Matthew's sore hand. Still shouting, she pointed at the food bowls. He backed against the frigid wall.

With a smirk on his face, Domilo appeared from behind boulders further down the slope.

"You shouldn't have eaten that," he said. "That was forbidden food."

Forbidden food? Then why put it on display, unguarded? The churches back home would never do such a thing. Staring at Domilo, Matthew's face burned. That little cretin. He and his minions had eaten forbidden food first and fooled Matthew into doing the same!

As Namanti continued to jabber, he threw up his hands. "Hey! I was tricked into this! And *your* children ate this stuff first!"

A crowd of Vasfians clad in blood-red robes had gathered, their steely eyes cast in shadows by the heinous turnip. Namanti held the tallest skull staff while the others held shorter ones. They all rattled with the hollow echo of bones and death. Matthew's stomach sank; none of them seemed to understand his words.

He jumped as Namanti seized his elbow and pulled him down the path toward the water. Gnashing his teeth, he stumbled after her. He'd never been so humiliated—tricked by children, yelled at by a fat woman, and pulled around like a misbehaving cow.

"Why did you do this?" he shouted as he passed Domilo.

The boy jutted his chin. "Just because you're big, doesn't mean you get to pick on people smaller than you."

"What will happen to me?"

"Maybe get some cow pies to the face. My grandmother and her apprentices are talking, and they'll think of something."

Would cow pies be all? Something struck Matthew on the side, and he jolted. One of the druids with a shorter staff had hit him, and she shook the suspended animal skulls in his face. Barking nonsense, the old woman pointed toward the steamy spring below.

Multiple staves prodded his side and forced him to walk. Physical punishment was surely coming. They must know the consequences of hurting a Norman, but he was isolated from his troops. Chills racked his body, followed by a torrent of heat. Maybe he shouldn't have yelled at Namanti and her apprentices. All they could understand was his unapologetic tone.

Matthew glanced at the smooth surface of the hot spring below, then in the direction the water flowed. Somewhere out of view, it drained out into the rest of the world, into freedom. He squirmed with the urge to jump.

But jumping and swimming away wouldn't solve his problems or fulfill his goals. He was there to gather intelligence for Aliwyn's sake, was he not? Somewhere outside the cave, the Vasfians must be emptying the Boltans' crates and sorting through the real bounty. He needed to find that place.

Matthew snapped back to his senses. His feet stumbled close to the edge, but someone grabbed his arm and pulled him back.

"Don't even think about jumping." Domilo's fingernails sank into Matthew's flesh. "The water moves fast, and there are a lot of rocks."

"I wasn't going to jump." Matthew swallowed several times. He had perhaps one last chance to rectify things with the druids.

"Domilo, tell your grandmother I didn't mean to offend anyone. I can make up for it by doing physical labor." He raised a shaky finger toward the bonfire beside the hot spring. "I can help you chop firewood. Can you tell your grandmother that?"

The child's face became blank. He let go of Matthew's arm and spoke to Namanti, but the procession didn't stop chattering or moving. Matthew's chest heaved. He might just get thrown into a pit if Domilo mistranslated his message. Or perhaps Namanti would understand his intention to scout their territory and throw him into a pit anyway.

Finally, the old druid held up her arm. A hush came over the crowd. They halted suddenly, and Matthew almost toppled onto Domilo.

The boy turned back to him with a smirk. "My grandmother says to give you a shovel."

"What? I said I'll chop firewood."

"We don't need help with that. But there is a mountain of horse dung outside, by the stable." Domilo's grin grew until it was too big for his face.

Bitter laughter rumbled in Matthew's throat, but he didn't know why he found this amusing. At least he'd have a chance to leave the cave.

"Fine," he muttered. "Give me a shovel."

Domilo wrinkled his nose. "Bath first."

What was the point of bathing if he'd shovel manure right afterward? Yet, Matthew didn't argue. He strode downhill toward the hot spring while Namanti and a dozen druid aspirants followed.

CHAPTER 3
SMOKE SIGNAL

Matthew

THE BATH IN THE Vasfian hot spring felt nicer than Matthew cared to admit. Nearby, a few redheads knelt at the edge and cupped water into their mouths. He hesitated, then leaned down and drank from the surface.

Matthew dried off quickly, changed into Aelfric's tunic, and marched uphill from the spring with old women and giggling children trailing behind him. Every step reminded him of how foreign he was here.

He had work to do. Somewhere in this village, the Vasfians had to be sorting through the loot stolen by the Boltans. If Matthew could locate maps or letters, he might find a clue to Aliwyn's whereabouts.

He and the others exited the cave, which was situated in a rocky hill in the middle of the village with the opening at its peak. Below him, the hot spring poured out as a stream that sparkled in the afternoon sun and flowed into the forests beyond. Flocks of pigeons soared like a moving mosaic over the skyline.

Round houses with thatched rooftops dotted the settlement below. Wooden palisades surrounded the village, followed by concentric soil banks designed to confuse enemies. Matthew couldn't look for long before his fear of heights made him dizzy.

They walked for a long time around the village, passing only livestock, playing children, and villagers going about their chores. No one was sorting through what looked like loot.

Matthew chewed on his tongue. Would he have a chance to look elsewhere?

Namanti veered off the path toward a fenced-in stable. Inside, a muscular chestnut mare trotted in a wide arc. She was a fine warhorse, but Matthew barely had time to admire her before the Vasfians led him around the side to a shoulder-high mountain of manure.

Dread clamped around his stomach. He held his breath, his throat burning again, and stepped gingerly into the enclosure.

Domilo tossed a shovel at Matthew's feet.

"All of this goes onto that." The boy jerked his chin toward the cart parked outside.

Matthew gripped the splintered handle. He'd never get to search the village for anything of value if he were stuck here.

"This is too much," he protested. "I won't finish before nightfall!"

"Then you shovel until Reiya returns and takes you out of my village," Domilo said flatly.

Matthew glared at his spectators. The condemnation of their stares pressed heavier than the manure's stench. He was outnumbered. He had no control over where he could go. Shame flooded him as it became clear that his scouting attempt had ended before it began. He was useless to the royal army now, useless in the search for Aliwyn, and the rest of his men didn't even know where he was.

He glanced at the sky. The sun was dipping toward the mountainous horizon. So much time had been wasted already.

"Where is Reiya?" He struggled to sound calm. "She was supposed to be back at noon so we could leave for Barton-upon-Humber together."

Domilo lowered his eyes. "My sister sent a message saying she'd be late. But now...we're getting worried about her."

"Oh, so Reiya's your sister," Matthew grumbled. "Look, I only agreed to wait for her until noon. I'll shovel...a quarter of this pile, but then I must leave. My commander is in Barton. He expects me back."

He tried to steady the tremor in his voice. His fatigue was settling back like an iron curtain, and he'd be alone in the forest if he left now. It would be a long and risky walk to Barton, Jacques Verdun's manor and military base, but he had no choice.

The Vasfians only stared at him. Matthew swallowed hard. He'd joined Sir Verdun's troops to make himself useful in his tutor's absence, but he'd been anything but useful. "Please understand. My men must be worried about me."

Namanti spoke, and Domilo translated. "You keep shoveling until we think you've paid the penalty."

Matthew thrust his tool deep into the muck and hardened his jaw. What did they want him to do, fall onto his hands and knees and beg for freedom? He needed another excuse to get out of this pen.

"I can join a team to search for Reiya," he said. "Why not organize one? Just give me a horse."

Domilo chuckled. "If we give you a horse, you'll speed away and never give her back. Obviously."

Admittedly, Matthew had made a crude attempt to pilfer the majestic mare he'd just seen. He stamped down the rage surging within him. The last time he lost control, a child had plummeted down a ravine.

Now, he had no clever way out of his predicament. Matthew gritted his teeth and sent another pile of manure flying into the cart. How he'd ended up in such a humiliating situation was unfathomable. He was supposed to be knighted next spring now that he was twenty-one years old, but here he was sinking in horse turds.

Namanti soon departed, but several warriors, Domilo, and his cousin remained. The boy smirked and folded his arms over the fence.

"Don't you have something better to do?" Matthew shouted.

Domilo shrugged. "I could shell walnuts for the *Anuin* tomorrow. But I like this much better."

The *Anuin* must've been another absurd pagan ritual. Matthew's upper lip curled. Throwing a heap of manure at Domilo would've been so satisfying. Yet, shame began strangling him. He had been bested by a ten-year-old boy.

By the Devil's tail, Aliwyn. I'm sorry. I still can't look for you.

"You deserve this." Domilo straightened, his face becoming serious. "My villagers risked their necks to help save you. They carried you when you fell sick. Reiya told us to treat you well, so we tried to give you food and medicine, but you're just snobbish and rude."

Matthew's pulse throbbed in his ears. He tried to focus on shoveling, but the truth in Domilo's accusations descended like a thundercloud.

"You made my cousin cry and never even said 'sorry.'" Domilo continued. "Who do you think you are?"

Who do you think you are? Aliwyn said something similar just yesterday. The strength drained from Matthew's arms, and he couldn't lift his shovel. Since Aelfric had given him a second chance at life, all he had done was exasperate those who still talked to him.

He glanced at Domilo's cousin, whose face was blank as she pressed against the boy's side. Maybe Matthew could apologize to her, but it would come across as stilted. They'd mock him, and everything would be worse. Matthew shook with cold sweat.

Years ago, he'd tried to apologize to his father. Matthew's pet piglet, his secret of many weeks, had dashed into the great hall during a Christmas feast. The muddy pig had overturned dishes, disgusted the guests, and utterly humiliated his father. Matthew's sincere apology made no difference. His father had thrashed him and ordered his beloved pet slaughtered. Every Christmas since had been ruined with that memory. Matthew had refused to see his father again.

Now, for better or for worse, the man was dead.

Coughing again, Matthew struggled to speak to Domilo and his cousin. There was no place to begin. All he saw was his father's enraged face.

He slouched close to the muck, his arms numb as he leaned on the shovel for support. What felt like a long time passed.

The rising stench seeped into his skin. Once again, Matthew caught the scent of rotten eggs. He squinted at the pile. The texture wasn't right for pure manure, and his breath hitched.

"Domilo," he rasped, "what exactly am I shoveling?"

The boy kicked something wooden and hollow beside him, hidden by the wooden fence. *A crate?* Matthew's eyes widened. He struck his shovel into the ground.

Domilo scrunched up his nose. "We mixed the stuff from these boxes with water to make it stink less, but we still have to bury it outside our village."

Matthew wiped his brow and drew a slow breath. Perhaps the Heavens had granted him a reprieve, after all. "Was there...anything else in those crates?"

"No."

The boy kept a straight face, but he had tricked Matthew once already.

"Can I look at the crate beside you?" Matthew asked.

Domilo shrugged. "You can. There's a bunch here."

Matthew approached the far side of the fence, the part he hadn't seen earlier. Empty crates, not yet dismantled for burning, lined the ground near the corner. One box had something etched on its side.

He reached over and scraped off the dried mud. First, an "X" appeared, then a "V," followed by more Roman numerals. His pulse quickened. Beneath the grime emerged a faint circle with a cross through it. Below that, a second line in Danish runes.

Matthew couldn't read the runes, but something about the cross-circle nagged at him. Wait—he'd seen it before on tax records, back when his father had seized lands from Danish nobles after the last rebellion. The cross-circle was the Danish symbol for currency.

Gripping the fence post, Matthew scanned the other crates. They'd been turned every which way.

"This writing," he asked, "is it on the others too?"

"Yes." Domilo nudged another one with his boot. "Reiya says they're all curses, so we're burning them."

Matthew grabbed the closest crate and flipped it until he saw the same inscription, a Roman numeral followed by the currency sign. He strode along the inside of the fence while turning more crates.

Domilo and the three women watched him with bemused faces but didn't stop him. Each crate Matthew rotated revealed the same markings, though the Roman numerals differed. His throat burned with each breath.

Domilo approached with his eyebrows raised. "Can you read curses?"

"Those are not curses." Matthew pointed at a crate. "They're numbers. Price labels. And that's the symbol for Danish money."

"Really? Someone was selling this stinky stuff?"

Domilo and the other redheads leaned closer. Matthew was about to respond when it struck him. No one in England used Danish coins, but Tobias Boltan was part Danish. His uncle, a merchant named Edward, often sailed to Denmark. Matthew had learned this during their training together years ago.

Some kind of trade was happening between the Boltans and Denmark. Were the Boltans buying or selling?

Regardless, the possibility that Danes were involved sank in like fangs. The last time they came, His Grace had sent Matthew's father and uncle to burn the northern villages. It had been the only way to purge rebel hideouts. Aelfric's family had died in those fires. Aliwyn's too. Matthew was now old enough to participate in such a campaign. If His Grace ordered such a culling again, Matthew would be expected to wield the torch.

His chest clenched, and he hunched over the fence.

Domilo's small hand waved before his face. "Are you all right?"

Matthew stared at the boy. He was imagining the worst. All he had seen was Danish runes on some crates, not invaders on longships. He should be relieved he'd found a clue amongst the Boltans' possessions. Those rebels were probably travelling to the eastern coast to meet the Danes and do business with those crates.

Myton, the one town Tobias admitted his father was travelling to, stood beside a river that flowed east toward the sea. Matthew needed to tell the royal army stationed at Barton to focus their search along that river and the coast.

He wiped the sweat from his neck. He could only hope his interpretation was correct, even though it felt unsatisfying. How did trade surrounding those crates tie into the rebellion at large?

The tension between the English and His Grace never seemed to end. It had been nearly ten years since Matthew's people had left Normandy and settled in England. Nearly ten years of learning English, treating Aelfric like a brother, and treating English villagers with respect. Matthew even drank their horrible ale to fit in.

Where had he gone wrong? Why did the people keep rebelling?

Domilo tugged on his sleeve.

"*Now* are you fainting?" His voice was on edge.

Matthew only managed to shake his head.

The boy held onto his sleeve. His wide green eyes peered up from behind tousled red hair, and Matthew saw Emma's face appear over Domilo's. Aelfric would've been horrified by what Matthew had done by the gorge. Matthew had also abandoned Kato, a redhead who had kept Evelyn and Marie hidden from the Boltans, in a leper cabin. Those lepers would whisper of Matthew's cruelty as they begged in villages.

Many years ago, Matthew had also broken Tobias' arm over a lost chess tournament and infuriated Ransley Boltan. The mare's whinny pierced the silence, but all he heard was the crack of Tobias' arm and Emma's scream.

If the rebels claimed the Normans were merciless, Matthew had only perpetuated their lies. This was where he had gone wrong.

When Domilo and his cousin pulled Matthew by his good hand away from the manure pile, he stumbled after them. They led him to the rear of the barn, where the lone mare still whinnied and paced.

He came to his senses again when a fresh breeze, free of stench, cooled his damp forehead. Domilo pointed to the bundles of hay beside him and told him to sit. Matthew obeyed.

He still needed to convince the Vasfians to release him, but he decided to wait before asking again.

Three adult Vasfians and two children watched him with anxious eyes. A woman offered him a basket of bread and cheese and a bucket of water. His face grew hot. During the last uprising, the rebels had drawn allies from across the ocean. Here, he'd been alienating the ones standing before him.

Matthew rinsed his hands while a woman brought ointment and linen. He bandaged his bite wound before taking the bread.

"Thanks," he whispered.

Domilo watched him closely. "Welcome. But what is a Danish?"

"He's a person from another country," Matthew answered in between bites. "He comes by longship and raids the coast."

The boy's eyes rounded, and Matthew continued, "I believe the Boltans plan to meet the Danes along the North Sea for trading. Please fetch your grandmother. She needs to know."

Domilo relayed the message to one of the women, and she hurried off in his place. Matthew ate his meal quickly. As warmth spread through his stomach and strength returned to his limbs, he turned to Domilo's cousin. She stood hugging the leather ball the children had been kicking.

"I'm sorry for throwing you down," he murmured.

The girl stared at him, her short hair blowing about her face, until Domilo whispered something to her. A grin brightened her face as she responded.

"She says it's all right," Domilo mumbled, staring at his feet. Maybe the boy had yet to forgive him, and Matthew sighed.

His cousin pointed at herself. "Nissa."

"You have a nice name." Matthew smiled back.

Nissa settled beside Matthew on the hay and reached to touch his collar. She said something else, her eyes becoming moist, and Matthew shuffled in his seat. Last night, Reiya had also pulled on his collar embroidered with clovers.

"What is Nissa saying?" he asked Domilo.

"Oh, that she misses her English teacher," Domilo muttered, kicking at the dirt. "Though she never sat still long enough to learn anything." His gaze drifted to the grazing mare before he straightened. "Look. Grandmother's coming."

Namanti's weathered face was tight with concern as she approached. Her young apprentices, all holding skull staves, trailed after her like a living cloak. Matthew explained that the crates were labeled with Danish currency.

"The Danes may return to trade with the rebels," he said. "You have sister tribes along the coast, correct? You should tell them to guard their shores."

Domilo translated, but he stuttered constantly. Perhaps he lacked the vocabulary. Matthew rubbed his eyes. The ideal person to talk to would've been Reiya, but how could he convince her to partner with him again? And she was still missing.

Namanti and her followers muttered among themselves as Matthew waited for his chance to speak. Maybe he could persuade the Vasfians to take him toward Barton, and they'd search for Reiya along the way. If he wanted to defeat the rebels, he needed to commit to this alliance.

But before he could say anything, Namanti and the others departed toward the crates. She pulled out a tangled mess of crucifix pendants from her satchel and studied each one. Some bore dark stains of blood. Matthew sat back with a fresh wave of chills.

The pendants must've been pulled off dead "Outsiders." Why did she keep them?

As though he could read Matthew's thoughts, Domilo said, "My grandmother saves those necklaces for the writing. She collects them from soldiers from different places. The crosses help her identify their languages."

Matthew ran a hand over his face. He had a crucifix like that too, presented to him the day he became a squire. The priest had pressed it into his palm and reminded him to serve with honor. But he kept it locked away in his dormitory. Wearing it was only a reminder of all the virtues he lacked.

"I'm sorry," Domilo murmured.

Matthew scratched between his brows. A partnership with the redheads still felt like playing with fire, but if they'd killed Danes before, they could do it again. The Norman-Vasfian alliance must be maintained to crush the rebels.

"Tell Namanti I want to help find Reiya," he said. "I won't steal your horse. You have my word."

The boy nodded and spoke to his grandmother and her followers as they returned. Namanti remained solemn.

"She agrees with you that it's Danish writing," Domilo said. "And she thanks you for telling her. But as for finding Reiya... We'll find her on our own. A team has just left." His voice quivered. "She thinks you've had a change of heart, though, so you can leave."

The child rubbed his eyes, and Matthew hunched over as he sat. Maybe Namanti had displayed the bloody crucifixes to remind him of boundaries he couldn't cross. At least he was allowed to leave now. It was too bad Reiya was missing. He'd have to tell the Norman reserves at Barton-upon-Humber that Tobias had escaped without her present.

Matthew looked Namanti in the eyes. "Before I go, can I ask you something, and you give me an honest answer?"

Domilo interpreted his words and asked, "What is it, Matthew?"

"Tell me what those crates contained. Only those pebbles, or something else?"

His pulse thumped in his ears. If the druid lied now, he'd have no way to know.

Namanti circled a hand around her crown of gray hair and pressed her palm over her chest. It was a Vasfian greeting Matthew recognized.

"In the name of the mighty Lenus," Domilo said. "My grandmother tells you that we only found those pebbles. The Boltans were using them to pollute our hot springs, so Reiya wanted them destroyed."

"Pollute your springs?" Matthew straightened. "You've seen the pebbles before?"

"Yes. They dumped similar rocks many times, but this batch smells worse." Domilo rubbed his nose. "It's like the bad people are trying to make it stink more and more. Lenus is punishing us because we couldn't protect his springs."

Matthew rubbed the stubble growing on his chin. Tobias had admitted, while dangling upside down, that those rocks were used to start fires. Why were the Boltans so obsessed with this lackluster kindling?

"I appreciate this information," he muttered. Instinct told him he'd see the Boltans' enigmatic goods again.

Namanti raised her hand toward the sky, already colored with the hues of dusk, and Matthew took it as a sign for him to leave.

He pushed to his feet. At least he felt much stronger today after a long night's sleep. "I hope Reiya returns safely. Can I...can you show me where my belongings are?"

He expected Domilo to translate, but the boy's face had flushed down to his neck. Casting a pained look at Matthew, Domilo tugged Namanti's sleeve. Whatever he said made her face darken with anger. She shouted something and stabbed her staff into the ground.

Matthew sucked in his growling stomach. Domilo began to leave with his shoulders slumped.

"Wait," Matthew said. "What's going on?"

The child wiped his eyes. "I told her the truth, that I'd tricked you into eating the *kubozi* balls. Now I have to do the shoveling. Goodbye, Matthew."

Matthew frowned at the wall of disgruntled faces surrounding him. Domilo's trickery had been a blessing in disguise, giving Matthew a chance to explore the Boltans' loot. The boy had received only punishment for his honesty, and it seemed as though he was sorry.

"Hold on," Matthew called out, walking to Domilo's side. "It takes courage to tell the truth. Domilo is an asset to your village, and we couldn't have communicated if he weren't here." He paused, searching for the right words. "Please forgive him."

Domilo translated with a shaky and foggy voice. He took longer than usual, and Matthew tapped his toes inside his boot. Finally, unable to resist, he reached out and rubbed the child's shoulders. His movement was enough to rock Domilo back and forth, and the boy startled before resuming his speech. Matthew pulled back with a sheepish grin.

Nissa also added her voice to the plea. Finally, Namanti turned to Matthew with a guarded smile.

"She says I'd better not do it again," Domilo said. "I'll have to say a long apology to my ancestors tonight for eating their food, but I won't have to shovel. Thank you."

Matthew nodded, but Namanti was already pointing at the hill looming over them, the one housing the hot spring.

Domilo cocked his head. "Oh, there is smoke in the distance. Maybe it's a sign from your people? You should go see what it means."

Matthew licked his lips. If what they'd seen was indeed a smoke signal, it may have been sent by Sir Jacques Verdun himself. A thrill ran through him, and his weariness vanished. His troops must be closer than Barton-upon-Humber for the smoke to be visible. Maybe it was because Sir Verdun had already left Barton to investigate Myton.

"When did the signal appear?" Matthew asked.

"While you were shoveling. It's none of her business, but since you stood up for me..."

"Please take me to see it."

NISSA RAN OFF TO play ball while the others led Matthew uphill toward the cave entrance. As long as he didn't look down, his fear of heights stayed quiet. The autumn air bit into his skin. He breathed on his fingers, longing for the warmth of his padded gambeson.

Domilo followed at his heels. "How do your people put words into smoke?"

"We don't. The puffs are the message. One for 'all is well.' Three in a row for distress."

Domilo hollered to the women leading the crowd, and one of them turned. She held up three fingers of one hand and one finger of the other.

"Oh!" Domilo exclaimed. "What if there are two smoke signals, side-by-side?"

"What?"

This was unusual. Matthew lengthened his stride and looked over the redheads' yew wreaths and woolen hoods. In the distance, a single column of smoke billowed over the tops of evergreens. Three puffs rose adjacent to it, followed by an extended break. The pattern of three repeated itself. Matthew chewed on his tongue. The continuous column of smoke likely originated from a destructive fire, while the smoke signal called for help.

Matthew flexed his sore right hand. Had rebels started the fire? If he were forced to fight, would he stand a chance with his hand like this? Yet, his men had sent for help, and any loyal soldier who saw the plea was expected to investigate. Maybe he'd meet other Normans along the way.

"I should go," he murmured. If only he had a horse to ride on.

Domilo translated to his villagers, who murmured amongst themselves.

"If you go that way, we can't escort you," the boy said. "It's far outside of our territory."

"I understand that."

Matthew's pulse hammered. They probably thought him reckless, but his journey wouldn't be as risky if he borrowed a horse. Armored and mounted, he'd stand a much better chance. Matthew wiped his palms on his thighs. He'd ask for their mare and promise upon his head that he'd return it.

But the Vasfians kept talking and wouldn't give him a chance to speak.

Domilo tugged Matthew's sleeve. "Are you sure your people sent that?"

"It's a standard distress signal. Who else would use it?"

"Lepers. Their home is that way. There's nothing else."

Matthew froze. He'd abandoned Kato at a leper cabin to prevent the ale delivery boy from courting his cousin, Evelyn. Now the cabin was on fire?

"Something else must be burning," he stammered.

All the Vasfians turned to Matthew. They couldn't possibly know he'd abandoned one of their own with the diseased, could they? All the same, Matthew struggled to look them in the eyes.

"My grandmother says to take Porei," Domilo said. "She's the mare you saw earlier."

"Really? They'll let me take her?"

"Yes." The child's face flushed. "My English teacher named her after your favorite drink. He wanted you to have her if something ever happened to him."

Matthew almost toppled over. "Your teacher...what?"

"He named her Porei. Like poiré."

Was this a farce? Yet, Domilo's stare held no humor. Matthew didn't know where to begin with the questions. Namanti pointed her staff downhill toward the stable, and the villagers began to leave.

Domilo pulled Matthew along. "If Porei accepts you, she's yours."

"Who was your English teacher?" Matthew's throat pulsed. He already knew, but just couldn't believe it.

"We call him Afix, but you call him Aelfric."

Matthew's eyebrows twitched between a scowl and a grimace. When Nissa had wrapped her arms around his neck in that dim cave, she'd mistaken him for Aelfric.

"Aelfric said he traded with your tribe," Matthew said. "Why would he come here?"

"He's been my sister's friend since he moved to Brocklesby."

If this were true, then Aelfric had been Reiya's friend before he'd been Matthew's. Was this why her tribe had readily agreed to help Aelfric infiltrate Ransley's manor? Matthew clenched his jaw, trapping the storm inside.

"Aelfric never talked about Reiya."

"For a reason. But we've known about you for years."

Matthew looked at the boulders they shuffled past and wanted to crawl underneath them. He used to mock the Vasfians' appearance, and so did many others in Lord Seville's household. Aelfric had never joined in. Now Matthew knew why.

"How often did Aelfric come?"

"Every Sunday, before he left to serve the Normans. Afterwards, he spent two months with us each winter."

Aelfric was home in Brocklesby for only three months a year, and he'd spent *two* of those months in a Vasfian hillfort? Did Aliwyn and Miriam know?

"How did he manage that?" Matthew demanded.

"Easy. His supervisors thought he was in Brocklesby. The people in Brocklesby thought he was serving the Normans. But really, he was living with us."

Matthew scowled as unwanted anger heated his face. He'd thought he knew his friend like his own shadow until now.

They approached the stable. The sun was setting, and streaks of orange and pink painted the sky. Behind the fence, Porei stood watching the crowd with deft sways of her tail. The white star on her forehead seemed to shine in the sunlight.

Matthew stopped by the stable's fence, where the brown mare watched him with dark and pensive eyes. Matthew entered the enclosure and approached her with measured steps.

"Hello, Porei," he croaked.

He raised his good hand, and she lowered her head to smell him. Her ears flicked with curiosity.

Matthew caressed her neck with rhythmic strokes. Porei responded with a soft whinny and nuzzled his chest, as though searching for Aelfric's scent in the fabric. Matthew's throat tightened. Aelfric knew Matthew needed to buy a horse before his knighting ceremony next spring. It would be a dazzling celebration that he and his friend had talked about for years. Now only Porei could go.

"She's a beauty." Matthew ran a hand through her mane. Turning to the Vasfians, he continued. "But I should return her to you before the winter sets in. She's worth more than my yearly wages."

Domilo spoke to his grandmother before saying, "It's Samhain, and we've all felt Aelfric's spirit since you came." He lowered his eyes. "Aelfric wanted you to have her, but we all doubted at first that you deserved her. That's why we didn't tell you earlier that Porei is yours."

"I promise to take care of her." Matthew leaned against the mare's neck to steady himself. The Aelfric he'd known wore simple clothes and owned little. Yet here, he'd had a horse.

The questions stormed Matthew's mind, and a shadow crept over everything he remembered about his best friend. If Aelfric had kept his second life a secret for five years, what else had he hidden? Could his sister be hiding something just as significant?

"Porei likes you." Domilo grinned. "Aelfric said she would. He taught her the way he saw you teach other horses."

Matthew forced a smile back. "I'm glad to have her. And I'm—" his voice frayed. "I'm also ready to leave."

Namanti led him, Domilo, and other Vasfians toward the wooden palisades and gates of the hillfort. Dogs leashed to wooden posts barked upon his arrival. Two Vasfians waited beside a wheelbarrow carrying his helmet, padded armor, and chainmail.

Aelfric would normally help him armor up. Now, Matthew had to struggle into his chainmail alone. By the time he fastened the belt, he was sweating.

Domilo stood beside him and held Matthew's sword and sheath, the Nornsblade, in both hands.

"This is really heavy," he said, eyes wide. "I never knew swords were this heavy."

Matthew took the weapon and threaded the sheath through his belt. "Of course they're heavy. Didn't Aelfric tell you that?"

Domilo frowned, and Matthew pressed his lips together. He should have said something else. Anything else. Trying not to scratch his itchy bite wound, he pulled on the gloves the Vasfians had cleaned and dried for him. Someone had filled his water costrel and packed what smelled like bread into Porei's saddlebag.

Matthew's fever had broken overnight. Sleep and a good meal had restored his strength, but the lump in his throat kept him from speaking words of gratitude.

Gloves on and helmet secured, he mounted Porei. The mare shifted under his weight, then steadied. A click set her walking; a nudge brought her to a trot. How much time had Aelfric spent training her, all while pretending he knew nothing about horses?

Matthew hung his head as he guided her toward the open gate.

Redheads led him through the hillfort's winding earthworks while others trailed behind. They exited the dirt ramparts to the forest's edge, where a gust of wind carrying the scent of evergreens greeted him. A flock of birds soared in the sky's last burst of brilliance before the sunset began. Ahead, only a single path slithered into the trees. Matthew gripped the reins. Now the real danger began.

"Follow the road and turn right at the fork," Domilo hollered behind him. "And are you going to come back?"

Matthew reined Porei around. "You want me to?"

"Yes." Domilo didn't hesitate, but the adults nearby exchanged glances.

Matthew had already stayed too long. He'd treat the Vasfians as his allies from now on, but he saw no need to enter another hillfort.

"I don't belong here," he said.

He hadn't expected the boy's expression to fall. Hoping to bring him some cheer, Matthew added, "I'll inform my men that your sister fought hard against the Boltans. Tobias did escape, but that means we must work together to capture him." He managed a smile. "You were all very generous to an Outsider like Aelfric. Thank you for giving him this mare."

Domilo's mouth twisted. "Aelfric wasn't an Outsider."

Matthew almost dug his heel into Porei's side. "Of course he was. He was an Englishman. His parents were from Scotland, but he was born in England."

Domilo shrugged. "Go ask Reiya. But you'll have to come back to find her."

A sour taste crept over Matthew's tongue. *How many more secrets, Aelfric?*

"I hope Reiya returns, but I won't," he croaked.

He turned Porei toward the trees and urged her into a canter. The branches whipped past in a blur of lights and shadows, the forest air raw in his lungs. He should be thankful for this mount, not wishing he could grab Aelfric's shoulders and shake him for answers.

What did they mean when they claimed his friend wasn't an Outsider? Was Aelfric a Vasfian oddity born with black hair? Or a half-blood? Matthew shuddered.

Four years ago, Lord Seville had ordered Aelfric and other foot soldiers to bury redheaded thieves caught stealing eggs from the manor's outskirts. Starving and wretched, they had stood no chance against the militia. Aelfric had vomited while digging their common grave. That evening, Matthew found him crying in a ditch. He had carried Aelfric home on his back. The redheads deserved to die, Matthew had told the younger boy. Don't cry over those heathens. They're not worth it.

Aelfric had been silent the entire night.

Now the memory choked Matthew. What else had he said to Aelfric?

Wind cut through his helmet, chilling his damp forehead. Any more distractions, and a rebel's arrow would find his neck. Matthew focused on the smoke signal rising over the darkening trees. His troops must be out there searching for Aliwyn and the Boltans. He needed to rejoin them.

Putting away his costrel, he clicked his tongue. Porei trotted onward.

Chapter 4
The Stolen Warhorse

Matthew

The road ahead of Matthew grew hazy with smoke, and the thick air clung to his throat. Coughing didn't help. He couldn't gauge the fire's spread through the trees, but the stench of charred wood became unbearable. His heart pounded as he pressed on.

What felt like an eternity passed. This was becoming a far bigger blaze than he'd expected. Where was the Norman division that sent the smoke signal? He had seen and heard no one. *Bloody Kraken!* His luck never improved.

Then a familiar rotten-egg stench hit him, and he yanked Porei to a halt. Heat seared his face as he stared at the smoke rolling over the treetops like a thunderhead. The rebels must have used their putrid kindling. Those fools! What did they hope to gain by torching their own timber and hunting grounds?

Porei whinnied constantly and swayed her head as she sought to turn around. With the forest shrouded in shadows, unease crept up Matthew's spine. No allies. No clear path forward. The flames were still out of sight, but advancing. If he didn't turn back now, he and his mare might not survive.

Yet, who had sent the smoke signal? Had anyone else arrived to help them? Shoulders heavy, Matthew wheeled Porei around, still reluctant to leave.

Something stirred behind the drooping willow branches. He tensed, and his hand closed around his sword hilt.

A shape pushed through the trees.

Matthew narrowed his eyes, his heart hammering, but it was only a lone warhorse. The beast slipped from the thicket with his muzzle low to the ground. Sweat streaked his dark flanks, and his sides heaved as he drank from the stream. Matthew drew his sword in silence and scanned the woods for movement, but no rider followed.

An abandoned horse?

The fading sunlight caught the blue and yellow checkered cloth beneath the saddle. Matthew's mouth fell open. Blue and yellow were the heraldic colors of His Excellency, Bishop Geoffrey de Montbray. His troops had been here. One of his knights must've lost his mount while fleeing the fire. He could be wounded. Or dead.

The warhorse shifted, and fresh blood gleamed across the back of the saddle. His rider had been *attacked*, and Matthew's stomach dropped. The forest appeared dark and empty for now, but the assailant could be lurking. Matthew had to run.

But the warhorse was alone, and Matthew couldn't bear to leave this handsome beast in the encroaching fire. Gripping Porei's reins, Matthew steered her toward the stallion. The horse raised his head sharply, his ears pinned back in fright. With a swish of his tail, he turned and trotted into the bushes.

Matthew gritted his teeth. It was too risky to bark a command in Norman French. He pressed his heel to Porei's side, and she charged after the fleeing horse.

The warhorse stalled a short distance away with a high-pitched whinny. In the darkness, a hand seemed to extend from the undergrowth. Matthew froze. The thicket beside the stallion stirred, and branches snapped. A man with tattered clothing and braided blond hair staggered to his feet. He grabbed the reins, but the warhorse pulled back its head and stomped.

Matthew's vision tunneled. This man had the hairstyle typical of Danish raiders. Had he killed the horse's rightful Norman rider?

Withdrawing his sword, Matthew gripped Porei's reins and squeezed her side with his heels.

She obeyed his cue and charged with a mighty leap. The horse thief yelped and spun away to run, but Porei dashed toward him with her thrashing hooves. Matthew leaned over and swiped the man with his sword. Something prompted him to rotate his blade at the last instant, and he knocked the man aside instead of slashing him.

The Dane rolled onto all fours and rose onto his knees. With both eyes bulging on his grimy face, he raised his hands in surrender. His hair was shaved on both sides. Soot and blood covered his exposed scalp, and a disheveled braid grew from the vertex of his skull. Someone with such hideous hair would've been laughed out of every English village.

Matthew jumped off his horse, his breathing ragged and his sword still raised. His opponent wore an empty dagger sheath and seemed to carry no weapons. A thin gambeson covered his torso. He'd be easy to kill, but he was surrendering.

The stallion's whinnies were fading. Matthew licked his lips. Even if he bound the Dane with rope, he'd never turn his back on the man to pursue a horse. Slay the Dane now and capture the steed, or give up on the beast?

A moment of hesitation was all it took for the warhorse to vanish into the darkness. A growl rumbled in Matthew's throat.

"Who sent you?" He pointed his blade at the foreigner.

The Dane stared back. His chest heaved in quick gasps, but he didn't speak. Either he didn't understand, or he pretended not to, and Matthew squeezed the Nornsblade with his sore hand. The man's belt featured a stylized eye embroidered in green, something Matthew had seen on goods from Denmark.

No bandit could cross the North Sea alone. Where were the rest of his men? Were they here to take advantage of the civil unrest to steal a warhorse or two?

Matthew could arrest this man and make him talk. Danish interpreters wouldn't be hard to find in a large town.

"Turn around," he ordered.

Still on his knees, the thief didn't move. Matthew made a circling gesture with his hand. He barked the rudimentary Danish Lord Seville had forced all his soldiers to learn. *Turn. I arrest you.*

The man rose to his feet, his knees knocking but his face emotionless. Filthy tears marred his trousers over the knees, and he stood a handspan shorter than Matthew. His gaze darted constantly to Matthew's sword.

When Matthew shouted again in Danish for him to turn, the man shuffled a half-circle.

The stench of his blood and sweat filled Matthew's nostrils. He'd never arrested a man by himself before. He didn't even have rope to tie him with. Backing against Porei, Matthew rifled inside the saddlebag and retrieved the Vasfian cloth once used to wrap bread. It would have to do.

"Put your wrists together behind you," Matthew commanded.

The man's arms quaked, but he kept them raised. Matthew circled to the side, his pulse thudding, and approached from behind. Ideally, other men in his army would've surrounded the enemy with their blades drawn, and Lord Seville would've given the orders. Matthew struggled to unfurl the bread cloth while gripping his sword.

But even if he bound the man's wrists, how would he pull the prisoner back to the Mehi's hillfort without rope?

He'd have to worry about that later. Matthew reached for the Dane's wrists, but the man whirled around. His arm shot straight for the dagger sheathed at Matthew's waist. Matthew scrambled backward and raised his sword, but it was too late. The thief yanked out the dagger and thrust it toward Matthew's side.

Matthew jolted back. The blade struck the side of his torso with a metallic chink. Pain ripped through him. The blunt force of the blow left him reeling, and he stumbled to regain balance.

The Dane lunged again with a shout. He swiped Matthew's arm, and the Nornsblade went flying from his wounded hand. Panic flared. With chainmail weighing him down, he couldn't match the Dane's speed in hand-to-hand combat. The man reached to the side to grab Matthew's sword, but Matthew rammed his conical helmet into his opponent's chest.

They both plummeted to the ground, screaming and flailing their limbs.

Matthew struggled to pin the man down and choke him, but his adversary drove up his knees. He flung an arm loose and stabbed for Matthew's unprotected eye. Matthew dodged just in time. He bashed his helmet against the man's face. The Dane yelped. The stolen dagger clanged against Matthew's helmet instead.

Panting, Matthew pushed himself up and wrenched his dagger back. The man's scarlet nose flashed before him, and bile surged up Matthew's throat. He could plunge his dagger into the Dane's throat now and end the battle.

But Matthew stumbled back onto his feet with his vision washing in white. He'd never killed anyone before.

His adversary rolled onto his side, moaning. Matthew side-stepped toward his fallen sword. He picked up the Nornsblade as the Dane pushed to a sitting position, his eyes barely opening from the blood. He rose, one arm shaking in surrender, and chills washed down Matthew's back.

This wasn't combat training. This man had to die.

He lunged, and the man let out a hoarse cry. He raised an arm before his face, and Matthew's legs turned to lead.

The thwack of a loosed bolt echoed in the distance. Matthew ducked on reflex. A feathered bolt impaled the Dane in the neck, and its fletching flashed a vibrant green—a Vasfian bolt. Matthew froze, his eyes rounded, and so did his assailant. Pain twisting his face, the man slumped onto the ground.

Matthew turned to the side and retched. Thankfully, nothing came out.

He almost didn't hear Reiya as she shouted something from within the shadows. Matthew wiped his mouth and sucked in air that didn't satisfy. Footsteps everywhere rustled the leaves. The redheads had probably been watching the fight, waiting for clearance.

Matthew staggered toward the one figure he recognized as Reiya, but the Danish man lay in his way. Despite the bolt through his neck, he was alive and gurgling. Against his will, Matthew's boots ground to a halt beside him. The Dane brought a fist to his chest and tapped twice over where his heart would be. Matthew stared, and the thief tapped again. The corners of his mouth jerked upward.

He was begging for a mercy killing.

Now that he lay helpless, he resembled a poor beggar back home. Matthew's eyes burned. He lunged and thrust the Nornsblade through the man's heart. The thud of his sword on the ground reverberated up his arm. When he withdrew, the Dane grew limp on the ground.

"Something you should've done long ago," a voice hissed in his ear.

Matthew shook with cold sweat. Reiya and her warriors had pressed around him, and their rustling footsteps entered his awareness again.

"He surrendered," Matthew said, panting. "I wanted to question him—"

"Where are the rest of your men?"

A haunting orange glow filled the smoky sky, and the treetops whirled back into place. Matthew drew a long breath before he could focus on Reiya's dimly lit face. Strands of hair clung to her freckled forehead.

"I'm alone," he said. "But I saw a smoke signal, a distress call."

"I also sent a signal for the Norman army to come extinguish..." Her eyes widened, and her gaze swept Matthew up and down. "*Kaba* Lenus." She spat on the ground.

He chuckled without knowing why. "You were the one who called for the Norman army?" He shrugged. "Well, I am *it*."

Just his luck. He'd tracked the signal only to realize his men hadn't sent it. At least he'd found Reiya.

But the chief glared at him. She squatted by her warriors, who were pulling off the dead man's boots and unbuckling his belt with the emerald eye. The piercing gaze of that eye made Matthew's insides heave again. That symbol now looked familiar, but why?

He stumbled toward Porei, who hadn't fled despite the chaos, and threw his arm around her. No one had warned him his first kill would feel like this. Porei nickered in his ears, and her sturdy and warm frame steadied his nerves. Matthew's eyes stung. His second kill had better come more easily.

The thief had been *Danish*. It was too perfect to be a coincidence. Matthew had to search through the body for why he was here. Already, he was dreading the answer.

Wiping his sword against a mossy tree trunk, Matthew sheathed it. He turned around to face a snarling Reiya, who raised her club and shouted, "You stole our horse!"

"No, I didn't!" Matthew tilted back. "Your grandmother let me take her. Her name is Porei, and she was Aelfric's. Right?"

Reiya's jaw hardened. Her warriors surrounded Matthew with their crossbows, but he held his ground. The last time he'd seen Reiya, he'd been determined to leave and shame her before Norman troops. No wonder she assumed he'd stolen Porei. Sweat trickled down his back as he matched the intensity of her glare.

Finally, Reiya's lips twitched. Something about Aelfric's name seemed to affect her, and she turned away with a wave of her hand. Her followers lowered their crossbows. Matthew dared to inhale again.

But his relief didn't last long. One warrior offered an axe to Reiya, who muttered something in Vasfian and raised the weapon over the corpse. *Head harvesting?* Matthew clutched his stomach.

"Wait," he croaked. "Don't behead him yet. Let me examine him."

"This bothers you?" Reiya asked.

Matthew drew a shaking breath. He couldn't speak.

"Then I'll forgo it this time," she said. "The fire will consume his body as an offering to Lenus."

Matthew coughed in the thickening smoke and squatted by the dead thief. The man's gambeson was already stripped away, leaving only a threadbare tunic. Matthew pulled at a cord around the man's neck. A bloodied crucifix slid out from behind his collar. It, too, was marked by an emerald eye. Matthew flipped it over and squinted at what appeared to be Danish runes.

On impulse, he grabbed the man's emerald-eyed belt nearby. His fingers traced a series of Roman numerals burned into the leather. He froze. First, there had been numbers on the Boltans' crates, and now numbers on a Danish man's belt. Why?

"This writing on his belt," he said. "I've also seen it on—"

"Worry about that later," Reiya cut in. "You should know this man fought for the Boltans. He became separated from his group and tried to steal a horse from my team."

Matthew stared up at her. "Tobias Boltan attacked you?"

"No. I didn't see him, but I ran into his father and his men. I smashed that scoundrel's head with my club, but he escaped." She handed her axe back to a warrior. "We'll see what happens to Ransley Boltan. Now get up."

The bruise on Matthew's side twinged as the full brunt of her news sank in. The dead Dane was one of Boltans' *recruits.* The Boltans weren't simply trading with those foreigners.

"What did Ransley's other soldiers look like?" he stammered.

"They all looked like this man. Get up!" Reiya almost kicked him. "We might get attacked again!"

They all looked like this man. Each word landed like a slap. If this revolt mirrored the last, then the rebels had once again recruited hundreds of Danes on their side. Maybe the first foreign scouts were already slipping into England. Did Reiya understand the peril behind discovering even one Danish recruit?

They needed to talk once they escaped the forest.

His hands shaking, Matthew pulled the pendant from the dead man's neck and pocketed it. Leaving the crucifix to burn would only worsen his wretched fortunes.

"Off to my hillfort," Reiya said as Matthew stood. "I must evacuate everyone. The smoke will suffocate us all."

He raised his heavy helmet and wiped his brow. With so much work ahead of her, she'd have even less time to talk. But she was his ally, and he had to try.

Vasfian warriors led their mounts and the runaway warhorse, finally recovered, out from the shadows. Reiya tossed the newly plundered belt onto their lone cart. It was already cluttered with gambesons, a black chest, and other belts. Matthew's chest heaved. Once they reached the hillfort, he'd ask permission to see her loot. The Danes were using numbers for something, and he had to figure out what.

Reiya swung onto her gray mare, and Matthew mounted Porei. They took off at a trot with the Vasfian warriors riding at the rear. Hoofbeats and rustling leaves echoed through the smoky woods.

Matthew nudged Porei into a trot beside Reiya and said, "After we evacuate your hillfort, we'll go to Barton and report Tobias missing as planned. Correct?"

"Correct. And I will return that warhorse you found." Her jaw tightened. "He's Norman's horse."

Matthew blinked. "Norman? Norman Rochefort?"

"Yes, that one. Kato's mentor." She held Matthew's gaze. "Norman came to us riding that horse. His name is Vaillant."

Matthew's eyes widened, and Reiya continued. "Ransley Boltan escaped south. Norman chased him on horseback, but only Vaillant returned to us. Then that bandit stole him."

Norman must've borrowed Vaillant from Jacques Verdun's manor in Barton-upon-Humber. No knight, even one who'd had his knighthood degraded, would abandon such a prized warhorse. Matthew pressed his weight onto the stirrups. There had been blood on Vaillant's saddle. All of him screamed that Norman was dead.

"Why did Norman come to you?" he asked.

"He found us. He'd been riding back to the leper cabin to fetch his apprentice, whom someone had left rotting there." She raised an eyebrow at Matthew. "Norman helped us fight Ransley's men before he disappeared. I waited for his return, but the lepers' shelter began smoking in the distance. The fire spread unlike anything I've ever seen. I tried to extinguish it with no success, so I called for backup. All I got was you."

She rubbed a scratch on her cheek and sped ahead. Matthew followed with his shoulders slumping. The horses' hooves thudded against the ground as they trotted in the surreal light of the flames behind them, glowing brighter than the fading sun.

There was no ignoring the lump of guilt in his chest. Norman had been his father's friend and drinking partner. They'd fought many battles together, but Norman's swordsmanship wouldn't extinguish blazes. Hopefully, the man had galloped to safety before somehow losing his steed.

And there was the person Norman had tried to fetch. Matthew squirmed in his seat. When Reiya slowed her horse back to a trot, he called out, "Did you find Kato?"

Her braid bounced behind her fur cape. "Why do you care?"

"Because...he was good to my cousins. I shouldn't have left him at the leper colony."

"Consider him dead, unless you want to search through those flames."

Matthew clenched his jaw. "It sounds like you were at the cabin. Why didn't you take Kato with you?"

"There's much that you don't know." Reiya smoothed the bandages over her arm. "Kato is a traitor, just like Aliwyn. They both helped Tobias escape the leper colony."

"What?"

"I only arrived at the cabin after both Kato and Aliwyn had disappeared, but your cousin saw everything." Reiya twisted around on her saddle. "Evelyn, you can't hide from him forever!"

Matthew spun around, his rigid back tearing. A familiar face peered out from behind the large chest on the horse cart. Brown hair was matted against her forehead, and dirt streaked her cheeks. She braced her knees to her chest.

"Evelyn?" Matthew cried. "What are you doing here? I left you at St. Peter's for a reason!"

His cousin glowered at him and leaned back to hide behind the chest. Matthew's chest burned. All this time, he hadn't worried about his cousins because he thought they were somewhere safe. He pulled on Porei's reins and guided her toward the open cart.

"You should've known better!" he shouted. "You left Barton to look for Kato, didn't you? And where's Marie?"

Evelyn pulled off the hood, shadowing her features.

"Marie is safe in the church." Her upper lip curled. "None of this would've happened if you hadn't left Kato with lepers. You think I wouldn't find out you did it?"

Matthew swallowed hard. "I...I wasn't thinking straight at the time."

Evelyn ignored him, and his mouth ran dry. She must've seen him fight the Dane. Still, she'd chosen to huddle amongst dirty gambesons to avoid seeing him. Matthew struggled to compose himself as he searched Evelyn for injuries. Dried mud caked her tunic and knees.

"Are you all right?" His voice softening, he directed Porei to trot behind the cart. "What happened at the colony?"

Strangled laughter escaped her throat. "Kato and Aliwyn betrayed us. They plotted together and hid Toby in the leper's cabin. I saw Toby escape right before my eyes, but I couldn't stop him."

Matthew froze. "Whatever you said, say it again."

Evelyn repeated herself. The words echoed in Matthew's head until their message crashed into him. He threw up a hand.

"Why would Aliwyn betray us?"

"I don't know."

"How do you know she hid Tobias?"

"Because she said so. Right before Toby rode off, she told me she hid Toby in the leper cabin. Kato saw it all but said nothing until Toby escaped."

If Kato had unveiled Aliwyn's lie, those repugnant lepers would've killed her along with Tobias.

"But Aliwyn had no reason to betray us!" Matthew cried.

Evelyn looked out the side of the wagon, her chest heaving. He had never seen her eyes so swollen. Had anyone checked her for injuries?

"Reiya," he called out. "Can you pause the procession? I want to sit with Evelyn."

"Stay on your horse," she snapped. "I can hear you just fine."

Matthew set his jaw, but it shook all the same. "Tell me everything from the beginning. Start from when you arrived at the leper colony."

Her face contorted. She recalled how she'd returned to the leper's colony to find both Aliwyn and Kato. Neither said anything about Toby. Soon afterward, one of the lepers returned asking for help, saying he'd found a group of injured Vasfians by the river.

"Kato and I went to help that group. I found Reiya, but Aliwyn ran off alone into the forest. When I returned to the cabin, she confessed to hiding Toby. He stole my horse and escaped."

"Where is she now?"

"Kato made her speed away with his donkey. All the lepers chased after her, but I ran back to the river where Reiya was. I shouldn't have left Kato on the ground. I shouldn't have..."

Matthew's body seemed to sink in on itself. "You're telling me Aliwyn is also in that fire?"

"I don't know where she is. Reiya and I traced the cart's tracks. We found it by a river, but Kato's donkey and Aliwyn were gone. There were clumps of gray horsehair on the bushes and horseshoe imprints everywhere. I recognized some of the imprints. They belonged to the silver horse Toby stole from me."

"Aliwyn reunited with Toby," Reiya said simply. "She's a traitor."

The forest seemed to spin around Matthew. Aliwyn's figure appeared in every passing shadow between the trees, only to disappear in a blink. In his mind, he saw her shy smile and heard her delicate voice as she said she'd follow him. He tasted her ginger tea and followed her up those creaky stairs again to where Aelfric used to sleep.

Reiya was wrong. Aliwyn wouldn't betray him after tending to him just hours before.

"The rebels attacked her cart!" Matthew shouted. "They took her against her will and set the forest on fire! Probably the cabin, too!"

Reiya frowned over her shoulder. "Then why did she lie about Tobias' identity?"

"He could've threatened to stab her!"

"*Kaba.*" Reiya pinched the skin between her eyebrows. "I'm wasting time with this loud imbecile."

She spurred her mare ahead. Belts rattled against the chest on the cart ahead of them, and Evelyn scowled at Matthew with red-rimmed eyes. Chills radiated down his limbs.

"And why would Kato betray us?" Matthew called out to Evelyn.

"I don't know. I never got to talk to him. When Reiya and I returned to the leper cabin, he was gone." She wiped her eyes. "He must've fled from the lepers. I couldn't find him anywhere."

It was all Matthew could do to keep Porei on the dark, meandering road. Kato tired easily after being poisoned. Without his donkey, he couldn't have made it far, and Matthew couldn't risk riding into the fire to search for him. The redhead's inevitable death sank into Matthew's conscience, followed by an onslaught of guilt.

"After I evacuate my village, we'll leave for Barton-upon-Humber," Reiya shouted.

Matthew couldn't look at her. Whatever happened to Kato wasn't entirely his fault. Or so he told himself.

"You must rejoin your men and eliminate the Boltans," she continued. "That's where your focus should be."

The thunderous horse hooves brought Matthew back to the present. The Boltans. Fury spread as heat down his chest. Those blasted militants had burned the forest, driven the Vasfians north, and vanished south. Yet, they had dropped possessions along the way. The Danish belt they had just stolen had writing, possibly clues to their next destination.

Matthew's stomach clenched at the thought of Aliwyn's plight. Danish raiders like those serving the Boltans sold their female captives as thralls overseas. How long did Matthew have to find her before she shared the same fate?

If there was any hope, it was that she still had value to them. She was alive. She had to be.

Reiya rode ahead with her red hair and cape flying in the wind. Studying her loot could be Matthew's only chance at tracking down the Boltans and Aliwyn before she was lost forever.

He doubted Reiya could understand Roman numerals. Would she allow this "loud imbecile" to go through her plunder?

CHAPTER 5
A HEALER'S DECEIT

October 2, Aliwyn

THE MORNING FOLLOWING THE Vasfian attack on the *Lady Fortuna*, Aliwyn stirred awake in blissful unawareness of what lurked below deck. It took her a moment to remember why the ground beneath her rocked and why men murmured in the background. Then the scent of burnt pottage wafted to her nose, and everything came flooding back.

She was on a ship sailing toward the barrier islands. The crew would moor today to replace the broken yard, and she needed to convince Toby he mustn't sell his destructive compound to the Danes. When would she find time to speak to him alone?

The urge to move seized her, but her body was bound snugly by the hudfat, a Norse-style sleeping sack, and the warmth behind her. Toby's arm was still draped over her waist, his rhythmic breaths comforting against her back. Aliwyn smiled faintly. Despite the uncertainty, his closeness felt like a refuge.

Opening her eyes, Aliwyn was about to turn around, but Emma's doleful gaze met hers instead. The girl had lowered her cheek to the floorboards, and Aliwyn blinked in surprise.

"Good morning." Emma smiled. "I was wondering if you'd wake up."

Aliwyn grinned back. "I could almost feel you staring. Do you need something?"

The girl hesitated and twisted her small hands on her lap. "I have to empty privy pots, but I still hear Loki downstairs. Can you come with me?"

"Oh, of course I—"

Before Aliwyn could finish, Toby shifted behind her. His arm tightened around her waist, and the stubble of his beard brushed against her cheek as he leaned close to her ear.

"Good morning, Ali," he murmured.

Her breath caught, and she turned to face him. Toby's hazel eyes, flecked with gold and green, met hers with a warmth that made her chest flutter.

"Good morning," she whispered back. "Did you sleep well?"

He propped himself up on one elbow with a tired smile. "The best sleep I've had in weeks, thanks to you."

Aliwyn's cheeks flushed as she smiled back. Would he still look at her with such contentment after she challenged his goals? She reached out to curl her fingers around his, and the warmth of his hand sent her strength. May she be as bold today as Toby was last night when he'd braved the Vasfians' assault on his ship to protect the crew.

"I'm glad you slept well," she said. "You don't have to get up yet. Emma said she wanted help emptying the privy, and only I need to go."

"But I should check on my father." He lowered his eyes. "His head still hurt last night. He was so worried about seeing sunlight that he slept below deck."

As a mercenary walked past their hudfat, Toby pushed himself up to his knees. He moved carefully but still winced and pressed a hand to his side, where the redheads had shot him. Aliwyn's brows knit. She sat up and pushed Toby's gambeson aside.

"Let me tend to you first," she said. Turning to Emma, she continued. "Can you please help me fetch a basin and washcloths? I'll follow you downstairs afterward."

The girl smiled. "Of course."

Aliwyn thanked her, and the girl stood. Walking past where Zelrin slept, she shook her head and flipped his blanket back over his legs. This boy of roughly fifteen had fearlessly pelted rocks at the redheads last night. Now, he slept like a tavern drunkard, facedown and with sheets flung everywhere. Aliwyn grinned, but not for long.

An acrid stench of soot and decay had swallowed the ship. The wind must've carried this caustic mix of soot and condensation from the recent fires, and the sun was reduced to a cocoon of grey. A similar haze had engulfed her birth village after the Normans had razed northern England. Chills prickled Aliwyn's nape. Now she was aboard a ship of former Norsemen, turned rebels and mercenaries, who seemed intent on repeating that destruction on a far greater scale. In three days, they'd meet the Danes in Ravenser's Point to supply them with potash compound.

She couldn't let it happen. She had to convince Toby to dump the wretched cargo into the sea before he sailed to Denmark, where his inheritance awaited him.

Farther down the deck, the crew had rolled away their hudfats. Many men sat cross-legged as they sipped what smelled like horribly burned pottage.

Toby's uncle, Edward, sat against the opposite railing of the ship. His greasy blond hair stuck up in all directions as he sewed a small gash on his gambeson. Watching him stab the fabric with a tiny but sharp object made Aliwyn tense. Her lip still throbbed from his beating the day before. She had three days to turn Toby against this older man, the captain, and scuttle their mission.

Would the confrontation be today?

Emma returned with a water basin filled with floating handkerchiefs. Aliwyn mindlessly rolled back the sleeves of her purple cloak and picked up a cloth. She rotated her shoulder, the one nicked by a Vasfian bolt, and was relieved to find it painless. Turning back to Toby, she gasped. He had already taken off his tunic and was wiping his face with a handkerchief. Other than the bandages wrapped around his side, his torso was bare.

Emma giggled and placed Toby's orange tin of ointment beside Aliwyn.

"I'll go find bandages," the girl said.

As Emma skipped back toward the cauldron, Toby stopped wiping his face. A red tint colored his cheek.

"Did you want to do this later?" he asked. Picking up his tunic, he began pushing his arms back into the sleeves.

Aliwyn shook her head. "I-I'm ready."

Grabbing a rag, she rubbed her face with its icy dampness to steady herself. She had work to do, no matter how handsome the patient was. Ignoring the sounds of men walking and muttering around her, she tugged on Toby's bandages and unwound them. The scent of mint and bitter herbs wafted over her.

"Can you lie down?" She couldn't look him in the eyes.

Toby did as he was told. Aliwyn scrutinized his wound, but a flicker of warmth at her neck betrayed her awareness of his toned arms and his lean torso still sun-kissed from the past summer. The shallow arrow wound appeared red and puckered where the hot knife had sealed the flesh the day before. At least it was dry.

Aliwyn gathered ointment onto her finger and dabbed the wound, trying not to tremble when the muscles of his side tensed under her touch. The overcast sky did nothing to diminish the blue and purple bruises covering his chest. With time, the swelling in her throat grew unbearable. How many more injuries would he endure if she pushed him to follow her way?

Emma returned with the cheer gone from her face.

"All the bandages were used up," she murmured as she knelt beside Aliwyn. "We don't have much fresh water left, either."

Aliwyn glanced at Toby's injury again and swallowed. With clothes rubbing over his side, he'd be in constant pain. And without fresh water, she couldn't even wash the dirty bandages to reuse them.

"Thank you all the same, Emma." Aliwyn smiled. With her clean hand, she tucked the girl's hair behind her ear.

Movement flickered behind Emma. Aliwyn stiffened as Axlan, one of Toby's few allies on the ship, sprinted across the deck with another mercenary. They halted before Edward just as he tore the thread with his teeth.

He stuffed the sewing kit into his belt pouch and stood. Aliwyn's hand clamped around Toby's arm, afraid Edward would elicit another fistfight with his nephew, but the older man simply turned toward the ocean. Through the thinning mist, the jagged outlines of conifer treetops appeared. The barrier islands were coming into view.

"Ali, what's wrong?" Toby asked. "Don't worry about bandages. I'll be fine."

He lay on his back watching her. She struggled to shake the image of him, fallen, while his uncle towered over him to deliver the killing blow. Toby might be blind to the possibility, but she wasn't. What could she do to keep him safe? As the makeshift yard groaned above her in the wind, an idea struck her. Maybe there was a way to get rid of Edward for a few hours after all, and she could speak with Toby in peace.

When Toby sat up and reached for her shoulder, she leaned toward him.

"Who is leaving to fell the yard?" she asked. "Can it be Edward? Please...please don't leave me here with him."

Genuine fear entered her voice. Toby gathered her close, and she wrapped her arms around him.

"I'll discuss what to do with them," he murmured in her ear. "Both my father and uncle."

"When has this ever been a point of discussion?" a surly voice boomed.

Aliwyn's stomach knotted as she looked up. Edward laced the front of his gambeson while he glared at her and Toby with dark, sunken eyes.

Marching forward, the older man said, "You are leading the logging team. I'm the captain of this ship, and I stay."

Toby's arm tightened around Aliwyn. She wanted to squeeze him back in return, but instinct warned her it would only aggravate Edward further.

"I can tend to Father's needs while you go," Toby said in a steady voice.

Edward bared his teeth in a snarl and spewed out several sentences in Danish. Although Toby didn't speak, his chest rose and fell with erratic breaths. Aliwyn caught Edward's furious glare flick to her several times. She carefully loosened herself from Toby's hold and squeezed his good hand one more time.

"Ask your father," she murmured, barely audible over Edward's rant. "Don't agree to go yet. I'll go empty the privy pots now."

She hoped against hope that Ransley would stop his injured son from being sent. Toby's anxious gaze matched her own, and he nodded once. The fact that he'd said not a word against Edward made her chest ache, but there was nothing she could do.

Aliwyn stood and reached for Emma's hand. The girl had turned gray since the yelling began, and her breaths came in fleeting puffs in the cold air. Toby should've refused to take part in this mission and taken the child elsewhere. Aliwyn drew Emma close, and the two of them hurried toward the black hole of the stairwell. At least down there, it was quiet.

Footsteps followed her. Aliwyn's heart shot to her throat. She spun around.

"Young lady." It was Axlan, holding his hat between his hands. "These men all need their wounds looked at, if you'd please."

He gave a hesitant smile with two missing side teeth. Beside and behind him stood nearly a dozen men with swollen eyes and sliced lips from the night before. Dirty bandages appeared everywhere she looked, all in need of changing, and something tugged in her chest. But if she helped these men, would they only turn against Toby within a few days? After all, only Edward paid them.

Unable to think, she said, "Give...give me a moment."

She glanced again at Toby. He had stood up and pulled his tunic back on, but the way his shoulders slumped while Edward gestured this way and that tore at her heart. Why couldn't he stand up to this bully of an uncle?

A small voice urged her to speak to Ransley, but the thought of speaking to a murderer face-to-face again made her shudder.

Aliwyn was halfway downstairs with Emma when the girl looked to the side and halted.

"Zel is here," she said.

Zelrin dragged his feet up to them, holding a rush lamp in one hand and rubbing his eyes with the other. Wisps of his wild, sandy brown hair flew out beneath his sackcloth hat.

"Hey," he said, gaze downcast. "I want to help."

He stomped onto the stairs, stepping down two steps at a time, and soon passed Aliwyn and Emma. Something was brewing beneath his surliness. Last night, he had called Toby's mission "blasted stupid" when it became clear another Norman would rise to power even if the rebels toppled King William.

Aliwyn needed to gather all the allies she could find, and she called after him. "Are you all right, Zel?"

He didn't answer.

The three of them arrived at the base of the stairs, and Aliwyn covered her nose with her sleeve. It reeked down there, and the flickering glow from Zel's rushlight did little to illuminate the ship's hull.

Zelrin placed the rushlight on a nearby crate, far from Ransley's straw mattress, and marched toward the privy at the ship's stern. Aliwyn stared at the man lying on his bed. Somehow, he slept right through the stench, and again she felt an urge to speak to him. She could no longer hear Edward or Toby upstairs, but she couldn't imagine the confrontation turning peaceful.

"We all hate it when Toby and Ed argue," Emma said, her large brown eyes peering up at Aliwyn.

Zelrin reappeared from behind the back door, balancing a full bucket. His face was scrunched up from the stink.

"It's worse than arguing," he said in a strangled voice.

Aliwyn swallowed and approached him. "What did Ed say in Danish?"

When Zelrin brushed past her in silence, Emma trailed after him. "Tell us, Zel. Is it really bad?"

After more questioning, Zelrin finally lowered the bucket beside the stairs and muttered, "Ed says Toby's mother shouldn't have had him."

Emma gasped, and a twisting pain began in Aliwyn's stomach. If she understood the meaning behind that statement, things were getting dangerously out of hand.

"Zel, Emma, can you two haul the privy pots upstairs? I will—" Her breath hitched at the thought, but she calmed herself. "I will speak to Ransley."

"He's still sleeping," Emma whispered.

"He can't anymore."

Aliwyn walked toward Ransley's mattress, hoping the man would stir given all the noise the two youngsters had made. He lay with his back turned under two layers of linens, and his frame didn't rise with breathing. Aliwyn's mouth ran dry. She quickened her pace. Stopping by the cot, she patted Ransley's shoulder.

"Sir," she said.

His broad shoulder was still warm, but there was no response.

Aliwyn struggled to call him again through the ball in her throat. Zelrin and Emma soon shuffled beside her; the girl was already whimpering.

Holding her breath, Aliwyn pressed on Ransley's shoulder and rolled him onto his back. He was limp. Half his face was grooved from the uneven blankets, and his dried lips were parted. One eye was cracked open, the other shut.

A sickening twist coiled in her gut, and Emma screamed. Zelrin pulled her back and buried her face in his chest.

Aliwyn tried again to shake Ransley awake. There was no vomit, no blood on his pillow. What had happened?

Uneven footsteps thudded down the steps, and Toby's shadowy figure approached them in the dimness. "Emma! Are you all right?"

His gaze fell on his father, and he stiffened.

"He's not responding," Aliwyn stammered.

"I don't want to see!" Emma screamed into Zelrin's tunic.

Aliwyn could scarcely draw a breath as Toby strode forward, his wide eyes fixed on the motionless man and his disheveled blankets. More footsteps thundered as men streamed downstairs, and Edward shoved his way to the front.

"Rans!" His raw cry boomed in Aliwyn's ears.

What followed was a chaotic blur. Edward charged toward Ransley's mattress as Aliwyn struggled to push Emma and Zelrin out of the way. Shouting echoed in the hull in a monstrous cacophony. Aliwyn felt Toby's presence against her back, shielding her and the two youngsters through the crush of bodies. But by the time they scrambled up the staircase, Toby was gone.

Aliwyn and the two others stumbled on deck. Fog had engulfed the ship, and only the dark, jagged tops of evergreens on the closest island peeked through the haze. The mist did little to cool the fire in Aliwyn's throat. She cradled Emma to her chest while Zelrin leaned against the rail and hung his head. The few men still upstairs hovered near the stairwell, panic etched on their faces. Emma's sobs had faded into quiet whimpers, but Aliwyn barely noticed as she stroked the girl's hair. This couldn't be real.

Ransley may have been confused yesterday, mistaking Aliwyn for Toby's fiancée and forgetting what Toby's destructive thundercrashers could do, but he was still walking and talking. Without his presence, who would defend Toby against Edward? Fears for herself and Toby battered her already scattered thoughts, but Aliwyn clenched her hands. She had to lock this dread inside.

"What are they saying?" She turned to Zelrin, her voice eerily calm.

He tore off his sackcloth hat, gripping a handful of his hair as tears brimmed in his eyes. "That Rans isn't answerin'. He has a pulse, but it's like he's..."

Zelrin's voice broke, and a stab of grief made Aliwyn shudder. She reached for his arm, but he jerked out of her reach and leaned over the railing again.

"Now they're blaming Toby," he spat. "Ed's claimin' he gave Rans bad medicine!"

Aliwyn stiffened all over. Sedatives and anesthetics could be fatal if given in the wrong doses, and Ransley could be near death. What if Toby had truly made a mistake?

When a cry of pain rang out from the hull, her chest seized. It sounded like Toby, like someone had punched him. Instinct screamed for her to run downstairs.

She loosened Emma's grip from her waist. "Sweetheart, I have to go."

Aliwyn spun toward the stairs, but Zelrin's arm shot out to block her. "Don't be stupid!"

His glare jolted her back to her senses. Rushing downstairs without a plan would only make things worse. But what could she do?

An idea, wild and untested, bloomed in the haze of her fear. Even if Ransley's deterioration *was* Toby's fault, she could turn the blame away from him. She must.

Clenching her fists, she shouted down the staircase, "Bring Ransley up here! I'll show you what's wrong with him!"

Aliwyn tensed at the authority in her voice, one she didn't feel. To her amazement, the worried muttering from the darkness below died down. Uncertainty seemed to hover in the air.

The memory of Toby's bruised and smiling face from earlier that morning threatened to crumble her composure. Her limbs twitching, she fought the urge to rush downstairs and seek him. It was too dangerous.

She was about to shout again for the men to ascend when the first of many footsteps thudded on the steps.

The rocking ship groaned as mercenaries trudged up the stairs. Their grimy hands gripped the corner of Ransley's blanket as they carried him.

Aliwyn held her breath. Edward dragged himself onto the deck with red-rimmed eyes; Toby followed with one side of his pale face flushed. Had Edward slapped him? She resisted running and wrapping her arms around him. Edward's devastation was one sliver away from murderous rage. She had to tread carefully.

As the rest of the men crowded around her, Aliwyn steeled herself.

"Lower him here." She pointed before her feet.

The men obeyed, and the blankets fell back from Ransley's face. Thinning blond hair clung to his forehead, and his unkempt beard did little to disguise the pallor of his skin. With another wary glance at the surrounding men, Aliwyn knelt beside Ransley. She felt his neck for a pulse and found it, faint and irregular, but his chest didn't rise. Her scalp tingled with chills. This man was alive...without breathing?

"How to wake him up?" Edward croaked.

"Wait." She shot him a commanding glare, but sweat beaded at her hairline.

Aliwyn spread her hand over Ransley's forehead. The warmth of his skin startled her, and an unbidden sorrow made her quiver. No matter what he had done in life, this man was still Toby's father. Toby stood beside Edward with a fine tremor in his hands, and she forced herself to turn away from his grimace.

"Didn't the wrong medicine do this?" Edward growled.

"No," she snapped. "There...are other reasons."

Aliwyn scrambled to recall every detail of the conversations she'd heard between Ransley and the others. "Ransley was injured before we set sail. A Vasfian had hit him on the head, remember?"

On the head. Aliwyn blinked quickly as the pieces fell into place. She used her thumb to lift one of Ransley's eyelids, then the other. Her heart gave a great leap. "Look at this. His pupils are not the same size."

Even in the grey morning light, the difference between the two was stark. Edward, Toby, and half the mercenaries leaned over to look. The others shuffled in place with their mouths twisted downward. Zelrin stood to one side with his arm tightened around Emma's shoulders. He looked green.

"Uneven pupils are a classic sign," Aliwyn said confidently. "Ransley was also confused and forgetful yesterday. Afraid of sunlight. This all points to bleeding within the skull and—"

Before she could finish, Ransley's chest shuddered. A slow and rattling breath scraped from his lungs.

Aliwyn jerked back her hand and nearly lost her balance. Around her, the deck erupted with the sound of creaky footsteps and frightened cries. Men backed away from the blanket, some of them muttering in English about a curse. Ransley continued to take heaving breaths, faster and faster.

"What...what did you just do?" His mouth falling open, Edward stepped forward.

"Nothing." Aliwyn squeezed the edge of Ransley's blanket. When Ransley's wheezing breaths decreased in rhythm, she fought the swirl of emotions inside. The bewilderment. The fleeting release of knowing justice had been served, followed by a suffocating dread.

If only she could grab Toby and the two youngsters and run.

"This kind of irregular breathing is terminal," she said, turning to the men. "The bleed within Ransley's head is already too great."

"It isn't too late." A sob escaped Edward's throat. "Can't you make a hole? Drain the blood?"

This massive, loathsome man was crying. Repeating that Ransley would soon die wouldn't appease him, and blood pulsed in Aliwyn's ears.

"I don't have any tools," she stammered. "And I lack the train—"

"I'll get you tools."

"But she isn't comfortable doing it." The fear in Toby's eyes matched her own. "Ali, it can't be too late. My father is still breathing."

He stepped forward as though to reach her, but he shouldn't have.

Edward spun around and grabbed Toby by the collar. "Rans was bleeding, and you said nothing!"

Toby shoved himself free, his teeth bared, and Aliwyn could almost see a fist flying for his face. She shot to her feet.

"Stop!" she cried. "What's the use of blaming anyone?"

Edward's glare flashed to her, his eyes volatile with panic, and Aliwyn licked her lips. He wouldn't leave Toby alone, no matter who was at fault for Ransley's condition. A plan bloomed in the haze of her mind.

"Maybe it isn't too late for Ransley after all," she said, her chin held high. "You want only the best care for your brother, yes? Then you must bring him onto land. There should be a priest or a surgeon with the tools and experience."

Murmuring swept over the men. The muscles of Edward's jaw worked, his scowl still fixed on her. This vengeful man would never believe the truth that his brother's erratic wheezing would be his last. So be it. Aliwyn needed to get Edward off the ship before he turned violent.

"The islands will think His Excellency's men have arrived to help an injured man. To fix a ship." She tilted her head toward the blue and yellow sail just above her head. "There isn't time. If you want to save your brother, you must act now."

A wall of distraught faces stared at her, and Aliwyn swallowed. Yes, she wanted the men to leave. She wanted Toby to herself. But what if the crew screamed at her for trying to doom the mission? For tricking them into leaving the ship?

But one of the hired hands with a blond, braided beard turned to Edward and voiced a different concern. "Ransley's condition is surely an ill omen. The gods do not strike a man down without cause."

"Nonsense. He's still alive." The bridge of Edward's nose twitched. "And you will be paid."

His face flushing again, he strode forward, and Aliwyn backed away just in time to avoid him falling on his knees. Edward gripped Ransley's shoulders and muttered something in a hoarse and cracking voice. Aliwyn stared at him with equal measures of pity and revulsion tightening her stomach.

Finally, Edward straightened just as Ransley began another episode of rattling breaths.

"I'll take him onto land," Edward said. He passed a hand over his face. "Who will go with me? You will be compensated."

Aliwyn kept a blank face while most of the men around her nodded and seemed to mutter their interest in going. Did they not find this mission risky? It was unbelievable how easily they were swayed by the promise of money.

Turning back to Aliwyn, Edward dipped his chin and uttered words she could scarcely believe. "Thank you."

She swallowed, her tongue dry. Edward would waste time no matter what he did, but he'd refused to accept the truth. Now, she'd finally get rid of him for a while.

A quick search of the crowd revealed that Zelrin and Emma had disappeared. Toby hung his head with his forehead wrinkled in misery, and her ribs twinged. How was she going to talk to him about his mission and his cargo if his heart was in a thousand pieces?

On a whim, she approached him and placed her hand on his elbow. "Stay on board with me?" she whispered.

Toby reached around her back and pulled her into a tight embrace. His chest heaved and shuddered. The raw scent of his wounds drifted over her, and Aliwyn squeezed her eyes shut.

"I'm so sorry," she whispered. She was sorry in more ways than one, and she couldn't shake the fear he'd soon despise her.

Edward raised an arm as he surveyed the men around him, his eyes piercing again. "Send scouts on the canoe."

CHAPTER 6
IN FIVE DAYS

September 30, Matthew

HUGS, TEARS, AND CHEERS. Matthew didn't have to speak Vasfian to understand how much Reiya's people appreciated her return. The wooden gates of Blaithin hillfort had barely creaked open before they swarmed around her mare, disregarding him and Evelyn like wrinkly apples in a feed trough. Torches held aloft by the enthusiastic crowd flickered in the hazy night air.

Domilo and Namanti were the loudest. As Reiya swung down from her saddle, they wrapped themselves around her. Matthew had never cared to be squeezed or cried on, but something about the scene tonight, and his exclusion from it, made his throat tighten.

Evelyn didn't even look at him. Matthew took off his helmet with his damp forehead tingling. He may as well not exist. If his kin ignored him, what did he have left?

He still needed to ask Reiya for permission to examine the Danish belts, but he wanted to speak with Evelyn first. Maybe even apologize for leaving Kato at the leper colony. He just needed some time with her alone.

Reiya finally pulled off Domilo's arms and straightened. Scowls now darkened the crowd's faces, their voices turning somber as they watched the encroaching smoke. Matthew suppressed a cough as Porei snorted beside him in distress. The fire shouldn't reach the hillfort, as it was surrounded by dirt mounds with nothing to burn, but the smoke was becoming unbearable.

Reiya shot Matthew a glance and nudged Domilo toward him. As she led her villagers away, the boy bounded over.

"My sister said a bad person almost stabbed you," he called out.

"Yeah." Matthew's armor felt ten times heavier. "But she loosed a bolt at him, and I dealt the final blow."

Domilo grinned. "I'm glad you're all right."

His words meant more than Matthew could express. He gave a slow nod, his throat tight. "Guess I came back after all."

"And you're back with family." Domilo's smile grew as he turned to Evelyn. "Reiya said you're Matthew's cousin. My name is Domilo. Pleased to meet you. Welcome to Blaithin." He extended a freckled hand.

Evelyn shook his hand, but her face soon wrinkled with sorrow. She pulled back and turned away.

Frowning, Domilo turned to Matthew. "I thought Normans shook hands?"

Matthew sighed. Kato's hands were also covered in freckles. Maybe the redhead had already perished in the fires outside the leper colony.

"Evelyn's had a difficult day," he mumbled.

Domilo nibbled his lower lip. He pushed all his red hair underneath his checkered headscarf. "Miss Evelyn, I can show you our guesthouse, although we'll be leaving soon. My family owns a second hillfort beside the River Humber."

"You plan to pack everything?" Matthew asked. "The fire shouldn't enter the village."

"It can. The wind can blow fire sparks very far." The boy lowered his eyes. "The bad English people have burned my village before."

"I...see." It was odd to hear a Vasfian boy talk about what Aliwyn's people had done. "Please take me to the stable so I can tend to Porei."

"No need. My villagers will help with the horses. Are you both hungry? I know where food is."

Evelyn finally spoke. "No, thank you. Please show me where I can stay."

Matthew wanted to protest and say she must eat, but he swallowed his words.

He stroked Porei until two villagers came to take her reins. Nickering softly, she departed with the women with her tail swinging. Matthew watched his companion disappear with an ache he couldn't explain.

Domilo led Matthew and Evelyn through the village, where hideous glowing turnips sneered at him before every doorstep. Smoke drifted from the conical roofs of their roundhouses. Matthew dragged his feet and suppressed a yawn. The burn of his throat spread through his chest.

They stopped before a roundhouse with overlapping circles painted on its wooden door. A woman with a water bucket greeted them, and Evelyn followed her inside.

Matthew drew a steadying breath. Now was the time to make amends with his cousin.

He turned to Domilo. "Wait here. I'll remove my armor inside."

The boy nodded, and Matthew slipped through the doorway.

Smoke and burning lard thickened the air. Flickering light from two carved turnips cast shadows over fur-lined floors. Wooden ladles, smoked meats, and bundled herbs hung from the beams beneath the conical thatched roof.

Evelyn helped the Vasfian woman light the hearth while Matthew lingered near the wall. After what he'd done to Kato, he didn't belong here.

He found a bare patch of ground, shrugged off his chainmail, and exhaled as the weight left his shoulders. The metal needed scrubbing, but he was too tired. As Matthew loosened his gambeson, he caught Evelyn watching him in the firelight.

He forced himself to speak. "I can bring you something to eat."

"Don't bother." Her gaze was stern. "Kato used to bring me food every day when Marie and I lived on the streets. You disappeared for seven years."

Matthew's throat constricted. If only he'd been there when the Boltans sank his family's ship and left his cousins homeless. "But I...I wrote you letters every season. I never forgot your birthday. I just didn't want to see my parents next door."

"Your parents moved to Marcottesville." Evelyn turned her back on him. "You still didn't visit."

"They only moved last year." Unwanted anger surged in his chest. "I planned to visit you this Christmas. And it's not true that I disappeared for seven years. I saw you in Beverly for Easter five years ago."

"That was just for four days, and your parents weren't there. They sent you many letters from Marcottesville. You never opened them."

Why would he? Matthew used to receive letters full of curses when he was younger, telling him his love of painting was for fools, not knights. Matthew clenched his hands. He could only change the subject.

"Why did you never visit me?" he challenged. "I spent every winter alone in Lord Seville's manor."

At the worst moment, the pain of spending many Christmases alone cut through his old scars.

Evelyn bowed her head. "Leave me alone. I only want to see Kato."

A creak came at the door, and Matthew turned to catch Domilo's red hair retreating from the entrance. The anger draining out of him, Matthew frowned at his feet.

"I'll sleep elsewhere," he mumbled.

The words to apologize for Kato's disappearance wouldn't come. So much for trying to make amends.

He strode to the door, his mind wandering back to happier days when he'd receive Evelyn's letters sealed with twin blue roses. Her messages helped him feel connected to some kind of family, even if reading about her holiday travels with her parents made his throat tighten every time.

His own parents only noticed him when he failed. His father was either drunk or away in Sicily. His mother locked him away with servants every night after he'd caught her in a tryst with another man. By age seven, he'd been sent away as a page.

Evelyn never had a reason to interact with him. He was a splinter at the edge of her perfect life.

Matthew exited the roundhouse, where the chill of the night enveloped him again. Domilo stood right outside with his arms crossed. Matthew sighed. To be alone was impossible.

"Who's Kato?" the boy asked. "That's a Vasfian name."

"He...forget about him." Matthew sighed. "I need to see your sister, please."

"But Reiya's talking to my elders."

"I need to see her. I saw writing on the belts she stole from Ransley Boltan. Maybe it will help us track them down."

Domilo hesitated, but he turned around to lead. "I don't know where my sister is, but we can start by walking this way."

Matthew followed the boy down a path where the scent of boiled meat filled the air. The fragrance made his stomach growl, but his mind was elsewhere. "Domilo, did your grandmother send the messenger pigeons to the coastal tribes to warn them about the Danes?"

The boy turned around with an apologetic look. "No, she didn't."

Matthew clenched his jaw. He had suspected the Vasfians had only paid him pleasantries so he'd leave. He'd have to discuss the matter with Reiya.

Finally, behind a tall dirt mound where villagers fired clay pots, Matthew heard Reiya's voice. He and Domilo circled the structure and halted.

Reiya squatted beside a black chest and an open crate with belts hanging over the edge like dead snakes. Matthew stopped a short distance away and swallowed.

Reiya and her warriors must have killed a dozen of Boltans' men to collect so many. Druid apprentices crouched beside her, holding torches, as she frowned and ran a belt through her hands section by section. They all spoke in tense voices. Matthew squinted; there were rows upon rows of letters burned into the leather. *Interesting.*

Domilo pointed to a hearth where a Vasfian man ladled stew onto flatbread, serving a gathering nearby, but Matthew declined to eat. The boy left him and joined the others as Matthew squared his shoulders. Reiya wouldn't throw him out just for asking questions. Would she?

As he stepped closer, a few apprentices noticed him and quickly beckoned one another to lift the black chest. It was the large one taken from the Boltans. Its dark colors had once blended with the shadows, but now the torchlight revealed varnished wood and caulked edges. They were the features of a watertight chest. A gold stripe decorated each side, while a large padlock secured the object.

The apprentices strained to carry it behind a roundhouse. Matthew's pulse quickened. Were they shielding it from him? He wasn't here to steal, but that chest looked expensive and heavy. Maybe the Boltans had locked chainmail inside. Or gold.

"What are you doing?" Reiya spoke just behind him.

Matthew spun around. She had approached without a sound, and her eyes flashed with displeasure.

"Looking for you." He kept his tone light. "Were you trying to read something on those belts?"

"Yes, and I will do it by myself." She glared at him. "You're supposed to be sleeping, not wandering around my village."

Matthew swallowed. He resisted looking at Domilo and getting the boy into trouble.

"But can you read the alphabet?" he asked. "Because I can."

Reiya crossed her arms. "I know a thing or two about your culture. I once spent months at a Norman convent."

Matthew raised an eyebrow at that, but now wasn't the time to ask why she'd stayed in such a dreary place.

"Look," he said. "I'm just here to help you translate—"

"I don't trust the intelligence of a man who kneels for a woman who just spat on him." Reiya lowered her chin, her eyes glinting under the orange torchlight. "You're still obsessed with that traitor, aren't you?"

Matthew suppressed a cough. So, this was about Aliwyn.

"Reiya," he said. "I had a best friend I thought I knew well, but now I know he kept many secrets. Maybe because I never gave him a chance to talk."

She inhaled slowly, and Matthew squashed the urge to ask if Aelfric was of Vasfian descent. What if the answer brought fresh wounds instead of closure?

Unexpected grief swept over Reiya's features. "Why are we talking about Aelfric?"

"Because I never gave Aliwyn a chance to explain herself, either. I can't assume I know the truth about her."

Reiya's frown returned in an instant. "Or you're diverting my attention while you plot a way to steal something. My warriors saw you staring at our loot."

"I'm not a thief." He met her gaze. "I'm trying to prove this alliance matters to me. When you were missing earlier today, I offered to help your grandmother search, but she refused. You can ask her to confirm this."

"Or I can confirm it," Domilo hollered.

Matthew grinned at the boy, who sat on a stool by the eating table and swung his legs. Reiya exchanged a few words with her brother. Finally, unfolding her arms, she beckoned Domilo over.

The torches held by the druid apprentices flickered over her and Matthew as they squatted by the crate. She fingered the belts with a deepening frown.

"All war spoils must be blessed at the celebratory feast before we touch them. These are belts we scavenged from the Boltans' soldiers who died outside Aelfric's mill, and the gods have already blessed them." She turned to Matthew. "Now, tell me what you see."

He kept a frozen grin. "Just give me some time."

"We don't have time if the rebels plan to strike again soon." Reiya pulled belts from the crate and laid them flat. "Look. The writing on each belt ends with the same symbols."

She pointed at the last row of numbers. Two pairs of numbers, IX XX and X V, appeared in the firelight.

Matthew picked up another belt, then another. The same two pairs of numbers appeared, like she'd said, at the end of long lists of numbers. Yet, the preceding numbers were often different. Matthew scratched between his eyebrows. These numbers told him nothing. So much for offering to make sense out of this.

Domilo handed Reiya a flat bread covered with meat stew, then left a plate of the same thing beside Matthew. His mouth watered at the fragrance of roasted carrots and rabbit, but he refused to eat until he solved this numbers puzzle.

"These are Roman numerals," he mumbled. "The last pair always reads nine-twenty, ten-five. And none of the numbers exceed thirty-one."

Reiya sat cross-legged, studying them. "Could they be dates?"

Matthew blinked. The first number of each pair ranged from one to twelve, and the second ranged from one to thirty-one. His scalp tingled. Impressive. Despite Reiya's bloodshot and tired eyes, she was still sharp.

"You could be right," he said. "So, let's assume we have lists of dates, but September twentieth and October fifth are at the end of each list."

Reiya's sigh came out like a growl. "That's not useful."

Matthew struggled to stay calm. His mind turned back to the emerald eye embroidery he'd seen on the Danish thief. He turned all the belts over to the external side. A few featured emerald eyes, whereas others displayed golden boar heads or a horse with eight legs. A buried memory resurfaced. Following the previous rebellion, Lord Seville had brought home round shields as spoils of war. Matthew had to clean them.

"I've seen these emblems before on the back of enemy shields," he said. "They represent different mercenary groups from Denmark."

Reiya had been gnawing on a bone, but now she grew still. Matthew wiped a sweaty hand on his thigh.

"I'll tell you what I think is happening," he continued. "Danish mercenaries are here to aid the rebels. Those belt markings are the dates of their contracts. The last date is October fifth...meaning they have a mission in England ending in five days. And knowing the Danes, they won't leave without a raid."

Reiya's eyes widened, an expression he'd never seen her make, and he swallowed hard. He'd strung together several predictions, a strategy he'd often employed to curtail an opponent's moves while playing chess. But this wasn't a board game.

"It's a plausible theory," he argued. "The Danes were here during the last uprising. I told your grandmother the Boltans used Danish runes on their crates, like there was trade happening between them. And we killed a man who looks like he'd just sailed from there."

Reiya picked at the bandages on her arm. "Either you're brilliant, or you're trying to squeeze milk from turnips. You told my grandmother to warn the coastal tribes to guard their shores. That means dispatching warriors to the sea while rebels still roam inland. She didn't like it. My sister tribes won't either. They won't move their warriors."

"Not even for five days?" Matthew asked. "I'll also ask Sir Verdun to secure the coast."

He looked up at the sound of muttering. Namanti and three other redheads stood nearby, their frowns flicking over him. Reiya spoke with them before standing.

"Eat your food, Matthew. And my elders tell me I need to sleep." She handed her unfinished plate to another villager.

His stomach dropped. "You'll do nothing with what I've just said?"

Reiya took a moment to embrace her grandmother, and Matthew struggled to be patient. The older woman spoke gently to Reiya before departing with the other Vasfians.

Reiya watched them go. "My doves cannot navigate without the sun. I can't send warnings till morning. And also..." Her mouth twisted to one side. "My written language doesn't have a word for 'Dane.' Only 'Outsider.' So, I don't know how to communicate your warning."

She looked away, tapping her fingers on her belt.

"There's a way around that." Matthew waited until she looked at him again. "You can tell your sister tribes to attack any ships that land. His Grace's ships won't trespass like that. And why use words? I can draw you a griffin surcoat as part of your message."

Her scowl lifted. For the first time, she smiled at him. "I like that idea."

"I'm glad you do." Matthew breathed again. "Give me parchment and I'll draw it tomorrow."

She nodded. Rubbing her eyes, she continued.

"My sister tribes should agree to watch the coast if it's only for five days." She spoke to the druid apprentices before turning back to him. "These men will take you back to the guesthouse. Tomorrow, I'll leave you and your cousin at Barton-upon-Humber."

She turned to leave, but Matthew called out, "One last thing. If your sister tribes ever find a woman on board, ask them to keep her alive and well."

Reiya spun around, scowling again, but Matthew stood his ground. The only person who had treated him tenderly in the last year had been Aliwyn, and he hadn't even thanked her.

"I've already told my sister tribes to keep that peasant alive," she muttered.

As she departed, the tension eased from Matthew's shoulders. He had achieved something tonight, at least. Domilo looked back at him one more time and waved. He and his sister disappeared around a bend.

ON HIS WAY BACK to Evelyn's roundhouse, Matthew picked up an extra serving of flatbread and stew. He lowered it beside where Evelyn slept. Maybe by the time he was knighted next year, when he finally inherited his father's manor and gave her a home, she'd speak to him again.

His head lowered, Matthew exited and pushed three haystacks together for his makeshift cot. He should be warm enough with his gambeson and cape.

A heavy weight pressed on his chest as he lay down. He hadn't slept well since Tobias lured him into Wynthorpe with a letter claiming his shipwrecked parents had taken shelter there. It had been a trap. If Aelfric hadn't helped the Vasfians breach Wynthorpe's ramparts, Matthew would have perished.

He shivered and coughed. The only way to thank Aelfric was by saving his sister. Wrapping his cape tighter, he reached into his belt pouch for the golden pig ornament Aelfric had given him. His friend had cast it after melting a brooch he'd won in a chess tournament. The tiny pig bore Matthew's name and was the only thing the Boltans hadn't stolen. They must've missed it.

Rubbing his thumb over its pointy ears, Matthew smiled. The Boltans had failed to take Aelfric's first gift. That had to mean something. Clutching it tight, he finally fell asleep.

October 1

MATTHEW COULD HARDLY PEEL his eyelids apart when someone shook his shoulder.

"Why are you sleeping outside?" Reiya asked.

Matthew squinted up at her. She had wrapped a cloth around her nose and mouth, and the rest of her face was too blurry for him to read.

How long had he been sleeping? His dry throat burning, Matthew muttered, "Evelyn doesn't want me inside."

There was a pause.

"It's time to go," she said.

Matthew pushed himself into a sitting position. At least she didn't comment on his family's problems, but he wasn't grateful for long. Reiya dumped a heavy cloth on his head. He yelped and pulled it off, only to realize it was a colorful, woven blanket and not a medicated sack. Sighing, he wound the blanket around his shoulders and pulled it up over his nose. It smelled of wild roses. The scent teased him with a memory just out of reach.

"You can sleep on one of my carts," Reiya said. "Stand up."

The whinnying of horses echoed to his ears, and what looked like sunlight now cast the smoky sky in a pale glow. Despite the cloth covering his nose, Matthew gagged in the smoke.

"Is Porei—" he began.

"She's also ready to leave. We took care of her, don't worry. Want your chainmail?"

The thought of donning such heavy armor made his head spin. "No, my gambeson is enough. Also, the chainmail isn't mine. I borrowed it from Sir Verdun. Is it packed?"

"Yes. Follow me."

Matthew rubbed his eyes and rose to his feet. He trudged alongside her, and each cough worsened the pain from his bruised torso where he'd almost been stabbed. As he sucked water from his costrel, Reiya turned to him and unfurled her fist. A glistening black ball rested on her palm. It was twice the width of her thumb and smelled pungent, even an arm's length away.

"You refused my grandmother's medication yesterday," she said. "This one is mine. Will you refuse it also?"

Matthew wrinkled his nose. "What is this made of?"

"Black mushrooms, garlic paste, and oregano powder. Mashed with a pestle." She pinched a small piece, lifted her scarf, and placed it into her mouth. "Not poison."

Something told him he'd regret refusing the Vasfians' offering again. Holding his breath, Matthew picked up the sticky ball and shoved it into his mouth. It packed enough flavor to season an entire cauldron and set his throat ablaze. His eyes tearing, Matthew gulped down more water.

"The burning will pass," Reiya said. "You'll cough less for the next while."

Matthew massaged his throat. Reiya's voice had softened despite her stern gaze, unless he was imagining it. He covered his nose again with the blanket she'd given him.

They approached over a dozen carts parked in a clearing, where villagers loaded bags and rolled barrels up ramps. Porei shuffled restlessly beside the wagon she was tethered to. Evelyn sat upon the warhorse, Vaillant, with her back straight and her face obscured by her hood. When she turned to Matthew with a cold stare, he pretended to check his scabbed right hand.

Had she eaten the flatbread he'd brought her? Should he bother asking?

"I shouldn't have accused you of stealing Porei," Reiya said just then.

Matthew looked up in surprise. "You...were making a rational assumption."

"All the same, I apologize."

Her eyes were downcast, and Matthew swallowed a few times. Chiefs should not apologize so readily; she'd lose the respect of her followers.

Reiya led him toward the village exit as gusts of smoke heated Matthew's face. The sky burned orange. Birds shrieked as they escaped the treetops, skittering between the torrents of rolling smoke. Fear finally pierced his exhaustion. When he turned to Reiya again, her eyes glistened above her scarf as she watched the escaping animals.

He'd hate to be in her position. And despite everything, she had cared enough to make him a medicine ball.

"You...are you all right?" he asked.

She fussed with Porei's stirrups. "This fire is my fault."

"How?"

After a long silence, she answered, "The Boltans polluted our springs for months. I killed their men without asking what they dumped or why. I assumed it was garbage. Feces." She glanced at the smoke overhead. "But my grandmother said...the Boltans must've been trying to make whatever started this. And they dumped into our waters what didn't work."

Matthew looked down. The royal army had also missed the rebels' schemes. "This fire is still not your fault."

Squeezing the edge of Porei's saddle, Reiya closed her eyes and leaned her forehead on the leather. Aelfric's old saddle. Matthew sighed; he needed to change the subject.

"Can I help with something? Maybe load those?" He turned to a few youngsters straining to load chests onto a covered wagon. The watertight chest was already on board.

"No, you can't help them." Her gaze was sympathetic. "They're my grandmother's apprentices. Only the druid class can touch our spoils of war until the next *Anuin*. It was supposed to be...today."

Her voice frayed, and Matthew felt a tug in his chest. "What is an *Anuin*?"

"Our worship feast for our gods and our ancestors. It's when we bless our plunder. Pray to Lenus for healing." Her eyes grew bright again, but she wiped them dry. "Anyway, if you want to help, there is something..."

"What?"

"I sent scouts north toward Barton-upon-Humber since we're heading that way. They tell me Jacques Verdun is outside the Brocklesby town walls."

Matthew blinked. "Isn't that good news? Brocklesby is closer than Barton-upon-Humber. I'll reunite with my men, and you'll get rid of me sooner."

"No, it's not good news. Jacques has seen how the suspension bridge is not burned, like I said it would be. He's seen Tobias gone." Her rounded eyes lifted. "When you see Jacques, perhaps you could...speak well of me."

Matthew stroked Porei's neck. "I already agreed to speak to my men with you, didn't I?"

"Yes, but I had hoped to meet a different knight in Barton. Not the man who robbed Aelfric's watermill."

"You were there?"

"No, but a few village children watched from a distance."

Matthew scratched between his eyebrows. He had tossed Aliwyn's chickens out of the men's reach while yelling for them to stop ransacking the mill. No one had listened. The memory still left a sour taste in his mouth.

"I'm sure Sir Verdun had a lapse of judgment," Matthew muttered into the blanket. "He was knighted for his bravery during the conquest of England. He's one of His Excellency's most experienced soldiers. He should be willing to hear your story."

"So you say." Her scowl didn't ease. "What will you tell Jacques Verdun about Tobias' disappearance?"

Matthew hadn't seriously considered this question. Head buzzing with fatigue, he followed Reiya toward the edge of the crowd and their herd of sheep. Bleating and barking filled the air. Hunting dogs circled villagers loading the last bags into overstuffed carts. Within the wagons, Domilo and Nissa lay sleeping beneath checkered blankets. Other children and the elderly huddled beside them.

A lump formed in his throat. One day ago, he wouldn't have cared about anyone here.

He caught up to Reiya. "We can discuss what we'll say on our way to Brocklesby."

"You're not going to sleep?"

"I'll sleep later. This is important."

A warmth filled her eyes above her scarf, and Matthew swallowed. She was unrecognizable when she looked like that, and he didn't know how to respond.

"I'd appreciate that discussion," she said. "Porei is waiting for you."

She left for her horse nearby. Matthew mounted Porei and twisted his back side to side. The cart hitched behind her carried a harp, overfilled yarn sacks, and two crates of chickens who stared back at him all silent and puffed up. He stared back. Why did they look familiar?

Sleep deprivation, probably. He adjusted the blanket over his nose and coughed. Looking up, he found Evelyn approaching him on horseback and braced himself for the worst. But her hard expression had faded to quiet sorrow.

"Thank you for the food," she said. Her eyes were red from crying.

Matthew tried for a smile. "You're welcome."

"I'd still like to have some distance from you. I hope you understand." She sighed and continued in Norman French, "Everyone here reminds me of Kato. I just want to go home."

Matthew nodded once as she turned her horse toward the village gates. Maybe his silence was the distance she wanted.

Finally, the gates opened outward. Hunting hounds surged outward with frenzied barking. Wagon wheels groaned as the procession rolled into the forest, away from torrents of orange smoke rising in the air.

Evelyn wove through the crowd to the front. Matthew shifted in his stirrups, fighting the urge to follow. He had to respect her freedom. At eighteen, she would've been married in Normandy if the Boltans hadn't attacked their ship on the way.

Reiya waited near the road. Something had changed about the way she looked at him. There was a bit less irritation in her eyes, maybe. Matthew directed Porei to canter toward her.

"Here." She raised a fist and held out the Nornsblade.

He pulled up beside her and took the sword.

"You trust me with this?" he asked, strapping it to his belt.

"I trust you not to be a fool. We have crossbows. You wear no armor."

Matthew grinned wryly behind the blanket covering half his face. Reiya held his gaze for a moment before turning her mare around. Wavy red hair flew between the layers of her scarf as the dust kicked up by the procession drifted about her. The lump in Matthew's throat returned.

Sir Verdun might not take news of Tobias' escape well. If his meeting with Reiya turned sour, Matthew would have to side with the royal army. Reiya must understand this. Even so, she had returned his sword.

"Are we talking or not?" she called over her shoulder.

Matthew tried to relax his posture. Clearing his throat, he urged Porei to Reiya's side.

CHAPTER 7
WOLVES AMONG SHEEP

October 2, Aliwyn

ALIWYN'S BREATH CAUGHT IN her throat as she peered at the militiamen of the Driftmere harbor front. It must be close to noon. White flags bearing the Normans' red cross fluttered from the sailboats and longships moored at the dock, and militiamen crowded everywhere. So far, they only smiled at Edward and his mercenaries as they carried Ransley on his blanket onto land.

Edward wouldn't be gone long. She still needed to convince Toby to dump his cargo, but what would she say? None of the ideas spinning in her mind felt right.

Snippets of conversation reached her ears. Edward proclaimed that he had come in peace as one of His Excellency's knights, was staying until afternoon, and needed help for his injured brother and damaged ship. None of the Driftmere militiamen questioned him.

As the rebels populated the rocky beach, monks emerged from the dense fog shrouding their island to assess the unconscious Ransley. Fishermen surrounded other mercenaries to sell barrels of dried cod. The mercenaries, in turn, took out their purses.

Aliwyn pinched her fingertips. *Just unbelievable.* The militiamen themselves spoke Danish, and some even grew forked beards in the Danish style. They didn't seem to suspect that the Boltans were rebels. This island must've been too isolated to hear of their crimes.

A few women and children wearing clothes embroidered with foreign patterns wandered on the beach, collecting driftwood. Oh, how they resembled Brocklesby's villagers! But the people here, unlike back home, were Danish settlers. Perhaps they were the militiamen's families. Meanwhile, Edward's hired hands were a different kind of Dane altogether. By now, Aliwyn was certain they were former raiders.

The breeze tangled her hair with the scent of drying fish. Gulls shrieked in the gray sky, their cries lost in the chatter of traders and creaking ships. Everything looked ordinary, but goosebumps still skittered over her arms. Edward's hired hands had better behave on this island.

She sank below the railing and reached for Emma's hand. They'd been ordered to stay hidden at the stern, where the privy vent reeked. A makeshift curtain of capes and the raised platform kept them hidden. Edward didn't want questions about a woman and child aboard.

Emma looked up at her and whispered, "When is Toby coming back?"

"Soon," Aliwyn said, combing the girl's curls. "Let me braid your hair. I promised you I would."

Emma smiled and leaned closer.

Although Aliwyn patiently braided the child's hair, her restlessness grew. Toby *was* taking too long. Finally, clopping hoofbeats prompted her to rise again and peer over the rail. On the quay, an ox cart pulled to a halt beside Ransley. Mercenaries lifted his makeshift stretcher onto it.

Toby stood nearby, clad in his gambeson and speaking with two elderly monks in black woolen habits. They clasped his hands in prolonged shakes, and smiles brightened their wrinkled faces. Aliwyn gawked. How did the monks of Driftmere know Toby?

Other monks began carrying full buckets of water aboard. Through the curtain of capes, she heard Zelrin directing them to refill the ship's drinking barrels. The floorboards vibrated with their footsteps. Aliwyn frowned at the sound of splashing water. She appreciated it, but the monks didn't understand who they were helping.

She dared to check on Toby again. He stood beside his uncle, and watched the man with sympathy. Meanwhile, a monk patted Edward on the back and addressed him by name. Another monk applied salve to Ransley's temples as he lay on the cart.

How strange it was to see the Boltans and the religious order interacting like old friends. And why did Toby still look at his despicable uncle this way?

Aliwyn nibbled on her lip. Maybe the Heavens had brought everyone to Driftmere so she could get answers. Her instincts whispered that to sway Toby into dumping his cargo, she would need to unearth his past and perhaps exploit his apparent attachment to the peace-loving monks.

Aliwyn finished Emma's braid with a satisfied smile. She now knew what to say when Toby returned.

Toby

THE MIST CLUNG TO the shoreline like wool. Now that the hired hands had departed to cut a new yard, Edward barely spoke anymore. His eyes hollow, he climbed into the cart beside Ransley.

Toby watched with his chest aching. Would the salty ocean scent and the chime of the abbey bell stir the old Edward awake? Driftmere was where they'd first met, over a decade ago. Edward had brought Toby sweets and hoisted him onto his shoulders.

Toby was willing to overlook all their fights over the last few years if it would bring his uncle cheer again. As for Ransley, Toby didn't know what to think. It was a relief to see Edward's vulnerability without Ransley's smug interference.

Brother Dunstan, the abbot and leader of the monastery, adjusted his satchel. "Come home with us, Toby. We have your favorite white cheese."

Toby hesitated. Driftmere didn't feel like home anymore. His home was his cause and his ship. He'd also promised Aliwyn he'd stay, especially with Cilebi ordered to remain on board as punishment for hiding last night while other mercenaries braved the Vasfians.

"I can't come," Toby said. "The ship is in poor shape. I need to do maintenance before we sail again."

The words sounded honest enough, but sweat beaded at his hairline. Dunstan mustn't know that Toby had brought a young woman. It would lead to too many questions, and Aliwyn wasn't his only secret. Twenty-four chests of thundercrashers lay nestled in the hold. Dunstan would never approve. Despite suffering a slash to the face years ago, dealt by a Norman sword, the old abbot obeyed the crown and groveled for charity.

Dunstan smiled. It lifted half his face, but the scarred half only quivered.

"Well, my boy, you're now a busy man. But you're welcome back anytime."

Toby inhaled slowly. "Thank you."

He hadn't visited Dunstan since Odrianna had passed. They'd speak again when the tyrant king was toppled and the bells of Driftmere rang in a free England.

Edward's voice rasped from the cart. "Watch the *Fortuna*."

Toby turned. His uncle sat and stared at Ransley's labored breaths. The minty ointment Brother Claude applied to Ransley's scalp wound failed to make him stir.

For a heartbeat, Toby saw in Edward the man who'd taught him to whittle swords from driftwood. The man who had tucked him in at night when he visited Driftmere.

Toby stepped closer.

"Uncle Ed," he murmured. He hadn't addressed Edward like this since the Norman invasion that had killed his wife and unborn child. Yet, in front of Dunstan, who expected such a greeting, Toby had an excuse.

"Please remember to eat," Toby continued. "And that kitten you used to feed...if she's still alive, she'll find you soon."

Edward had been so fond of that cat, but he didn't stir. There was no hint of a smile, not even a glance. Toby fought the chill in his chest.

"I'll take care of the *Fortuna*. You take care of yourself," he finished.

Dunstan waited beside the ox. "He's in good hands. And if you change your mind about visiting, the old garden's still there. So is your bench. Some things don't change."

Toby gave a stiff nod and stepped back.

Soon, the fog swallowed the departing oxen cart, the marching mercenaries, and Edward's slouching form. Toby sighed and turned toward the

Fortuna. Edward would come around. They'd lost their belongings and their home to the Normans. All they had left was each other and the cargo. Only by selling it to the Danish prince could they secure passage to Denmark and escape the gallows for treason and murder in England. Edward would have to cooperate for the sake of survival, if not for family.

A wisp of brown hair caught Toby's eye. He looked up as Aliwyn's forehead ducked behind the railing. Had she been watching? He scowled with a prick of irritation.

Not only had she risked being discovered, but now she'd ask about the monks and why Toby hadn't once knelt by Ransley like a proper son. And how could he tell her the truth without losing her respect?

He lowered his gaze and limped onto the gangplank. Let her wonder. He'd hide below deck with his journal, the one Edward had given him when Toby was six. The pressed flowers and old memories would steady him. Perhaps Aliwyn would forget to ask her questions.

His boots thudded onto the deck. Schooling his features into a smile, Toby greeted Cilebi and Zelrin. Behind him, the mist closed in again.

Aliwyn

CHURCH BELLS RANG THE noon hour through the impenetrable mist shrouding the island. With time, the beach became deserted. Toby and Axlan retrieved the gangplank and raised the entry rail, which was a hinged section designed to be lowered for boarding.

Aliwyn strained to hear Toby's voice. Finally, uneven footsteps approached where she and Emma hid, and the curtain flew back.

Toby appeared with a smile and a bucket of water. "Emma, Ali, come drink your fill."

Emma jumped to her feet with a muffled squeal. She nearly dunked her face into the clear liquid, and Aliwyn grinned despite all that had been happening. When Toby lifted the bucket toward her, she gulped down the blissfully cool water that spilled down her throat and calmed her nerves.

She finished drinking, and Toby smiled at Emma. "Beautiful braids, young lady."

The girl beamed, fingering her two pigtails, and he winked at Aliwyn.

Aliwyn wiped her mouth and smiled back, but her chest was tight. It had been so strange to see Toby stare at Edward while completely ignoring Ransley on the cart. And now, the circles beneath Toby's eyes made him hardly recognizable. Something was still upsetting him. Would he want to talk to her at all?

Finally, she broke the silence. "It was kind of the monks to bring us water. How come you know them?"

A frown flickered over Toby's brows, and she swallowed. He backed away and gulped from the bucket. Turning his back, he poured the leftover water into a barrel along the railing.

"I spent part of my childhood here," he finally answered.

Aliwyn's eyes widened. Why had Toby been living here?

Beside her, Emma exclaimed, "What? Are you saying you and your family moved in with monks?"

He looked up and chuckled. "No. Only I did. The two brothers who left last, Dunstan and Claude, were my mentors."

"Why?" Emma asked. "You're not a monk, and I'm glad you aren't. Monks can't get married!"

Aliwyn wanted to smile, but she thinned her lips instead when Toby turned to frown at the nearly invisible island. Rich families sometimes offered their children to monasteries as oblates, or living sacrifices, to be raised as future monks. But as Emma had said, Toby was no monk. Neither did he seem willing to talk about what happened.

She finally stammered, "It must've been peaceful, living here."

"Yes." Toby lowered the bucket with a thunk. "Anyway... Can you prepare some pottage, Ali? The men have an endless streak of burning it."

"Oh, I'll do it." She tried to sound casual, but it bothered her that he'd stopped making eye contact.

"Also, I don't appreciate you watching me when you were supposed to stay hidden." A muscle in his jaw twitched.

Aliwyn swallowed hard. Before she could speak, Toby took a step back and tugged at his gambeson. "Please excuse me."

He hobbled toward the stairs and passed Zelrin, who had been standing nearby with his arms crossed. As Toby disappeared below deck, Aliwyn clenched her hands. How would she talk to him now?

Emma looked up at Aliwyn and stuck out her lower lip. "Toby almost never talks about when he was little. It's annoying."

"He must have reasons," Aliwyn muttered.

Chasing him downstairs now wouldn't help, but bringing him food would be a good excuse to see him. Swallowing her impatience, Aliwyn took Emma's hand.

"Let's make some good pottage," she told the girl.

Emma smiled, but Zelrin's expression remained somber as he stood beside the staircase. Aliwyn stopped beside him.

"Are you all right?" she asked.

He only frowned at his boots, and her heart sank. Ransley's plight must be haunting him, too, but there seemed to be something else. Aelfric had sometimes been similar at that age, his emotions simmering under the surface while he remained stubbornly silent. Then he'd disappear to practice slinging in the Vasfian forest all afternoon.

Her throat ached at the memory. Whatever had troubled Aelfric, she could never address it now. Reaching for Zelrin's shoulder, she said, "Let me know if I can help you."

Zelrin only glanced at her. Aliwyn contented herself with knowing he was following as she led Emma toward the sandbox.

The three of them had just passed the stairwell when boots stomped up the steps. Aliwyn flinched and pulled Emma close. Cilebi's shiny, bald head soon emerged from the staircase, followed by Axlan's sackcloth hat. Both men carried privy buckets with their faces scrunched in disgust. The stench trailed after them as they hurried to the edge of the ship and emptied four buckets overboard.

Cilebi turned around with a glower and dropped the buckets, leaving Axlan to rinse them out. A sour taste filled Aliwyn's mouth. Why hadn't she seen this coming? Not all the mercenaries would leave the ship.

"Pleased to see me?" Cilebi crossed his arms, his black beard twitching.

Aliwyn appreciated Zelrin's presence, but the hairs on her neck rose.

"Thank you for emptying the privy pots," she said coolly.

"You think I volunteered?" the man snarled. "It's because of your accusation last night that—"

Axlan gripped his shoulder. "This isn't punishment. Sir Edward wanted us to stand guard against stowaways."

"You mean rot in rat feces." Cilebi's dark eyes flicked back to Aliwyn. "Make food, wench."

Aliwyn strode to the sandbox and cast a wary look behind her. So, cleaning the privy was Cilebi's punishment for crawling under the back platform during the Vasfian attack last night. Edward should've dismissed Cilebi altogether for being a coward. Now, she was trapped with another dangerous man.

Cilebi and Axlan soon squatted near the anchor line to play dice made of bones, and she scowled at them from the corner of her eye.

She kept Emma and Zelrin close as they tried to ignite the kindling. Despite all three of them blowing, the flame was reluctant to start. In contrast, fire from the thundercrasher yesterday had erupted with incredible ease. Aliwyn's jaw tightened at the memory. May it never happen again.

They finally nursed the smoking kindling into a usable blaze. Aliwyn lifted the empty cauldron over the fire and filled it with water. If only pottage could cook faster! She wanted to race downstairs to feed Toby and tell him why he couldn't hold on to his cargo.

Without warning, Zelrin shot to his feet and scurried toward the stairs.

"Zel!" Emma cried.

But he was already gone. Emma's call only prompted both Cilebi and Axlan to look up from their game. Cilebi licked his upper teeth, and Aliwyn curled her bare toes. It was the first time she had been on deck with neither Zelrin nor Toby nearby, but it probably wouldn't be the last.

Thankfully, Axlan drew Cilebi back into the game.

From downstairs, both Toby's and Zelrin's voices began to escalate. Soon, they were yelling, and Aliwyn sighed. She could only hope she'd fare better with a bowl of food in hand. A moment later, Zelrin ran back up the stairs with a thundercloud darkening his face. Toby followed at his heels, but when he saw Aliwyn and Emma by the hearth, his scowl relaxed.

"Zelrin can't leave you here," he said, glancing in Cilebi's direction.

He opened his mouth as though to say more, but his face flushed instead. A moment later, he descended again.

Zelrin sat and rolled back against the rail with a hollow thump. His brows knit, he tore off his woolen cap and grabbed at his hair.

"Want to help us cook, Zel?" Emma asked.

Zelrin didn't answer, and his wet eyes glimmered in the fire's glow. Aliwyn knelt by his side and reached for his gloved hand.

"What were you trying to say downstairs?" she asked in a hushed voice.

Zelrin's fingers quivered under her hold. He looked at Cilebi and Axlan, who were engrossed in their game at the opposite end of the ship, and turned back to Aliwyn.

"Maybe you should talk to Toby," he whispered.

"About what?"

"Remember how I said...Edward was saying things about Toby's mum?" His nostrils flared. "Then the mercenaries started calling Toby 'the Baseborn' instead of by his name. I couldn't understand all that Danish, but this be a very bad sign."

How dare those men insult Toby as soon as his father fell unconscious? Toby may have been oblated as a child, but he was still Ransley Boltan's son. Aliwyn put her arms around Emma and pulled her close. What had Edward said to his men in Danish, and why hadn't Toby defended himself?

Zelrin wiped his eyes. "I told Toby he should take all of us onto Driftmere and let Edward continue this blasted stupid mission with his seadogs. He didn't like that."

Aliwyn stared at him, then leaned close to his ear. "You want us to get off? What about the cargo?"

"Who cares? Those seadogs also blame Toby for the accident last night and all the repairs they be needin' to make. Remember what I said, that every time I sleep I have fits that something will happen..." Zelrin's eyes brimmed again. "Just convince Toby to get off before dark, please."

"Go to Driftmere?" she mouthed.

"Where else? The monks even wanted him to stay. I heard 'em."

Aliwyn's pulse thrummed. Both she and Emma were in peril if the mercenaries lost respect for the only man on board who could protect them.

Problems she hadn't considered tumbled into her mind. Edward could be furious upon realizing his brother would never recover. The mercenaries could mutiny over this wasted effort. She drew a slow breath. The ship's stillness was but an illusion. Was it a mistake, then, to send all the men onto land? Regardless, it was too late for regrets. She, Toby, and the youngsters needed to move before Edward and the mercenaries returned.

But the ship! The crates of potash compound and chests of thunder-crashers still sat in its belly.

Emma crawled next to Zelrin, and the two whispered to each other. Aliwyn scooped oats and dried peas into the cauldron. The water's surface swirled with the heat like the thoughts in her mind. She'd never expected to find people who cared about Toby in Driftmere. Could she convince him to abandon the ship?

She could then ask the monks to relay a message to the king's army about how Edward planned to meet the Danes at Ravenser's Point on October fifth. This was all information she'd gathered while living on board. The Normans would sweep down the Humber with unmatchable wrath, destroy Edward's ship, and confiscate the flammable cargo. He and his men would fall to their schemes. She and Toby and the two youngsters could board another ship for Denmark and leave this nightmare behind.

Was this plan clever, or madness? What if the Normans never got her message?

"Look out!"

Zelrin's cry jolted her back to attention. He got there just in time to tilt the cauldron off the fire before it boiled over.

Aliwyn's face heated. "I-I'm sorry."

She had become blind to her task. As Zelrin steadied the cauldron, she stooped and threw sand under the cauldron's tripod legs to tame the flames.

"We found you shoes," Zelrin said from above.

What a strange time to worry about footwear. Aliwyn straightened to see Emma holding up boots, stockings, and loops of twine. The soles were caked with mud, and Aliwyn hesitated.

"They're not stolen." Zelrin jutted his chin. He glanced toward shore. "Hard to run if rocks be ripping your feet."

Aliwyn could hear Cilebi and Axlan speaking behind her, and unease turned her stomach. Anything could happen tonight. Emma handed her a damp handkerchief, and Aliwyn cleaned her feet before slipping on stockings, tying them with twine, and pulling on her boots.

"They fit you?" Zelrin asked.

"A bit big, but I can wear them."

Emma smiled wistfully. "That's 'cause Lukas had bigger feet. You're wearing his spare ones."

Aliwyn held her breath. Embossed vines decorated the boot leather, and the same pattern spiraled around Zelrin's shoes. She remembered the bodies washed up near the leper colony. One of them must have been Zelrin's twin. Her ribs tightened.

"Thank you, Zel."

"Don't thank me," he said, his voice thick. "I'm making you do something I can't."

She studied his large, deep-set eyes and the broadening jaws just at the cusp of manhood. If the mercenaries turned against Toby tonight, they wouldn't spare Zelrin for his youth. Nor would they spare Emma. Nor her. A vision of Toby and Zelrin lying injured and dying flashed in her mind, and she quivered.

Perhaps Providence had brought them to Driftmere for one final chance at saving themselves. She could only manage one thing—convince Toby to throw away his cargo, or take him ashore and save his life. She chose the latter.

"Is pottage ready, young lady?"

Axlan's question snapped her from her thoughts. He approached her carrying a stack of bowls, and Cilebi stood beside him with the same conniving frown. Aliwyn ignored the Norseman.

"It's ready," she said.

The ship swayed with the waves, and she only filled each bowl halfway. Maybe both men she fed would soon perish. Axlan had been a kind Englishman, but, like the former Norsemen who'd joined Edward's cause, he shouldn't have joined the Boltans' mission.

Once everyone was sipping their portion, Aliwyn carried the last bowl toward the staircase.

Leaning toward Zelrin's ear, she whispered, "You didn't make me do anything. I'm going to see Toby because I want to."

For the first time that day, a smile tugged at his lips.

Chapter 8
Battle Belongs

October 2, Aliwyn

Aliwyn balanced the bowl of pottage and descended the stairs. Toby might crave solitude in his grief for Ransley, but she had to convince him to flee the ship. Driftmere could be their only chance at survival. Once Toby escaped with her, she'd alert the Norman authorities so they'd capture the *Lady Fortuna*.

An oil lamp lit the hull, which was cluttered again after the crew had carried down chests and crates before docking at Driftmere. The scent of pottage offered a small cloud of comfort as the stench of urine closed around her.

The ship continued to rock. Her nausea was gone, but her pulse raced. The wind had also grown stronger upstairs. She prayed they would not be struck by a rainstorm.

Ransley's boots and a chest of what might be his belongings stood beside his cot. His belt rested on neatly folded blankets. Toby must've arranged everything, but where was he?

Squinting in the dimness, she took two paces below deck before a voice called out, "I told you to stay upstairs!"

Aliwyn flinched. She retreated until her ankle dug against a step. "Toby, it's me."

Silence. Chills sprinkled her scalp, but she stood firm.

Another light flickered on at the far back, behind a row of boxes tall enough to hide someone sitting behind them. Someone shuffled across the floorboards behind those boxes, and the light brightened. She drew a slow breath. Toby had fenced himself in between a line of boxes and the privy door in the back, where he'd be completely deaf to voices upstairs.

He wanted silence, but she couldn't give him silence.

Aliwyn rehearsed the words she had prepared and waited for Toby to appear. Yet, the first thing that emerged was a war axe and its overstretched shadow floating across the floorboards.

Toby's darkened figure stood holding that weapon as though he were rising from a fiery pit. Flickering light lit his weary expression in a coarse pattern of amber and black. Aliwyn scowled. Her rational mind battled her instincts to flee.

Finally, he lowered his chin. "Sorry. I thought you were Zel."

"He's still upstairs, but I brought you pottage. Not burned."

She tried for a smile, but her mouth ran dry at the sight of Toby's axe. Despite its short handle, its blade was as big as her head. What was he doing with that?

Toby lowered the blade to the ground and scooted it aside. "I didn't mean to frighten you with this. It belongs to my father. I was cleaning it."

He showed her a rag in his hand and said something else, but his words were lost in the water splashing outside.

Aliwyn's fingers curled around the bowl as she stepped forward. "You must be hungry."

Toby's expression grew troubled as she approached. Dirty tear marks tracked down his face, and his blond hair stood on end. Grief seeped into her like a cold mist. She understood all too well the desire to be alone, and yet she couldn't leave him be.

Toby folded his cleaning cloth into a tight square and slipped it into his belt pouch.

"Thank you for the pottage," he said quietly, "but I'll fast until my father returns safely."

"But he's..." Aliwyn blinked rapidly. Ransley wouldn't return alive, and she had yet to convince Toby of this. A stone settled in her stomach.

"Why don't you have the pottage instead?" he asked. "Did you eat?"

Aliwyn struggled for words. She had longed to comfort Toby with food before talking to him, but he was already ruining her plans.

"I-I'm not hungry," she objected.

The ship's swaying made her stumble to one side, and the pottage came to the verge of spilling.

"Let me help you." Toby exited his fort of boxes and hurried toward her.

He reached for her bowl, his hand covering hers, and his other hand landed on her back.

"You're always taking care of others," he said. "Please take care of yourself, too."

His hand was gentle, and the concern in his eyes made Aliwyn's stomach flutter. How could she refuse the pottage now? She sipped from the bowl but tasted nothing. The gulp only deepened the sorrow in her heart, the ache of wishing Toby had never stepped onto this floating prison.

When she lowered the bowl, his gaze seemed sharpened with fear. Maybe he sensed she wanted to prod for anything to weaken his convictions.

Aliwyn swallowed. "Zel and Emma and I are worried about you."

"Thank you for your concern." His chest rose and fell. "I have a lot to think about."

She needed some excuse to stay. Searching between the crates he had stacked together, she noted one large, tarred chest in the back. It seemed to be filled with...books?

"Are you reading?" she whispered.

She didn't have to feign her wonder. Only the wealthiest owned books, and she'd never seen so many in one place.

His expression softened. "I like reading."

"Oh, please show me your books!"

When Toby hesitated, Aliwyn tried again. "Please, Toby, I've never even touched a book before."

Still, the silence stretched on. She met his scowl with pleading eyes, and Toby finally murmured, "I did say I wanted to show you something last night, and I'll keep my word. It's my journal and plant collection."

He beckoned her to follow him toward an opening between the crates, and Aliwyn squealed inside. She shuffled after him with the unfinished pottage in her hands. Genuine curiosity made her heart race.

Despite the damp and oppressive air of the hull, the makeshift room Toby had made for himself felt welcoming in the oil lamp's glow. The flickering light highlighted the crate serving as his table, on which a single book lay open. It featured two leather straps with metal clips to secure it when shut. Aliwyn's breath caught as she gazed at the neat calligraphy flowing over each page.

"You wrote this?" she whispered. Raising a hand to touch the book, she checked herself and turned to Toby for permission.

"Go ahead," he said with a smile. "And yes, I wrote this. Brother Dunstan trained all the boys in the scriptorium."

The scent of lavender lifted from the cool, smooth pages, and Aliwyn felt a tug of sorrow. Despite his neat penmanship, Toby had turned to killing and stealing. "Why were you in Driftmere, and why did you leave?"

Toby's smile vanished. Would he send her upstairs now that her questions had begun? Aliwyn held her breath. To her relief, he sat cross-legged before his book and began turning the pages.

"My father decided where I went," he muttered. "Anyway, what I wanted to show you is this."

He turned toward the back of the book, where the pages were covered with vibrant flower petals. Aliwyn gasped. She'd also tried to collect pressed flowers, but they never lasted long in her humid watermill, so she'd resorted to collecting pretty pebbles instead. Without warning, all the longing for home, for Miriam and Aelfric and her hens, came crashing back. Her hands quivered for her feathery friends, but Aliwyn steadied herself. She had decided to follow Toby, and there was no going back.

"This is beautiful," she said quietly, blinking to refocus on Toby's collection.

He grinned and patted the empty floorboard beside him. As though in a trance, Aliwyn sat with the pottage bowl in hand and snuggled against his warmth. Yet, part of her screamed inside. This was not why she'd come.

Toby named the plants on each page. He read his notes about how to grow them and their culinary uses. Time passed quickly. His sorrow seemed to lift, and in another maddening moment, Miriam's smile reappeared on his face. Aliwyn blinked hard. It must be the plants bringing back her mentor's memory. If only she could fly with Toby off the ship and walk through this garden of his past. With this, a nebulous idea formed in her mind.

"What is the first flower you collected?" she asked.

For better or worse, his face became blank.

"I'll show you." His thumb twitching, Toby flipped the book to two pages whose corners had been folded together, hiding what was between them. He carefully separated the pages.

What appeared made her eyes widen. Toby had arranged blue rose petals on the page to resemble the flower again, and the circular display was stunning. Along the edge, he had also pasted blue wax seals imprinted with twin roses. Had he saved them from letters he once received?

"This rose is gorgeous," Aliwyn said. "Where did you find a blue one?"

"I have yet to find wild ones." A grin lingered on his lips. "This one is from a friend who dyed white roses blue. It's her signature flower."

"Odrianna?" Aliwyn asked gently. Maybe Toby's fiancée had sent him letters sealed with the twin roses. Now, after losing her, he couldn't bear to see any blue roses again.

To her surprise, he answered glumly, "No. I received this before I courted her."

"Oh. Was it from someone in Driftmere?"

Toby glanced at her, a look of warning, and Aliwyn bit her inner cheek. But he answered calmly, "It doesn't matter. She never writes to me anymore. Have a look at the other plants."

Who was this mysterious *she*? Even Aliwyn wanted to poke herself for being so nosy. As Toby turned the pages, she struggled to focus on the rest of his collection.

"I've never seen some of these before," she said. "Are they from Driftmere?"

He scowled at his book. "Yes."

His discomfort was building, but she couldn't stop now. "Did you ever want to live in Driftmere again?"

Toby sighed and shut his book with a thump. "Did Zelrin send you? To preach his fanciful ideals that I can't possibly follow?"

Aliwyn's chest thudded at the edge in his voice. "Why not?"

"I said it last night, before the Vasfian attack. The tyrants in power have evicted me and my household. I have no place in England now. And those tyrants must be disposed of."

He turned to face her fully. The cool patch he left on her shoulder made her shiver, but his frown still wavered with a vulnerability she ached to protect.

"I remember what you said." Her eyes locked with his. "But while you slept, I heard Edward say you didn't exist. Like he wants to dispose of you. We must leave before he returns."

"He was just upset about the yard snapping, understandably." Toby hunched over, his elbows sinking into his knees. "Also, Ed needs me. He doesn't know how to handle the cargo safely, as he demonstrated."

"You and your uncle don't agree on how to handle those things at all. Why stay together?"

"Because this is his ship." Toby ran his hands through his hair. "Please don't comment on my family's affairs. You didn't hear what we discussed last night in the hull. We agreed to have my uncle take full control as the captain, and I'd only support him."

Dread clamped around her throat. "You can't let him take control. He'll burn another town like Myton."

"He promised my father he wouldn't do it again."

"And you believe him?"

"If I don't believe my family, who am I supposed to believe?"

He was angry now, but she didn't care. "Ed shares your family name, but that means nothing. He started calling you Baseborn in front of the entire crew this morning. You never even defended yourself!"

Toby picked at the bandages on his right hand, his upper lip curling. "So, Zel was your trusted interpreter?"

Aliwyn's stomach twisted. "Yes. But it's because he cares about you."

Toby's frown deepened. He kept picking at the swollen skin of his palm where the bandages didn't cover. She reached for his hand to stop him.

"You deserve more respect." She closed her fingers around his. When Toby finally looked up, she continued. "Listen to me. If you hide in Driftmere, even for a few days, Edward can sail alone wherever he wants. Then you leave for Denmark without him and claim your inheritance."

He blinked rapidly. Was he at all tempted by what she said? She was about to speak again when he interrupted her thoughts.

"What do you think I inherited in Denmark?" he asked. "A house and field? A manor?"

"Yes...?"

Toby pulled his hand free, the muscle of his jaw tensing. "I didn't know how to tell you this, or tell Zel and Emma. My inheritance is nothing but swampland Ransley's legitimate sons didn't want. And now that William has seized my family's holdings in England, that cursed marsh is all that's left to me."

Aliwyn's mouth fell open, the words stolen from her breath.

Toby continued. "And unless I finish this mission and earn something to drain it, it'll remain a swamp. I'm homeless, Ali."

His words echoed ceaselessly in her mind. Just before she boarded this ship, one of the mercenaries detaining her had called Toby a baseborn. Back then, it had made no sense, but now... Aliwyn clapped a hand over her still gaping mouth. Monasteries also accepted children born out of wedlock. Was Toby's mother a servant? A prostitute?

"Ransley ruined my life before it even began." Toby's voice shook. "He separated me and my mother so no one could spread rumors about why I exist. He left me in Driftmere and never visited until the Normans killed his wife and legitimate children during the conquest. Suddenly, he needed an heir. So he pulled me out of the monastery and forced me to train as a knight, where I was spat on and beaten..."

Aliwyn ducked her head to hide her burning face. So this was why the other squires in his school didn't like him, why they didn't defend him when Matthew so cruelly broke his arm.

"Ed was the only family who used to visit me," Toby murmured. "He took me for walks and gave me the journal you just saw. But he changed so much after his wife and unborn child died." His voice cracked. "I'm still waiting for him to become his old self again."

The last thing Aliwyn wanted was for Toby to remember why he tolerated that beast of a man. Her nostrils flared, but she could say nothing.

Toby's voice was eerily low when he spoke again. "Now tell me, was Ransley's breathing truly terminal?"

His eyes were bloodshot but fierce, and Aliwyn swallowed hard. All his mourning earlier on deck was...fake?

"It was terminal," she stammered. "But no one believed me."

"I believe you now." Toby picked up the pottage and drank. "It's most fitting that Ransley dies in Driftmere." His forehead wrinkled. "Odrianna wanted me to love him. I tried. We had some good moments. I did always...want a father."

He tried to set his bowl on a crate, but his shaking hands could scarcely hold on. Aliwyn took the bowl from him, only to have Toby suddenly push to his feet.

"Why did I tell you that?" He hobbled away. "Now you know I'm an imposter."

Aliwyn stiffened all over. She was even worse.

"Wait." She wanted to stand, but her legs felt like stone. "I'm sorry I was quiet. I don't blame you for how you treated Ransley, and I don't think any less of you."

Toby turned halfway, his eyebrows twitching between a frown and a grimace. "I'm the product of sin, and you...you were too offended to wear stolen stockings."

Had he overheard her last night, refusing Zelrin's suggestion of stockings after she had lied countless times, sabotaged the ship, and almost killed everyone on board? He still didn't know, and she could never tell him.

Shame surged as hot tears in her eyes. "I'm no better than you, or anyone else."

She struggled again to stand. After a moment, Toby limped back to her. His face still ashen, he extended his hand and pulled her up with a firm grip. Aliwyn wanted to embrace him, but he drew back. Something in his posture had changed, and shame still clouded his downcast eyes. Aliwyn's lungs stung with each inhale. Resentment must've spilled into her voice when she spoke to him yesterday, when she'd assumed he lived a pampered life and could never understand a commoner's suffering. She had been so wrong.

Another storm brewed in the back of her mind. Toby just admitted he owned no housing in Denmark. Her plans were tearing at the seams. She could only sputter another apology as she struggled with what to do next.

Toby adjusted Odrianna's cloak around her shoulders.

"I'm also sorry," he murmured. "I gave you false hope for a watermill I can't afford."

She blinked back more tears. "I don't need a mill. I just want you to be safe. Even if we'll be homeless and living in churches, I'm willing."

"But I cannot enter Denmark without the prince's permission, and he'll only give me permission and the funds to reclaim that swamp if I give him what he wants. In three days." Sighing, Toby surveyed the surrounding crates. "Ed negotiated a deal. I now see his wisdom in doing so."

It was not wisdom, but coercion. Edward would undoubtedly gain handsomely from exploiting his nephew. Aliwyn studied the resignation in Toby's eyes. He was a scribe turned knight, and finally an outlaw, all against his will. Her breath scorched in her throat. Only now did she grasp how trapped he was, and she saw no way out.

Finally, Toby stepped back. "I understand you're worried about safety, and I've already made plans. I'm meeting my allies soon. Then I'll leave you and the two young ones on a peninsula."

Aliwyn gasped. "Why?"

"Because I'll sail into battle afterward."

"Then how will we see you again?"

Toby's brows furrowed, and he walked toward the stairwell. "If I win the battle, I'll return on this ship. If I don't, then…" He paused with his back turned. In her mind's eye, Aliwyn heard Aelfric saying something similar as he'd approached the door of their watermill for the last time.

He never returned.

Her shaking breaths almost drowned out Toby's voice as he said, "Then you tell the Normans I abducted you and two children as thralls. That I forced you to lie about me back in Myton."

He shifted to look behind at Aliwyn. The tension in his gaze finally ignited something within her.

"You're telling me to lie," she snapped. "I refuse. And I'm not getting off."

"You must. I can't take the three of you into combat. I hope you had the foresight to know we must separate."

She didn't. Despite the fury boiling within her, a sob escaped her throat. Toby was highly educated. Who knew how much plotting he had done with his uncle and father? She couldn't save Aelfric, and this rebellion that wouldn't end was about to claim more lives. Aliwyn crossed her arms and struggled to lock in the storm inside.

She had utterly failed to convince him to leave this cursed ship. And Toby clung to his cargo more than ever.

The waves tossed the vessel. Aliwyn stumbled and struck a nearby crate. Toby hobbled toward her, but she backed away and bumped into more of those loathsome crates. They were so heavy, so filled with potash compound, that they didn't budge. Aliwyn gnashed her teeth even as Toby extended an arm toward her.

"Don't you want to build a mill in Denmark?" he asked gently. "When I have the funds, I'll replicate Miriam's home, and all of us can live there. You, me, Zel, and Emma. We'll finally have the life we want."

"No matter what I want, it isn't worth the violence." Her voice broke. "The killing. Risking my life."

"Ali." He held her gaze. "Perhaps training as a healer makes you opposed to violence, but you must understand...that sometimes we must fight back. Even if it means taking lives."

She wrapped her arms so tightly around her stomach that she felt nauseous.

His expression unreadable, Toby turned back for the stairwell. When he straightened and seemed to study the ceiling, she imagined his body going slack as it dangled from a hangman's noose. A wave of dread swept through her. That was his death if the Normans ever caught him. Toby had never wanted this. If there was anyone she should be angry at, it was Ransley and Edward for the corner they had forced him into.

"Toby," she croaked. "Wait."

The waves swallowed her voice, but he nonetheless turned around. Aliwyn's vision swam as she shuffled forward. Her jumbled thoughts could scarcely put together the words for a prayer, one that sounded like a scream for help. She had to be on this ship for a reason. There must be a way forward. She just couldn't see it.

As she drew close, she reached for him and touched his gambeson. Toby placed his hands on her shoulders again.

"It means a lot to me that you care," he said.

Reaching up, he cupped her face and gently wiped tears from her cheeks. His warmth brought her comfort, and the condemnation she had seen in his eyes was gone. Yet, Aliwyn still quivered. He didn't know what she'd done with Ransley's dagger, how she had cut their rigging. Perhaps she would confess many years from now. She swallowed and pushed aside the dread of that day.

"Emma and Zelrin care about you, too," she said. "Please don't follow Ed as though you're blind. Please tell me you'll still use your head."

Toby looked aside with a frown. Then, meeting her gaze again, he brushed his thumb over where Edward had bruised her lip the day before.

"All right," he whispered. "I promise I'll intervene if he becomes abusive again. And can you do something for me in return?"

"What?"

The muscles of his neck constricted. "I need to know that you have faith in me and what I'm doing. Please."

Unfinished and incoherent prayers still tumbled in Aliwyn's mind. "I...I have faith that the Almighty One knows what He is doing."

Toby's brows lifted. How was he going to respond to this? His gaze seemed to look past her and into something unseen, and Aliwyn's chin trembled. Finally, he turned back to her with a smile she hadn't seen since that morning.

"I hope you'll understand that fighting is sometimes necessary, but you're right." He tucked a strand of her hair behind her ear. "The battle has always belonged to Him."

Aliwyn mustered a smile. A pleasant tingling radiated from the warmth of his touch. She reached out and wrapped her arms around his padded torso.

Toby returned her embrace, the stubble of his beard grazing her forehead. The scent of pine sap and woodsmoke from his clothes drifted over her.

He stood unwavering in his cause, driven by a conviction she couldn't help but admire. It was rooted in his resolve to do what was right, something they both shared, even if it placed them on opposing sides.

She remained determined to stop the thundercrasher assault. Whose prayer would the Almighty answer? The question churned in her mind as she pressed her forehead against Toby's chest. The side that lost would almost certainly die. She squeezed her eyes shut, fighting the tide of anguish rising within her.

She still had time before they docked at Ravenser's Point. Until then, until the moment *Lady Fortuna* offloaded its cargo onto Danish longships, she wouldn't give up.

Toby held her steady despite the rocking of the ship. She didn't hear the footsteps and worried voices from upstairs until he whispered in her ear, "Seems like the anchor isn't holding. I'll go check."

He loosened her arms from around him and, for the last time, swept aside her bangs and smiled at her. A moment later, boots pounded toward the stairwell's edge, and Aliwyn looked up with a jolt.

"Are you deaf or just daft?" Cilebi's raspy voice rang from above. "The anchor's gone, and we're drifting! I can't see the shore no more!"

Aliwyn gasped.

In front of her, Toby's hand flashed to his sword's handle. "What happened to it?"

"Who knows? But the anchor line is broken!"

"Why didn't you warn me earlier?" Toby shouted. "Didn't you see the shore receding?"

"No, because of this blasted fog! And don't you go blamin' me when all you do is hide downstairs!"

With that, Cilebi's voice faded with a ruckus of quaking floorboards. Another violent tilt of the ship forced Aliwyn and Toby to brace themselves against the wall. Her mind spun in chaos. If *Lady Fortuna* had drifted, could this mean...that Edward couldn't get back on? Joy sparked within her, but it was soon smothered by dread.

Without an anchor, the ship could be washed anywhere. It could accidentally beach on Vasfian territory again. And this time, Aliwyn hadn't cut anything.

"What do you think happened?" She squeezed the rail.

Toby's jaw worked. "Sabotage."

He began trudging up the stairs. Aliwyn swallowed and hurried after him.

CHAPTER 9
RETURN TO BROCKLESBY

October 1, Matthew

MATTHEW AND THE VASFIANS departed Reiya's hillfort before dawn and travelled all night. When the sky softened to a hazy gray, the church spires of Brocklesby rose to their left and across the ravine. Colorful flags fluttered above canvas tents erected outside the manor walls.

The familiar sight made Matthew's pulse quicken. Soon, he'd rejoin his men. Soon, he'd warn Sir Jacques Verdun about the Danish markings on the Boltans' crates and the need to secure the eastern coast.

Reiya had already dispatched messenger pigeons to her sister tribes with the same news.

Matthew and his procession plodded toward Brocklesby Bridge alongside a sea of peasants and their groaning carts. Exhaustion lined every face. The air buzzed with talk of villages displaced by fire, and a bitter taste filled Matthew's mouth. Blasted rebels. He'd make them pay.

The bottlenecked crowd spilled past Aliwyn's watermill as they waited to cross the bridge. Just outside, a dead wolf lay sprawled with a bloody wound on its head. An unexpected pity stirred within Matthew. Maybe the beast had been alone when it had breathed its last. Given the way Matthew's life had been unfolding, he'd probably die the same way.

A moment later, Evelyn urged her steed into a canter and surpassed him.

Matthew gasped. "Wait!"

But she didn't turn around. Her warhorse pushed through the congestion and cantered onto the Brocklesby stone bridge.

Matthew gripped Porei's reins. The irony. Just when he feared he'd die alone. His cousin was rushing into the Norman encampment and not into danger, but the ache in his throat remained.

"You don't care if Evelyn leaves us?" Reiya spoke for the first time in an hour.

Matthew stared at Sir Verdun's half-black and half-red flags, flapping alongside His Excellency's heraldry across the stone bridge. "I care, but she wants some distance from me."

After a moment, Reiya said, "You made the correct decision to leave Kato behind. Make sure she understands this."

Her words turned over in his head. "Why would you say that? Kato is one of your own."

"No, he's not," she spat. "His mother was a thief. My mother banished her years ago. Kato's face is nearly identical to hers, except he lacks freckles. So unsightly."

Matthew scratched between his brows. So that was why her warriors had been reluctant to treat Kato's poisoning. Heaven forbid Reiya condemn Matthew, too, based on what his predecessors had done. And did she also find him ugly for lacking freckles?

He closed his eyes for a moment. Enough of that.

"An ominous sign," Reiya said just then.

Matthew opened his eyes and followed her gaze across the ravine. Far above the Norman tents, vultures spiraled near the Brocklesby town gates.

Dread churned in his gut. Those birds often circled over the corpses of farm animals or humans. Had Jacques Verdun discovered how Brocklesby's residents helped Matthew cross the bridge? Matthew wanted to believe Sir Verdun wouldn't execute anyone for a minor offense, but he didn't know the man well. The knight was merely the first Norman soldier Matthew had found after fleeing the Boltans.

There must be a way to cross the Brocklesby Bridge faster. When Matthew saw a cluster of foot soldiers up ahead, he called out, "Matthew Marcotte and Reiya, the Mehi chief, here to see Sir Verdun!"

He repeated the words in French. It worked. The soldiers shouted in French for the crowd to part. Their spears rose above the crowd as they pushed their way through.

Matthew pulled his horse to attention. He wore only Aelfric's tunic and a Vasfian's green and red blanket wrapped around his torso. *Flying Krakens.* He must look ridiculous! His armor had better be in the carts.

"Matthew," called a deep voice in Norman French. "Where is the Vasfian leader?"

Reiya pulled back her hood. With a heavy accent, she answered in French, "Present."

Matthew's breath caught. She understood his language, after all.

The man who had spoken stepped into view, followed by several other soldiers. He was one of Sir Verdun's older men, and his helmet seemed to squeeze his rotund, clean-shaven face.

"Sir Verdun wants to speak with her," he said, his dark eyes fixed on Matthew.

"Why won't you speak to me directly?" Reiya asked. Her French grammar was clumsy but understandable.

The man only glanced at her in response. "Both of you dismount and walk with me."

His dismissive tone made Matthew tense, but Reiya said smoothly, "I appreciate the opportunity to speak to Sir Verdun, but I won't leave my people. Please make space so my tribe can cross with me." Her knuckles blanched as she gripped her reins.

The soldiers muttered amongst themselves. Matthew's pulse tapped in his throat. Sir Verdun chose Normans, rather than Englishmen, to be his foot soldiers. Less chance of encountering traitors, he'd said. But that also made his warband more haughty than most.

"Follow us." The portly man finally stepped back.

He barked orders to his men, who barred more peasants from crossing. Levelling their spears, they pressed those already on the bridge to one side. Reiya surged ahead and vanished behind the dust stirred by her village's wagons. Dozens of Vasfians followed on foot. Smoke tinged with the metallic scent of blood drifted from up ahead.

Matthew swallowed. He grounded himself to the rhythm of Porei's hooves clopping against stone.

The Norman encampment sprawled around Brocklesby's timber walls. Stained tents and charred shields blurred in and out of the smoke from the hearths. Outside each tent, pairs of boots marked where men had entered to sleep. The scent of roasting meat mixed with horse manure made Matthew hold his breath. Between the tents, soldiers played chess on barrels or sorted through boots and armor. The stripped surcoats they shoved into bags featured familiar heraldry, but of which household again?

Regardless, those men were dead.

Thank Heavens neither Aliwyn nor Aelfric was here to see their village like this. Matthew's shoulders remained slumped as he guided Porei off the bridge and onto muddy ground. Reiya sat nearby on her horse, watching while her people's wagons circled into a protective ring around the villagers. The Norman encampment began a few paces to the right.

"Someone is bringing Sir Verdun to see us." She turned to Matthew as he rode up. Even without her face scarf, her expression remained unreadable.

Matthew nodded. Did so many Norman tents unsettle her? Or did that look reflect how she regarded all Outsiders?

To his left, vultures still circled above the town gates, which curved out of view along the ramparts. Matthew approached a nearby soldier standing with a spear held at attention.

"Has there been an execution?" Matthew asked.

The man grinned. "Yes. Yeaton and his sons are dead. Their heads are impaled outside the gate."

Matthew forced a smile back. Yeaton had been the lord of Brocklesby, who feigned loyalty to the Norman king but secretly allied with rebels like the Boltans. How had Jacques Verdun caught that traitor so quickly? He'd receive a sizeable award from His Excellency, and Matthew could claim no part of it.

Worse still, he knew what often befell the peasants of a condemned lord—public whipping, foot amputation, or worse. Aelfric and Aliwyn had been innocent. Matthew wanted to believe the rest of Brocklesby had been as well.

"What happened to the Brocklesby peasants?" he asked. "Were any of them arrested?"

"I arrest whomever I wish, Matthew Marcotte."

Matthew tensed at the sound of Sir Verdun's voice. He'd not heard the knight riding toward him, still clad in his chainmail and a blue and yellow surcoat. His massive black warhorse huffed under the man's weight. Two whiny dogs, a greyhound and a Norman bloodhound, scurried around the horse's legs.

"Greetings." Matthew forced himself to focus on the man's bloodshot eyes.

The knight was around the age of Matthew's father, but he looked much older this morning. All the rancor Matthew had faced for defending Aliwyn's watermill resurfaced in the man's gaze. When Sir Verdun grinned, revealing a missing front tooth, the rest of his face did not.

"Greetings to you, too, Matthew. Imagine my surprise when your cousin reported your presence across the bridge..." He raised an eyebrow at Reiya. "With the Mehi chief."

Matthew searched the tents nearby, but he couldn't find Evelyn. He crumpled the reins. Having a family member's support would've helped.

Sir Verdun cleared his throat. "Where were you and Miss Reiya when the insurgents burned Myton last night? The village could've used your assistance."

Matthew and Reiya glanced at each other, and Matthew hardened his jaw. So the rebels had burned Myton after leaving the leper cabin ablaze. Blasted militants.

"We were escaping from another fire, sir," Matthew said. "I...I see that you've captured that traitor, Yeaton. Congratulations."

"I caught a rebel close to Myton who confessed that Yeaton never left Brocklesby. He'd been hiding in tunnels beneath his own manor. My hunting hounds sniffed him out." He gestured at the dogs by his feet.

The sound of crying infants amplified in Matthew's ears, but he kept a stony face. "Very clever, sir."

"But the three knights who served their dear lord Yeaton, the Boltans, are still missing." Sir Verdun scratched his stubbly chin. "Miss Reiya, why is the rope bridge not burned?"

"Matthew and I can explain," Reiya said, her back straight. "During the rain two nights ago—"

The older man raised a hand. "Unfortunately, Matthew cannot be a part of this."

Reiya hadn't even finished one sentence of the narrative they'd prepared. Matthew fought a wave of chills. "Sir, I was also present during the incident."

Sir Verdun's scowl skimmed over him, then Reiya. "Matthew Marcotte is not a leader. He's only a subordinate squire, and recently, a deserter of the royal army."

Matthew's eyes rounded. "A what?"

"You said you'd return two days ago with an English woman. You didn't. In my latest report to His Excellency, I announced your desertion."

"I'm not a deserter." Heat flooded Matthew's face. "There was heavy rain two nights ago. I couldn't return."

Sir Verdun grunted. "Imagine if all my men decided to disappear for two days at a time in pursuit of women? Imagine if they all walked away with expensive equipment that belongs to me?"

"I kept Matthew in my village for one night," Reiya said, adding quickly, "because he was ill."

The knight smirked, but his eyes remained weary. He switched to speaking in Norman French. "Why, Matthew! I see you've had better luck with Vasfian women."

Matthew's gaze snapped to Reiya. She must've understood, but she didn't even blink!

"Nothing happened between us!" he retorted.

Sir Verdun switched to English. "Matthew will take a bucket from the camp and water my horses. Reiya, you and I will speak as leaders."

"So be it," she said.

A headache pierced Matthew's temples.

"I'm not a deserter," he stammered, strangling his rage at the last instant.

"We'll discuss that later." The knight glanced at him. "Or do you wish to be called disobedient also?"

"Go, Matthew," Reiya said through her teeth.

Matthew tugged on Porei's reins. His arms felt as heavy as iron as he turned the mare away from the meeting. He couldn't help looking back at Reiya. Wasn't she flustered? All that time they'd spent rehearsing their speeches had been wasted. Yet there she was, speaking to Sir Verdun with a steady posture and the occasional hand gesture.

Matthew swallowed hard. Maybe she'd be all right without him, but he was not all right by himself. What was he going to do about this accusation of desertion?

It was a serious offense. If His Excellency acted upon Sir Verdun's report, Matthew would be expelled from the army. He'd never be knighted or inherit his father's land without serving in the military. He'd become homeless, his cousin Evelyn forced to marry within weeks if she didn't want the same fate…

Matthew passed a hand over his face. He still needed to fetch water. Jumping off Porei, he tied his mount to one of the royal army's covered wagons. Porei lowered her head to graze as Matthew asked a nearby soldier for a bucket. The man gave him one that stank of mold.

"Where do I get water?" Matthew asked.

"Down there. The gorge." The other soldier pointed toward the Brocklesby ravine, its waters roaring even from this distance. "Take the path starting this way."

A chuckle rumbled in Matthew's throat. This had to be a nightmare. Did Verdun know he was afraid of heights? He trudged toward the ledge, his stomach already heaving at the thought of heights. A woman soon called his name.

"Matthew!"

Evelyn's voice rang again through the haze in his mind. Turning around, he found her standing amongst a group of women and children. Smoke drifted before their frightened faces, and his throat constricted. He recognized some of the peasants. They'd given him food for Aliwyn. Amongst them stood the bailiff's wife and four children, wearing their drab nightgowns and wrapped in linen sheets. The oldest was probably only twelve.

The woman stared at him, her arms bracing a sniveling toddler. Her husband was absent. So were all the adult men. Some stood barefoot, as though driven out of their homes with haste. Had the entire village been accused of treason?

The ache in his throat intensified.

"Are you all right?" Evelyn asked.

"Yes." Matthew lifted his empty bucket. "Just need to fetch water."

He couldn't bear to see Aelfric's people treated like this, but what could he do? He was also on the brink of losing his father's inheritance. He didn't even know how to tell Evelyn. Ducking his head, Matthew marched toward the path leading to the ravine's edge.

"We have plenty of water here," Evelyn called out. "Take some from us."

Matthew halted. Before him, the cliff's edge and smoky horizon tilted to one side and then the other. If he didn't accept her offer, he might soon be vomiting. His eyes lowered, he returned to Evelyn and accepted a full bucket from her hands. Water splashed onto the ground. Clear streams mingled with bloodstains on the grass, and an icy dampness seeped into Matthew's stockings.

His face grew numb, then tingled. There were worse things than being called a deserter, like losing a spouse or father. He looked at the bailiff's wife and her children, how the wind shifted the hems of their night tunics. The woman tried to wrap her woolen mantle around her toddler, and her brown hair clung to the edge of her swollen eyes. Two days ago, she had given him cheese for Aliwyn. Now, the warmth on her cheeks had faded into ash.

He couldn't just ignore her.

"Hello," Matthew croaked. The terrified expression of her children unnerved him. "What happened to Leofsige?"

Leofsige was the name of her husband, and he still remembered.

The woman hardened her lips. "Norman soldiers arrived at dawn and arrested Leo. They arrested all our men." Her voice rose with a fury Matthew didn't expect. "They'll undergo an inquest at Barton-upon-Humber, or so I was told. Your men took everything we owned, but we knew nothing about Lord...about Yeaton's treachery."

Matthew shuffled his feet. She should be grateful for the inquest system, something his people had established in England for men accused of treason. Inquests were more sensible than trials by ordeal, but mentioning their benefits now felt useless.

Finally, he said, "You'll have everything returned if the inquest council finds your men innocent."

"We have no clothes, almost no food." Her glower persisted. "The soldiers forced their way into our homes. They took all our money and wouldn't respond to a word I said. What are we going to do now?"

Matthew drew a slow breath. The air hung thick with the stench of sweat, which a fleeting aroma of buttery pastries did little to redeem. Verdun's men were consuming what they'd confiscated from Brocklesby, hauled out of all the bakeries and inns. As the noise of the feasting army permeated his senses, Matthew hung his head. He had no authority to ask for the return of her possessions.

The peace he had hoped to maintain as a future knight felt like a distant dream. What could he still offer to Aliwyn and Aelfric's villagers? The Boltans had stolen all his valuables except one. Matthew reached into his belt pouch and found the piglet figurine. Stroking its ears with his thumb, his chest tightened. Could he truly do this?

The bailiff's wife pulled her children closer until they huddled under her free arm.

"Sir, I apologize." Fear now strained her voice. "Please don't be offended."

Matthew withdrew the golden pig from his pouch. The ornament glimmered on even a sunless day. He'd never know how Aelfric carved such an intricate, tiny mold to make casting the pig possible.

"Take this." He offered it to the woman. "It's pure gold."

She frowned. "Why me?"

"It came from someone who loved Brocklesby."

"Who?"

"Just take it. Sell it in the next town and use the funds to travel to Barton-to-Humber with your townsfolk. The church will feed you while your men wait for the inquest."

Regret burned in Matthew's throat, but he forced his hand to remain open. The pig, after all, was recast from a brooch Aelfric had won at a chess tournament. It was Aelfric's gold.

The woman's eyes filled. She braced her whimpering child with one arm and collected the piglet from Matthew's palm. Her three other children smiled at Matthew. One of the girls grasped her mother's wrist for a better look at the figurine. Next to her, Evelyn's gaze carried a sympathy he didn't remember seeing. Matthew mustered a grin back.

"Thank you, sir." The woman smiled at him for the first time. "My name is Fritha, and you..."

Her eyes dropped to the pig.

"You're a Marcotte?" Her eyes widened. "Matthew Marcotte?"

Drat. So much for wanting to remain nameless; the piglet bore his name, and Fritha could read.

Evelyn stepped forward. "Yes, this is my cousin, Matthew."

"Aelfric spoke often of you," Fritha said, rolling the figurine with her thumb. Her voice shook. "If you're here, where's Aelfric?"

"And what happened to Aliwyn?" asked one of the girls. "Why is her mill empty?"

A numbing sensation spread down Matthew's forehead. "Aliwyn is...I'm bringing her back. But Aelfric is gone."

"Gone?" Fritha asked softly. "Aelfric is gone?"

Her children looked startled, and Evelyn bowed her head. Matthew released one sob, then coughed to pretend it was nothing. The urge to stab Tobias Boltan right then sent heat flaring down his chest.

"Good luck," he managed to say. "Good luck to you and your people."

He turned and trudged toward Brocklesby Bridge, his bucket swaying and splashing. He had once dreamed of making Aelfric his bailiff when he became a knight of his own manor. Now Aelfric was dead, his sister kidnapped, and the manor slipping away because of Verdun's false accusation.

Jacques was likely still furious that Matthew had so fiercely resisted the raid on Aliwyn's watermill. He wanted to make an example of Matthew. A knight like that didn't deserve the title "sir."

Matthew wouldn't lose his inheritance without a fight. He could challenge Jacques to a trial-by-combat, but such duels often ended in death. While Jacques could hire a champion, Matthew could only rely on himself. If he died, who would care for his cousins?

He licked his lips. There had to be a better way to prove his loyalty as a Norman soldier.

Walking in the shade of the town ramparts, he approached the Brocklesby Bridge gates where he had left Reiya and Jacques. He was sidestepping piles of armor and grain when inspiration struck. What if he offered Jacques a grand gesture to clear his name? Aelfric would have liked this plan, though Matthew preferred to settle matters with his fists. He fingered the clovers on his sleeve and blinked away the mist in his eyes. Maybe Aelfric wasn't completely gone.

Back by the stone bridge, the Mehi tribe and their sheep stood behind a ring of horses and carts. The oldest villagers sat on a cart in the back. Domilo and the other children stood in the shadows of the closest wagons.

Seeing the Vasfians' most vulnerable across from dozens of soldiers, the same soldiers who'd robbed Aliwyn, made Matthew's stomach turn. The Vasfians needed to leave as soon as possible. He'd negotiate with Jacques afterward. Maybe he could help Reiya and Jacques finish their conversation quickly. Matthew wrapped her red and green blanket tighter around his shoulders and ran toward them.

Both Reiya and Jacques had dismounted. She stood facing the knight with several warriors standing behind her. Meanwhile, Jacques paced before a row of foot soldiers, his head bowed and his face flushed beneath his conical helmet. What had happened?

"So I let him escape once, and so have you," Reiya said, glancing at Matthew as he approached. "But we will not be made fools again."

Matthew arrived, panting. He lowered the sloshing bucket beside Jacques' steed. "Who did you let escape, sir?"

Jacques gnashed his teeth, and his light brown eyes flashed. "I was deceived by a traitorous wench and a child."

Matthew swallowed, his mouth dry, as Reiya turned to him. "I'll leave you with Sir Verdun to discuss Tobias' escape from Myton last night."

He stared at her. "He escaped again?"

Reiya dipped her chin and pinned Matthew with a knowing look.

"Then the forest went up in flames. We think Tobias must've found other rebels, and they together started that fire."

Turning back to Jacques, she continued. "Let's not blame each other for Tobias' escape. Instead, I'll continue searching with my warband, and you with yours. May blessings be upon our endeavors."

Tobias had been sighted again last night, only to slip away? Matthew shook his head as the news sank in, but Reiya spoke first.

"Matthew, come retrieve your chainmail from my wagon."

Restlessness flickered in her eyes as she turned from Jacques, and Matthew held back his questions for now. She and her whole village must depart.

He had taken only two steps with Reiya when Jacques spoke from behind.

"Wait. What about the crates?"

Reiya inhaled audibly before turning around.

"We confiscated the crate of belts from enemy soldiers, and we will keep them." She glanced at Matthew. "Matthew claims to have deciphered the writing on those belts, as I've mentioned. Ask him to explain his reasoning."

"Not the crate of belts," Jacques said, his voice icy. "I'm referring to the crates of black matter."

"You told me to dispose of them. My people mixed the matter with manure and water. We buried it all."

Jacques's frown only deepened, and a dull ache began at the back of Matthew's head.

"I don't believe it." The knight straightened to his full height. His soldiers shifted to attention.

"Why won't you believe me?" Reiya tilted her head.

"It's impossible to bury all that black matter so quickly."

"I was in their village," Matthew called out. "I saw the black matter mixed with manure, as Reiya said."

Jacques only kept his eyes fixed on Reiya. "Prove that your wagons don't carry the black matter. We now know it's very dangerous. I must take any remnants to His Excellency."

She widened her stance. "How can I prove that I have none? By letting you search through all our belongings?"

"You have nothing to fear if you're telling the truth." Jacques gestured for his men to move forward.

Reiya's hand slid toward her crossbow. Matthew sucked in his breath and bumped her arm with his hand, but the movement failed to dissuade her. She stepped past him while gripping the wooden frame of her weapon.

"I object," she declared. "I gave you my word, Sir Verdun, and you have no right to sift through my belongings."

She marched toward Jacques's group of soldiers. The few warriors beside her also gripped their crossbows and shuffled past Matthew. At their advancement, Jacques' soldiers slowed to a stop, but chills rained down Matthew's back.

Only a narrow strip of grass separated the Vasfian wagons from the Norman tents. Domilo, with the younger children huddled behind him, stood beside the cart carrying the village's elderly. The boy gripped a leather sling despite his frightened expression.

By the Devil's tail. One fired projectile, and it would be a bloody disaster. Could Reiya talk herself out of this?

"I'm evacuating my village," she said, facing Jacques. "We're carrying sacred objects that only druids are allowed to touch."

"But the black matter isn't sacred." Jacques smiled. "If you have nothing to hide, why do you fear being searched?"

Behind Reiya's back, Norman soldiers camped closer to the bridge began to stir. Several crossed the grassy strip toward Domilo, with their spears angled forward. Matthew's mouth fell open. As he'd feared, Jacques's soldiers were targeting the most vulnerable.

"Reiya!" he shouted.

Before she could respond, he grabbed his bucket of water and bolted toward the row of spears. He didn't dare draw his sword; he could only block the soldiers' way and hope they'd back off.

This was the end of his knighthood before it ever began. Matthew's feet pounded onward nonetheless.

Ahead of him, a rock shot out from between two wagons. It struck a soldier's helmet with a clang moments before he reached the wagon.

"Leave us alone!" Domilo shouted.

The soldier staggered back onto his startled companions but regained footing. Snarling, they charged again with their shields pressed together and spears raised, but another barrage of rocks aimed at their boots beat them back. Meanwhile, Vasfians bearing crossbows flooded outward from between the wagons. Matthew's vision went white.

"Stop!" he shouted.

Lunging toward the men, he thrust the contents of his bucket. Water flew out in a glistening arc and splattered over the soldiers' helmets and faces. They yelped and stumbled, their spears knocking into each other.

Reiya shouted something in Vasfian, and her followers lowered their crossbows. Matthew sprinted the rest of the way to Domilo's cart. He bashed his bucket against the other soldiers' shields, the violent thunks throbbing in his ears until the men retreated across the grassy divide.

"What are you attacking?" Matthew shouted in Norman French. "The Vasfians are our allies! How will you win this war if you attack your allies?"

The soldiers he'd driven back straightened their spears again, their dripping faces warped with anger. Matthew's chest heaved. He widened his stance before the Vasfian cart as other men rushed to the scene from either side.

Matthew swung out his free arm. "Put down your weapons!"

"Why are you giving orders?" Jacques hollered. He marched forward and shouted a command in French. The soldiers approaching Matthew halted.

Matthew released a tense breath. The water dampening his stockings sent chills up his legs. What had he just done? The sight of his cracked bucket, dangling from his hand, drifted in and out of focus.

"I saw a chest that looks like it belonged to the rebels," one of the foot soldiers finally said in English. "I wanted to see what's inside."

"That chest didn't belong to the rebels." Reiya's voice came closer than Matthew expected. She squeezed behind him, her shoulders pressing against his back. As he turned around, she placed her hand on a wooden chest carved with ornate vines and flowers. It was secured by a large padlock.

"An Englishman crafted this chest as a gift to my tribe," she said.

Matthew knew who that Englishman was. Shaking with cold sweat, he let the bucket slip from his grasp. Reiya unlocked the padlock and lifted the lid. Her jaw set, she presented the chest's contents with an upturned palm.

"This is the suit of armor Matthew borrowed from you, Sir Verdun," she said. "Take it back, but leave me the chest. There shall be no further search of my people's belongings. I gave you my word that we carry no black matter."

After a moment of silence, the knight muttered, "Very well. I accept your oath."

Matthew breathed again, but the emotionless tone of Jacques's voice kept him on edge.

Reiya and two other warriors pulled out the helmet and clinking chain-mail. They dumped the objects on the ground for Jacques's men to collect, and Matthew felt a small hand grip his shoulder. Domilo whispered his name, but he resisted the urge to look at the boy. Matthew already appeared enough of a traitor to his own.

"Give me that sword," Jacques said, stepping before Matthew's bowed head.

Wanting to sink into the ground, Matthew unstrapped the Nornsblade. The weapon wasn't his. He'd named his borrowed sword after the real Nornsblade, his most expensive and prized possession of five years, to dull the pain of losing it to the Boltans. The hilt had featured a red lion, the emblem of his family. He'd never see it again.

Jacques grabbed the sword from his right hand, and Matthew pressed his bite wound against his tunic to temper the stinging. His mind spun in a void as voices floated around him.

"Miss Reiya, I apologize for the misunderstanding," Jacques said. "You see, my men have been marching all night from Myton. They're in a foul mood."

"They need to retreat farther," she said coldly.

The image of the royal army lying dead, impaled with arrows, burned in Matthew's mind. Jacques must've known his men were in no condition to fight. When the knight ordered his soldiers to return to their hearths, the tension drained from Matthew's limbs. The footsteps of soldiers receded. A collective sigh of relief hovered over the Vasfian gathering. Matthew expected their wagons to begin rolling, but Reiya stood her ground.

"Why did you confiscate Matthew's sword?" she asked.

There was a pain in her voice that Matthew didn't understand. He crossed his arms to stop shivering and stared at his boots.

"It isn't his," Jacques answered. "He also doesn't deserve it."

"Are you discharging him from your warband?"

Jacques chuckled. "Why do you ask? Would you want a subordinate who gives orders without permission?"

"Let me..." Matthew forced himself to speak. "Let me explain myself. In private."

In truth, he had no words to defend himself. The stabbing pain in his gut worsened with each breath. He looked up at Jacques with as much poise as he could muster.

"Fine, Matthew," Jacques said. "Let's talk in private. However, you're better off on your own. My men will leave for Barton-upon-Humber, and you'll return to your tutor to explain why you're a deserter."

His last words almost buckled Matthew's knees. He could hardly move as Jacques sauntered away. The Vasfians muttered in the background. Reiya didn't need to stay anymore, and Matthew would face his problems by himself.

"Godspeed," he said, turning to her.

His face screwed up in ways he couldn't control. He may have just insulted her. They didn't even believe in the same gods.

Reiya scowled back, her face still red.

"Can you be forced to leave Brocklesby alone?" she asked.

He nodded, dread already swelling in his throat. He could only scurry back to his tutor. Lord Seville was in Norwich, many days' walk away.

"I need to settle this accusation of desertion as soon as possible," he muttered. As a last resort, he could beg for Lord Seville's assistance, but he feared his tutor would be more furious than willing to help.

Reiya shifted so she could see Jacques better. "Sir Verdun, will your conversation with Matthew take long?"

Jacques had stopped a short distance away. "No, not long."

"Then I'll wait here for your decision to keep Matthew or not."

The knight grinned. "Why?"

"If you dismiss him, I may accept him as one of my warriors."

"What?" Matthew mouthed.

From behind him, Domilo spoke Vasfian in a pleading tone. Matthew wanted to crawl out of his skin. It was one thing to defend the Mehi's young and elderly, but another matter to be enrolled under their chief's command.

"I haven't decided yet," Reiya continued. "While you speak to Matthew, I'll discuss with my elders."

"Certainly." Jacques' smile broadened.

He turned to leave, and Matthew hung his head. Just days ago, he had eagerly joined Jacques' cause to prove himself in Lord Seville's absence. His mind wandered back to Aliwyn. If he left now, he wouldn't be there to defend her innocence when she was found.

He dragged his feet after Jacques, and a hand lifted from his shoulder. Domilo had been holding onto him this whole time.

"Thanks for helping us," the boy said.

Despite everything, a warm sensation stirred within Matthew. He turned around.

A cart full of children and old women gazed back at him with sympathetic smiles. Chickens clucked in their crates. Matthew recognized them. They were the same hens he'd rescued when Jacques had robbed Aliwyn's mill. The fluffy birds had kept him company as he sat alone on a stump in the clearing. Now the Vasfians had taken custody of them.

Today, Jacques had failed to steal any chickens. The heaviness in Matthew's chest lifted, and he smiled at Domilo. Uncrossing his arms, he strode after the knight who would decide his fate.

CHAPTER 10
STEALTH TRAINING

Matthew

THE BROCKLESBY PEASANTS WATCHED as Matthew followed Jacques between the tents, and their scrutiny made him tense. Amongst the crowd, he caught sight of Evelyn standing beside Fritha and other women. They looked worried, but he didn't know how to respond. He'd talk to his cousin later.

Jacques and Matthew reached a stained canvas tent at the edge of the encampment, where the knight tied his greyhound and bloodhound to a post outside. He scratched behind their ears. They had stopped whining, and their skinny tails wagged in the air.

Nearby, a young man with wavy brown hair sat on a stump and wiped chainmail draped over his lap. A black greyhound lay contentedly at his feet, while a shortbow leaned against a tree. As Matthew approached, the man glanced up with a polite but distant expression.

Jacques smiled. "This is my squire, Vincent. He joined me in Myton last night."

Matthew forced a grin. He'd wondered where Jacques' original squire had gone. Had Vincent been visiting family in Myton? Too tired to ask, Matthew trudged behind the knight as they approached a waxed linen tent.

A flash of bright red stitching caught Matthew's eye. He looked up to see Latin words embroidered over the tent's entrance: A merciful soldier is a dead soldier.

The statement left a sour taste in his mouth. Before the revolt, he would've debated against it. Now, he wasn't so sure.

Jacques lifted the tent flap. "You appreciate the maxim I teach all my recruits?"

"It's good advice, sir," Matthew answered flatly.

The knight grinned. He made a sweeping gesture with his palm up, inviting Matthew to enter. "After you."

Matthew ducked inside. The air within, thick with smoke and damp earth, clung to his throat. Dim sunlight filtered through the worn fabric walls. A woolen blanket and pillow lay to one side, while crates and sacks lined the perimeter of the simple space. Yet, despite these meager provisions, a double-edged claymore and three long daggers stood on display on wooden stands.

Matthew tried not to stare. How many weapons did one man need? And yet, Jacques had confiscated Matthew's only blade.

"Have a seat," Jacques said.

Matthew sat on a crate and shuffled his stiff legs. Jacques lifted his plumed helmet from his matted brown hair, set it on a nearby box, and sat across from Matthew. He propped one foot over his other knee.

"Congratulations," he said. "You have won the sympathy of that pagan redhead."

His statement was as out of place as his smile, and Matthew leaned away from him.

"Let me redeem myself," Matthew said hoarsely. "Keep me in your division, and I'll prove myself not a deserter. Is there a caravan you want me to lead, or—"

"Ah, so impatient." Jacques smiled. "Wait a moment. Let me tell you what's happened in Brocklesby. I've had a new lead today. Under coercion, Yeaton's youngest son confessed that the Boltans are sailing east toward the North Sea. They have a meeting along the coast."

Matthew nodded slowly. He had suspected from the start that the Boltans were sailing somewhere. If they remained close to English shores, then so did their captive, Aliwyn. Perhaps this was good news, but it also meant Aliwyn was confined with several dozen men unless she dove overboard. She desperately needed rescue.

This worry was soon overshadowed by another. "Are they meeting the Danes?"

Jacques raised an eyebrow. "Good guess. Yes, the rebels have recruited those cretins once again. I extorted that information from Yeaton the elder himself, telling him I'd spare his youngest son." He smiled. "It's times like these that heroes are made."

Matthew stared at the blackness between Jacques's teeth with a sinking stomach. After all the deliberation over Roman numerals with Reiya, he'd still hoped he was wrong, and the Danes hadn't returned to empower the rebels. What if His Grace retaliated with another razing of English villages?

Struggling to draw a breath, Matthew asked, "Are the Danes attacking in four days?"

Jacques crossed his legs and smirked, though his eyes remained narrowed. "Interesting. Who was your informant? I have the same information."

Matthew told him about the dates he'd discovered on the Vasfians' looted belts and their significance.

Before he could finish, the man threw back his head in laughter. "Chicken scratch was your informant?"

Punching out his other front tooth would've been so satisfying.

"I uncovered the same information as you," Matthew growled. "So, did *your* informants tell you where the Danes are landing?"

"No." Jacques looked aside and turned the conical helmet beside him. "All the Yeatons expired before I could ask."

"You shouldn't have killed all of them."

Jacques's eyes sparked with fire, and Matthew clamped his jaw shut.

"I just sent messengers to seaside villages telling them to evacuate," the man muttered. "I'll soon join the troops guarding our shores. It doesn't matter where the Danes land. We'll be ready. They'll be facing trenches, hidden archers, and iron spikes to cripple their warriors. Meanwhile, what have you done?" he sneered. "Slept in a Vasfian hillfort?"

Curses clamored in Matthew's head, but he checked himself. "Reiya and I killed a Danish mercenary in the woods."

"That's nothing. You said you wanted to redeem yourself to the royal army, correct? There is something you can do."

"What?"

Jacques fingered through his belt pouch and withdrew a brown ox horn half the length of his hand. A cork stopper sealed the opening of the horn, and a long leather strap wound around its body.

"Find the black matter amongst Reiya's spoils and collect a sample in this."

Matthew stared at him.

"You want me to spy on the Mehi?" he whispered.

"Call it scouting, if you wish. His Excellency has ordered me to collect a sample, and Reiya is hiding a cache. That's why she didn't want to be searched."

"I don't want to spy on our allies. His Excellency can arrange with Reiya for a better time to—"

"To what?" Jacques raised an eyebrow. "To search her hillforts? She'd hide everything if she knew we were coming."

"What if I find nothing in their hillforts? And what if I get caught?"

Jacques pushed to his feet. He loomed over Matthew, stinking of sweat and clad in enough chainmail to sink a canoe. Matthew held his breath.

"I expect better from Lord Seville's squire," the knight said. "You didn't see what I saw, how the fire spread over the black pebbles outside Myton. This substance is incredibly flammable, incredibly dangerous. And I'll tell you why I'm so certain the Mehi are hiding it..."

He began pacing the tent. "Out of the ten hounds I owned, only two escaped the fire outside Myton. The rest...trampled by horses in the chaos."

"My condolences," Matthew murmured.

"My two surviving hounds have learned to equate the scent of black matter with danger. With death. Hence their fear when we were beside the Vasfians."

He turned around and faced Matthew's wide eyes.

"I know my dogs," Jacques continued. "They've never feared the red-heads, but they were terrified as soon as Reiya arrived. They *smelled* the black matter. This is why I'm certain she is hiding the substance. Once the revolt ends, the pagans will turn against us the way they've fought the English for generations. They'll burn our long ships and manors with a spark..."

Matthew slumped over in his seat, his elbows pressing into his thighs. Could Reiya be a liar? He hardly knew her. At the same time, he hardly knew Jacques, either. Who was he going to believe?

"What about the Boltans?" Matthew asked. "They must have more of the black matter. Why not focus on finding them instead?"

"Of course, we'll capture them in addition to exposing the Mehi's treachery." Jacques smiled. "Some alliances are made with the wrong people."

What felt like invisible insects crawled down Matthew's neck. "I don't know where to start looking."

"Sure you do. I saw the Mehi transporting a few chests with flat lids, built in the English style. Concentrate your search on those. Here, I'll even make it easy for you." Jacques uncorked the horn and inverted it. Out slipped slender lockpicks. Matthew sucked in his breath.

"You've received stealth training, I assume?" Jacques asked.

"Yes...sir."

All the squires knew how to pick locks for breaking out of prisons and for escaping from shackles. And now, apparently, for cracking open chests like a thief. Unbelievable.

"Now put those skills to good use," Jacques said with a smile.

The black chest Matthew had been watching had a flat lid. He struggled to appear calm. "If I find anything, what will you do with it?"

"I'll send part of the sample to His Excellency. I'm sure he'll confront Reiya about it in a civilized manner. But of course, he'll end the alliance."

Matthew had heard good things about His Excellency, Geoffrey de Montbray, but maybe that was all flattery. Matthew had never met the bishop himself. He wiped his sweaty palms on his tunic. He had to agree with Jacques on one thing. If the Vasfians did still harbor the black matter, it needed to be found and confiscated.

"What if Reiya finds the Boltans before I can find the black matter?" Matthew asked. "The mission will be over. She'll send me home."

"The solution is simple. I deserve to find the Boltans first. If you want more time with the redheads, stall them. Set their tents on fire. Crack their wagon wheels at night."

"You—" Matthew's mouth fell open. "You want me to rob *and* sabotage our allies?"

Jacques slammed the horn on a nearby crate, and Matthew flinched.

"They are not allies," the older man hissed. "They smile and feed you only to chop off your head at night. What do you think happened to my brothers?"

Matthew panted, his throat searing. The tip of the horn curved like a fang toward his face.

"Yes or no, Matthew Marcotte?" Jacques leaned over the crate with his gloved hands spreading over its surface. His voice turned sickly sweet. "Do you want me to withdraw the charges of desertion? Say it was all a little misunderstanding?"

It was useless to tell him about Aliwyn's plight and how she needed to be rescued. Matthew shuddered in cold sweat. He couldn't return to the royal army today, no matter what he did.

He grabbed the ox horn. "I accept the mission."

"Good." Jacques adjusted the fit of his leather gloves. "Meet me in Norwich the last week of October. I want that horn filled."

His Excellency held court monthly in different towns to settle disputes, award his followers, and punish others. The next session was in Norwich.

Matthew felt as though he exhaled steam. "Yes, sir."

He stuffed the horn in the inner pocket of his gambeson. Jacques watched him, his greasy face split by a tarnished nasal prong.

"I'll convince Reiya to take you as one of her soldiers." The knight grinned. "Although if you ask me, she is already convinced. Who knew you could be so charming with women?"

Matthew gnashed his teeth as Jacques strolled to the tent's exit. With a flick of his wrist, the man flung open the canvas and stepped out into the gray daylight. Matthew stood and strode after him.

Ducking out of Jacques' tent, Matthew squinted in the smoky haze. The camp was alive with the clatter of men slicing onions and dunking coarse bread into steaming pots of pottage. The smell made his stomach clench with hunger, but he kept walking.

"Wait, Sir Verdun."

Jacques turned around, and Matthew followed suit. Vincent stood behind them, holding two wooden bowls of pottage.

"I scraped the last servings." He smiled and offered both bowls.

Matthew had done nothing to deserve this food, and he hesitated. But when Jacques grabbed the pottage and began gulping it down, he accepted the second bowl and sipped slowly. His chaotic thoughts kept him from tasting anything.

"This is how a squire should behave." Jacques grinned and returned the emptied bowl to Vincent.

Matthew's nails dug into the bowl. Muttering his thanks, he returned it to Vincent.

"We trained together, didn't we?" Vincent asked. "Under Sir Devereux."

The words hit harder than Matthew expected. Sir Devereux had been his first tutor. Now that he thought about it, Vincent seemed familiar. He'd been one of the squires who trained alongside Matthew when he'd fractured Tobias' arm.

"We did," Matthew said quietly. After Sir Devereux had expelled him, Matthew had been too ashamed to maintain contact with the other trainees.

"I heard about what happened to your family," Vincent said quietly. "My sympathies."

"Thanks."

Matthew kept his eyes downcast. Maybe he should've tried to keep close friends other than Aelfric, but painting and chess had always been more interesting than what the other men did—hunt and talk about women.

Vincent lowered both bowls to the ground, where the black greyhound wagged its tail and began licking them.

"I've just been assigned to look for the Boltans myself," Vincent said, standing again. "Tobias fooled me and Sir Verdun once in the forest, but he won't again."

Matthew managed a smile. "Appreciate the support. Maybe I'll see you after the war."

"I'll look for you." Vincent nodded, then looked fondly at his dog. "We'll take Garrick hunting."

The two of them bid farewell, and Matthew followed Jacques back toward the Brocklesby Bridge.

Evelyn stood conversing with Reiya in the distance. His cousin fidgeted with her hands, her expression bleak, and Matthew sighed. Reiya must've told Evelyn about his predicament. Behind Reiya, the cart of Vasfian children and elderly observed the conversation, but only Domilo folded his arms over the wagon's railing and seemed to understand.

As Matthew trudged onward, both women turned toward him. A breeze fluttered the sleeves of his damp tunic, and goosebumps prickled his arms.

"I discharge this squire from my warband," Jacques said as he stopped beside the two women. Evelyn drew a shaky breath, and Matthew averted his gaze.

"However," Jacques continued. "If Reiya takes him and he helps her capture the Boltans, he may redeem himself before His Excellency."

"Redeem himself from what?" Reiya asked.

"The accusation of desertion. You see, a deserter of the army cannot be knighted. His Excellency will reallocate the Marcotte estate to someone else." He grinned.

"I understand," Reiya said. "But Matthew won't lose his inheritance because I do accept him as my warrior. And we'll find the Boltans first."

Matthew's eyes widened. They didn't even know where the Boltans were going!

Jacques laughed. "You sound so certain!"

"It's impossible to catch someone second, correct?" Reiya grinned. "It'll be a competition between my warriors and yours, Sir Verdun, and I like competitions. Let's say whoever captures all three Boltans, dead or alive, is the winner."

A dull ache began behind Matthew's ribs. Jacques was lying to her. Catching the Boltans had never been a requirement to clear his name. Matthew had also been ordered to stall her progress and steal her loot. He was entering her warband as a traitor.

Shame sank into his bones, and he stared at the ground.

Next to him, Jacques began to chuckle. "What does the winner receive?"

"Well, the honor of killing the Boltans," she said. "If you find them first, you may subject them to Norman trials. If my people find them first, we'll burn them as per our traditions."

Jacques smiled broadly. "How delightful. I agree to your terms, young lady. Good luck."

His last words dripped with sarcasm. Maybe Reiya wanted to punch him as much as Matthew did.

The man's heavy footsteps departed, and Matthew forced himself to look up at the Mehi chief. *Flying Krakens.* This woman his age was now his commander, and he'd soon return to the land of skulls and turnips. What a disaster. And when would she stop giving him that unreadable stare?

"I can help you with your horses and donkeys," he stammered.

"Oh yes, Matthew!" Domilo thumped the cart's side.

Reiya put her hands on her hips. "No Norman has ever served me. I'll only keep you if you're useful. Jacques told me earlier that we have four days to determine where the Danes and the Boltans will meet."

"Matthew will serve you well," Evelyn said. She placed her hand on Matthew's forearm. "Reiya, can I speak to him for a moment?"

Reiya nodded, and Evelyn led him aside.

"What is it?" he asked.

She smiled and grasped his right hand, avoiding the still-swollen bite marks.

"I have ointment for you," she said, retrieving a tiny, corked jar from her belt pouch. "It's from Fritha."

"Oh...thank her for me."

Matthew took off his glove. A lump lodged in his throat as Evelyn smeared something cold over his wound. Aliwyn had done something similar before he'd lost her, just a few paces away.

"Make sure you ask Reiya to help you with it," she said, wrapping bandages around his hand.

"Right."

"I'm proud of you for defending Reiya's people. And for giving your piglet to Fritha."

Her gaze was gentle, her face framed by brown hair like his own. Matthew fought to keep his composure. Despite all he'd done to hurt her, Evelyn had probably spoken to Reiya and encouraged her to keep him.

"You're not a deserter," she said. "You will clear your name."

Maybe he wasn't a deserter, but he was about to become something he despised. Memories of stealing his parents' spice box haunted Matthew as the cow horn pressed against his chest. On a whim, he grasped Evelyn's hand. He may have a price to pay for his sins, but she deserved an easier life.

Her gaze grew distant on the Vasfians behind him, now chattering with excited voices. Matthew swallowed. He couldn't bring back the one redhead she longed for.

"I'm sorry," he said.

"About what?"

"You already know."

Her eyes brightened with tears, and he sighed.

Releasing her, he said, "I'll be in Norwich at the end of this month for His Excellency's court. Then I'll meet you back in Barton."

It took all his self-control to hold back the details of his new mission. She didn't need to share his burden.

"Marie and I impatiently await your return," Evelyn said.

"Thanks. Please stay safe."

She smiled and gestured at her sword and sling. "You know I will be."

CHAPTER 11
NOT WITHOUT TOBY

October 2, Aliwyn

THE WIND CHILLED ALIWYN's still-wet eyes as she followed Toby upstairs. The two of them had been leafing through his journal downstairs while the others idled on deck. There had been no battle, no storm. How could the ship's anchor have gone missing?

Emma ran toward Toby and cried, "Toby! I'm scared."

He bent down and hugged her, murmuring something in her ear. Dense fog obscured the bow. The taste of ash lingered in Aliwyn's throat, and she fought a wave of chills. How far had the ship drifted into the sea?

Zelrin stood leaning against the mast with a questioning look. Aliwyn shook her head. Judging by the way he thinned his lips, he understood that she'd failed to persuade Toby to escape onto Driftmere and abandon the cargo.

It was hard to know if the drifting ship was a curse or a blessing in disguise.

Cilebi and Axlan stood by the capstan, the vertical axle turned by several men to pull up an anchor. The anchor's rope lay limp on the floorboards with nothing attached. Toby released Emma into Aliwyn's arms. Hobbling forward, he grabbed onto the rail for balance as the ship swayed. Aliwyn hung back and pinched the edge of her cloak. Maybe he was frightened, too, and forced himself to hide it.

"He be very stubborn, I know," Zelrin murmured, walking beside her. "Now it's up to Providence. This drifting is no accident."

Aliwyn blinked. He sounded pleased. Had he noticed they were drifting, but said nothing?

His next sentence answered her question.

"We can drift to Denmark without the seadogs comin' back." Zelrin smirked, then wiped his mouth to hide it.

Aliwyn drew a slow breath. His optimism was unfounded. Whoever had been so cunning and cruel as to cut the ship's anchor line might still be on board, hiding. She hugged Emma's shoulders. Her gaze wandered to beneath the ship's back platform, where the three-pronged fishing spears lay behind a stack of spare round shields. The sight of the sharp weapons made her shoulders rigid.

Toby picked up the twine, tarred on the outside to protect it against the weather, and fingered the frayed end. "When did anyone realize the anchor was gone?"

"Not long ago," Axlan answered with a nervous lilt. "Cilebi and I were taking a pause. We thought the waves were just rough, but the ship's rocking became mighty bad."

Cilebi spat over the rail. "Don't blame me. The anchor line looked intact when I turned the capstan earlier. And I've done nothing to it since."

"I'm not blaming anyone." Toby removed a piece of kelp from the line. "But this twine is not as rotten as the rigging, and there was no storm to strain it."

Axlan scratched his thinning hair. "Err...you think someone cut it?"

"Yes," Toby muttered. "Cut the twine partially, then let it snap on its own."

Aliwyn swallowed and widened her stance to keep balance. When Cilebi turned to her with his eyes narrowed, she glared back at him. This time, it couldn't possibly be her fault.

"Could it be a stowaway?" she asked.

Cilebi grunted. "We've looked long enough for non-existent stowaways."

Toby looked each of his crew in the eyes. "Someone may have compromised the line while we were moored near Myton, then escaped before we set sail."

"A tall tale," Cilebi mumbled.

"Is it?" Toby frowned at him. "The Vasfians pursued my father on his way to Myton, and Ed and I arrived late. This ship was poorly guarded for a while." He lowered the broken rope as the ship groaned and tilted. Bracing his side, he stood. "Regardless, we need an anchor. Cilebi, Axlan, please go downstairs and see if we have a spare."

Cilebi grumbled something in Danish. Nonetheless, he followed Axlan to the stairwell and descended.

Toby shifted back to Emma and Aliwyn, his gaze softening.

"The rest of you search the fishing nets in case the anchor got caught," he said. Hobbling away, he added, "I'll climb up and locate Driftmere. Ed will know what to do once we return."

He gripped the rope ladder extending along the mast. Stepping onto the first rung, he tried to stabilize his injured ankle, but his mouth twisted with pain. Aliwyn approached him with her pulse thrumming. Part of her still couldn't believe what a bind they were in. Toby had almost no crew, and she was useless.

"Zel," she called out. "Can you go up instead?"

Zelrin let go of the pulley used to crank in the netting. "Oh, Toby, your ankle be bad still. I can go."

"No." Toby pulled himself up another rung. "I recognize the landmarks around here." He closed his eyes for a moment. "And I recognize bounty hunter ships when I see them."

Bounty hunters. Ice wrapped around Aliwyn's stomach, but maybe she shouldn't be surprised. The farther they drifted into the open sea, the more dangerous the waters became.

"Blazin' sards." Zelrin rubbed his eyes. "Why didn't you say this earlier?"

Silence. Toby pressed his forehead against the rope. The wind tossed his blond hair, and panic simmered in his lowered eyes. Aliwyn's throat swelled. Of course, he was frightened. Why was this happening? Was it Providence giving her more time to convince him to abandon his mission?

Zelrin pulled out his sling and shook out the leather strap. He cleared his throat. "I'll get more rocks for my sling and warn the other two." He ran to the stairs and soon disappeared below deck.

Aliwyn squeezed Emma's hand as Toby pulled himself up another rung. His weakened ankle wobbled with every step, but he continued with a scowl.

She had to put aside her doubts and find that anchor. Leaning toward Emma's ear, she whispered, "Let's go check those nets."

She would never guess what lay waiting.

The first nets they reeled in through the pulley systems yielded nothing but dripping seaweed. Zelrin hauled a sack of rocks on deck, tied it against the rail, and joined them in the search.

Finally, they pulled up the net hanging from the back platform. Something metallic glinted from within the black and moldy twine. It was too small to be an anchor. Aliwyn froze. Instinct screamed for her to plunge the netting back into the water, but it was too late.

"Oh, look!" Emma jumped. "It's Ransley's knife!"

Aliwyn's knees almost buckled. She had dropped that knife when cutting the rigging last night, and never did she expect... Her mouth dry, she struggled to appear calm as Zelrin reeled up the net to his eye level.

"Sards." He rummaged through the meshwork and untangled the weapon. "Who tossed it here?"

The face of a spiteful griffin, carved onto the blade's hilt, glowered at Aliwyn. She wanted to knock the ugly thing into the sea forever.

"We can show Toby later," she stammered. "Let's keep looking for the anchor."

"Did you find something?" Toby called out from the rope ladder. He clung precariously to the top rung and had to twist around to look at them.

"Not the anchor, but your papa's knife!" Emma cried.

A numbing sensation washed over Aliwyn's face. *Emma, no...* At the child's sharp cry, Axlan and Cilebi's footsteps below deck stuttered, then turned back toward the stairwell with deliberate force.

Zelrin walked away and raised the knife for Toby to see. The glinting blade sent a fresh wave of dread coursing through Aliwyn.

In her mind, last night's chaotic scene flooded back. Before she'd shredded the rigging, the ship's relentless sway had jostled her hand from rope to rope. She had sawed at any twine within reach, maybe even the...

Aliwyn's eyes widened. It was her. She had compromised the anchor line, and it had just snapped entirely.

Axlan called from the stairwell, "We couldn't find a spare anchor, but you found *what*?"

He and Cilebi stomped upstairs, and Aliwyn's chest swelled with terror until she couldn't breathe.

Both men approached Zelrin and stared at the knife. The youngster gestured at where it had been retrieved, exactly where Aliwyn stood. She wanted to shrivel and disappear.

Cilebi's glare burned into her skin, and the man barked a laugh.

"Caught like the rat you are!" He put his hands on his hips and shouted up at Toby, "Now do you believe this wench cut our lines?"

Emma turned around with a worried look, and Aliwyn's face burned. Lies to save herself again swirled in her mind, but this time, she clamped her mouth shut. No more lying.

She couldn't see Toby's face from behind, but he seemed rigid as he stood high on the rope ladder.

"You found my father's knife," he said. "But it doesn't mean she cut anything."

Aliwyn's tongue lay thick in her mouth. Part of her wanted to scream the truth.

Cilebi threw up his hands. "By Thor! She stole the knife! She hid by the lines last night and cut our rigging and the anchor!"

"I'll deal with the knife later." Toby tested his wounded ankle on a lower rung but hoisted himself back up. "I still haven't found land. Both of you, keep searching for a spare."

"I agree we deal with the knife later," Axlan said. He clapped a hand on Cilebi's shoulder, but the bald man jerked away. Axlan shrugged and departed alone for the stairwell.

Cilebi marched to the mast with his fists swinging.

"You bloody fool!" he shouted up at Toby. "The culprit is right here!"

He jabbed a finger at Aliwyn, who had pressed herself against the rail. In her mind's eye, she saw the soldiers again pouring into her watermill, forcing her against the wall and almost killing her. The scene was repeating itself. This time, Toby wouldn't reach her in time. She glanced at the ship's stern, cluttered with familiar fishing spears, but her stomach heaved at the thought of fighting a man.

"Leave her be." Toby's voice cracked as he began to descend. "My father was confused. He could've dropped his own knife."

As he spoke, Aliwyn guided a whimpering Emma toward the ship's bow. Pins and needles shot through her arms. She clung to the hope of avoiding a fight until Cilebi's boot stomped in their path. Emma shrieked.

In a flash, Zelrin darted in front of Emma. He shoved Cilebi back and brandished Ransley's knife. "Leave them alone!"

"Go downstairs!" Toby ordered, but his injured ankle buckled with the next step down.

Cilebi again burst out laughing, and chills rained down Aliwyn's spine.

"You dare push me?" he roared.

He threw a punch toward Zelrin's face. The youngster ducked, but Cilebi grabbed him and threw him down like a sack of barley. Aliwyn's vision tunneled. Zelrin's cry of pain rang in her ears. She teetered backward and shouted for Emma to run. The girl scampered away. Then the sounds around her cut off.

Time seemed to slow. From the depths of her mind, Matthew spoke again. *Ever stabbed someone with that fishing spear of yours?* The memory of his tired grin in her watermill sent her a jolt of strength.

Aliwyn startled back to attention as Cilebi swung at her. She ducked, and his blow swiped open air. Pivoting on her new shoes, she bolted for the ship's bow and the fishing spears lying in the shadows. Cilebi's crashing footsteps quaked the floorboards beneath her, thundering in her ears, until she dove for the weapons.

Aliwyn seized a spear and tore it free from behind the heap of toppling round shields. Scrambling to her knees, she swung the weapon in a sharp arc. Its triple points sliced the air toward Cilebi.

He froze, his eyes wide.

With a cry, she aimed at his legs and thrust. At the last instant, she shifted her aim and trapped his shin between two sharp prongs. The man howled. With his lower leg immobilized, he toppled forward. His torso descended like a shadow and crashed onto the rail behind her. Aliwyn scrambled out before his knees buckled over her. Her wobbly legs wouldn't stand again, and she crawled away with fire in her veins.

Yelling filled her ears. Aliwyn pushed herself up to sit against a mast and turned around. Toby and Axlan were prying back Cilebi's arms.

"Easy now, C-man," Axlan said. "You must be wanting some mead. We have one barrel left. Right, Toby?"

Toby, red in the face, said nothing. He wrung his father's knife out of Cilebi's grip, and Aliwyn's chin trembled. *Dear Heavens!* Cilebi had grabbed that dagger from Zelrin and nearly slashed her, but she hadn't seen it. The fear of knowing would've crippled her. Maybe she should feel proud about fighting, but the memory of that confrontation made her shudder.

Matthew, how did you know I'd have to...

It was the memory of his voice that had triggered her self-defense, but she couldn't thank him anymore, or see him again. Her eyes stung. He'd hate her if he knew what she'd done, and she had best forget about him.

Cilebi hollered in Danish as the other men marched him toward the stairwell. A sour taste flooded Aliwyn's mouth. Toby still believed in her innocence, but for how long? She staggered to her feet and walked toward Zelrin and Emma, who were huddled together with bewilderment marking their faces. Zelrin looked alert, at least, without blood anywhere. Aliwyn managed a smile.

"Thank you, Zel..."

"Looks like you didn't need me." Despite his sullen tone, he grinned. "Good aim there."

Tears welled in Aliwyn's eyes again. This drifting was her fault. Her fault. When Emma reached for her, Aliwyn fell in a heap beside the child. Emma snuggled against her and smiled.

"I want to be brave like you," the girl whispered.

Aliwyn's throat tightened as she held the child close. Turning toward the men, she waited for Toby to give Cilebi his due punishment. At least, she expected as much.

Axlan was still consoling Cilebi with the promise of mead below deck when Toby said hoarsely, "Wait. He's not going downstairs."

Aliwyn stiffened all over. Both of Cilebi's arms were still pinned behind his back. He shot Toby a spiteful glare, but Toby continued in a calm voice, "Climb the mast yourself and tell me what you see."

The man's nose twitched. "Are you jesting?"

"No. You are one of the strongest fighters Ed hired, and you deserve to see what I saw. Then we'll discuss what to do next."

The two men locked gazes, and Aliwyn clenched her hands. What was Toby doing? Cilebi was a coward, not a fighter. And after his outburst, he should be taken below deck and tied down.

Cilebi cocked his head. "What did you see?"

Drawing a slow breath, Toby murmured, "Longships. Bishop's colors."

Axlan's bushy eyebrows shot up, and Aliwyn's heart lodged in her throat. The Normans, like the Danes, loved to sail on longships. She braced Emma's small frame even tighter.

Cilebi smirked. "Ah, Skinheads. Let me see."

Moments later, the burly man was climbing the rope ladder with fervor. His movements made the mast groan. Once he was a safe distance above, Aliwyn shuffled toward Toby with her back drenched in cold sweat. He hobbled toward her with worry darkening his eyes, but a smile lit his face when Emma and Zelrin walked ahead to meet him. Extending his arms, Toby hugged both youngsters and kissed Emma on the head. Aliwyn wrung her hands. This was his little family, and she had endangered everyone. Again.

"Y-you saw Norman longships?" she asked.

He nodded, his brows drawn as though in apology. "I also saw Driftmere to the west, but the winds are not in our favor. If the longships come to investigate, we cannot escape."

"But we're sailing the bishop's colors." Zelrin jerked his chin toward the sail. "Isn't it authentic enough?"

"They know their bishop didn't send a hulk ship into the North Sea."

Zelrin rubbed his nose. "Well then, let's start escaping now." He nodded at Axlan. "Axlan and I will trim the sails...and flamin' sards if I don't kill the one who cut our anchor." He grabbed a rock from his belt pouch. "We're going to find him, aren't we?"

"If he's still on board, yes."

The men spoke some more, and tears fell from Aliwyn's eyes. She fought the urge to bolt away.

"Thank you for defending her, Zel," she heard Toby say. "And...I'm sorry about earlier."

Zelrin grunted. "Sorry about what earlier?"

Toby only smiled and lowered his eyes. He also thanked Axlan for his good work, then sent the two men toward the lines controlling the direction of the sail.

When he turned to Aliwyn, as though expecting her to say something, she could only squeeze her eyes shut. Toby was doing everything to hold his tiny crew together, and she had done everything to ruin his life.

Cilebi's voice made her jump.

"Aye, Skinheads!" he called down. "By Thor... At least three ships fully lined with shields. I wager twenty men on each ship."

"Help me steer back to Driftmere?" Toby called back.

"Aye..." Cilebi frowned into the distance and chuckled bitterly. "Driftmere or straight to Valhalla."

What did Valhalla even mean? Aliwyn stumbled backward when the former Norseman began to descend.

He glowered at her, then smirked. "I will tell Captain Ed about the dagger."

Aliwyn's face heated beneath her tear tracks. To protest that it wasn't her fault would be lying to Toby again. She couldn't do it.

Cilebi's footsteps thudded on deck, his eyes still fixed on her. "Even if Ed doesn't kill you, he'll sell you as a thrall, have you whipped—"

"Enough," Toby said. "I decide what happens to her."

Cilebi grunted as he marched toward the lines controlling the sail's angle. Aliwyn's chest heaved. The threat to her life was over, for now.

Although Toby approached her next, she couldn't stand his presence. Turning away, she hurried to the cauldron and ladled water into a dirty bowl to rinse it. She dumped the murky liquid overboard only to see Toby standing nearby again, watching her, as though waiting for her to speak.

Maybe he did suspect her after all. Her screams echoed in her mind. At any moment, he'd start interrogating her—

"What's wrong?" Toby asked in Vasfian.

Aliwyn's stomach squeezed. She dropped her partially cleaned bowl with a thunk and scrambled for a response. "Those longships. Aren't you worried?"

Resentment for her own backstabbing ways came out in her voice, seething and biting. The wounded expression on Toby's face made everything more unbearable.

"Fear won't keep the longships away," he said. "I'm more concerned about getting you, Zel, and Emma off the ship if there's an attack." He gripped the rail to steady himself. "I need to ask you...why didn't you answer when I called you during the incident last night?"

His look of melancholic condemnation made her shake.

Aliwyn dipped her chin. "I was scared."

It wasn't a lie, but not the full truth, either.

"I see. It's normal to freeze when one is scared. But...look at me, Ali."

She managed to meet his gaze.

"You just defended yourself. You're stronger than you think. If I call you again tonight..." The knob in his throat bobbed up and down. "If I tell you to get into the canoe with Zelrin and Emma, you do it. Don't freeze. Don't look back."

Aliwyn stared at him. He was dense. Incredibly dense to her treachery and yet so insightful in other ways. Why did that make her angry?

"Why won't you come with us?" she asked, her breaths quickening.

Toby stared at the choppy waters. "I'd rather die at sea than face Norman wrath on land. If the ship is taken, my battle ends here."

Not more of the same foolish bravado that sent Aelfric to his unmarked grave. Fury swelled in Aliwyn's chest.

"You still have a future without battling anyone and without facing Norman punishment," she seethed. "You just don't see it."

He blinked. "What?"

"Dump your cargo. Escape onto Driftmere with me and take another ship anywhere. It doesn't have to be Denmark."

The wind flipped back Toby's hair. He smirked, then chuckled. "So, you want me to run away? I can't do that. And I can't dump the cargo. It's the only thing on board worth anything."

"What about our lives? What about your life? What good is your cargo if you're dead?"

All humor vanished from his face. "That cargo is all I have to bargain for a future."

"You still have one without it. If you must choose between me and the youngsters and all this—" She stomped the floor. "What would you choose?"

Toby's lips thinned, and his face darkened. This time, she had pushed too far, and her chin trembled. Without another word, Toby turned for the ship's bow and limped away. His foot dragged more than before.

Aliwyn wiped her eyes. She'd tried everything to extract Toby from his obsession with "defeating tyrants" except one—setting his cargo on fire. The thought had tempted her last night, and now it became irresistible. Ducking by the hearth, she grabbed a fire striker and flintstone from the sack.

Grasping the frigid objects sent chills down her spine. A few sparks in the right place, and the ship would burn from bow to stern, forcing Toby to escape by canoe. Forcing him to live.

Her eyes refocused on Emma, who was wiping the bowl Aliwyn had discarded. With her forehead crinkling, the girl glanced at Aliwyn, then at the destructive intent in her grip. Aliwyn swallowed. The girl might not understand Vasfian, but she seemed to understand the situation.

In that moment, Aliwyn saw the danger in her plans. The fire could burn out of control. It could take the ship, the cargo, the mercenaries, and the child in front of her. Everyone.

Her fingers spasmed. Starting a fire was reckless, but what else could she do as a last resort? For now, she tossed the objects back into the sack. She could always return to them later.

Smiling through her tears, Aliwyn reached for the girl's braids and stroked them. "Emma, if we need to leave this ship, will you come with me?"

The girl grimaced. "Not without Toby."

Aliwyn rose to her knees and hugged Emma close, feeling the child's breathing against her own. If only she could take this girl to a real home.

"I know," Aliwyn whispered. "I'm still trying to bring him with us."

Her gaze lingered on the sack with the fire strikers hidden within.

Toby believed that completing his mission, earning funds, and building his dream home justified any sacrifice. He couldn't see that Edward's return meant death for them all, followed by death for hundreds in England once the Danes bought the cargo.

Aliwyn gritted her teeth. She would give Toby more time, but unless he abandoned his ship or dumped the cargo before Edward returned, she'd have to do the unthinkable.

CHAPTER 12
TWO LIARS

October 1, Matthew

WITH THE ROYAL ARMY lingering by their tents, Matthew climbed into a cluttered wagon beside Domilo. Part of him still couldn't believe he was entering Reiya's warband after Jacques accused him of deserting the Norman army.

Evelyn's figure vanished as the wagon circled the Brocklesby town walls, but her voice lingered in his memories. They'd rarely spoken as friends. This was his fault. When he saw her again, he'd be a better cousin.

They were heading north. The ox-pulled wagon rumbled along the dirt road, its wheels clattering over the occasional rock. Aliwyn's chickens, safe within two crates, clucked at the rear. The stink of manure faded into the crisp scent of evergreens. Domilo smiled and taught Matthew Vasfian phrases, but he barely listened.

Four days. Four days to find Aliwyn *and* steal some black matter, all without angering the Vasfians and getting expelled. Or worse. His stomach twisted as the last Norman flags fluttering outside Brocklesby vanished behind him.

"Where are we going?" Matthew asked. "Another hillfort?"

"Yes," Reiya called out. "Jethran is close to the River Humber. It means 'waterfall' in my language."

Matthew flinched as she rode up to the cart where he sat. She motioned for the driver to halt, tied her mare to the wagon, and climbed aboard. Wind tugged her vest and hair as she sat beside him.

"We'll reach Jethran by afternoon," she said, sipping from her costrel. "My sister tribes will send doves tomorrow if they see men wearing the griffin surcoat."

Matthew scratched his scabbed hand. "What if they have nothing to report? We don't even know where the Danes are landing."

Scowling, Reiya corked her water pouch. "That bothers me, too, but the answers don't always come at once. Let's wait for the messenger doves and plan from there. For now, we should eat and rest."

Matthew sighed. It was hard to be patient and rest, but his sore throat and dry eyes demanded otherwise. Reiya pulled over a drawstring bag and reached inside, her face calm. Why wasn't she worried about the enemy's arrival? He tried to mirror her ease.

But as she rummaged within the sack, her red sleeves flashing like bursts of blood, Matthew tensed. In just four days, he could enter the first true battle of his life.

She withdrew a triangular loaf of bread.

"Thank you for helping my people today," she said, offering him the food.

"Don't mention it." Matthew stared at the bread. Saliva pooled in his mouth, but he didn't deserve to take it.

Her face seemed paler in the brightening daylight, and she dipped her chin. "I was careless back in Brocklesby."

"No. You couldn't control what the soldiers did."

A smile tugged at her lips. "Now that you're under my leadership, do you have any questions?"

He blinked. "N-no. Everything's clear. No questions."

"Really?" She chuckled. "So, eating our offerings to the dead won't happen again?"

Matthew shook his head. As the wind chilled his sweaty neck, he averted his eyes and braced his empty stomach. The longer he talked to Reiya, the more likely he'd say something stupid. Like revealing his true intentions.

"You should ask questions." Her voice took on an irritated lilt. "Better ask too many than act the fool, especially around my druids."

"I...just don't have any."

"I'm trying to help you, but you don't seem grateful."

Matthew tugged on his collar. "Do you want to be addressed differently?"

"Hmm... What are the options?"

"There's M'lady Reiya." He grimaced at the awkwardness. "Or Madame Reiya. Or—"

Reiya burst out laughing. "*Kaba nao*! Just call me Reiya. My warriors do the same."

"Fine...Reiya."

She grinned at him. Did she still want to talk? Because he was done.

But Reiya continued. "We need a smoke signal that only the two of us understand. This way, I won't call for the Norman army and get you instead. Any suggestions?"

"N-no."

Her smile faded. "How about alternating short and long puffs? Whoever sends it wants the other to come."

"Fine."

He was being so agreeable, and yet the displeasure on her face grew. Matthew's pulse throbbed in his ears as he looked away.

Domilo busied himself with sliding small bowls of grain into the chicken crates. Reiya spoke to the driver, Namanti, whose loaded crossbow remained by her hip. The conversation around him sounded friendly, but the glint of Namanti's bolt tip unnerved Matthew.

Should he stall the Vasfian's progress for more time to find the black matter? *But Aliwyn...* Matthew scowled and rubbed the clovers she'd embroidered on the sleeves of Aelfric's tunic. Now his tunic.

"Matthew, look at me," Reiya muttered.

She sounded angry. His shoulders stiff, Matthew turned around. Reiya grabbed his left hand, pressed the triangular bread onto his palm, and tossed a water pouch onto his lap. His fingers dug into the bread's crust.

Reiya jutted her chin. "You're torturing yourself over a woman who doesn't matter."

Matthew looked away and shoved bread into his mouth. "I promised Aelfric I'd keep her safe."

"That's because he didn't know she'd turn traitor. Did Jacques tell you which woman had fooled him into letting Tobias go?"

Matthew took bigger bites until he pushed all the food into his mouth. The bread, stuffed with mushy vegetables and nuts, made him gag. He gulped down much-needed water.

"No. He didn't say." Matthew wiped his chin dry, but unease welled in the pit of his stomach.

"Jacques used to grind flour at the Brocklesby mill, so he recognizes the people who live inside." Reiya arched an eyebrow. "Do I need to say the traitor's name?"

She sounded pleased. Too pleased. The air around Matthew seemed to thicken, and shadows darted over his face as the wagon careened into the woods.

"No," he mumbled.

Why, Aliwyn? He wanted to hurl every object he saw off the cart. Didn't she know siding with the rebels meant torture or death? He ducked his head, his face flushing, but there was no escaping Reiya's scrutiny.

"So you admit Aliwyn's a traitor? No one threatened to kill her if she exposed Tobias' identity, but she lied anyway." Reiya leaned in, her brows knit. "Stop caring about her."

Domilo had grown still while watching their conversation, and even the driver twisted around.

Matthew's throat pulsed. "How did you make Jacques realize his error?"

"I told him Aliwyn and Tobias were likely traveling on horseback, based on the hoof prints Evelyn had seen. Jacques said he'd seen Aliwyn last night, outside Myton, with a man and a child. Then he realized that man had been Tobias."

"Flying Krakens. Jacques didn't recognize Tobias?"

"No." Reiya gripped her kneecap. "At least Jacques and I are even. We both let that imbecile escape once."

Water stung Matthew's cracked lips, the only sensation that still grounded him to the conversation. Had Aelfric been alive, what would he have thought? What would he do?

"I don't understand," he muttered. "Why did Aliwyn lie?"

"Who cares? She can be dead or alive. She's nobody to us."

"But Aelfric talked about his sister all the time."

"His sister?" Reiya sat back, her eyes rounded. Then she hunched over and rubbed her temples. "I see. Is that what Aelfric told you?"

"Of course." Yet, even as Matthew spoke, dread began shackling him down. "Miriam adopted both Aelfric and Ali as sib—"

"That isn't true."

Matthew chuckled. "Of course it is."

"No. It's a lie."

What felt like laughter rumbled in his throat, but it was a deep and tortured sound he didn't recognize as his own. Aelfric had uttered only one thing before he died: *Ali.* Matthew had promised to find and protect his best friend's sister. The memory still burned, laced with the scent of blood and lit by the fire engulfing Wynthorpe's ramparts. This last exchange between them...had been based on a lie?

"I don't believe you," Matthew croaked. "Aelfric would never lie to me."

Reiya glanced at him with her forehead crinkled. She was finally quiet. Matthew folded his legs and stared at the soot-covered railing beside him.

On his other side, Domilo murmured, "Aliwyn isn't Aelfric's sister. Me and anyone in the village can tell you that."

Hadn't Aliwyn also said she wasn't Aelfric's sister? Matthew no longer remembered. He only recalled making her so angry she'd pulled a dagger on him. A hollow ache spread in his chest. He should've listened.

Reiya said in a quiet voice, "Aliwyn and Aelfric both trained under Miriam. But Miriam never adopted them as siblings."

"Why?" Matthew asked. "Why did Aelfric lie?"

"I have a theory. He wanted to court Aliwyn, but she wouldn't accept him. It wounded Aelfric deeply. I think calling her his sister was his way of coping, a way he could stay close and feel accepted."

Matthew hung his head. He never knew Aelfric had trouble with women. The women servants used to swarm around Aelfric, but he'd simply told Matthew they weren't for him.

"He lied to my whole family," Matthew murmured.

"Aelfric met you when he was still a boy," Reiya said. "He never told me he'd lied, either. He must've regretted it."

Matthew leaned back against the sacks behind him. The wagon's tossing rocked him back and forth, shaking out the frenetic energy of that morning. Pines blurred past on either side. The cloudy sky cracked into powdery chips with sunlight piercing through. Aelfric had to be up there, listening, desperate to explain himself. Matthew wanted to believe that, anyway. Wind chilled his wet eyes, and the aching for answers went unfulfilled.

"Do you think poorly of Aelfric now?" Reiya asked, her voice on edge.

"No. But I wish I could talk to him. He still cared about Aliwyn."

Something about her silence prompted him to look at her. Reiya sat cross-legged beside him, her braid unraveling in red strands over the side of her scowling face. Matthew held her gaze.

"I still want to know the truth," he said.

"You just heard the truth."

"No, I mean the truth behind Aliwyn's motivations. You say Aelfric had lied for a reason. I want to know what Aliwyn's reasons are. I still want to find her."

He braced himself for an angry retort, but Reiya only tucked her hair behind one ear. Her frown lifted.

"Fine," she said. "I applaud your pursuit of the truth. I won't try to stop you anymore."

Matthew drew a long breath. They'd finally agreed on something.

"But be prepared." Reiya narrowed her eyes. "Because you may only find Aliwyn's body. And if she's not dead, then the Norman punishment for treason is still death, isn't it?"

His toes curled. "There is no use in fearing the worst. Or talking about her sentence right now."

Reiya shot him one last scowl before turning to Domilo. An image of Aliwyn with a noose around her neck flashed in Matthew's mind, and chills racked his body. It would not happen. Not to someone Aelfric loved and trusted, even if she wasn't his sister. Something in Aliwyn's story must exonerate her from blame.

By the Devil's tail. What was the whole truth, and why was it so hard to obtain?

And was Reiya telling the truth about not possessing the black matter? He needed answers.

Only one path forward gave Matthew peace. He wouldn't sabotage the Vasfians' carts to stall their pursuit of the Boltans. He had to find the black matter before the rebels were caught and his time among the Vasfians ended. In four days.

To succeed, he needed Reiya's favor.

Clearing his throat, he turned back to the Mehi chief. She had wrapped her arms around Domilo with a grimace tightening her face. Had he said something wrong? Or was she also upset about Aelfric's lie?

His mouth dry, Matthew waited until Reiya released her brother. "Can I help you unpack when we reach Jethran?"

His skin crawled at how sincere he sounded.

Reiya wiped her eyes and pulled a blanket over herself. "You need to sleep. I don't want to haul your body around again."

"I still want to help. Please wake me up."

She sighed. "All right. Then sleep now."

Matthew smiled to himself. That wasn't so hard. But unpacking the Mehi's belongings wouldn't be enough. He had to learn where the Vasfians kept their war spoils and how to reach them unseen. He had to approach the chest's padlock to scrutinize its keyhole.

"Reiya," he said, his voice squeaky. "I do have a question."

"Yes?"

"The *Anuin* you talked about last night. The one where you worship your gods. Can I attend one?"

Reiya's eyes grew still. With a blanket wrapped around her shoulders, she looked thinner and almost vulnerable sitting there. He hated this look, this reminder of the young woman beneath the leader.

She began spreading out blankets for Domilo and Nissa to lie down on. "Why do you want to attend?"

"So I can understand your faith better. And so I won't do something like eat *kubozi* balls again."

Reiya gave him a teasing grin. Yet, her lips trembled, and whatever annoyance Matthew felt was soon drowned by guilt. He only cared about the

Anuin because that's when the Vasfians dedicated their loot to their gods. Surely, the black chest she'd stolen from Ransley Boltan would go on display.

"I'll ask my grandmother," Reiya said. "We do need to reschedule the *Anuin*. It can even be tomorrow."

Something thudded in his chest. "Really?"

"Yes. My mother is sick and needs prayer. The *Anuin* has been delayed for weeks because of the war."

She sighed, and Matthew bit his tongue. It sounded like the Vasfians offered their spoils in hopes of healing from divine forces. And here he was, planning to break into and desecrate...

Matthew stopped his thoughts right there. He was doing everything for his men. Knights like Lord Seville had trained him since age seven and given him purpose. Now, he would prove his loyalty.

Looking Reiya in the eye, he said, "I hope your mother gets better."

"Thank you. I'll speak with my elders about letting you join. It's time a Norman soldier saw our ceremonies. I want the rumors to stop." Her forehead creased. "We don't sacrifice boys or drink blood."

"I-I'm sure you don't."

Reiya covered Domilo and Nissa with blankets. Lifting her gaze, she said softly, "Thanks for being the first Norman to ask."

Matthew nodded stiffly.

Reiya unlocked a nearby chest and pulled out red-and-green-striped blankets. She placed them beside Matthew and murmured, "I don't feel like we finished talking about Aelfric. He wasn't perfect, but he still loved you as a brother. I hope you never questioned that."

"I didn't. He'll always be my best friend."

She smiled, then spread her blanket and lay down. "Sleep, Matthew."

His face burning, he unfurled his woven blanket and lay down. Sacks and a roll of tapestry separated him from Reiya and her siblings on the other side.

Namanti shifted in the driver's seat, scowling back at him before returning her gaze to the road. One act of bravery hadn't earned her trust. Understandable. The other elders would be watching him, too.

Reiya's face relaxed as she slept, but Matthew's pulse raced on. Aelfric would hate what he planned to do, but pulling a heist on the Mehi was Matthew's assignment.

He needed to behave himself before the *Anuin* to continue winning the Mehi tribe's trust. And what would Reiya's mother be like?

Closing his eyes, he tried to sleep.

CHAPTER 13

DONKEY AMONGST WOLVES

Matthew

A PIERCING, NASAL CRY echoed in the woods and shook Matthew awake.

He sat up with a flash of chills. A war horn? Had the Danes arrived early?

But no one else stirred in alarm. Overhead, afternoon sun filtered through the branches. Reiya lay nearby on the cart bed with her face upturned and her eyes closed. Domilo slept beside her with his small body wrapped in blankets. Other Vasfians chattered in the background over the trickling of a stream, and their horses grazed around them. The procession had paused beside a rocky outcrop. Matthew sighed and rubbed his eyes. Maybe he'd had a nightmare.

He was about to lie back down when the sound rang out again. Now he recognized the noise as a donkey's loud and miserable braying. It wasn't a war horn, after all.

Maybe one of the Vasfians' donkeys was injured. On a whim, Matthew craned his neck to peer between the wagon's side planks. Porei stood by the stream with her coat glowing in the late sun. She looked fine, but the braying continued, and none of the redheads tending their animals seemed to notice.

Strange.

Matthew scooted toward Reiya to tap her shoulder, but her eyes opened anyway when the hunting dogs began barking.

He wanted to mention the donkey but doubled over coughing. Reiya threw off her blanket and sat up, rocking the wagon. As he wheezed into his elbow, she thumped his back so hard he nearly toppled.

"Hold on, Matthew. I have another medicine ball somewhere."

She crawled to a chest at Domilo's feet and hastily unlocked it. Opening the lid, she withdrew long seashell garlands and mosaic colored glass plates. They were odd but beautiful items that looked expensive. Gold and silver beads glimmered from sinew strands dangling from each shell. No wonder she wouldn't let Jacques touch them. Matthew sipped from the costrel she'd lent him, but the coughing began anew.

Reiya scowled. She carefully set down the items and dug deeper, rummaging through herb satchels, garlic bulbs, and wooden bowls. The scent of thyme and wild roses drifted around him.

He could hardly meet her eyes. He wasn't worth this hurry. Nothing here smelled like black matter either, and she had nearly emptied the chest without pause. Was she trying to prove she had nothing to hide?

Finally, Reiya grabbed a corked jar, pulled off the stopper, and sniffed the contents. "Good. This one is still fresh."

She offered the jar to Matthew, who removed the medicine ball and swallowed it without hesitation this time.

"Thank you," he croaked, sipping from his costrel.

The back of his throat tingled with a cooling sensation. Now that he'd stopped coughing, the donkey's braying and the dogs' barking again filled his ears. Matthew wiped his mouth with a frown.

"What's wrong with your donkey?" he asked. "Maybe I can help him."

"Nothing's wrong." Reiya took the empty jar and corked it again. "While you were still sleeping, my warrior told me she tried to pull him along, but he wouldn't move."

Matthew raised an eyebrow. *Nothing's wrong?* He'd never allow Porei to keep crying like this.

"Let me see the donkey," he said. "Do you have a carrot I can give him?"

"No." Reiya began repacking the chest. "Don't worry about him. We're leaving."

"What?"

Reiya ignored him and spoke to the driver. She leaned over the railing and waved at two warriors who stood beside their wagon. A few terse words later, the women who had been watching their animals graze began leading them back to their wagon. Other drivers climbed on board.

"You're leaving your donkey?" Matthew cried.

"He's not my donkey."

She rubbed her nose, and Matthew recalled where he'd seen that look of disgust before—when she had stated that having no freckles was ugly. And who had a donkey but no freckles? Matthew's eyes widened.

He pushed to his feet. "Is that Mils? Kato's donkey?"

When the driver raised her crossbow, he flinched and put up his hands. Reiya waved at the other woman, who lowered her weapon.

"So what if it's Kato's donkey?" Reiya muttered.

"Is Kato with him?"

When Reiya only glared at him, Matthew's heart thudded. Her silence was enough. He stepped cautiously toward the wagon's rear.

"Hey!" Reiya shouted. "I didn't say you can wander!"

He took another step. "I'm not wandering. I'm investigating under your full supervision."

Her nostrils flared. Matthew could imagine fire coming out of her ears.

"Kato's not welcome in my tribe," Reiya snapped. "Get back here before someone kills you by accident."

She'd just implied that Kato wasn't dead. Elation swelled within Matthew, but that joy soon shriveled. If Mils continued to scream, why was Kato so quiet?

A dozen redheads now gathered around Matthew with various weapons dangling from their hips. Namanti stood amongst them, and her glower sent dread rattling through him. Yet, he wouldn't let Evelyn down again.

"I owe it to my cousin to find Kato," Matthew said. "And he's Norman's apprentice. You said Norman helped you fight Rans—"

"Yes, but Kato helped Aliwyn and Tobias escape." Reiya rose to her feet. Matthew froze as her hand hovered over the crossbow strapped to her hip. Yet, she didn't grab it.

"My mother banished his mother and all her descendants," Reiya continued. "That woman stole from us and made everyone suspicious of each other. The Mehi almost disbanded until we caught her." Reiya surveyed the crowd around them, and her expression matched their darkened faces. "Now sit down. Kato's not welcome, and that's not my decision alone."

Matthew hardly heard her. A familiar brown sack hung from Namanti's arm as she gripped her animal skull staff. It was the type of medicated bag that had rendered him unconscious. Now he knew why Kato hadn't made a sound.

None of the Vasfians had raised a crossbow yet. With a final tightening of his jaw, Matthew spun around, jumped off the wagon, and bolted into the nearest row of trees.

"Hey!" Reiya shouted.

He darted between trees to make himself a harder target. Twigs poked through his stockings as he thrashed through the thicket, his heart lobbing in his throat. The tribe shouldn't condemn anyone for being born to unlawful parents. If Matthew had to pay for all his father's sins, celestial fire would've consumed him at birth.

The ground sloped upward. Where was that donkey? He pressed on through the shadowy trunks, guided only by sound. Damp air crept beneath his tunic. Wait—he carried no weapons. Matthew grabbed a long branch from the ground. He'd probably need it.

Leaves crunched behind him. He spun, but there was no one. Was Reiya following at a distance? He didn't know why he still hoped for her help.

The braying grew louder. He scrambled up a rocky rise and glimpsed the rump of a pack animal. Sunlight pierced the evergreens overhead, shedding light on a donkey braying and prancing over gnarled roots.

Mils!

Matthew's mouth fell open. Two shadows darted from the thicket. Before he could blink, the donkey charged and stomped with both front hooves. A sharp yelp rang out. The attackers bolted, bushy gray tails flashing, and left behind a man with clumpy red hair sprawled face-up in the rotting leaves.

Wolves. Mils and Kato had been surrounded. Matthew waved his arms and bellowed at the top of his lungs. He smacked tree trunks with his stick. The wolves, a pack of four, showed themselves again before scattering.

Mils' braying softened as though he sensed help had come. Stick still raised, Matthew strode forward. Sunlight lit Kato's pale face and the beige tunic sagging over his concave chest. His arms were bent and resting by his ears.

Chills ran down Matthew's back. Had the Vasfians sedated him, or worse?

There were no wolves in sight now. Only Matthew's panting filled his ears. Mils stepped close and snuffed Kato's hair, matted and full of leaves. With a last glance at the woods, Matthew knelt and felt for a pulse at Kato's neck. The warmth of his nape still reached Matthew's fingers, but even fresh corpses could feel warm.

Scrapes covered Kato's forehead. His lips were parted, as if he'd died gasping. Dread coiled in Matthew's throat. He should drag Kato to safety and check for life later, but his legs refused to move.

A bowstring snapped.

Matthew looked up just as a bolt zipped overhead and slammed into a tree. Gray tails rustled away into the brush. "Idiot!" Reiya's voice rang out. "Get out of here!"

Matthew released a tense breath. She charged toward him and waved for her warriors, all bearing crossbows, to fan out and cover them. A strange delight filled him to see her enraged face as she slammed another bolt onto her drawn crossbow. When her gaze shifted to watch for predators, Matthew dared to slide his arm behind Kato's shoulders. She didn't object.

Kato was limp and heavy. The back of his mantle was wet from lying on the ground, chilling Matthew's hand. As he lifted, the younger man twitched and slumped against Matthew. He was still alive. The knots in Matthew's throat loosened. Grimacing at the donkey stench emanating from Kato's clothes, Matthew staggered to his feet with the redhead in his arms.

Then a wet tongue met him between the eyes.

"Mils—" Matthew dodged before the beast could lick him again.

Two large donkey eyes stared back at him, and Matthew grinned. He hadn't felt proud of himself in a long time.

"Move!" Reiya shouted.

She and half her warriors backed toward him with their crossbows poised, while the other half began to exit the forest. Matthew adjusted Kato's weight between his arms and hurried after the retreating Vasfians.

Chapter 14

Fire

October 2, Toby

THE WIND FINALLY PICKED up, snapping the sails with a vigor that sent hope surging through the crew. "Pull toward port!" Toby shouted.

Although the *Fortuna* had lost her anchor, she was making substantial progress toward Driftmere. Toward Edward.

Toby gripped the rigging and ignored the throbbing of his hand. Zelrin worked beside him with sweat streaking his brow. On the opposite end of the sailcloth, Axlan and Cilebi released the ropes in small sections to adjust the sail's angle. All four men had discarded their gambesons from the heat of their efforts.

The hulk leaned into the breeze and cut across the waves. For the first time that day, their destination felt attainable. A hazy strip of land hung on the horizon behind jutting rocks. As the sun set, its rays diffused through the fog in streaks of gold.

Hold on, Ed. I'm coming back. Toby's chest heaved at the thought. Only his uncle had visited Toby while he'd been confined to Driftmere. Now, it was Toby's turn to sail to him, though not under ideal circumstances. The *Fortuna* must return to Driftmere before the sun set, the sea darkened, and the waves bashed the anchorless ship against a rock.

Zelrin was panting but jubilant. Following Cilebi and Axlan's lead, he wrapped his line around a belaying pin. "We're goin' to lose them."

Toby tugged at his sweaty tunic. "Don't let your guard down." The longships had disappeared in the heavy fog, but the anxious burn in Toby's throat never eased. If the longships were suddenly to appear, the hefty *Fortuna* couldn't outsail them.

He glanced behind at the aftcastle. Aliwyn and Emma sat tucked in the shadows beneath the platform. They had wiled away the afternoon cooking a second meal and wiping the privy. Other than cleaning Toby's wounded hand, Aliwyn had avoided him.

The sight of her sullen stare cut deeper than he wanted to admit. Aliwyn, who had tried to make him abandon ship and everything he'd worked for. Aliwyn, who may indeed have taken Ransley's dagger and—

No. She had never been seen holding that weapon. As Miriam's apprentice, she wouldn't do such a thing, either. Toby sighed and turned back to his men.

Wind filled the golden and blue striped sail above their smiling faces. *Thank Heavens.* Picking up the ladle, Toby served his men water. Cilebi leaned against the rail and sipped from the costrel of mead Toby had allowed him to have.

The brief respite was all they enjoyed before footsteps from the stern pattered toward him. Toby turned to see Aliwyn hurrying across the deck with her purple cloak swirling behind her. The hem's golden flowers caught what little light remained, and her honey-brown hair scattered about her pale face. Toby's heart quickened. Perhaps she was finally coming to pledge her support, to tell him she believed in him.

But Aliwyn grabbed his forearm with a scowl. "Emma and I heard a dog barking. Over the water."

The words sliced through his flicker of hope. "A dog?"

She nodded, her expression grim. He placed his hand on her shoulder to steady her as much as himself. They hobbled toward the stern, where Emma sat huddled below the aftcastle. Toby crouched beside her and strained to listen. For a moment, only the slap of waves against the hull reached his ears. Then a sharp bark cut through the haze.

Toby's fist curled against his thigh. Not now. Not when they had finally begun to make progress. He turned back toward his crew, who had been watching him for an order, and sliced a downturned hand through the air. The men's faces darkened. They knew what it meant—longships.

Zelrin, Cilebi, and Axlan ducked below the level of the rail and scrambled to the back. Soon, everyone was crouched together and panting with the smell of sickly sweet mead and sweat hovering between them. The men threw their gambesons back on and checked their slings and daggers. When Emma whimpered, Aliwyn pulled the girl onto her lap. Toby circled his arm around Aliwyn's shoulder and felt a glimmer of relief when she leaned against him.

The dog continued to bark. Louder. Had Edward or Ransley been here, they'd have taken the lead without hesitation. Toby had never captained a ship without them. Frowning at his filthy glove, he silenced the disparaging voices in his head.

The dog continued to bark. Louder. His pulse thrumming in his ears, Toby crawled beneath the rail and dared to rise just enough to see over it.

Three longships with gilded prows and blue and yellow striped sails approached. Soon, they were close enough for the conical helmets of each soldier to be counted. About twenty per ship, as Cilebi had said. The wind may have filled the sails of *Lady Fortuna*, but it had also propelled the lighter and faster longships directly toward them. Perhaps they'd been hiding all along behind the rock formations.

A lump swelled in Toby's throat. More than ever, he regretted bringing Zelrin and Emma aboard, but the two youngsters had refused to stay behind in England. And now, everyone was here because of him. How far would he go to keep them safe? To keep them together?

All was quiet except for the sound of water lapping the ship's hull, but Toby knew in his bones the day would end in bloodshed.

Finally, a man spoke from on board the closest longship.

"I still say it looks abandoned." It was an Englishman with a native accent.

"Perhaps, but it's still not supposed to be here." The second man spoke English with a light French accent. A Norman.

Cilebi flexed his massive arm, his jaw tightening, but Toby placed a firm hand on his shoulder. For now, they'd only listen. And why did the Norman's voice sound familiar?

"Look at the snapped yard," the Englishman said. "The whole ship is covered in mold. It's just an abandoned ship. We should return to shore."

"Garrick doesn't bark like this unless there's someone on board, dead or alive."

Garrick. Toby narrowed his eyes. Now he remembered why the Norman sounded familiar. For years, he'd trained alongside a squire named Vincent who taunted him endlessly for being the "prostitute's lad." And Vincent had owned a puppy named Garrick.

Toby had evaded Vincent and the knight he served, Jacques Verdun, once in the forest. He doubted Vincent would be fooled again. As soon as Toby showed his face, the longships would attack. He tightened his arms around Aliwyn's shoulders as Emma sat on her lap. Memories of his last naval battle against the Normans flashed through his mind, and he blinked hard.

Another longship sailor grunted. "A boat full of corpses sounds like a good reason to go home."

Footsteps paced the longship. "Sir Verdun told me the Marcottes' ship disappeared around here."

"You're saying this is their ship?"

"It's my guess," Vincent answered.

Aliwyn's brows furrowed, and she tensed under Toby's hold. He held his breath. When she tried to shift away, taking Emma with her, he didn't resist her. She might be upset, but any mention of the Marcottes' vessel also tore through him like a jagged knife.

Someone finally hushed the barking dog.

"The Marcottes' corpses have never been found," the first Englishman said. "And they've been dead for months."

A low muttering from the longships hovered above the waters.

"We can still retrieve the remains and give them a proper burial," Vincent said. "I saw two Marcotte heirs in Brocklesby. They'll want to know."

Two heirs. Did Vincent mean he'd seen Evelyn also? Toby's chest heaved with a glimmer of hope. He'd last seen Evelyn outside the leper colony. Perhaps she had survived the Myton fires after all.

The smell of newly tarred rigging wafted from the longship and brought him back to his senses. Cilebi, Axlan, and Zelrin stared at him with the whites of their eyes gleaming, waiting for his signal to move.

A moment later, grappling hooks flew toward the *Fortuna*, each clawing onto her rail with an earsplitting scrape. Everyone under the platform flinched.

Toby grabbed Cilebi's arm before the man could shoot to his feet. His pulse tripping, Toby caught Axlan's gaze and jerked his head toward the mast.

"Go," he mouthed.

Cilebi had turned grey. Nonetheless, he stood and shuffled out from beneath the aftcastle. Toby had told him what to do in case the longships ever drew close, but his plan would never send the Normans away. Only distract them.

Shouts rang out from the longships as their crews strained to pull their vessel closer. The *Fortuna* sat higher in the water than the longships, making the approach awkward. Toby flexed his good hand. Now he'd make them regret trying to approach at all.

Placing a hand on Aliwyn's back, he whispered in her ear, "I'll be back."

"Greetings, sirs!" Axlan called out from beside the steering oar. "I apologize for not coming to see you earlier. I was asleep, y'see." He gave an unconvincing chuckle.

Silence. The grappling hooks slipped slightly as the longships' crew stopped pulling. *Good.* Toby scooted toward starboard and pushed aside the folded hudfats stacked below the rail. The outline of a square, just the width of a man's shoulders, came into view on the floorboards. A trapdoor. He had unlocked it from the privy an hour ago and rubbed a candle along all its hinges to silence them.

As he lifted the lid, Aliwyn crawled to his side with her eyes wide. He'd never told her about this door, and there were many other things she didn't know about.

Back on board the longship, Vincent called out, "What are you doing on the North Sea? His Excellency had ordered all non-military ships to return to port."

"She's a very old ship, sir." Axlan sounded as though he were being strangled. "She lost her anchor. She's drifting, but my crewmates are comin' back with a new anchor."

Toby winced as he lifted the trapdoor lid. That wasn't what he'd told Axlan to say.

"Where is your crew?"

"Er... Driftmere."

Another piece of information Axlan wasn't supposed to give. Toby thinned his lips. Perhaps he should've kept the thundercrashers on deck, but it was too late for regrets. He extended a leg down the trapdoor, feeling for the privy's vent hole where he could wedge his foot and ease himself down. He found it and began lowering himself, his ribs twinging as he supported his weight with his arms.

Aliwyn and Emma watched him on their hands and knees. Fresh tears covered the child's face, and Toby felt his composure crumbling. But now wasn't the time.

"Remember the canoe," he whispered.

He didn't know what to make of the frown shadowing Aliwyn's face. Distracted, his foot touched the floorboards below at an angle, and he slipped. His ankle buckled, and he fell hard on one knee. The thump echoed upward. Toby looked up, fearing an arrow, but only Aliwyn and Emma looked down at him.

"Close the door," he mouthed.

With prickly heat crawling up his neck, he turned from the dim square of light above and exited the privy.

Outside the dark and cluttered hull, Vincent's voice rang forth. "Show me His Excellency's signet ring."

Axlan had no ring, and he'd better come up with a good excuse. Toby struggled to even his breathing. In the faint light streaming from the stairwell, he grabbed a plain bag he'd kept hidden within his chest of valuables. These thundercrashers were the real ones from China, the ones he'd kept for further study. He hobbled as fast as he could toward the staircase.

He had one chance to save the *Fortuna*. One chance to save this mission. Himself. Ed. Still, this wasn't how he wanted it to unfold. If Brothers Dunstan and Claude knew what he was doing, after years of teaching him that vengeance only poisoned men's souls...The bag suddenly felt too heavy to carry, and he collapsed to his knees. With shaking arms, he began crawling up the stairs while dragging the bag along.

"Who are you, and what are you doing on this ship?" Vincent yelled.

"Please don't shoot us!" a shrill voice cried.

Emma! Toby's head snapped up toward the gray square, but his vision darkened. She was supposed to stay hidden!

"Hold!" Vincent shouted. "Who was that?"

"My daughter, sir," Axlan stammered.

Toby squeezed his eyes shut. This was spiraling out of control. The Norman loyalists encroaching on the Fortuna must die.

Dunstan, Claude...forgive me.

He could almost hear them insisting that mercy could bridge even the deepest divides. But mercy hadn't saved Odrianna. Mercy hadn't stopped the Normans from taking his everything.

A shadow soon blocked the stairwell. Toby looked up in a panic, but it was only Cilebi crouching above him.

"Fire," he mouthed.

The gleam in Cilebi's eyes sent a jolt through Toby's limbs. He should have hesitated, but as Cilebi grabbed his arm and hauled him up, a zeal he couldn't explain fired through his veins. Together, they scrambled toward the hearth, now pinned between grappling hooks on either side.

The dog erupted in furious barks. Both Toby and Cilebi froze.

But what he saw was more terrifying than any dog. Emma, along with Zelrin and Aliwyn, stood beside Axlan and faced the longships. Axlan had wrapped his arm around Emma's shoulders, and the girl clung to him.

Toby almost lunged into the open. *Axlan, you fool! They're going to shoot all—*

"Here are my children and m-my sister, sir." Axlan said.

No arrows came, only Vincent's emotionless voice. "Why are they on board with you?"

Toby grabbed a thundercrasher from his bag and held its long, protruding cork to a glowing ember. His shaking hands could hardly hold the object. Why wasn't it igniting? Had it been stored for too long? Beside him, Cilebi followed his example and held two thundercrashers to the hearth, but nothing caught fire.

Something prompted Toby to look up just then. Aliwyn glanced behind her, and her eyes widened with horror at what he was doing.

"I lost my signet ring," Axlan said, his voice thick. "It's true, honest. Please have mercy on us."

Silence for a moment. The thundercrasher's cork smoked but didn't burn, and Toby gritted his teeth.

Finally, Vincent said, "All of you will board my ship. I'll pull your vessel to Driftmere to be inspected."

Then everything would be lost to the tyrants in power, again. Toby painstakingly extended the thundercrasher deeper under the cauldron's tripod, his gloved fingers searing in the heat, until he saw a flash of light. Ignition.

He withdrew his hand, his chest heaving. The cork was smoldering toward the clay sphere, and the pungent stench of sulfur blew over him. Now he had to wait until the right moment to throw it.

A reckless elation surged through him. Today, he would make history.

Cilebi pulled out two glowing thundercrashers, his dark eyes lit with glee. Back by the rail, Zelrin abandoned Axlan's side and swerved toward Toby.

"Where are you going?" Vincent demanded.

A jolt shot down Toby's spine. He rose to just above the level of the rail and peered down. The Norman longship was only half the height of the Fortuna. Even with his helmet on, Vincent was easy to identify with his jeweled scabbard and embroidered gambeson. He stood between shortbow archers while other soldiers struggled to extend a gangplank to bridge their ships.

Too late.

Toby rose to his full height and flung the thundercrasher toward their tarred rigging and sail. Cilebi did the same.

Vincent's mouth fell open. His gaze flicked to his assailants just as Toby bolted toward Aliwyn and Emma.

"Release!" Vincent shouted.

But his soldiers were too startled to release their arrows. The three thundercrashers struck the longship where they were most volatile. Each burst with a deafening boom. The sound swelled in Toby's ears. Men screamed. Aliwyn shielded Emma with her body as clay shards and searing particles shot through the air. Toby grabbed her shoulders and pushed her down onto the floorboards.

He wrapped his arms around her to cushion the impact, but Aliwyn shrieked with Emma still in her embrace.

She thrashed to free herself until he wheezed in her ear, "Ali!"

Aliwyn gasped and stilled, but Toby ached all over from her clawing and kicking. He let her go; he rolled her onto her side so that her back faced the rail. Her eyes brimmed with tears as soot and smoke stung his own eyes. Against his will, images stirred in the depths of his mind.

Evelyn lay unconscious on her family's ship with her forehead covered in blood from the hired hand who had struck her. Marie clung to her sister's stained nightgown, sobbing like Emma did now.

Chills rattled through Toby. He cupped Aliwyn's face, and the cool tears under his thumb grounded him to the present.

"The aftcastle," he said hoarsely. "Go. Grab a shield."

Something sparked in Aliwyn's eyes, that look of determination he'd admired many times before. She pushed to her knees and hooked a slender arm into the shield's back strap. Pulling Emma upright, she raised the shield and ran with the girl toward the back platform. Cilebi's boots pounded around her as he hurled more thundercrashers. He and the other men had already flung off most of the grappling hooks tethering the *Fortuna*.

Longship soldiers climbed up the fishing nets onto their ship, but Zelrin and Axlan beat them back with rocks, their vicious faces lit by the growing inferno below.

Toby grabbed a shield and rose to his feet. Out on the water, all three longships burned. Fire consumed their sails and rained sparks across the deck. Soldiers covered their eyes and rolled with fire licking their clothes; others dove into the frigid waters. Vincent was nowhere to be seen. He must've jumped overboard already.

The smoke around Toby seemed to swirl with lights and shadows. He didn't want this, but he also had to win. This was but a small taste of how his household would shock all the Normans into submission.

He drew his sword and slashed the next Norman loyalist who dared to climb aboard Edward's ship. Hobbling to the hearth, he gripped Cilebi's arm before the man could grab another thundercrasher.

"Enough of that," Toby said. "I want their anchor!"

CHAPTER 15
BLUE ROSES

October 1, Matthew

THERE WERE CONSEQUENCES TO saving a life. Not always good ones.

Matthew carried Kato out into the clearing with his arms aching. How could this pile of bones and rags be so heavy?

The Vasfian druid class, with their seashell necklaces and skull staves in hand, strode toward him with stark frowns. Matthew swallowed hard. He had just defied their wishes by saving Kato, whose mother had been a thief in their tribe. The other Vasfian adults stared with their mouths twisted in disapproval, but their children watched with curious and wide eyes.

Matthew halted at the clearing's periphery as Reiya walked past him and shot him a glare. So much for wanting to win her approval. He chewed on his tongue as she spoke to her people.

What felt like a long time passed. Matthew eased Kato onto a bed of brown leaves and squatted beside him. *Flying Krakens.* He couldn't understand anything the Vasfians said. What if Reiya expelled him now and sent him scurrying back to Jacques? But he couldn't throw Kato back out as wolf fodder and expect to sleep that night.

A slurred voice spoke just then. "Ravenser...Jacques didn't..."

Matthew blinked. Kato was awake. He looked down with a surge of excitement, but it didn't last. He had never rescued a dirtier wretch.

Wrinkling his nose, Matthew forced himself to tilt his ear toward Kato. "Didn't what?"

But the redhead's eyes closed again. It could be a long time before he was awake enough to speak, and it wasn't time Matthew had to waste. He thumped on Kato's chest as Mils walked beside him and sniffed the young man's face. Other than the erratic jerks of his chest, Kato didn't move.

Matthew had never seen a pack animal so attached to its caretaker. The thought of failing Mils now, donkey or not, struck a new level of anxiety within him. Maybe water would liven up Mils' owner. Matthew had just grabbed his costrel when boots crunching over twigs made him stiffen. Reiya marched toward him with the other Vasfians surrounding her.

The braid over her shoulder frizzled in all directions. "Kato can't stay. My warriors caught him stalking us since we left Brocklesby. He wants to rob my tribe."

"How do you know?" Matthew asked, his voice squeaky. "He just said something about Jacques."

"What?"

Her stare dropped to Kato, whose eyes remained closed.

"What can he possibly know about Jacques?" she demanded.

Matthew gripped Kato's bony shoulder. "Let him wake up and explain."

The wall of Vasfians gathered around him, growing loud and disgruntled. Reiya turned to address them. Mils continued to nuzzle against Matthew's neck, a furry warmth against his clammy skin he appreciated more than he could express.

Domilo's boyish voice cut through the clamor. "This is the Kato you talked about? Why doesn't he have freckles?"

The child stood with his lips pressed together. Blood pulsed in Matthew's ears. If Kato's mother had been banished, she could only have conceived Kato with an 'Outsider.' Domilo's expression made it clear that such half-bloods weren't wanted. Kato would be flung back out unless he argued for himself.

Bloody Kraken, Kato. Wake up. Matthew uncorked his costrel and splashed water onto the younger man. A bit too much. It soaked his neck and seeped into his collar. Kato's face scrunched, but he stayed silent. Matthew groaned and was about to pinch his nose when Reiya turned around.

"He can't stay," she said.

She looked mad enough to stomp Kato's head. Matthew leaned over and gripped Kato's opposite shoulder, glaring up at her and shielding the younger man from any blows. His stance seemed to make her hesitate.

"Why do you hate him so much?" Matthew asked. "Just because he's a half-blood?"

"Partly, yes." Her fist clenched and unclenched. "His existence is a disgrace to our ancestors. It's even more insulting because he's here right before Samhain. He cannot enter my village."

Matthew steadied himself. "Aelfric was also a half-blood, wasn't he? But you all accepted him."

Reiya straightened to her full height. All the same, her voice faltered. "Aelfric was...different. His Vasfian grandmothers were never banished. They only moved to Scotland."

Matthew blinked. He fought to keep calm before the gathering. He'd finally received confirmation of a truth he'd feared. For five years, Matthew had called the Vasfians uncivilized creatures deserving of eternal condemnation. Useful only for target practice. Pain tore through his chest, but it was too late to say sorry.

"You make a distinction without a difference," he stammered. Somehow, defending another half-blood now reined in his ravaging guilt.

Reiya threw up a hand. "Of course there is a difference!"

The Vasfians behind her had quieted down, some frowning with their arms crossed, others fidgeting with unease. Reiya's nostrils flared, but she, too, had fallen silent. As Matthew had hoped, talking about Aelfric had distracted her, but the memories also flooded him and made him shake. Whenever Aelfric returned from Brocklesby, he'd pull Matthew in for a tight embrace. He'd sneak wooden boards into Matthew's quarters so he could paint by candlelight, despite his father's disapproval. No one, not even Matthew's family, had ever been so happy to greet him in the mornings, before meals, after jousting...

Matthew blinked away the haze in his eyes. As Mils' lowered head entered his peripheral view, he lifted Kato against his chest and rubbed his back. Had Aelfric been born looking like Kato, with red hair, they would never have spoken. A colossal mistake. It was too late to do anything for Aelfric, but not for the person he'd just saved.

The Vasfians began muttering again. Reiya and Namanti's voices grew sharper, and chills racked Matthew's body. He pinched Kato's already bruised nose, causing the young man to grimace and writhe. Pity swelled in Matthew's throat, but he held on.

Finally, the redhead opened his eyes. "I have..."

But before he could finish, his hand jerked toward his waist and fell limp there. His eyes shuttered again. Matthew swallowed his vexation as he looked down. Kato's fingers now graced a beige object that protruded from his belt pouch alongside the braided cord of a sling.

"Oh, a scroll!" Domilo cried.

The boy was right, but why would an illiterate man carry parchment? With Kato still slumped against his chest, Matthew tugged loose the small roll. The parchment's external surface featured the image of stylized roses.

"This is Evelyn's seal," he whispered.

In her parents' manor, she would've stamped it with blue wax. She could only dip the stamp in ink this time, but the seal was unmistakably hers—two roses with stems joined at the top like a teardrop.

"A letter from Evelyn?" Reiya asked. "How did Kato even find her?"

"You'll have to ask him."

Matthew had seen her just hours ago. What if she needed help already? With jittery fingers, he untied the string securing the roll and unfurled the letter.

Inside was a short message written in Norman French.

Jacques knew the Danes would arrive at Ravenser's Point. He's going there now. He didn't tell you, but I overheard his men. Warn the Vasfians. Attack on October 5th.

Her words swirled in his head. The full weight of the message evaded him for a moment, and he scrutinized the elegant penmanship. "This is my cousin's handwriting. I'm sure of it."

As he translated the words into English and read them out loud, the implications of the letter sank in.

Jacques knew all along where the enemy was landing. He must've extorted this information from the Yeatons, only to tell Matthew that he'd failed to do so. Ravenser's Point was a tiny island at the mouth of the River Humber and was a plausible place for the Danes and the Boltans to meet.

Matthew gritted his teeth. He rolled up the parchment again. Tucking it into one of his belt pouches, he met Reiya's sullen gaze.

"Kato wasn't here to rob anyone," Matthew said. "He came to deliver a message. Let him stay. Maybe he'll have more to say."

Reiya made no reaction. Did she not hear him? Maybe she was angry enough at the Jacques' deceit and withholding of information to strike Matthew instead. The hairs on his nape rose, but his fear was short-lived. With a grimace wrinkling her face, she ducked her head.

In a moment of maddening silence, she reached for Kato's belt pouches and began tearing out their contents.

What was she doing? Matthew gave a start, but he dared not stop her. Out came an orange tin, a corked jar, a checkered handkerchief, a deer bone for storing needles, and a wooden plaque painted with an ale barrel. She unclasped Kato's sheathed dagger and flung it onto the ground. All the while, the young man sat slumped against Matthew, unable to protect his belongings. Indignation burned in Matthew's throat, but he had other matters to address.

"What will you do now?" He glowered at Reiya. "About Ravenser's? About Kato?"

She only pulled off the tip of Kato's deer bone and peered inside. There was a subtle widening of her eyes, and Matthew balled his hands into fists. What was so interesting about a sewing kit?

"Did you hear me?" he demanded.

"I heard you," she muttered, still staring down the hollow bone. "Kato's message...needs verification."

"Verify however you want, but let him enter your village to rest. He'll be out of your village long before Samhain."

Reiya rose slowly to her feet. Turning aside, she began speaking with her grandmother, who passed over a faded knapsack Matthew guessed belonged to Kato. Reiya stuffed Kato's belongings inside but pocketed the deer bone herself. Why did she want it? Matthew thought he'd burst with impatience when her frown turned back to him.

"Kato may stay one night," she said. Then, as though mocking Matthew's relief, she curled her upper lip. "But I'm locking both of you in a round-house."

"What?" Matthew inhaled what felt like fire. "I'm supposed to help you unpack. And attend the—"

"I changed my mind, and this is not my decision alone." She gestured at the people standing around her. "You don't understand the significance of Samhain, or how insulting it is to have this wretch amongst us. He carries his mother's spirit."

Blood roared in Matthew's ears. He hardly heard Reiya's order to lift Kato onto a cart. His nose scrunching at the donkey smell, Matthew hauled Kato back up like a sack of turnips and staggered toward the wagon. Mils ambled alongside and tried to lick his owner's dirty face.

Ahead of him, Reiya tore off all the blankets she'd spread out on the wagon. Domilo and Nissa stood to the side, startled, until Reiya put her arm around them and led them away. She flashed Matthew a piercing glare. The other Vasfians returned to their places in silence.

Matthew's shoulders slumped. All ruined. Everything he'd done to build rapport with this tribe he'd never understand.

Could he drop Kato on the ground and apologize to Reiya for offending her? But Kato was shivering, his face and neck cold and damp, and all his belongings had just been confiscated. Matthew couldn't let go. He clambered up the cart's ramp and lowered Kato between two sacks of grain. The younger man's tunic was threadbare. That rotten Namanti must've stolen his cloak back in the forest before rendering him unconscious.

From the corner of his eye, he saw Reiya pass Kato's knapsack to Namanti. She then stood beside the cart where Nissa sat and wrapped a blanket around the child. With no blanket for himself, Matthew pushed sacks against Kato to shield him from the wind.

Then he shot to his feet and gripped the rail.

"We're supposed to be allies!" he shouted at Reiya. "How can you treat an ally—"

"But you saved a thief and insisted I keep him."

Matthew blinked. She had spoken in French.

"A thief?" he asked in French. "Kato's not a thief. He worked for Norman and sold ale from a donkey cart."

Reiya's face flushed as she marched toward Matthew's cart and strode up the ramp. He squared his shoulders and blocked the path to Kato, but she knelt before reaching him.

From her belt pouch, she withdrew the hollowed deer bone and inverted its contents onto her palm.

To his amazement, a handful of metal pieces spilled out. They looked like keys, except these had hinges designed to manipulate the inner workings of a padlock.

"Lockpicks." Her eyes flashed with anger. "Who else but a thief carries lockpicks?"

Matthew gawked. His mind leapt to his drinking horn, which hid the same terrible secret.

Reiya slid the condemning objects back into the bone case and snapped the lid shut. "I had a choice," she said coolly. "Tell my tribe I found lockpicks on Kato and let you watch him get clubbed to death...or pretend I never saw these."

She slammed the bone onto the floorboards. "In the end, I decided not to tell my people." She switched to English. "And I'm letting him stay for one night. You have nothing to complain about, Matthew Marcotte."

His heart sank. Maybe Kato *was* the same as his mother.

Reiya glared at something behind Matthew, and he turned around. The younger man had pressed himself against the rail. The sound of the bone striking wood must've startled him awake, and his eyes widened on the object in Reiya's hand.

"I haven't used those in a year," he stuttered. "I kept them in case I need to free myself—"

"Why should I believe you?" Reiya demanded. "I'm driving you out to-morrow."

She launched herself off the cart. Marching toward her mare, she waved her arms with a shout. Her villagers began to mount their pack animals.

Kato's gaping mouth quivered. His gaze darted to Matthew, then away again. Matthew rubbed his eyes until he saw stars. Evelyn never mentioned that Kato was a thief, but of course she wouldn't. Back home, Matthew and Aelfric used to stand in crowded marketplaces to protect the merchants from pickpockets and bandits. He couldn't blame Reiya for being so irritated.

Fisting his hands, he turned around. "What did you once steal?"

Kato looked up with a start. "P-pennies from the tithe box. Bread." His forehead crinkled. "But I knew I'd get myself killed, so I stopped stealing and found work."

There was no way to verify if that was true. As Matthew glared at him, Kato ducked his head. He pushed onto all fours and crawled toward the rear of the cart.

Matthew grabbed the back of Kato's tunic. "Where are you going?"

The cart jostled, and the movement sent Kato crumpling onto his side. Matthew's hand landed on the younger man's shoulder, pressing him down despite his wiggling.

"Don't be stupid!" Matthew said through his teeth. "It's getting dark, and the wolves are still out there."

A manic look filled Kato's eyes, and Matthew fought to suppress his panic. He had yet to figure out his next steps. Hooking his arm around Kato's, he lifted and settled the redhead back against a sack.

"Reiya doesn't want me," Kato stammered. "I need to leave. Find Norman."

"We don't know where Norman is."

"He's in Barton—"

"No." Matthew swallowed the guilt he was tired of feeling. "He left to find you. Then he disappeared in the fire near the leper colony."

Silence. Kato blinked several times. "He's dead?"

"There's a chance he still lives." Matthew wrung his sore right hand. "After all, I just found you alive. But you should at least stay the night."

There was a long silence. Matthew watched warily in case Kato tried to escape the cart again, but the redhead drew his knees to his chest. He seemed to repeat Norman's name, silently, until Matthew couldn't bear to watch.

"I didn't expect the Mehi to attack me," Kato said, hardly audible. "To hate me this much. I'm the son of a thief? My Mum never said…"

The rawness of his voice sent a shiver through Matthew. Evelyn once told him that Kato's mother died when he was a small boy. Matthew scowled at the redhead's dog-chewed hair, struggling for something comforting to say… But the *Anuin*! Because of Kato, he could no longer attend!

"Of course she never told you she's a thief," Matthew muttered.

"But I am not a thief anymore." Kato's eyes brightened with tears. "Please believe me. Norman will tell you I'm an honest worker. I never stole anything."

"But I *can't* ask him."

Matthew sounded madder than he intended to, and Kato's teeth chattered. A red drop gleamed at the edge of his nostril before he pressed a sleeve against it. The top half of his face flushed.

Nosebleeds. Matthew had forgotten how easily Kato bled since the Boltans gave him a drink with arsenic. From what Evelyn had said, Ransley Boltan blamed the redhead for spying on his manor on behalf of the Vasfians. Kato had delivered ale to the Boltans' household and had been their first suspect. The real spy, of course, had been Aelfric.

Matthew unlaced and shed his gambeson, his arms almost too heavy to lift. Evelyn and Marie had been trapped as vagabonds within Ransley's sprawling seaside manor, but they'd gone undetected for weeks. Kato carted them everywhere to keep them safe. It was a miracle that Matthew had never thanked Kato for, but the words of gratitude still stuck in his throat.

"Evelyn said she'd find an antidote for you," he said, offering his gambeson to the young man. "Did she?"

Kato stared at him, then at the gambeson, with his sleeve still covering his nose. Matthew sighed. He leaned over and spread the gambeson over Kato's huddled figure.

Kato lowered his arm. His eyebrows twitched into a look of surprise. "Thank you. Blue gave me two jars of antidote. I ate everything. She said I just need to rest and eat well now."

Neither condition was being met. Matthew whittled at the guilt trapped in his heart. "Good. That you got enough antidote."

He had committed worse sins than stealing from the tithing box. What were a few pennies compared to ending the life of a child? Now, at least, Matthew could no longer be blamed for Kato's disappearance. Evelyn had even seen him alive. He allowed himself that bit of relief.

Kato turned to the side of the cart again and gripped the railing. His shifty side glances made it clear he still wanted to jump. Between wolves and a horde of pagan head-hunters, which was worse? Matthew rubbed the back of his neck.

"I can't tell if you're still a thief or not," he said. "But for tonight, I'll keep us both safe. So stop trying to jump."

The knob on Kato's throat slid up and down. "You mean that?"

"I just pulled you out of the forest, didn't I? You were about to become wolf supper."

"I-I thought I heard howling in my dreams." Kato gave a quivering smile. "Thank you for getting me out."

Matthew flexed his hands, the same ones that had shoved Kato against the leper cabin's door. He couldn't speak.

When the younger man sneezed into his sleeve, Matthew scooted beside him. The gambeson Kato had covered himself with became wedged between them, and warmth spread through Matthew's right side. He might not be unpacking the Mehi's belongings tonight, but he refused to question his decision to save Kato. Once they arrived at Jethran, he'd persuade Reiya to let him attend the *Anuin*.

There had to be a way. Shouldn't good deeds like saving someone merit good luck in return? And Reiya...he still wanted to believe she was more reasonable than her grandmother.

CHAPTER 16

JETHRAN

Matthew

At sunset, the Vasfian carts rolled through a maze of dug-out ramparts. A waterfall cascading from a tall mountain peeked through the top of the dirt slopes. Matthew's anxiety spiked at the sight of water plunging from such heights.

Even worse was knowing he'd been excluded from the *Anuin* ceremony. It was his best chance of approaching the Boltans' chest and collecting the black matter Jacques wanted. How could he regain the Vasfians' trust?

He needed to speak to Reiya immediately.

They arrived at the foot of a large hill on which the Mehi had erected concentric wooden palisades. From where Matthew sat, staring up from the base, only the tips of roundhouse roofs within the village were visible. The warriors guarding the gate frowned as his cart rolled past, and Matthew scowled back at them. Why did some of them look familiar? Kato, meanwhile, had curled up beneath the gambeson in a sleep that Matthew could only envy.

Reiya, Domilo, and others he knew by name were gone by the time his cart passed what looked like a market square. Here, the familiar scent of woodfire permeated the air. Villagers drew water from wells for their thirsty pack animals, pushed firewood-laden barrows, and herded sheep between crowded roundhouses. Chickens pecked and scratched along the dirt roads. The sight was reminiscent of English villages, save for the tiered palisades.

The cart stopped before a thatched roundhouse flanked by glowing turnips on fence posts. Warriors in fur vests surrounded the building. Some held torches, others gripped clubs. The driver turned around to watch Matthew with her crossbow on her lap. Farther down the road, Aliwyn's speckled hens flapped free of their cages with clucks of excitement, and Matthew groaned. Since when did he envy chickens?

"Excuse me," he called out to the driver. "Can we go in yet?"

She wore her hair in a braid like other Vasfian women. Pointing at herself, she said, "Yana."

He rubbed his eyes. "No. Try again."

Behind Yana, the warriors spoke amongst themselves. Their steely expressions struck Matthew with a flash of recognition. Some of these men had forced themselves into Aliwyn's watermill the night she'd disappeared. Perhaps Reiya had sent them to Jethran.

Matthew hardened his jaw. He had never cared to see these warriors again.

As the Vasfians muttered amongst themselves, Matthew scooted to Kato's side and patted the redhead's shoulder.

"Wake up." Matthew snapped his fingers. "Tell me what those men are saying."

Kato opened his bleary eyes. After a moment of listening, he drawled, "They say...the bad sons are here. That's us. And we bring curses."

Matthew chuckled, although nothing was funny. "Us? Bring curses?"

"They want us out of the village." Kato's gaze sharpened with fresh fear.

"Reiya makes the decisions. I'll talk to her."

Just in time, rustling footsteps approached from behind. He spun around. Reiya and Namanti approached amongst villagers who carried carved turnips. Reiya now wore a thick golden torque around her neck, but it was a woman on a stretcher who held his attention. Two villagers carried her between them. She lay flat on her back, covered in bright red and green striped blankets. Her exposed hand fingered the seashells on her necklace.

Matthew narrowed his eyes, but it was too dim to see her face clearly. Who was she?

Now wasn't the time to wonder. As the procession drew near, the gathered warriors made a circular gesture around their heads. Reiya and Namanti smiled and reciprocated, but Matthew tensed. He couldn't bring himself to raise an arm.

"Reiya," he called out. "We need to talk about my imprisonment."

Her lips thinned. "That can wait. I want to know if the letter Kato brought is trustworthy. My mother and I are here to see it for ourselves."

Her expression softening, she gestured at the woman on the stretcher and said, "We pray she will walk again."

"Your mother?" Matthew cried. "She can't walk?"

Reiya glowered at him, and heat crept up Matthew's neck.

"I don't mean to yell," he stammered. "I'm just surprised."

"Her name is Abithi," Reiya said. "She was injured, but Lenus will heal her at the right time."

What a hopeless belief. Matthew struggled to keep a blank face as Abithi's eyes roved over him. Her lips twitched with disdain, and she muttered something in Vasfian.

"*Amah*," Reiya said, "please speak in English so Matthew understands you."

Abithi grunted and said with a heavy accent, "Why you bring worst son? He run away when father try to visit. He leave family to die."

Matthew's jaw dropped. How did she know he used to run away from Lord Seville's manor to avoid his father? A retort thundered in his head, but he had the sense to snap his jaw shut.

Reiya massaged her temples. "That's not what you had said in our language, *Amah*. I brought Matthew here because of the Alliance. We both want to capture the Boltans."

"Why you not bring good Norman sent by bishop? *This* man sent by Jacques." Abithi's glare could shoot lightning bolts. "Jacques Verdun who rob Miriam's home."

"Matthew wasn't sent by Jacques," Reiya said, her voice on edge. "Jacques accused Matthew of deserting the army because—"

"You tell to me already. But Mattoo still come from Jacques. The Jacques who almost rob us."

Chills swarmed Matthew's scalp. Not only did this former chief see straight through his guise, but her English was functional. He'd better be wary of her eavesdropping in the future.

Matthew licked his lips. "I...am here to offer assistance."

Reiya jutted her chin. "From now on, address my mother as Honorable Abithi."

"Honorable Abithi," he muttered.

Reiya approached him with a stiff gait and extended a hand. "Now show me the letter."

Her face was pink. This conversation with her mother wasn't pleasant for her, either, and a twinge of pity settled Matthew's nerves.

Tugging open his belt pouch, he withdrew the parchment and offered it over the cart. "Have a look, but my people's lettering is beyond you."

He regretted saying that. With a huff, Reiya plucked the letter from his hand and opened it. A warrior approached her with a glowing turnip, and the light illuminated the circles under her eyes. Her brows drew into a look of longing.

Matthew exhaled through clenched teeth. She obviously couldn't understand anything. The symbols of circles and lines he'd seen her write to her sister tribes, the Vasfian language, looked nothing like the alphabet.

"You're sure this is Evelyn's handwriting?" she asked.

"Absolutely certain. She wrote me letters all the time. And the twin roses insignia belongs to her." He pointed at the flowers. When Reiya's expression remained doubtful, he continued, "Kato, tell us how you found my cousin in the first place."

Kato remained curled against the rail. "I was in Brocklesby last night, in Aliwyn's mill. Then this morning, a big Norman army passed by. I was afraid to get out until most of the soldiers left."

Matthew recalled what he'd seen earlier that day. "The dead wolf outside the mill...were you the one who killed it?"

"Yes, with my sling." Kato sighed. "I think the wolves kept tracking my nosebleeds."

"And how did you travel to Brocklesby?" Reiya asked.

"By riding Mils. He came back to me outside the leper colony. He had a burned tail..."

Reiya seemed to think this over. "You still didn't tell me how you found Evelyn in the crowd."

"I was watching the scene through the mill's smoke hole." Kato locked his arms around his stomach. "I saw Blue... I mean, Evelyn, riding a horse across the bridge. When the army left, I went to find her. She was really worried about the Danes going to Ravenser's Point."

Fear crept into his voice when he spoke Evelyn's name. Matthew realized he'd been listening with a deep scowl.

"I see," he mumbled.

Matters between Kato and Evelyn would have to be discussed in her presence. Never again would Matthew try to do away with someone she cared about.

Reiya turned to her mother and presented the parchment. The two talked amongst themselves with looks of confusion wrinkling their foreheads. Matthew's stomach growled with hunger, and he gripped the edge of the wagon. When would those two give up trying to read?

"Why can't you accept that Kato's message is authentic?" Matthew called out. "There is no reason to suspect it's fake, since it comes from my cousin."

Reiya's fingers whitened as she pinched the parchment. "I suppose I'll have to believe you."

"And you should. I want to kill the Boltans as much as you do." He took a deep breath. "So...can you please not trap me in this roundhouse?"

To Matthew's vexation, Reiya looked again at her mother, who then looked at *her* mother, Namanti.

"I want to see this Kato," Abithi said.

Matthew glowered at Reiya. She was the chief; why did she need her mother's or grandmother's approval? Back on the floorboards, Kato folded into a tighter ball instead of showing himself, and Matthew finally grabbed his arm and pulled him upright. Kato squirmed as he faced the woman on the stretcher for the first time.

Abithi's eyes narrowed. "You look much like your mother. How old are you?"

"S-seventeen."

"Reiya say you sold ale to Boltans, yes?"

Kato's lower chin quivered. Reiya finally said in a low voice, "I found a wooden plaque amongst his belongings. It had the Boltans' griffin and a barrel of ale." Her eyes flicked to Kato. "That was your license to sell ale, correct?"

The young man sagged in Matthew's hold.

"Answer the question!" she thundered.

"I did sell them ale," Kato stammered.

Matthew hardened his jaw. Kato should've thrown away that blasted permit a long time ago. Anything with the Boltans' heraldry should be burned.

"What you see in their manor?" Abithi asked. "What they trading?"

"P-perfume and wool."

"And the fire pebbles?"

Matthew had never thought of asking Kato about these details, and his pulse quickened.

Kato hung his head. "I never saw them. Or smelled them."

"How Boltans keep so much fire pebble, and it no stink?"

"I don't know."

Abithi's nostrils flared. She beckoned with a finger, and Namanti leaned close to her daughter on the stretcher. The two of them whispered to each other; the way Namanti's eyes narrowed and slid to Kato made Matthew's skin crawl. Yet, he couldn't glean anything from their conversation.

Namanti finally retreated to her position, and Abithi said, "Kato think all night and give me new answer tomorrow. This the only reason I let you stay, understand?"

"Y-yes., Kato answered.

Chills crawled down Matthew's back. He believed Kato. The Boltans would never let any servants or merchants sniff out their plans. How Tobias and his father kept everything secret in a bustling manor was something only they knew.

Reiya turned back to her mother. "You should go for your prayer ceremony. Both these men will be locked inside." Her hand on her hip, she met Matthew's gaze. "Don't try anything foolish."

He opened his mouth to speak, but Abithi said, "Reirei, you bring bad men. Think next time before you make mistake."

Matthew resisted rolling his eyes at Reiya's silly nickname.

She pressed her arms against her sides. "*Amah*, I'm being faithful to the alliance with His Excellency. Good night. See you at the *Anuin* tomorrow."

So, it *was* still happening tomorrow. Matthew's fingers twisted Kato's tunic until the fabric nearly ripped.

Abithi narrowed her eyes. "Norman man must stay in roundhouse until he fight Danes."

Fire shot through Matthew's veins. "But that's in four days!"

Reiya performed the circular gesture for her mother. "Understood."

The villagers carried Abithi away, and Matthew wanted to tear down the trees around him. What had happened to the young chief who had faced Jacques with poise? Reiya was spineless now, and the urgency to free himself by the *Anuin* gripped him by the throat.

"Why am I your prisoner?" he shouted. "We need to talk."

To his surprise, Reiya turned to him and raised an eyebrow. "We do indeed. First, lock Kato inside."

CHAPTER 17
TWO HUNDRED LONGSHIPS

October 2, Toby

THREE DYING FIRES REFLECTED on the black waters and illuminated the night. The acrid stench of burning pitch and wood filled Toby's nose and mingled with the sea's salty tang. Smoke coiled from the masts where flames chewed through ropes and sails. Dark and looming, the longships' hulls remained intact while their shadows stood stark against the glow.

Toby and Axlan pushed the capstan's spokes. They had bound the longship's anchor to the Fortuna's anchor line and were reeling it in. Meanwhile, Zelrin and Cilebi had boarded the enemy's ship and were dragging the anchor along its deck to facilitate the transfer.

They had almost lost Zelrin when he'd leapt onto the closest longship. A surviving Norman loyalist had tried to impale him, but Toby shot that man with a stolen shortbow. Still, it had been close.

The anchor line screeched through the pulley as the capstan turned. Toby's teeth kept chattering even though his skin flushed with heat. The thundercrashers from Asia were even more impressive than he'd thought. It was the first time anyone had fought with them on English soil. He had made history. He had defeated three longships with a crew of three men. Wasn't he now the most powerful man in England?

Toby smirked, but the dread twisting within him strangled his breath.

His contacts overseas had told of bloody battles unlike any other because of the potash compound. That was simply the reality of war whenever a new weapon was discovered. All the same, his teeth chattered again.

Axlan huffed as he pushed the capstan bar beside Toby. The wood groaned as the capstan turned, and there was room for more hands. Toby turned toward the forecastle, where Aliwyn hadn't made a sound.

She'd spent a long time by the hearth earlier, poking at the embers instead of offering aid.

"Come help me?" he asked hoarsely.

No answer. The dark outline of her figure, still clinging onto Emma, sat unmoving beneath the platform. Toby bowed his head. The cries of men drowning in the sea and the still-barking dog suddenly pierced his senses. When would she talk to him again?

Finally, the slimy and sharp anchor rose above the longship's deck. The *Fortuna* tilted from the added weight. Toby and Axlan stopped turning, then reversed directions so the anchor could be lowered back into the water. The hulk groaned, then stabilized.

Zelrin gave a whoop of triumph. He and Cilebi jumped onto the *Fortuna's* fishing net to climb back on board. They yanked the salvaged shortbows and quivers off their shoulders and tossed them beside the mast.

Toby straightened, panting, and used his sword to pry off the last two grappling hooks. It was too late to return to Driftmere, but with the replacement anchor, the *Fortuna* wouldn't crash against the rocks tonight. They could rest for a few hours.

He turned and put a hand on Axlan's shoulder. The man once led a peaceful, prosperous life shearing sheep and selling wool, but he was now pale and tremulous. Perhaps he hadn't seen so much death since losing his estate.

"Good work today." Toby squeezed Axlan's padded shoulder. He wished he could say something more useful.

Axlan's lips twitched, his eyes glistening, and Toby pulled the man in for a tight embrace. Axlan trembled slightly. Toby held on, uncertain who needed the comfort more.

As for the dog, when would it stop barking and whining? His throat swelling, Toby looked out over the waters. A canoe bobbed beside Vincent's wrecked longship. Inside, a black greyhound paced in circles, its tail tucked between its legs. Toby gripped the rail. There must've been a canoe in tow behind Vincent's longship, and he had tried to save his dog.

Moments later, Zelrin and Cilebi scaled the ship's side and hauled themselves onto deck beneath the aftcastle.

Cilebi picked up a shortbow he'd tossed on board from the longships. "That mutt won't be feasting in Valhalla."

Toby's chest seized, and he pushed down Cilebi's arm. "No. He's just a dog."

"A dog covered in soot who smells like last year's eggs." Cilebi raised an eyebrow. "And he's loud. The Normans will find him."

Zelrin wiped his nose, panting. "Cilebi is right. They'll know it's us."

"A dead dog is also covered in soot." Toby licked his lips. "The Normans will eventually know it was us, but it'll be too late. Prince Cnut will meet—"

Fast footsteps pattered toward him from behind. Toby tried to turn around, but Aliwyn shoved him hard and almost pushed him into Cilebi.

"Enough!" she cried.

Toby staggered, too stunned to speak. Aliwyn stepped forward with her tear-streaked face glistening in the firelight.

"Haven't you killed enough?" Her voice cracking, she jabbed a finger toward the canoe. "Leave the poor dog alone!"

Toby swallowed hard. "I wasn't—I wasn't going to let him shoot. You misheard me."

A sob escaped her lips. She backed away, then turned again for the forecastle. Toby ignored the men muttering behind him and reached for her.

"Ali." He took her by the elbow.

To his relief, she didn't try to jerk away. He turned her gently so that she faced him. Her swollen eyes, still glimmering with tears, made his stomach twist.

"I'm sorry you had to see that," he said.

Her upper lip curled. "Sorry I had to see that, or sorry you did it?"

"I had no choice."

"That Norman was showing us mercy!"

"No." Toby squared his shoulders. "He was about to pull this ship onto land, find the cargo, and send us all to the gallows. When you showed yourself, when you pretended to be Axlan's family, you made it clear you were a rebel sympathizer."

Aliwyn's chest heaved as if every breath was a battle. Smoke curled between them, and her eyes remained locked on his.

Toby steadied himself for his next words. He prayed silently she'd be willing to listen.

"I've tried negotiating with the Normans before. It was when Rufus Marcotte razed Fiskerton because he said my ports stole his business. When he killed Odrianna." He hardened his jaw to bite back the pain. "I asked for justice. I camped outside Rufus' manor and hoped to see him. He ignored me. I challenged him to a trial by combat, but he sent an innocent thrall instead. I forfeited the match. Rufus called for my eviction from England, and the crown granted it."

Toby drew a slow breath. He hated talking about this, but Aliwyn needed to understand.

"Those in power are tyrants, not rulers," he said hoarsely. "All mercy and patience are wasted on them."

Aliwyn's brows knit. For a moment, the only sound was the lap of waves against the scorched hulls as they drifted away.

"Who is Rufus Marcotte?" she asked.

"Evelyn's half-brother." Toby dipped his chin. Even the mention of her name summoned more grief. She never wrote him another letter following Odrianna's death.

Aliwyn pinched her fingertips. "I'm sorry about Odrianna. And about Fiskerton."

Was he finally getting through to her? But then she met his gaze again, and her next words stabbed through him. "But don't you see? Now *you* are the tyrant. You burn England and say you're saving it."

Anger flared within him, but he forced it down. "I'm fighting for a better future."

"A future with how many Englishmen left?" Her voice rose again. "Those ships were full of our own. There was only one Norman!"

Heat rose up his neck. Why was he still talking to her? And yet, the squeezing in his chest rooted him in place. "More people will die if I don't fight. I want to end the rebellion in a few days. It'll save many lives."

"How will two hundred longships burning up ports save people?"

Toby stared at her and the horror spreading across her face. Pins and needles sank into his scalp.

His hand slipped from her elbow. "Two hundred. Who told you that?"

She covered her mouth with one hand, her eyes wide.

"She's been eavesdropping!" Cilebi shouted from behind.

Toby's eyes burned. He stepped back from her and rasped, "Tell me the truth. How did you know it's two hundred?"

Aliwyn

SHE HAD MADE A horrendous mistake. Even worse, she had pocketed a fire striker and flintstone while the men had been salvaging the longship's anchor. Voices within her screamed for her to tell more lies. She made up so many on a whim, but now they lodged in her throat. Zelrin and Axlan watched her with their brows drawn, as though afraid of hearing her answer, and she wanted to melt into the floorboards.

"I overheard," she finally whispered.

And now, everything would unravel. Her knees wobbled.

Cilebi's face twisted with fury. "She's a spy. A filthy Norman snake!" He stomped forward, his fists clenched. "And you cut our lines, didn't you? I'll tear the truth from you!"

Toby raised an arm and blocked the man's advance, but a grimace contorted his face. "What is the truth, Aliwyn?"

She crossed her arms, and the floorboards seemed to tilt beneath her. Watching the Norman longship captain and his entire crew get slaughtered for trying to recover Matthew's family's remains had shattered something within her. All her plotting and deceit hadn't saved a single Englishman tonight. Toby hadn't seen how they appeared genuinely concerned about her and the two youngsters drifting on this rotten dump.

A few had reached out to take her hand so she could walk over the plank they'd extended. She had seen Matthew's face and his reserved sympathy in the Norman captain. Her eyes smarted with tears again. The clash tonight had exposed a side of Toby she'd known was there but had been afraid to see. There would be no changing his mind about his mission.

She was so tired of this war. Both sides were to blame. If the rebels killed her now, at least she could die with some scrap of dignity by telling the truth.

"Did you cut the rigging? And the anchor?" Toby demanded. The harshness of his voice snapped her out of her thoughts.

Her eyes were too blurry to see, and she was glad for it. She stumbled back against the rail. Its heated planks seared through her tunic.

"You were ready to kill your own countrymen with those thunder-crashers." She mustered what strength she had left. "Yes, I cut both."

Cilebi roared something unintelligible in Danish and charged, his hand shooting toward her throat. Yet, before his fingers could grip her, Toby shoved him aside.

"I decide what happens to her!" Toby shouted.

"Kill her now, or our pact is done!"

Aliwyn's pulse drummed in her ears. There was nowhere to run.

"Enough fighting!" Axlan threw up his arms and stomped between them. Gripping both men's shoulders, he pried them apart. "No more—"

A whistling hiss cut through the night. Aliwyn's head jerked toward the noise, her heart slamming against her ribs. An arrow streaked past Axlan's ear and buried itself in the ship's side with a solid thwack.

Not all the longship archers were dead.

Aliwyn screamed as chaos erupted around her. Cilebi and Toby lunged for their shields. Across the deck, a figure rose from behind the rail. His short hair, matted with blood and gleaming in the fire's light, framed a face twisted with wrath and sorrow. The Norman captain.

Before Aliwyn could draw another breath, he loosed a second arrow. It grazed the back of Zelrin's neck. The boy collapsed with a yelp and sprawled onto the planks.

Aliwyn's vision tunneled. She bolted to Zelrin's side. Diving beside him, she wrapped an arm around the back of his trembling shoulders.

"Zel!" a high-pitched voice cried from the forecastle.

Aliwyn's head whipped toward the sound. "No, Emma!"

But the girl had already darted out with her braids flying. She pattered across the deck and flung herself over the other side of Zelrin.

An eerie silence descended over the ship. Aliwyn looked up as the world spun in a whirl of shadow and smoke. The Norman archer hesitated, his arrow nocked but his hands wavering. His dark frown settled on both her and the child. Aliwyn's chin trembled. She pressed her cheek against Emma's warm forehead.

He didn't shoot.

From beneath the back platform, Toby charged with his sword raised. The Norman loosed an arrow, but Toby angled the shield and caught it with a dull thud. He closed the distance in a heartbeat with his blade flashing. One swift stroke, and the captain staggered back with a choked cry.

He vanished from the rail. A splash erupted from the waters below.

Aliwyn squeezed her eyes shut. Once again, she had seen Matthew's face over the captain's features. He couldn't shoot a woman and child.

Zelrin struggled from underneath her.

"Get off me," he rasped, pushing against her arm. She released him, and he sat up. Blood trickled from a shallow cut on his nape.

Emma hovered close to him, her brown eyes round with worry. "Are you all right?"

The boy touched the back of his neck. His fingers came away bloody, but he shook his head. "Just a nick." His gaze darkened as it settled on Aliwyn. "Did you hear? She cut our lines!"

Emma's lip trembled as she looked between them, her small hands fisting the hem of her tunic. Grief sliced Aliwyn's heart. She couldn't speak.

Across the deck, Axlan sat slumped against a barrel with his chest heaving. Cilebi knelt beside him and muttered words Aliwyn couldn't discern. The older man reached for Cilebi's forearm.

"Enough killing," he croaked.

Cilebi turned his glare on Aliwyn, his black beard twitching. She curled into herself. Tears blurred her vision as she wrapped her arms around her knees.

Cilebi would strike her on the head with a rock, or maybe it would be Toby who finished her. Her ribs shuddered; she wanted it to be Toby. Killing her would serve as justice for everything she'd put him through.

But no one attacked her. Toby stood clenching the rail where the Norman had fallen. Still panting, he asked someone to help him salvage the rowboat the captain had steered to the far side of the ship for his assault.

Zelrin and Axlan approached Toby, picking up twine along the way, but Cilebi only balled his hands into fists. He marched toward Aliwyn. Her eyes throbbed, but she didn't move.

"Leave her alone!" Emma scrambled to her feet, her tiny frame but a shadow as she stepped between Aliwyn and the advancing Norseman.

With a bemused smile, Cilebi hesitated.

Tears surged in Aliwyn's eyes. "No, Emma—"

Toby was already hobbling toward the scene, his bloodied sword swinging at his side.

He gripped Cilebi's shoulder. "Any more fighting puts us at risk. Stand down."

"It's over between us." The Norseman jerked away with a huff. "I followed you because you had the potash. But now I know you can't kill a rat in broad daylight. I'm not fightin' for you anymore, only Ed."

With a final, venomous glare at Aliwyn, he turned and strode toward the forecastle.

Toby lowered his gaze and pointed the tip of his blade toward the floorboards. His face pale and strained, he turned to Aliwyn. A strange relief tingled down her scalp even as a rising sense of doom made her ears hum. Whatever punishment he chose, she would accept it. But when Emma clung to her side, Aliwyn buried her face in the girl's shoulder and let the sobs come.

Toby's uneven footfalls approached her, and the dog's barking faded into the night.

CHAPTER 18
THE SABOTEUR

Toby

THE WIND ROSE BEHIND Toby's back with the sharp scent of rain. He stood a few paces from Aliwyn, his damp hair plastered against his brow. The way she and Emma clutched each other reminded him of two other women on the Marcottes' ship. He shuddered. His grip slackened, and the tip of his blade tapped on the floorboards.

"You could've killed all of us," he said hoarsely.

Aliwyn pulled back from Emma's shoulder. Strands of brown hair clung to her cheeks, and tears rimmed her light blue eyes.

"I'm sorry," she murmured. "I only wanted to slow down the ship...and save you. But now I know I can't."

She'd cut the rigging and risked the entire crew to *save him*? Toby's chest tightened with each breath.

"What else did you steal, besides Ransley's knife?" he demanded.

Aliwyn's chin trembled in silence. He marched toward her. Grabbing her arm, he hoisted her to her feet. He rifled through the inner pockets of her purple robe. Odrianna's robe.

Out came a fire striker, a flintstone, and curls of wood shavings perfect for kindling. As the objects fell onto the floorboards, bitter laughter escaped him. He remembered now, how Aliwyn had hovered around the hearth when it needed no attention.

Squeezing her arm, Toby muttered through clenched teeth, "What were you planning to do? Burn the ship?"

She recoiled from his grip. "I wanted you to see fire so you'd leave with us. On the canoe."

Her words struck a wound within him he couldn't name, and his jaw locked to contain the smoldering wrath. Not in front of Emma.

He pointed his bloody sword at the stairwell. "We're going down."

"Why?" Aliwyn gurgled.

Even now, the sound of her sobbing tore through him. For longer than he wanted to, Toby studied her delicate frame, remembered the warmth of her body against his just hours ago, how she felt when she breathed, the scent of medicinal herbs in her hair. To hurt her tonight...

His shoulders sagging, he glanced at his shaken crew. The men roped in the dead Norman's rowboat while Zelrin's neck dripped blood. There had been enough violence for one day. Toby wiped his blade clean on a nearby sack and sheathed it.

"I'm locking you in the privy." He limped to the rail and picked up the shackles Aliwyn had discarded the night before.

The chain and cold metal rings felt heavier than they should. To think he had been the one who had helped her unlock them...Toby closed his eyes briefly and looped the chains around his forearm. He had been blind.

The wind snapped through the rigging above, and a sudden gust scattered the arrows strewn on board. Gripping Aliwyn's forearm, Toby pulled her toward the staircase.

Behind him, Emma's small voice cut through the impending storm. "Why are you locking her up?"

"She cut our lines! And stole that fire striker and flint—"

He immediately regretted shouting. Aliwyn's footsteps faltered beside him, and her arm trembling within his fist deepened the ache in his throat.

"But we all do bad things." Emma frowned. "And you just did worse things."

Toby almost laughed. Had he taught her to think like this? The irony.

"Then it's because I can't trust her anymore," he said. "Stay upstairs."

"No."

He was too tired to argue. As he led Aliwyn down the steps, the dangling shackles swinging with his momentum, Emma followed close enough to step on his heels.

"How long are you goin' to lock her up?" the girl asked. "What if she's hungry?"

Worse, what would he do with Aliwyn when Edward returned and wanted to kill her? Toby couldn't answer.

Two days earlier, he'd taken Aliwyn down these same steps and introduced her to Ransley. He'd earnestly hoped to keep her safe, partially out of respect for Miriam and later because...It didn't matter. He had been a fool. Aliwyn had been on Aelfric's side since the beginning, and therefore, on the side of the Normans.

How much of her affection had been fake? Had everything between them been a lie? What felt like fire tore down his chest.

Aliwyn staggered beside him, crying, before finally collapsing in the darkness. On reflex, he lunged to catch her. She clung to his collar and huddled against him. Toby stiffened, but Emma stared at them with tears streaming down her face, and he couldn't shove Aliwyn away. His own eyes burned.

Aliwyn's betrayal was exactly what he deserved for pretending to love Ransley, for squandering the man's fortune on potash experiments, for using his death as an excuse to finally shed tears for Miriam. One of his greatest regrets was never seeing her one last time. Ransley barely mattered. The man had shuffled his baseborn son off to Driftmere so Miriam's infant wouldn't elicit gossip and ruin the Boltans' reputation.

Aliwyn's whimpering broke into his thoughts, and he sighed. At the end, Ransley was still his father. The Heavens had deemed fit to repay Toby in kind.

He carefully pulled Aliwyn back and steadied her shoulders. Emma's small hand grasped the hem of the cloak Aliwyn wore.

"Please don't hurt her," the child whispered.

Her breaths shallow and broken, Aliwyn hung her head. Her grief appeared genuine. The lump in Toby's throat grew unbearable.

He met Emma's gaze. "I won't."

Really? After all she had done to ruin his life's work? Edward would have his way with her as soon as he returned. Toby tried not to think further, but when Aliwyn looked up with swollen eyes, the images of Odrianna and Evelyn came tearing back. Both women lay unconscious and bloodied in his arms. There was no escaping the pain of losing them both, one to death, the other to hatred.

He wouldn't repeat what Rufus had done to Odrianna. He wouldn't allow Edward to abuse a young woman. All the same, the blackness of the hull seemed to close in. What, then, would he do with Aliwyn tomorrow?

His voice cracking, he looked at Emma and asked, "Can you light a candle for me?"

The child nodded. She left his side and approached the beeswax candle caged above where they'd slept two nights ago.

Whenever Toby tried to release Aliwyn, she swayed. Her hands jerked to her neck as though she feared being strangled. Toby frowned at the chains around his arm, how they pinched his flesh like the rope around his ankle when he'd hung upside down. He'd vowed to Heaven then to do as much good as he could if he survived. Whatever "good" even meant in this war.

"Aliwyn," he said hoarsely. "Why can you not see...that if I abandon this mission, if I don't shock the Normans into submission, many more Englishmen will die?"

She stared at him, silent, and he shook his head. He could never make her see. He could only take her somewhere so she'd stop tormenting him.

He finally whispered, "I'll carry you."

Candlelight glimmered in the gloom. The tiny flames brightened her eyes, still fearful but rounded with surprise.

He stooped to hook his arm behind her knees. She didn't resist, and he straightened again with her cradled in his arms. His battered knees throbbed in protest, but he held firm. Aliwyn rested her head against his shoulder and trembled.

"Why?" she whispered.

Leaning against a post to steady himself, Toby didn't answer. Her face, glowing in the moonlight last night, and the way she'd pulled him close within the sleep sack—everything had seemed real. He chose to believe, if only for his sanity, that her care for him had been genuine. But they were still on opposing sides of a war.

Toby limped onward. He couldn't tell Aliwyn that carrying her gave him the fleeting illusion of rewriting the past. A past where he wouldn't lose Odrianna and Evelyn after carrying them both this same way.

Every creaking step in the dank hull unearthed more memories. The screams from Rufus Marcotte's assassination, and the household massacre that followed, seemed to echo from the walls. Toby never knew his childhood friend and her whole family would be on Rufus' ship, sailing to her wedding. The mercenaries Ransley hired attacked anyone they saw on board.

No matter how Ransley tried to console Toby afterward, saying neither he nor Edward knew about Evelyn's wedding, Toby couldn't forgive himself.

He stopped before the privy. Just before he lowered Aliwyn to the floorboards, she snuggled against his neck. Her damp cheeks cooled his skin. Grief pierced him. Despite his hunger for revenge, he knew Aliwyn couldn't undo what she'd done. Likewise, he could do nothing to make amends with Evelyn, the young woman whose letters he had once cherished.

Firelight flickered at the edge of his vision. He couldn't change the past, but tomorrow, he'd have a canoe and a newly salvaged rowboat. An idea sparked within him.

Toby opened the privy door and carried Aliwyn inside. Nudging aside the empty buckets with his foot, he turned to her and spoke in Vasfian. "I'll release you on a canoe tomorrow at dawn when we approach one of the deserted barrier islands. You'll have to get yourself rescued."

His decision came with a risk. There was a slim chance she'd alert the Norman authorities in time about Prince Cnut, and an even slimmer chance the Normans would believe a peasant woman's warning. Yet, it was a risk he had to take. The alternative was to kill her or watch Edward do it.

Aliwyn folded her arms around her waist, the corners of her mouth tightening. Was she worried about getting rescued afterward? Toby couldn't afford to care.

Emma tugged on Aliwyn's sleeve. "What's Toby saying?"

Aliwyn hesitated before stroking the girl's ear. "He told me how to avoid Edward tomorrow." Turning back to Toby, she asked in a quivering voice, "But why are you doing this?"

Toby looked away, the image of her large eyes and heart-shaped face lingering in his mind. He couldn't answer without breaking.

"Let's go, Emma," he said, stepping outside the privy.

Her gaze downcast, the girl followed him. "When are you going to let her out?"

"She'll be out tomorrow." Before Emma awakened again, he'd make sure Aliwyn disappeared.

Toby closed the door and leaned his forehead against it for a moment. The chains he carried clinked softly as he looped them around the privy handle and an iron ring on the frame. Finally, he clasped the shackle rings together.

Aliwyn's light footsteps shuffled inside. Her gait was identical to Miriam's when she used to hurry about her mill, and he used to journal by firelight. He'd considered telling Aliwyn the truth about Miriam and himself, but now he was glad he hadn't. There was no purpose in tarnishing Miriam's reputation.

He stepped back from the door. The sound of Zelrin and Axlan talking on deck reached his ears. His men needed him.

Toby was about to leave, but Emma's downturned face and the way she toyed with her frayed braids made him pause. For two days, he'd believed he'd found her the perfect surrogate mother. Now, he feared the nightmares she'd have.

"Emma," he said softly. "I'm sorry for everything today."

He knelt and lowered his head. Emma stepped forward. Silently, she wrapped her arms around his neck and rested her cheek against his ear.

Toby smiled and returned her embrace, treasuring her warmth even as a heaviness remained on his shoulders. With her small body nestled against him, his mind drifted to all he'd told himself during those endless nights perfecting the potash compound. He'd convinced himself he had nothing to lose, that this mission would rekindle his bond with Uncle Ed, the kind man who once collected plants with him in Driftmere. But Uncle Ed had yet to recover from his family's death. Every day reminded Toby that he did have much to lose. Maybe Emma and Zelrin would've been better off as homeless exiles in Denmark. At least there, they might have escaped the violence.

The image of Vincent's arrow flying toward Zelrin resurfaced, and Toby's stomach clenched. His doubts swarmed, thick and unrelenting, until Emma pulled back and kissed his forehead. Her steady gaze held a trust he didn't deserve. Yet, it gave him hope.

He still had Emma and Zelrin. He still had his ship and its twenty-four chests of eighty thundercrashers each. The thought of so much power under his control stirred a rush of grim determination. With Aliwyn out of his way, he'd align with Edward and end the rebellion.

Toby stood and reached for Emma's hand. He couldn't bear to look at his father's empty mattress. What was Edward doing now? Would he return in a fit of rage over Ransley's death, or would his brother's passing finally convince Edward to accept Toby as the only family who remained?

With tears stinging his eyes, Toby prayed for the latter.

He and Emma were close to reaching the stairs when Zelrin hurried down the steps.

"Toby," the boy called in the dimness. "Are you all right?"

Zelrin strode forward with a rush lamp in his hand, but he halted with uncertainty wrinkling his forehead. Maybe he remembered how he'd been rebuked the last time he'd descended. Toby pressed his lips together.

"I'm all right," he answered. "Let's go upstairs."

Lights and shadows wavered over Zelrin's features as Toby and Emma drew close.

"What are you going to do about Aliwyn?" the boy asked, frowning at the chained privy door.

Toby lowered his gaze. "I'll explain later."

"I...I should've watched her better." Zelrin bowed his head. He pressed a gloved hand to the wound on his neck, where blood had already seeped through the fabric.

Toby draped an arm around Zelrin's shoulders and pulled him close. "You're alive. That's what matters. We keep fighting, Zel?"

The boy's gaze shifted to the stacked explosives. His jaw tightened, as if now grasping their power.

After a beat, he nodded. "I'll go where you go."

Toby smiled. He hobbled to Ransley's mattress and slipped the dagger Aliwyn had stolen back into its sheath. With Emma and Zelrin following, he ascended the stairs.

The wind carried an acrid tang of smoke through his hair. On deck, the cool bite of a drizzle clung to his skin. Shifting storm clouds overhead glowed orange from the three floating fires now drifting away. By dawn, they would sink. He had won a decisive victory.

Such an accomplishment would've compensated for Aliwyn's betrayal had it not been for the faint cries of men still echoing over the waters. Some must've found debris to cling onto. Toby's stomach sank. The calls for help were in English. Yet, he couldn't risk taking any survivors on board and endangering his own crew. Vincent's soldiers would freeze to death overnight.

Toby staggered back from the rail and turned as Emma and Zelrin hesitated on the stairs. It was going to be a long night. How was he going to explain this to her? And what kind of example had he just given Zelrin?

Toby exhaled, his head lowering. The thundercrashers had given him victory, but at what cost?

CHAPTER 19
IMPRISONED

October 1, Matthew

THE PRISON ROUNDHOUSE INTENDED for Matthew and Kato smelled dank, like no one had lit the central hearth for weeks. Matthew hauled Kato inside while Reiya followed him, carrying a glowing turnip. The flickering light illuminated two cots, a few stools, and a table. Matthew pulled a seat for Kato, who flinched even at the sound of Reiya setting the lantern on the table.

Matthew's anger faded. Kato was worse off. Tomorrow, Abithi would demand to know how the Boltans had transported their pungent black matter without the world noticing. Just because Kato had delivered ale to the Boltans didn't mean he knew anything. He might have to invent answers, and at his own peril.

The younger man sat and wrapped the gambeson around himself. He was shivering. Sighing, Matthew decided against taking back his armor.

"Have this tinderbox," he said, taking the object out of his belt pouch. "Start yourself a fire."

Kato looked up with swollen eyes and nodded. He appeared starved. Matthew didn't know where their next meal would come from or why he felt so responsible.

Turning to Reiya, he dared to ask, "Are Mils and Porei being fed?"

"Of course." She jerked her head toward the door. "Come, I'll show you."

The tribe treated pack animals better than Kato. But before this day, Matthew had treated the half-blood no better.

His shoulders heavy, he followed Reiya outside and shut the door behind him.

The warriors once crowded around the roundhouse had departed, at least. A breeze scattered browned oak leaves around Matthew's shins and stole the warmth beneath his tunic.

Reiya secured the door with a wooden plank. "Porei and Mils are over here."

He followed her along the roundhouse wall to its rear, where a sloping plain stretched into the fading evening light. Crickets chirped near and far. A dozen pack animals, including Porei and Mils, grazed with the breeze sweeping over their black manes. The familiar scent of hay steadied Matthew.

They neared a dovecot, a short wooden tower riddled with holes. Aliwyn's chickens pecked around its foundation. As Reiya and Matthew drew near, a few pigeons huddled within the tower's holes took flight in a flurry of clapping gray and white wings. Matthew watched them merge with a larger flock overhead, and his stomach sank. The flock he'd tried to rejoin had rejected him.

Lowering his gaze again, he shuffled to a stop beside Reiya, who had been frowning at the ground. Matthew pushed aside his troubles for now.

"You know what I want," he muttered. "So you talk first."

Her chest rose and fell. "I need to admit...I don't know where Ravenser's is."

Matthew arched a brow. A sharp laugh escaped before he caught himself. "Oh, really? Well, I can tell you. Is that why you wanted to talk without your mother listening?"

She shot him a glare, her fingers tightening around the torc at her neck. "Most villagers assume I know everything about the Outsiders just because I spent a year with nuns. I don't. Ravenser's must have another name in my language."

"I doubt the nuns knew much about geography, anyway." He watched her frustration with a flicker of amusement but decided not to provoke her further. "You did learn Norman French, though. That's impressive."

"Thank you. French is much harder than English."

"I disagree." Matthew smirked. "But regardless, grant yourself more esteem for your accomplishments. You don't need your mother's advice for everything."

"Please don't comment on my household's affairs." The edge in her voice was obvious. "I just need to know where Ravenser's is."

"I'll trade you. Lock me up for only one night and let me attend the *Anuin*. Then I'll tell you where Ravenser's is."

She jutted her chin. "Your commander kept crucial information to himself. The least you can do is tell me where Ravenser's is."

"What Jacques did to you was unfair—" Matthew hesitated and looked around. There could be serious repercussions for speaking against a superior, but no soldiers stood nearby to report his comment.

Reiya's brief grimace shuttered back into an unreadable stare. She was understandably hurt. Nothing she'd done deserved Jacques's belittling treatment, and Matthew softened his voice. "I'm not Jacques. I want to work with you. But that's hard to do when you lock me in a cage. If your mother were absent, would you still lock me inside?"

"I've only been chief for a month, and it's only because my mother was injured." She nibbled at her lip. "I'm still learning."

"It seems like you've learned plenty. You faced Jacques like a competent leader."

"If I were competent, I wouldn't have needed your help." She faced him fully, her gaze sharp. "Look, stop trying to flatter me. Just tell me where Ravenser's is."

There was something arresting about those large, green eyes. *Drat it all.* This would've been much easier had she been a hairy Englishman.

"I'll make you another offer." Matthew lifted his hand like a merchant presenting his wares. "Free me tomorrow for the ceremony, and I'll paint you a map of the coast. A detailed one. You'll see exactly where Ravenser's Point is."

"A map? You can draw one from memory?"

"Certainly. My ancestors were Norsemen, so I learned from the best navigators. And didn't Aelfric tell you I'm a talented artist?"

She raised a brow. "He said you painted flying pigs on your bylaws instead of studying them. Not sure that's talent."

By the Devil's tail, Aelfric. Why did you tell her that?

Matthew cleared his throat. "I drew an impressive griffin for your courier pigeons, didn't I? I can paint you a map on a wooden board. A very detailed one."

She seemed to consider his words, and he pressed on. "If I were free, I could help you fish, cut firewood, and tend to your horses. And I want to experience the *Anuin*. Then I can return to my troops and tell them the Vasfians were gracious hosts."

Matthew's pulse tapped behind his ribs like an offbeat drum. Listening to Aelfric heckle at the market must've taught him a thing or two. Reiya knit her brows, but there was a hint of something else in her eyes this time. Not frustration. Something closer to sorrow.

"My grandmother and mother said you can't attend," she murmured.

"But you're the chief."

"I know, but my elders reminded me of many things." She turned aside. "Don't you find the warriors here in Jethran rather cold?"

"Maybe. I also saw the man who tried to barge into Aliwyn's watermill."

"Yes. He and the other warriors in Jethran are the ones who refused to rescue you when Aelfric begged me for help. They stayed with my mother."

Icy tendrils crawled up Matthew's spine, and his throat blocked.

Reiya's eyes remained downcast. "They've heard of the way you deserted your parents for seven years. We see this as the worst kind of betrayal, deserving of divine wrath."

Aelfric must've told the redheads about Matthew's family situation, but it was hardly a secret. For years, Matthew rejected the letters from his father and refused to visit their new residence in Marcottesville.

"I see." His voice came out rough. "So, people here think I deserve retribution?"

"Yes. Aelfric intervened, and look what happened to him."

The words felt like a blow to his chest, and the roundhouses behind her dimmed for a moment. Nothing she told him was surprising, but Matthew's face still crumpled.

"I'm sorry." Reiya shifted toward him. "I shouldn't have told you that."

"No, I appreciate hearing the truth. Now I have even more reason to attend the *Anuin*."

"Why? I just told you why Jethran is unwelcoming. It doesn't help that you brought Kato here. I also had to explain to everyone that your commander is sabotaging my efforts. Now their perception of you is worse."

"Jacques is my *former* commander. I even opposed him for your sake."

"I told my mother this. She isn't convinced your intentions were pure. Because if you can even betray your parents, then..."

"How do I argue against that?" The hurt was now raw in his voice. "She sees in me whatever she wants to see."

Reiya squeezed the edge of her fur cape. "I agree. When you defended us, I didn't sense any deceit in you."

For better or for worse, she still didn't sense any deceit in him. Matthew stifled the pangs of guilt. "I don't like being judged for my reputation. It's easy to resent someone you don't understand. I can tell you that."

The sympathy in her eyes made him grow hot. He had been the resentful one. Only two days ago, he had threatened to ruin her reputation while they'd searched for Tobias and Aliwyn.

"Let me show your villagers I'm not just a wastrel of a son," he continued. "And that Aelfric didn't die for a fool."

Reiya searched his eyes. Matthew resisted looking away as he added, "I also want to prove my worth to your village. I want your mother to stop ridiculing your decision to bring me here."

That seemed to strike a wound within her, and Reiya blinked rapidly.

Dipping her chin, she murmured, "The ceremony will be behind the chieftain's hall. There will be prayers to Lenus and other gods for my mother to walk again. Chanting to ward off evil spirits. Can you tolerate that?"

"Yes." Matthew swallowed. He'd have to.

"The elders will all be there. Stay close to me and don't speak unless you're told to."

"All right." His breaths quickened. "So, you're letting me go?"

"Yes. I'll tell my mother and grandmother that you're coming." She thinned her lips. "And that this is my decision."

His scalp tingled with relief. "I appreciate that."

She returned his smile. "Can you draw the map in front of the crowd before our ceremony begins? I want everyone to see how capable you are."

"Then I'll do it."

"Good. Then I'll come fetch you tomorrow morning."

Reiya turned to walk back to the roundhouse entrance. Matthew followed with his mind muddled by a myriad of emotions. Why was he still nervous? Where was the satisfaction in winning the negotiation? Something had changed between them, and he couldn't put it into words.

Another question rose to the forefront, one that he had suppressed for days. Nearly a week ago, when Aelfric had come to ask for her help, why had she agreed to follow him and attack the Boltans' manor?

He almost bumped into Reiya when she halted.

"See, they're coming with food," she said.

Twenty paces away, Domilo, Yana, and a skipping Nissa approached along the dirt path where Abithi had been carried. The setting sun cast a copper glow over their red hair and Domilo's checkered hair scarf. Yana walked between the two children and held a basket handle in each hand. Matthew nodded at Reiya in thanks, but she only looked away, her expression shadowed with melancholy.

"Nervous about me attending tomorrow?" he asked.

"There's that," she said. "But I'm more worried about the Danes. My mother once fought them when they raided the coast. Soon, it will be my first time."

"There is always the first time for everything."

She glanced at him. "You don't seem at all worried. Why is that?"

Matthew chuckled, then turned to meet her quizzical stare. "I was wearing a mask. The battle ahead will also be one of my first. Of course I'm worried."

She smiled faintly. "I see. You had me fooled."

"Y-you, too."

"Much of being chief is theatrics."

Matthew was still contemplating her last statement when Domilo called out his greetings and waved his free arm. He pulled out a flatbread from the covered basket, flapped it in the air, and ripped off a piece.

Stuffing it into his mouth, he cried, "Look, Matthew! It's safe to eat!"

While he spoke, Nissa reached into Yana's basket and withdrew what looked like a small tart with dried apricots. She giggled and began eating it as well.

Reiya rubbed her forehead with a sheepish grin. "*Kaba.* Those little ones will eat everything by the time they're here."

Yana and the children soon encircled Matthew, introducing the flatbreads, pies, and nuts inside the basket. He smiled at them, but his mouth filled with sand. Reiya's mother had correctly sensed his deception, but her children had not.

"Thanks," Matthew managed to say, accepting a basket. "How do you say that in Vasfian?"

"*Sankei.*" Domilo grinned.

Matthew repeated the word, and the boy beamed.

As he and Nissa followed Yana to feed Aliwyn's chickens pecking around the dovecot, Reiya said, "My elders will have advice regarding the battle. I look forward to your thoughts as well."

Matthew nodded stiffly. Had she known why he was sent here, she'd never want to see him again. He'd also envisioned pulling Aliwyn out of the chaos and bolting away with her on Porei. His mandate had never been to help Reiya fight, and his shoulders sagged.

They carried the baskets toward the roundhouse. After such a long day, Reiya still smelled like wild roses, while Matthew could hardly stand himself. He tried to walk downwind of her.

When the others were out of earshot, he said, "Can I ask you something?"

"It depends on what you ask."

"Why..." he steadied himself. "Why did you agree to help Aelfric rescue me? You had never met me."

They walked into the shade of the roundhouse, where one turnip on its doorstep had burned out. Reiya released her basket and picked up the lantern, stroking its surface with her thumb.

"I heard a lot about you, and..." Her voice faltered.

Matthew tensed. Had she heard mostly good things? If so, she must have been thoroughly disappointed with what she ended up saving. The lump in his throat grew.

"Never mind," she said. "You say Aelfric was your best friend, but he was mine, too. That's all you need to know."

She walked him inside the roundhouse, bade him goodnight, and began to leave.

"Reiya," he called out.

She turned, her eyes wet, and he swallowed hard.

"Ravenser's Point is a tiny island at the mouth of the River Humber," he said. "Just off the tip of the peninsula."

Her face softened into a smile, though sorrow still lingered. "Thank you. I'll start thinking tonight about preparing my galleys."

Matthew blinked. For some reason, he had assumed the Vasfians only had small canoes incapable of naval combat. How naïve he had been.

"I'm still allowed to go to the *Anuin* tomorrow, right?" he asked.

"Of course. I keep my word."

Still smiling, she closed the door behind her. The plank outside fell back into place.

Matthew stared at the door with the warmth of the hearth at his back. He had never known Reiya was so close to Aelfric, and he wished he didn't. His mission was growing more complicated with every moment. Firelight stretched his shifting shadow across perfectly straight wooden planks.

His mind drifted back to the first time he had smelled wild roses. It had been just after she'd thrown a bag over his head. The scent had come with a warm cover, like a dream, but he'd smelled it again while awake. Reiya must have covered him with her cape even back then.

She should have kicked him a few more times instead.

Other thoughts crowded in. If Reiya truly hid the black matter, why had she accepted him into her tribe? Why had she agreed to take him to the ceremony? The pieces refused to fit together. Jacques could be wrong, and maybe his dogs had been reacting to something else. That possibility shook Matthew to the core.

He could be chasing a phantom, wasting time on a mission that led nowhere while losing sight of why he had come to Brocklesby in the first place—to find Aliwyn. He should be negotiating for a double saddle so she could ride with him. He should be searching for a lance to impale the Boltans.

Matthew raked his hands through his hair. For the first time, he felt an urge to ask Reiya to show him everything she had taken from the Boltans. He wanted to go home and declare, with a clear conscience, that Jacques was mistaken and that she possessed no black matter.

But if he dared to ask, the Vasfians would know he was a spy. He'd be expelled, or worse. And Jacques would be furious. No army would cover him while he tried to rescue Aliwyn. What was he going to do?

No answers came. A creeping fog dulled his thoughts as exhaustion settled in. He needed to sleep on the matter.

But a knock on the door made him jolt.

Domilo's voice came from the other side. "Matthew? Why did you go inside so fast?"

Matthew sighed. "It's not that I want to be inside. I was locked in here."

"Oh..."

Matthew heard the boy murmur in Vasfian to an adult woman, probably the guard outside his door.

There was a sigh, and Domilo said, "I thought Sis wasn't serious about locking you up. I'm sorry."

"It's not your fault."

"I...wanted to play chess with you."

"Chess?" Matthew smiled at the door. "You know how to play chess?"

"Aelfric taught me. He also carved me a chess set." Domilo's voice grew cheerful. "I love it so much. It's a box that opens into a board, and it can hold all the pieces inside. I want to show you."

A ball lodged in Matthew's throat. Years ago, he'd taught Aelfric how to play chess. Aelfric was the only one Matthew didn't mind losing to.

Pressing a hand against the door, Matthew muttered, "I can't play tonight."

"Tomorrow?"

"I don't know."

Silence. Matthew could feel the boy's disappointment through the door. He coughed into his elbow. "But I can teach you some Norman French. Can you guess what my favorite chess piece is?"

"Uh...the king?"

Matthew chuckled. He'd never want so much responsibility. "No, it's the knight."

He spoke the Norman French word for 'knight.' Domilo gleefully repeated it, his pronunciation improving, until Matthew's vision swam. He'd taught Aelfric French in the same way.

"How do you become a knight?" Domilo asked.

"Not easy. A lot of training for battle and proving myself in the field. If my superiors think I'm worthy, they knight me at a ceremony. They may grant me some land, but I'll have to fight for them to keep it."

"Oh." Domilo sounded almost disgusted. "So much trouble! My *Apah* just gave me his house when he passed. But I need to grow up first."

Matthew grinned wryly. *Apah* must mean father. Matthew wasn't so fortunate.

"That's very good, Domilo. I'll...I'll see you tomorrow."

The two of them bade each other goodnight, and the child's light footsteps scampered away. Matthew's heart felt too big for his chest. He shouldn't try to befriend the child when he had ulterior motives. For a long time, he faced the door as if it would speak words of wisdom.

"Matthew? What are you staring at?" came a voice behind him.

He'd forgotten Kato was still inside. Matthew inhaled slowly and turned around.

"I was just thinking of a few things." He faked a smile and gestured at the baskets. "There's food now. You should eat."

Kato stood before him with his arms crossed and his face unreadable. He had folded Matthew's gambeson on the table and had donned a clean tunic, one with clovers embroidered around the collar.

Matthew's eyes widened. "Where did you get that?"

"A chest under the table."

How dare he open Aelfric's chest and wear his clothes! His nape prickling, Matthew spun away and noted the clam shells suspended in a spiral pattern from the ceiling. Their iridescent colors gleamed in the firelight, and they twirled with the rising heat. Aelfric loved clamshells. This must be the roundhouse he once slept in, and Kato had just changed into one of his old tunics.

It was too much. Matthew stumbled backward, but there was no way out.

Something else was wrong. Kato appeared angry. Furious, in fact.

"We need to talk." The redhead uncrossed his arms. He held the brown cow horn that had been hidden in the pocket of Matthew's gambeson.

Matthew's vision went white. "Oh, my drinking horn. What's there to talk about?"

Kato uncorked the horn and inverted it over his hand. Out came five slender lockpicks, tinkling softly as they struck each other. Matthew wanted to pull out his hair.

Kato glared at him. "Who's the thief here?"

CHAPTER 20
LOCKPICKS

Matthew

"I didn't know those were inside," Matthew whispered, staring at the lockpicks. "Give them to me."

"No." Kato hid everything behind his back. "We'd better get rid of them."

Matthew bared his teeth. He marched forth with his fists clenched, and Kato gasped. Shuffling around the hearth, he almost tripped.

"S-stealing will get you killed, especially here," Kato said. "Then they'll chop off my head because you dragged me into this."

Matthew bristled with heat and chills. He didn't want to be in the space where Aelfric used to stay. Didn't want to hear another boy with a native English accent trying to reason with him.

"Matt, get rid of these," Kato said quietly. "Whatever you want from the Vasfians isn't worth it."

No one called him "Matt" without permission. Matthew gritted his teeth. "Who said I was stealing? You're the one who stole my horn. Give it back."

"I didn't steal." Sorrow creased Kato's face. "I couldn't find a cup, so I borrowed—"

Seeing his chance, Matthew grabbed Kato's shoulders and shoved him against the wall. Kato yelped. Matthew reached for Kato's arm to twist it, but the redhead ducked and lunged to the side. When he scrambled to get back up, his legs gave out. Matthew grabbed his arm and slammed him onto his stomach, ready to wrench the objects free. Just as his knee landed on Kato's back, the younger man tossed the lockpicks and horn into the fire.

Matthew screamed. He left Kato writhing on the floor and bolted for the fire, reaching out and almost burning his hand. With the flames scorching his face, he grabbed the first bucket he saw and cast its contents toward the hearth. A cascade of water pelted over the flames with a splash and a hiss. The roundhouse went dark.

He dropped the bucket with a thunk. The light from the lantern on the table flickered, and embers sizzled in the blackened pool. Kato pushed himself up, panting. They locked eyes. A thin line of blood trailed from Kato's nose. Matthew's throat swelled, but all he could think of was his lockpicks.

He squatted to pluck the objects from the hearth. The first one he touched burned his fingers. He deserved that. Withdrawing his hand, Matthew stood again.

"Kato," he croaked. "Are you all right?"

But the younger man crawled away. Huddling against the wall, he glowered at Matthew. The clothes he wore, *Aelfric's* clothes, were covered in dirt again.

Matthew hung his head. The heat of the moment had faded and left only the cold weight of shame. Eight years ago, he had sworn never to attack another boy after he'd broken Tobias Boltan's arm.

Pummeling the younger boy had tarnished Matthew's reputation and made recruiting English foot soldiers nearly impossible. Somehow, Uncle Henri had convinced Aelfric to give Matthew a chance, but the brute Matthew had tried to defeat still lived within him.

His chest tight, Matthew returned to the ash and retrieved the lockpicks.

Someone rapped on the door. He jumped. Could this nightmare get worse?

"Matthew!" came Reiya's voice. "What happened? Why so much yelling?"

The plank barring the door outside slid against its brackets. Matthew nearly toppled over. He grabbed the lockpicks and jammed them into the horn. "Stay outside! I'm bathing!"

The plank fell back into place with a thud.

Reiya sighed. "Do you always scream while you bathe?"

"I...I spilled cold water," Matthew lied, his hand trembling around the horn. The cork was missing. *Flying Krakens.* Where had Kato thrown it?

"Then do you need more water?" Reiya asked. The concern in her voice made his skin crawl.

"Uh...just more firewood because I..." Matthew froze. His eyes fastened on Kato, who squeezed a cork-sized object within his fist.

"I know," Reiya said from outside. "You doused the flames, didn't you? I'll bring firewood."

Her footsteps departed, and Matthew's knees almost buckled. If she had seen the lockpicks...

He approached Kato with measured steps.

"Give me the cork." He extended an itchy right hand. In the dim light, Aelfric seemed to sit in Kato's place, as thin as when Matthew had first met him. "I'm sorry, but I need it back."

"Be stupid, then." Kato tossed the cork toward him.

Matthew was too tired to be offended. The cork bounced to the side. As he bent to grab it, Kato spoke again. "Why do you need those things?"

Matthew stood, unable to face Kato again. Pressing the stopper into place, he approached the remaining bucket of water and splashed his tunic to feign an accidental spill. The frigid liquid made his teeth chatter; it was the least he could suffer for lying. Two baskets of food remained by the door, but he'd lost his appetite.

He picked up a basket and placed it closer to Kato.

"Eat something," he muttered. "You need it."

"Abithi will kill you for having those things."

"Why do you care?"

Chills racked Matthew's body. Half-soaked, he couldn't don his gambeson again. He shoved the horn into the gambeson's pocket and left the garment on the table. At any moment, Reiya would knock again with firewood, water, and her well-intended concern.

Matthew cringed at the thought of her smiling face. He must send her away quickly and keep her away from his lockpicks.

But Reiya didn't return for a long time.

Finally, Kato murmured, "I found a crucifix in your pocket, too. I washed it and left it on the table."

Matthew had forgotten about the cross he'd salvaged from the Dane. Kato had dared to rifle through his pockets, but Matthew was too tired to yell.

He picked up the pendant from the table. The grisly bloodstains had faded, but he still tensed at the familiar shape of the cross. When he became a squire, he'd sworn to protect the innocent and to live an honorable life. A priest had handed him a crucifix much like this one. At thirteen, Matthew hadn't taken the oath seriously. Now, the words pressed heavy on his shoulders.

After all the training, he was here. Cut off from the army. Chastised by a thief. He wanted to kick over a stool, but Kato's petrified expression washed out his anger. Kato had avoided speaking the word 'lockpick' in case anyone overheard. Despite the risks, he had confronted Matthew.

"Thanks for...this." Matthew said quietly.

The crucifix belonged to the enemy, but he wanted to bury it out of respect. For now, he slipped it into one of his belt pouches.

Kato's eyes softened. "Who gave you the drinking horn? You didn't have one when I first met you."

"None of your concern."

"Was it the knight in Brocklesby?"

"I said, none of your concern."

His gaze lowered, Matthew paced the roundhouse. A small part of him appreciated that someone cared enough to pester him.

A knock came on the door, and it swung open with a creak. A slender woman with wavy red hair entered with her companion, who pushed a wheelbarrow. Matthew watched the door, waiting for Reiya to arrive so he could dismiss her.

"Sorry it took so long," said one of the women. "But I needed to cut more firewood."

It was Reiya's voice. Matthew did a double take. She already stood beside him, and the woman pushing the wheelbarrow was Yana. With her hair now falling to her waist, Reiya was hardly recognizable. She had changed into a dark red robe, cinched at the waist, that fit her just right.

"T-Thanks for bringing it." He tried to focus on her face, but his gaze kept sliding down to the woodcutter's axe hanging from her belt. What an unusual item to see on a maiden.

Yana lowered the wheelbarrow beside the hearth. Matthew sidestepped the damp patch he'd made and helped her unload the birch bark kindling and firewood. Meanwhile, Reiya picked up the glowing turnip from the table and approached him.

"You're still wearing your dirty clothes." She wrinkled her nose.

"Oh, I..." Why was it harder to talk to her now? "I didn't get to finish bathing, so I put my dirty clothes back on."

As Yana blew on a new bed of kindling, heat flooded Matthew's face. He'd just called Reiya a 'maiden' in his mind. Whatever it was he was feeling, it was awful. And his words to dismiss her tangled in his throat.

Reiya gestured at Aelfric's chest of clothes. "Did you find anything in there to change into? Some of Aelfric's clothes must fit you."

The chest Kato had opened stood beside the table. Its varnished vine and flower décor glistened in the firelight.

"I didn't look inside yet," Matthew said. "This place...was where Aelfric used to stay, right?"

"Yes. Also visiting priests. This is why the plank for the door is on the outside, so they could be locked inside at night. My mother didn't trust them, either."

"I...see."

"I didn't have another place for you to sleep. I should've warned you that Aelfric used to stay here."

He looked away. "It's all right."

Reiya told him that the rocks in the wheelbarrow could be heated in the fireplace and added to buckets of water to warm them. Matthew nodded but squirmed inside. She cared too much.

Kato still sat huddled on the ground against the far wall. The pensive look in the younger man's eyes deepened Matthew's guilt over their skirmish. He resolved to be kinder, to speak to Reiya a bit before making her leave.

Meanwhile, Reiya and Yana had knelt by the baskets to scowl at their untouched contents.

"The food isn't poisoned," Reiya said, her eyes melancholic. "Please trust me enough to eat."

"Oh, I believe you." Matthew struggled to meet her gaze. "I just didn't have time to eat yet."

Reiya pulled a stool into position beside the table and motioned for Matthew to sit down.

"You know the medicine I give you?" she asked. "It gives you energy and tames the coughing, but it doesn't mean you've recovered. You still have to eat and rest properly."

Matthew nodded. He walked stiffly to the stool and sat. Part of him wanted to...what? Confess everything? His chest tightened again.

"Oh, I know."

She smiled and strolled to the baskets. "I think you'll like this."

As she knelt, the hem of her robe folded gracefully around her ankles. Lifting the basket's checkered cloth covering, she withdrew what looked like a pie. "I call this 'baked pottage.'"

"What? Pottage can be baked?"

"I decided it can be." Her grin broadened. "I know your people love pottage, but it's not easy to carry around. So one day, I poured it into a pie crust and baked it."

She slid the pie out of its supporting dish. Breaking off a piece of the crust, she put it into her mouth. The fragrance of butter and oats wafted to Matthew's nose. He accepted the pie from Reiya and took a bite. Thickened pottage with pieces of sweet carrot and a rich dill flavor oozed from the dense crust.

Instantly, he was ravenous. He couldn't swallow fast enough to satisfy the expanding void in his stomach.

Reiya beamed and sat on a stool across from him. A rosy color tinted her cheeks, and her clear eyes held a sparkle of amusement. It was too bad she rarely looked like this. Once he was halfway through his pie, Matthew forced himself to pause and thank her.

"You're welcome," she chuckled. "Aelfric says you can eat even faster than he does. Now I believe it."

She spoke as though Aelfric were still alive. His lips quirking into a smile, Matthew unclasped the costrel from his belt and took a long drink.

"The pottage tastes like home." He wiped his mouth. "Except your carrots are much sweeter. How did your tribe grow them?"

It was supposed to be a casual question, but Reiya looked away with her chin lowered.

Matthew shifted in his seat. "If it's a farmer's secret, then don't tell me."

"I don't know how the carrots were grown." She smoothed her dress with her hand. "They came from His Excellency. So did the grain."

"Really? You've been trading food with him?"

"Yes, thanks to the alliance." She paused, as though deciding if she should continue. "The Boltans burned my farmland here in Jethran in the summer. It was too late to replant anything. The crops in Blaithin weren't enough to feed everyone, so I negotiated with the Outsiders for food. Your bishop, specifically."

Matthew frowned and set his costrel down. Domilo had once said the "bad English" burned his home. Now, Matthew understood. Because of the Boltans, the Vasfians had begun to rely on a Norman bishop for their winter provisions. Reiya had negotiated a treaty for more than just military support.

If Matthew reported the black matter, that alliance could break. Her people might starve.

As he sat there, tapping his index finger on the table, Reiya said, "Something's wrong. You're suddenly quiet."

Matthew's toes curled.

Her large eyes seemed to look right through him, and he said as smoothly as he could, "I'm just surprised you met His Excellency. He's very powerful. I won't even get to meet him until my knighting ceremony. What did he look like?"

To his surprise, Reiya giggled. "He was a short man and came dressed as a priest. His beard was so thick I could hardly see his face."

"What?" Matthew sat up straight. How could any self-respecting Norman wear a slovenly beard?

"I'm not jesting. After my farmlands were burned, he came and called himself Father...oh, I don't even remember. He had a very odd accent, too, but he offered to help us. My mother and I thanked him and sent him away. We never took him seriously. But two days later, two knights arrived with caravans full of food." Reiya raised her eyebrows. "One knight told us the priest we had seen was His Excellency himself."

"Flying..." Matthew's mouth hung open. What kind of strange bishop was Geoffrey de Montbray? "Does His Excellency still wear a beard?"

She shrugged. "I never saw him again, but one of his knights gave me this ring."

She raised her hand, displaying a silver ring with a falcon's insignia on her middle finger. "I can present this ring wherever he is holding court and ask to see him. He wants to learn Vasfian medicine and how to train messenger doves." She smiled. "I appreciate him. He seeks knowledge, not possessions."

Matthew clenched the tunic covering his thigh. Did she speak like this because she truly had nothing to hide from this bishop she appreciated?

"Your mind seems to be elsewhere," Reiya said quietly. "I'll let you rest."

Matthew blinked. As she stood, her hand lifted from a small satchel on the table. He hadn't noticed her taking it out.

"What's this?" he asked.

"A jar of honey and crushed garlic for your hand. And bandages." She turned away.

Matthew stammered his thanks. Unable to look at her face again, he fixed his eyes on the hem of her robe as it brushed around her bare ankles. His chest swelled with all he couldn't tell her. Just as he was about to bid her goodnight, Reiya's sandaled feet stopped walking.

"Oh, I almost forgot. I'll wash this for you."

Before Matthew could react, she hurried back and picked up his padded armor. It happened to be upside down. To Matthew's horror, the horn slid out, and Reiya caught it with perfect precision.

Matthew almost fell off his stool.

"Oh, no." He raised his hands to yank everything back, only to freeze when she looked up in surprise.

"What?" Her slender fingers tightened around the brown horn. "I know how to wash clothes."

"I-it's not that dirty."

"Really." She raised an eyebrow. "This house smells like a barn."

She gave the horn a shake. Matthew stopped breathing. Thankfully, the cork pressed the lockpicks down to the bottom, and they didn't rattle.

"I'll wipe my gambeson tonight." His voice had turned squeaky. "Please don't bother washing it."

He dared to pluck his padded armor and horn back from her hand. Reiya scowled as he slid the horn back into its pocket and hugged his clothes. A puff of acrid sweat and donkey stench rose to his face. He cringed. How was he going to wipe this clean?

"Good night," he forced himself to say.

"Good night," Reiya muttered. She glanced at Yana, who had been watching with a puzzled frown, before turning back to Matthew. "My roundhouse is next door. Please don't scream again when you bathe."

Both Reiya and Yana walked toward the door. It swung open, and Domilo stood outside with a stunned look on his face.

"Domilo! It's rude to eavesdrop." Reiya ruffled her brother's hair, and Domilo gave Matthew a sorrowful look. Before Matthew could say anything, Reiya shut the door.

Their departing footsteps echoed in his ears. He scowled at his boots. Perhaps the boy had still hoped for a game of chess, but Matthew doubted it would ever happen.

From behind him, Kato spoke again. Matthew sighed and turned around.

"Fine. You don't have to tell me who gave you that...*thing.*" The redhead pushed to his feet. "But if you understood Vasfian, you'd know that they hunt heads because those please their gods the most. Gods like Lenus are supposed to heal Reiya's mum."

The orange glow cast shadows beneath Kato's furrowed brows. Back in Lord Seville's manor, Matthew would've scoffed at all these impossible things the Vasfians believed in. But now, stuck in a roundhouse with no way out, his neck suddenly felt exposed.

"The Vasfians are not easy to rob," Kato continued. "I once had two friends, also half-bloods. The three of us tried to take swords from a tribe that threw swords into a river as an offering. Waste of good weapons, we thought.

So we tried to 'save' them." He lowered his chin. "The Vasfians came out of nowhere and shot all three of us. Only I escaped."

Matthew tried to inhale, but his ribs wouldn't expand.

Kato looked aside and murmured, "And I only survived because of Norman. He found me half dead and carried me to a church. My friends and I were skilled thieves, but we were still caught." His eyes met Matthew's. "Don't be their next head."

Matthew clawed at the padding overlying his deadly secret. Every instinct screamed to hurl the objects off a cliff. The Vasfians had ambushed the Boltans in Brocklesby without hesitation. If they caught him near the black matter, they could kill him and blame the rebels. Abithi certainly seemed capable of such a thing.

Dread churned in his stomach. What was he supposed to do? The safety of his countrymen depended on properly controlling the black matter.

As Matthew sat in silence, pinching the skin between his eyebrows, Kato shuffled around the roundhouse. By the time Matthew looked up, the redhead had changed into his old, threadbare tunic.

"I didn't know I was wearing your friend's clothes," Kato said, setting a food basket by his mattress. "I won't do it again."

He sat cross-legged on his cot and began eating a baked pottage. A lump rose in Matthew's throat. Kato had spoken with a boldness Matthew had only seen in Aelfric. The other servants who tended to him, after he left Normandy and settled in England, had been afraid of criticizing Matthew. To his detriment.

He still didn't know what to do about the black matter, but his filth was unbearable. Matthew stripped off his tunic, dipped it in water, and wiped himself with the cleanest patch. Yet, the rot lay deeper than that.

Kato remained in his fraying clothes and slept with his back turned. Firelight flickered and cast shadows on the walls. In the dimness, Matthew imagined himself crouched before a chest. Shouts pierced the air, followed by Reiya's furious scream. Arrows rained down and pierced him repeatedly. Goosebumps skittered down his arms. He had been fooling himself. Stealing from the Vasfians wasn't just risky. It was suicidal.

And why hadn't Jacques told him about the Danes landing in Ravenser's?

The answer came easily. To Jacques, the Vasfians were not allies worth informing. To Jacques, Matthew was expendable, but Reiya had risked her life to help Aelfric save a "best friend" she'd never met.

Her face appeared in his mind, stern and yet with a glimmer of compassion underneath. A new path took shape. Matthew could defy Jacques' expectations by asking Reiya for advice on how to save his knighthood. They also needed to have an honest conversation about the black matter's whereabouts.

Even if she had it, he'd convince her that the Vasfians and Normans needed to manage it together. No more lies. No more schemes. Her druids might believe the black matter was a valuable offering to their gods, enough to cure Abithi, but they'd have to find an alternative. He and Reiya could take the substance straight to His Excellency without Jacques' meddling. The falcon ring she wore would get them access.

Reiya had worked hard to build an alliance with the Normans. She needed it to feed her people through winter. Matthew would have to take a risk and trust that she'd listen to him. He couldn't abandon children like Domilo to starvation.

There had to be a chance after the *Anuin* ceremony to speak with her privately.

That was it. His mind was made up.

Matthew paced the roundhouse with the blasted horn in his fist. How could he hide the lockpicks before Reiya discovered them? Maybe by burying them? Squatting, he scratched the packed earth with the tip of the horn, but his frantic movements barely made a groove.

Kato sat up on his mattress. "What's that noise?"

Matthew squeezed the wretched horn. "I need to get rid of what's inside. Bury them."

"Hmm." Kato's scowl softened, and he continued in a hushed voice, "Well, don't bury them. You'll leave a mound of overturned dirt, and it'll be obvious."

"Then what do I do?"

The redhead grinned. "First, tell me what changed your mind."

Matthew's mouth twitched. "Reason. Now, how do I get rid of these things?"

"If you can't go down, then go up." Kato's eyebrows shot up as he glanced at the thatched roof. "Hide them in the straw."

"What? You're sure they won't fall?"

"Mm-hmm. I used to hide money I stole in the church's roof." Kato lowered his gaze. "I did it for years and was never caught."

Matthew stood and stared at the roof, his chest heaving. "I don't like this. Got other ideas?"

"You can throw them into the village privy pit, but that isn't smart. You need to stop carrying those things with you. Reiya will check your horn when she lets you out tomorrow."

"How do you know?"

"You're a bad liar." Kato cocked his head. "You looked terrified when she found your horn. We're both lucky she didn't yank off the cork. I guess she respected you enough not to do it."

A chuckle rumbled in Matthew's throat. A thief was criticizing him, an aspiring knight, for having poor lying skills. How much lower could he sink?

He tried not to glower at Kato as the redhead smirked and whispered, "I was awake wondering if I should pickpocket you tonight and shove your lockpicks up there. You saved me that trouble."

Matthew grunted. This ale delivery boy didn't look like much, but he had a good head.

"Fine," Matthew whispered. "Up they go."

The redhead nudged a stool with his foot. Matthew stepped on top and made the mistake of looking down, something he always avoided when mounting a horse. His head spun. Uncorking the horn, he dropped all five lockpicks.

Kato knelt to retrieve them. "Want me to do it?"

With a huff, Matthew jumped down and tossed the horn onto his mattress. Kato moved the stool to the edge of the conical roof and climbed up, his legs wobbling. How many times had his knees been bruised? Matthew hung his head. He had nothing to prove to the younger man. Stepping beside Kato, he steadied the redhead with a hand.

Kato reached into the straw with a determined frown. When he pulled back, the lockpicks were gone.

Grinning, Kato dusted off his hands. Nothing fell.

Matthew gripped his arm and helped him off the stool. "Good. Thanks."

"You're welcome. No one should find those 'til the roof needs fixing." Kato's smile faded. "But just in case, I'm leaving tomorrow with Mils. Abithi scares me."

Matthew held onto his arm. "You're sure? Reiya's warriors will likely head to Ravenser's Point, and I can drop you off in a village on the way."

"I'm sure," Kato murmured. "I was only meant to deliver a letter."

"Where are you going?"

Kato dropped his gaze and squirmed within Matthew's hold. Matthew suddenly understood—someone was waiting for him. Evelyn.

"You're going to Barton-upon-Humber?" Matthew muttered.

"Y-Yes. I still hope Norman will be there."

But Evelyn was the real reason. She had dispatched Kato with her letter and must be anxiously waiting for him in Barton. Ravenser's Point was in the opposite direction from where she'd be.

Matthew narrowed his eyes. A little discouragement was needed. "Did you know Jacques Verdun is the lord of Barton?"

"Yes, but I'm not going there to see him."

Matthew fought a reflexive anger. Trying to keep the redhead away from Evelyn hadn't worked before, and it wouldn't work now. He'd have to let them reunite and reason with his cousin later.

He released Kato. "I hope you find Norman. If not, Evelyn can speak to the soldiers in Barton. They'll help you search."

Kato's face brightened. He nodded, but his cheer faded as he turned toward his mattress. Maybe he was worried about leaving alone.

The least Matthew could do was to give Kato better clothing. He walked to the chest containing Aelfric's clothes and rummaged through it, his eyes smarting. Among the tunics he'd gifted his friend over the years, Matthew found a dark green mantle with a hood. It was just long enough to keep Kato warm.

"Take this for tomorrow," he said, holding it up.

Kato rolled around on his bed and squinted at Matthew's offering. "You're sure?"

"Yes." Matthew's voice cracked. "Aelfric wouldn't mind."

He dropped the mantle into Kato's hands and retreated to his own cot, where he knocked aside the Horn of Evil. Sitting, Matthew stared at the ground. It wasn't safe for anyone to travel alone, but Matthew couldn't make Kato stay. Shoulders heavy, he dressed his hand with the honey and garlic Reiya had given him.

Sleep wouldn't come, though his eyes burned with exhaustion. The mattress smelled of bitter herbs and nothing like his own. He longed for the mornings when he'd brush Lord Seville's horses and stroll along the lake with his best friend. They would try to outdo each other at skipping stones.

He'd gone through so much trouble to protect Aelfric's sister, who turned out not to be his sister at all. Matthew fought against waves of regret as he tossed and turned. There was still honor in keeping his oath. Aelfric had loved *Ali*. Matthew had a duty to save her from becoming a thrall, to hear her story, and to prove Jacques wrong. A merciful soldier was not a dead one.

"You all right?" Kato murmured from his cot.

"I'm...wondering what Aliwyn is doing. I promised Aelfric I'd protect her."

After a pause, Kato said, "She was a kind person. I hope you find her in Ravenser's."

Matthew pinched the embroidered cuffs of the tunic he wore and ran his fingers over Aliwyn's perfect herringbone stitches. Long into the night, he prayed for her safety. She had better still be alive.

Chapter 21

Beneath the Trapdoor

October 2, Aliwyn

Aliwyn paced the tiny, dark privy with squeezing bouts of pain in her chest. Even the revelation of her ugliest secrets had not ended in her death. Even in mercy, Toby had defeated her, and her punishment was living with his decision.

She had been carried there like a corpse in a strange form of farewell, but she wasn't ready to go. The space stank. Aliwyn shoved herself against the door, yet it wouldn't budge. She finally sat in the corner, opposite a privy bucket, with the ship's creaking her only company. The gnawing pain within found no relief. She had lost another person dear to her, even though this time, he wasn't dead.

Why had Toby let her go unscathed? The fact that he refused to tell her only salted her wounds.

She tilted her head back as the frigid floorboards sent chills up her spine. Maybe it was a good thing she hadn't set the ship on fire. No satisfaction came from doing her all to save English villages. She only wanted one person's forgiveness and affection, even if the rest of the world burned. But how could she be so selfish?

For a long time, she could scarcely breathe. The yearning for the heat and strength of Toby's embrace as he'd carried her made her hug her knees until her arms ached.

Heavy footsteps jolted her from her thoughts. Outside the door of the privy, someone was lurching about on unsteady feet. Then came the unmistakable scrape of an object being dragged across the floor.

"Where's the spigot?" a voice slurred. It was Cilebi.

Aliwyn pulled herself into a tighter ball. Why couldn't he be anywhere else?

There was a metallic click and the faint glug of liquid. Cilebi had probably opened the mead barrel and was filling his costrel. He'd already drunk so much since Toby had tried to appease him, and he was still—

A fist pounded on her door, making it jump within its doorframe. Aliwyn gasped.

Cilebi laughed outside. "I'll kill you!"

He couldn't get in, but Aliwyn's heart lodged in her throat as the banging thundered in the room.

"Now I see why the Normans massacred the English," the man shouted. "Weaklings, the lot of you! Toby's the same, too soft to finish even traitors. I hope the Normans do it again! Burn the whole bloody North to ash!"

Weaklings. His words rang in Aliwyn's ears, and she gritted her teeth. This churl of a Norseman. How dare he mock her people's suffering?

The chains rattled as Cilebi continued to laugh and pound on the door. Lightning flashed outside the privy's tiny vent and illuminated the trapdoor's faint outline above her. She had no strength to pull herself up and out, but as Cilebi's incoherent curses echoed in the room, she stepped onto an upside-down bucket. Shaking, she stared at the trapdoor, hoping someone would open it. No one did.

She was trapped. Trapped like Toby when he'd first turned from the law.

His voice echoed in her memories. *Why can you not see...that if I abandon this mission, if I don't shock the Normans into submission, many more Englishmen would die?*

Tears welled in her eyes. Toby had so patiently tried to reason with her. Pride had blinded her then, but now the thought struck her like a blow. King William could repeat the Harrying that Cilebi had described. Nothing stopped the conqueror king from retaliating in this way if the rebellion continued. What if Toby's surprise assault on the Norman ports *would* prevent the Harrying from repeating itself? Could she not, for once, consider his actions the lesser of two evils?

Lightning flashed outside, and thunder rumbled like the hoofbeats of Norman warhorses. In her mind, Aliwyn saw the fires that would burn villages like Brocklesby to the ground. She could hear starving mothers and children weeping over their husbands and fathers lying dead in the reddened snow. All because the revolt dragged on into winter. If Toby's plan worked, if it truly prevented such horror, then all she'd done was break everyone's trust and walk away with nothing.

Aliwyn squeezed her head between her hands. Her ragged breaths shuddered beneath Cilebi's laughter.

After what felt like an eternity, the man's footsteps thudded away. She lifted her sweaty hands from her temples.

"Toby," she croaked.

She wanted to tell him she was sorry and that she understood his reasoning, even if that was the last thing she said.

She called him again, but the rain falling outside drowned out her words. With a trembling hand, she withdrew a pretty pebble she'd collected in Brocklesby and threw it at the trapdoor. A sharp tap echoed in the darkness. She waited, but the door remained shut.

Aliwyn frowned and hurled another pebble. Then another. Meanwhile, Cilebi's footsteps staggered around the hull, and more crates scraped the floorboards. There was a faint creak of hinges as a door somewhere swung open. Was he searching for *more* mead? Aliwyn curled her upper lip and threw another pebble. May that man drink himself into oblivion!

Finally, footsteps shuffled up on deck, and the trapdoor flew open.

She gasped with anticipation. "Toby!"

But it wasn't him.

Zelrin's stark frown appeared in the dim light of a rush lamp as he snapped, "Stop that noise!"

She flinched at the anger in his voice. "Is Toby with you? I just want to talk to—"

"You want to what? Tear him apart again?" Zelrin's flashing eyes latched onto hers. But despite his yelling, his breath shook, and he fell silent for a moment. His face contorted with pain as though she'd stabbed him.

Aliwyn's chest tightened. "I'm sorry—"

"Shut it, you liar." His frown returned in a flash. "For some reason, he still wants to give you this."

Zelrin lunged to the side as though to grab something, and she wrung her hands. Was that...Emma whimpering upstairs? As Aliwyn shook with sobs, something bulky fell through the trapdoor and bounced off her shoulder. She flinched in fear, but the object proved to be only a soft, folded hudfat. When it tumbled beside her, its woolen layers unfurled to reveal a filled costrel and three hard biscuits. The scent of burned pottage drifted forth.

Her hands shook as she reached for it. This was the same sleep sack she had shared with Toby the night before. Remembering the tenderness in his smile that morning pierced her with longing.

"Zel—" she began.

But the trapdoor slammed shut with a dying thud.

Aliwyn's gaze lingered on the provisions, and the weight of Zel's words settled over her. She sank onto her knees, her fingers digging into the cold sheepskin exterior of the hudfat.

For many hours into the night, she lay shaking between the two layers of wool as the ship rocked with the waves. It became so dark she couldn't see her fingers before her face. The thunderstorm outside quieted to a drizzle. Then came a low grunt. The faint sound of footfalls. She froze, listening. More rustling. A few clinks of metal against wood. The sound of someone straining.

Aliwyn tensed and pressed her toes together within the hudfat. It sounded like Cilebi and maybe someone else, but who? The muffled voices of Axlan, Toby, and Zelrin all spoke from upstairs. Emma had claimed to have heard similar noises down here. Maybe this ship *was* haunted by some malevolent spirit. Aliwyn's pulse quickened in the oppressive blackness, but she steeled herself. No. There was no spirit. All she heard were shifting contents and a stumbling, drunk man.

The hinges of a door creaked one more time, then silence. She released a breath, but the unease creeping into her bones kept her wide awake for a long time. Should she alert someone upstairs? But what if they just yelled at her again? Aliwyn squeezed her eyes shut. No one wanted to see her again tonight. If she told anyone about the noises, it would be Toby when he returned the next morning.

It would be the last time she saw him. If she was lucky, she'd also see Emma and Zelrin one more time, but maybe they never wanted to see her again. Her mind numbed and drained, Aliwyn wrapped the hudfat around herself and waited for daylight.

CHAPTER 22
THE CARTOGRAPHER

October 2, Matthew

THE MORNING AFTER KATO hid Matthew's lockpicks, a much-anticipated knock came at the door.

Matthew shot to his feet. Today was the *Anuin*, where he'd prove his worth to Reiya's elders by painting a map. After the ceremony, he'd discuss with Reiya the need to scrutinize the Boltans' chest.

"Matthew?" Reiya called from outside. "Are you dressed?"

With a glance back at Kato, who was beginning to stir, Matthew hurried to the door. "Yes, I'm ready."

He straightened the embroidered mantle he'd found amongst Aelfric's clothes. Outside, the plank barring the exit lifted. The door swung open. A crisp scent of autumn leaves swept inside and blew back Matthew's tangled hair. He squinted in the brilliant morning sunshine.

When his eyesight adjusted, he gulped. Reiya, along with Namanti and Abithi on her stretcher, crowded around the door. The women wore beige robes and crowns of cheerful yellow flowers, but their faces held no emotion.

Matthew smiled faintly. "G-good morning."

Reiya was wearing her axe again. Maybe he should've worn his grungy gambeson.

"Good morning." She gestured at the clay flask Namanti gripped in one hand. "Would you like some tea? We always drink this blend before our dedication ceremony."

"Oh...what was it steeped in?"

"Mint preserved in pine sap and dried mushrooms." Her eyes dropped to his beltline. "Where is your drinking horn?"

"Beside my mattress."

"Go fetch it, please, so I can serve you."

Matthew swallowed. *By the Devil's tail.* Kato had been right about Reiya's suspicions regarding his horn. Matthew's costrel hung at his waist, visible to everyone, but she had not asked for it.

Appearing casual, he strode back into the roundhouse. The cow horn lay jammed beneath the cot. As he approached the smoldering hearth, Kato sat up and rubbed his eyes. Matthew knelt beside his mattress and waited for the redhead to look at him before retrieving the condemning object.

"Thank you," Matthew mouthed.

Kato blinked a few times. He glanced at the Vasfians crowding around the door, and a look of understanding came over his face. He smirked.

Reiya and Namanti entered the roundhouse with searching eyes. The wrinkly older woman struck her staff into the loosened dirt Matthew had dug up, but no one peered up at the roof where Kato had hidden the lockpicks.

Matthew returned to Reiya and uncorked the horn. "Here. Please fill it up."

Both Reiya and Namanti looked inside his horn. Namanti lifted her jug and filled it with mud-colored water. The two women exchanged glances. Reiya smiled, but her grandmother did not. Back by the doorway, Abithi glared at him from her stretcher. Matthew licked his dry lips. They weren't even trying to be subtle. Reiya must've told her relatives about his strange behavior last night, and they'd come to investigate.

Matthew sniffed his tea, which stank like moldy hay. He braced himself and took a sip. The drink tasted bitter, and a minty edge couldn't redeem the flavor.

He gagged. "It's refreshing."

Matthew forced himself to gulp down the liquid. As he slung the horn over his shoulder by its leather strap, Reiya beamed. She was *relieved*. Maybe she had wanted to prove him innocent in front of Namanti, and something twinged behind his ribs. The ceremony had better be short. He wanted to speak with her alone.

"Are you ready to go?" Sunlight brightened her hair into a flaming copper. "I asked someone to prepare a brush and paints for you."

"Yes. Only one last thing." He steadied himself. "Kato is leaving today. Please let him take Mils and depart peacefully."

"I question him first," Abithi called from the stretcher.

The former chieftain waved her hand, and her warriors carried her inside. One bumped the doorframe, but nothing fell from the roof. Matthew dared to breathe again.

Kato pulled his knees to his chest as he sat on his cot. "I have nothing to tell you. I just want my travel bag back, please. Someone took it when I was attacked."

"My mother have it," Abithi said. "Answer my questions, and she return it."

Matthew had no choice but to back away as Abithi's warriors carried her past him.

She shot him a look of disdain. "Leave now, Mattoo."

A ball lodged in his throat. What if she wasn't satisfied with anything Kato told her? When Kato's pleading eyes darted to Matthew, he widened his stance.

"Honorable Abithi, I believe Kato has told you the truth already. Manors are busy places with little room for secrecy. The Boltans shouldn't keep what you call 'fire pebbles' in their home because of how smelly it is."

And why was she so obsessed, anyway, with how the Boltans stored the black matter?

Abithi's jaw tensed. "I still have questions. Please leave."

"Then I'll go." Matthew drew a slow breath. "But regardless of how Kato responds, please give me your word that you'll let him depart safely."

She blinked a few times, her eyes sliding to gaze at him. "I give you my word, but you a Norman. Why you care for half-blood?"

"He—" Matthew's words caught in his throat. "First, thank you for giving me your word. As for Kato, he took care of my cousins after the Boltans attacked my family's ship. For this, I am grateful."

Kato stared at him from his mattress, his arms still locked around his knees and his eyes glimmering with tears.

Matthew turned to him and smiled. "Godspeed."

The younger man lingered in Matthew's mind as he followed Reiya and Namanti out of the roundhouse. Behind them, the door remained shut. Everything appeared peaceful. All the same, unease gnawed at Matthew. Abithi may have given her word to release Kato, but her expression had been full of contempt. Crossing himself, Matthew prayed Kato would travel safely to Barton-upon-Humber.

Namanti soon ambled down another road, presumably to fetch Kato's knapsack. Matthew trailed after Reiya's sandals.

An oxcart carrying bundles of dried fish passed them as they walked, and Reiya turned around with a smile. "So, you do know how to be polite."

Matthew returned a half-grin. He tried to focus on the tasks ahead. Drawing a map. Speaking to Reiya alone.

Morning light brightened the roundhouse roofs as smoke rose from cooking fires. Villagers tended to their herb gardens and chickens amid soft laughter and chatter. Overhead, a flock of geese flew past a mostly cloudy sky.

Matthew squinted at them. "Did your sister tribes send any messenger birds?"

"I was waiting for you to ask." Reiya smiled. "The Ahitan reported that a cargo ship tried to land on their shores. The crew spoke what sounded like Danish."

He scowled. "Tell me more."

"That ship beached in the dead of night, and the crew slung rocks at the Ahitan. The Ahitan fought back."

Matthew sucked in his breath. "Was it the Boltans?"

"See for yourself." Reiya reached into her belt pouch and withdrew a piece of crumpled black cloth. She shook it open; it was the size of her hand and featured the head of a golden griffin, the Boltans' ugly heraldry.

Matthew's mouth fell open. "This—where did the Ahitan find it?"

"North Sea coast, two days' walk south of us. The ship left behind several surcoats with this griffin." She pinched the beast's skull. "The Ahitans cut a piece and sent it with their bird. You told them to look for the golden griffins; it was a brilliant idea." Her brows knit. "Unfortunately...the ship escaped."

"But we know where they're going," Matthew said. The neat stitches running along the griffin's mouth caught his attention, and he reached for the cloth. "Can I see this?"

Reiya passed him the fabric, and Matthew stretched it out to inspect the stitching. It was perfect herringbone, tight at the corners, and finished with a double tuck. The pattern was as distinctive as someone's handwriting.

Matthew's pulse quickened. "This is Aliwyn's handiwork. I recognize it. She always sewed this pattern to mend Aelfric's stockings."

"I recognize it, too." Reiya's mouth twisted with disdain. "Why are you so happy? She's sewing the rebels' clothes."

"Yes, to leave this clue. She wanted us to know the enemy boarded a ship."

Aliwyn was alive. Not only that, but she wanted her allies on land to follow. He held his breath and hoped Reiya's face wouldn't darken on him. She blinked a few times, her long red eyelashes fluttering.

"Think about it," he continued. "Why would the Boltans throw their surcoats overboard and leave a trace of themselves?"

Reiya crossed her arms. Just as he thought he'd lose her, she murmured, "Maybe you're right."

Did she really say that? Matthew sighed with relief. "Then can you do something for me?"

"What?"

"Help me rescue Aliwyn. The Danes won't surrender easily, and I expect chaos." He sucked in his upper lip for a moment. "I won't know the best route to save her until the fighting begins. Can your archers cover me?"

Reiya's face drained of emotion. She turned and walked away.

"Please, Reiya." He strode after her back of cascading ginger hair.

"Aren't you fighting for me?" she called back. "That other woman isn't worth fighting for."

"I'll fight for you, too. Trust me. I want the Boltans dead as much as you do."

Reiya tugged at the cord suspending her whistle. "You admitted yourself the battle will be chaotic. Frankly, I don't see how you'd find *or* save Aliwyn."

"I'll find a way once I get there. I promised Aelfric I'd protect her."

"Even so, what you're doing is reckless."

"You don't want me dead?" He smirked.

Reiya jutted her chin. "I'd like to think I didn't help save an idiot."

Matthew suppressed a chuckle. "If you help me, I'd be more likely to find Aliwyn. And I wager we'll find her kidnapper as well." Matthew waited for Reiya's eyes to lift to his. "I'm talking about finding and killing Tobias. You want his head, right?"

The lines on her face eased, and her fingers wrapped around her axe's handle. "I see your strategy."

"Good." He exhaled. "So, how many archers will you give me?"

"We'll discuss that later. But I'm warning you...you won't like how Aliwyn reacts if she sees Tobias die."

"What do you mean?"

Reiya rolled her eyes. She quickened her pace, and Matthew followed with a scowl. Aliwyn might not want to witness the death of anyone, but this was war. What else did she expect? Within four days, he'd have her back to hear her side of the story.

"About your ships," he said. "Can I help you prepare them after the meeting? I can tar the hull and scrub the deck."

Reiya smiled. "Offer accepted."

Matthew grinned back. He'd speak to her privately then about the chest. Flexing his right hand, he prepared himself for a paintbrush. Then a sword.

He and Reiya passed through the gate of the middle rampart and entered the second level of the village, layered like a halved onion that was regrowing from the center.

The road wound past many roundhouses, a wheelwright's workshop, and a stable. Behind the buildings, a majestic waterfall sometimes revealed itself, its water cascading into the river that curved around Jethran. Porei and

Mils grazed at the edge of the river while Domilo, Nissa, and other children watched from the doorstep of one roundhouse.

A few of them waved. Matthew raised a hand, but it felt awkward. He had never waved to children before.

Reiya watched him with a wistful smile. "Aelfric used to carry those young ones on his shoulder or teach them slinging and English. Now they have someone else, but she doesn't speak English."

"I...I didn't know Aelfric liked children."

"Of course he did. He didn't tell you he wanted to be a father?"

Unease curdled in Matthew's stomach. What else had Aelfric discussed with Reiya but not with him?

"No," he mumbled. "We talked about food and weapons, and chess. Why would we talk about children? We couldn't even find the right woman."

Reiya laughed, and irritation flared within him. Was this...jealousy? He sighed and tried to clear his head. Aelfric was still his best friend, and that was the end of it.

He followed Reiya left around an oak and stepped onto a rocky outcropping. Gulping, he backed away from the ledge. They'd climbed high enough to see above the outer ramparts, and Matthew caught his breath. Charred farmlands stretched to the banks of Jethran's river.

"The Boltans?" he whispered.

"Yes." Her eyes flashed with anger. "We killed many of the men who polluted our springs. They burned our farmland in return."

"I see," Matthew murmured. No wonder Reiya had allied with the Normans for food. "Did the fires smell like rotten eggs?"

"No, not back then. That would've given away their secret too early." She turned to him, her brows knit. "Lenus punishes my people because those who polluted his springs still walk free. Just look at my mother."

Matthew resisted making any comments. He only nodded.

"We'll destroy all the black matter the Boltans possess." Reiya began walking again. "No one in England should possess such a monstrosity. Do you agree, Matthew?"

It seemed a shame to eradicate something powerful before it could be fully understood. All the same, Matthew forced himself to say, "Yes. I agree."

Her anguish over the black matter's existence appeared genuine. So, did she possess it or not? For the hundredth time that morning, Matthew prepared to confront her about the mysterious chest.

He'd fallen behind. Reiya turned to wait, and only then did he really look at her. Her yellow flower crown complemented her wavy locks, and a checkered red and green mantle flowed over her robe. The cloth rippled around her curves. It was nothing like the menswear she wore to battle. When she smiled at him, the melancholy that had filled her eyes vanished. He would've liked to paint a portrait of her.

At once, that awful, tingly feeling he'd experienced last night swirled up his shins again.

Matthew looked away with his shoulder blades cinched together. He was a fool. He'd be laughed out of town if he ever brought home a pagan woman. Purposely falling behind again, he stared at his feet.

They climbed a slope into the innermost circle. The evergreens were so tall that few pockets of sunshine reached the mossy earth. Behind the massive trunks, columns of smoke drifted from the roof of a large rectangular building. Furs adorned the sturdy doorframes.

"This is the chieftain's hall," Reiya said. She led Matthew behind the building. There, massive stones double his height encircled a sandstone platform, as did rows of fallen logs to seat spectators.

Reiya continued, "After the ceremony, my mother and I will go to the sacred grove for a private offering. You should stay here with Domilo."

Matthew glanced behind at the children following him, including Domilo, and nodded.

A gray stone archway marked the entrance to the stone circle. As Matthew was about to enter, something below caught his eye. From where he stood, above the middle ramparts, he could see the village stables. Kato buckled a bridle onto his donkey's muzzle while Abithi and her warriors watched. Namanti stood nearby with a beaten knapsack in hand. It was Kato's, most likely.

He was about to leave after all. A sense of loss tugged at Matthew.

Be safe, Kato.

To Matthew's surprise, Kato and Namanti began talking, gesturing. About what? Abithi started waving her arms as well, and Matthew tensed. He wanted to see Kato exit the village gates for good, but Reiya pulled on his arm. Matthew narrowly missed a bowl of *kubozi* balls on display beside the archway.

He grinned sheepishly as Reiya raised an eyebrow.

"Stay sharp," she said. "The painting board is ready for you on the platform."

Matthew clenched his clammy hands and stepped onto the sandstone platform carved with large, spiraling seashells. In the middle, a wooden board leaned against a rowan tree laden with red berry clusters.

He glanced back. Villagers were settling on the rows of logs. Some were Namanti's apprentices, judging by their striped robes and skull staffs. Others wore checkered red and green mantles and appeared confused to see him at the front. The warriors he'd clashed with in Aliwyn's watermill sat in the first row, scowling over the brim of their drinking horns.

Matthew averted his eyes. Only Reiya's steady gaze reassured him.

He picked up a brush and a clay board grooved with pools of black, red, and blue paint. The heady scent of egg yolk used to mix the paints filled his nose as he gathered a mental image of England's geography. He dipped the horsehair brush in black.

The strokes came faster as he outlined the River Humber. He swirled the brush in water to clean it. The troubles of the world faded as he painted.

Matthew had completed the eastern coast of England with thick lines of black and blue when a woman barked a word in Vasfian.

Matthew whirled around. A druid apprentice lifted his arms and released a roaring chant. The crowd echoed him. Other druids surrounding the platform began pounding their skull staffs against the massive stones encircling the site. Drumbeats joined in. The chant repeated in new words. The air grew hot, and Matthew's stomach flipped. Even the children were shrieking and leaping.

At the back, Abithi's warriors carried her stretcher forward. She seemed to grin at Matthew's bewilderment.

This had to be sorcery, and he was in the thick of it. With a shaking left hand, he crossed himself and turned back to his work. He dabbed red paint where Ravenser's Point would be. Let them yell. It couldn't touch him. He'd wait until it all ended to speak about his map.

But when he saw Reiya standing with her hands raised and her eyes closed, his throat tightened. He needed no reminder of how different she was.

Several more apprentices entered the stone circle. A few carried sacks and crates, while two others carried the watertight black chest. Matthew tried not to stare, but the aspirants stepped onto the stone platform and simply lowered the chest beside him.

He had gotten rid of his lockpicks, but were they now tempting him?

The scent of wild roses floated past his nose. Matthew flinched. Reiya had walked to his side, her brows drawn with concern.

"Are you alright?" she yelled above the noise.

"I-I think so."

"This is a great map. I recognize all the bends in the river." Smiling, she pointed close to the River Humber shoreline. "By the way, Jethran is here."

Matthew smiled back, his pulse racing from the cacophony and now something else that made his face warm. Still shaking, he struggled to paint a circle for Jethran. His brush ended up splattering the board instead, and he cringed. He was too embarrassed to look at Reiya again.

On the other side of the platform, the apprentices rattled their skull staffs over the chests and the sacks they'd brought. They reached into the bag and withdrew coins and jeweled brooches. These spoils glimmered in the sun as the robed men and women lifted them and joined in the chant.

Another apprentice knelt and inserted a sharp, bony tool into the keyhole of the padlock. Matthew's eyes widened. They were opening the chest next to him, just like that?

"This type of prayer only happens before Samhain," Reiya said. "It's supposed to scare away evil spirits."

"I'm sure it scares away many things!" he cried.

She laughed, but Matthew was too tense to appreciate it. A moment later, the padlock of the black chest tumbled onto the stone floor.

The thud shook Matthew to the core. Someone lifted the heavy lid a crack, revealing two swords partially wrapped in blue silk. Silk also lined the interior of the chest. All that silk would cost Matthew over a year's savings. The spoils were certainly valuable, and the Boltans' trade business would've given them access to silk. But would they really risk their necks to deliver silk and swords to Yeaton, the deposed lord of Brocklesby?

Matthew scratched between his brows. Something was amiss.

The apprentice lifted the lid all the way back, and sunlight illuminated symbols painted on the underside. What language was that? Matthew took a step toward the chest, but Reiya walked beside him. He almost tripped.

"Wait," she called out. "Don't sit down yet. You didn't present your map."

Matthew halted and hardened his jaw. The symbols were too small to study from this distance, but he didn't dare get any closer. He scuffled back to the tableau, sniffing the air for any rotten egg stench emitting from the chest. There was none.

"The chanting won't last long," Reiya said reassuringly.

Matthew nodded, but it wasn't the demonic chanting now bothering him. Instinct told him that opening this chest, right before his eyes, was a ruse. *Theatrics* was the word Reiya had used. Was this even the same black chest as the one he'd been watching?

"Is your map finished?" she asked.

He struggled to focus on her face. Could she be hiding something? Yet, the gaze of her green eyes was calm and sincere.

"It's finished," he finally said.

"Then I'll introduce you."

She raised her right hand, and the chanting stopped. Only a steady drumbeat continued as Reiya spoke to the gathering in Vasfian. Matthew's temples throbbed. Abithi's stretcher was tilted so that she could see him directly, and her glare could drill holes.

"You can talk now," Reiya said. "I'll interpret for you."

Matthew forced a smile. He'd better stop gawking at the black chest.

Walking back to his tableau, Matthew gestured at the map he'd painted.

"This is England. Every two handspans is the distance of a morning's walk." Sweat had beaded above his lips, and the stone faces below didn't help. He pointed at the blue marks he'd painted. "Here are Brocklesby, Barton-upon-Humber, and Myton. This river south of Myton is the River Witham."

Reiya interpreted for him. Matthew then tapped the crimson mark at the mouth of the River Humber. "And this is Ravenser's Point. It's a densely forested area where no one lives and is a strategic place for the enemy to meet. But there are also shoals and sandbars nearby for our ships to hide."

Before Reiya could interpret Matthew's words, Abithi declared, "I be chief for ten years before Reiya. I never hear of island you call Ravenser's."

"Understandable." Matthew twirled the paintbrush between his fingers. "Few people live in that area. The islands are often flooded."

"Then why you know about them?"

The background drumbeat matched Matthew's pulse. "My uncle Henri tried to start a trading post on Ravenser's, but the floods destroyed everything. He used to call the islands nearby the Sinking Shoals."

Why couldn't she see he was telling the truth?

"Reirei, you believe him?" Abithi asked. "You be sending ships to speck that no exist. A trap."

Matthew frowned. "Why would I set a trap?"

"I believe him." Reiya gave him a nod. "The Ahitans spotted the Boltans last night, about here." She pointed to the coast south of Ravenser's Point. "Tobias likely sailed the Witham to the North Sea, then turned north past the Ahitans. At this pace, they'll reach Ravenser's Point in four days."

She switched to Vasfian to speak to her people. Abithi spoke as well, and the crowd muttered amongst themselves. No one smiled. Matthew's breath scorched his dry throat. Painting such a detailed map had not earned him any respect. What if he discussed some battle strategy?

"Where are your galleys moored?" he asked, just as Reiya finished speaking.

She turned to him. "They're along the—"

"Reiya!" Abithi shouted.

Matthew only understood his name in the Vasfian that followed, but the distrust in her tone was obvious. His face burned. He was not gathering intelligence about their fleet so he could send the Norman army to destroy them.

"Then I don't need to know where your fleet is," he said. "I only ask because I can suggest hiding places for your galleys."

"I no need suggestions," Abithi snapped. "Tell me what I not know. How many ships your Jacques have? Where he be sending them?"

Matthew hesitated. "Sir Verdun didn't tell me."

"Really?" she leered. "Why you ask about Reiya's ships, but you know nothing about yours?"

Chills tingled down Matthew's face, and cold sorrow pooled in his stomach. There would be no pleasing this woman. Why was he even trying? His vision blurred for a moment, and he blinked hard to focus on Reiya again. At least she was glaring at her mother and not at him.

"Jacques was a despicable man," Reiya said. "He hid information from me as well."

"Then why you take his squire?"

"We talked about this yesterday. Matthew is not Jacques."

Thank you, Reiya. Yet, those words became strangled in his throat. In his mind's eye, he saw his younger self presenting his best drawings to his father. The man simply walked away. Ten years later, that still hurt. Matthew turned and slapped his paintbrush on the paint board.

Reiya continued, "After the feast, I will send scouts to see if Jacques Verdun is approaching Ravenser's as it is drawn on the map. I will also prepare my ships. I'm confident the scouting report will support Matthew's presentation, and that we can set sail tomorrow morning."

She then spoke in Vasfian. The crowd grew louder, like a swarm of hornets lifting from the ground. Matthew itched to get off the platform and out of the village. When Reiya nudged him on the shoulder, he almost toppled over. She approached the platform's edge and beckoned him to follow.

Abithi called out, "Talk to your elders, not Mattoo. Send him to fight. That be all."

Reiya frowned back at her. "I will not blindfold him until battle. What I see, he will see."

She glanced at Matthew, and the sympathy in her gaze stirred him into movement. He followed Reiya toward the last row of logs. There, the soreness of his throat wormed into his consciousness again. He slumped in his seat beside Reiya. Only the warmth of her elbow brushing against his arm reassured him.

"Thanks for that," he said quietly.

"You're welcome." She sat hunched over as though her stomach ached. "Once we set sail, you'll be free. You can roam the deck as you wish."

It was too bad she had to argue with her mother, who read sabotage into everything Matthew did and said.

Sabotage. The word began to haunt him.

On the platform, two apprentices easily lifted the black chest between them. But back in Blaithin, while the tribe was evacuating, two others had *strained* to lift the same chest. How come the chest seemed lighter now?

Abithi's scornful expression dominated his mind. She'd wanted him out of Jethran from the moment they'd met. Was it only because of the way he'd treated his parents, or was she hiding something? He grew hot all over. Maybe she had switched the contents of the chest with something else, then planned the ceremony so he'd see the chest opened with the wrong items inside. Then he'd leave to report that the Vasfians owned nothing of interest...

Matthew snapped back to attention to find the chest gone. The druid apprentices had also vanished. He twisted around to search, but saw only Vasfians with their furry vests whirling around him. Oxen carts with firewood and baskets of orange carrots and dried fish had arrived, and many villagers helped unload the carts.

Shivers rained down his back as the realization sank in—he might soon sail to Ravenser's, but he had also jeopardized his mission to investigate the chest. As soon as he set sail, he'd leave Jethran and the chest behind.

"Food will be ready soon," Reiya said. "Don't faint on me."

He shook his head. "I'm fine. Where are they taking the black chest?"

"To the sacred grove for a private offering, like I'd said."

"Where is that? And what will they do with it?"

She narrowed her eyes, but he was tired of skirting around the matter.

"Please tell me."

Crossing her arms, she muttered, "The sacred grove is at the top of the waterfall. We always throw our offering down the waterfall. For the things that float, we burn them." She bit her lower lip. "Aelfric always thought this practice was a terrible waste."

Matthew rubbed his face with both hands. It was worse than a terrible waste. He switched to French. "Do you understand what I'm saying?"

"If you speak slowly," she said, her jaw tensing. "Why?"

"I saw writing on the underside of that chest's lid," he continued in French. "I think it's important. Can you take me to your sacred grove so I can read it before it's burned?"

She shifted toward him, her frown deepening. "I didn't notice any writing. Why didn't you say anything earlier?"

"I was afraid to." Heaven forbid his hunch was wrong. "I think your family is hiding something from you. That chest used to contain something else."

"How do you know?"

"I saw people struggling to carry the chest in Blaithin, but not anymore. The chest is lighter." He braced himself against the hardening of her gaze. "The writing may tell me what used to be inside."

Reiya drew a slow breath. "I don't know how to say the following in French, but you'd best stay out of my family's affairs."

"Good advice, but can you read?"

She glowered at him. "You've been watching that chest, haven't you?"

Flying Krakens. He had begun the conversation he'd wanted privately with her at the worst place and time. Should he shut his mouth or continue? Reiya turned away from him, and Matthew tensed. He couldn't afford to lose her.

"Do you really believe the Boltans put swords and silk into their chests?" he said. "They were desperate to deliver something to Harold Yeaton. They even trespassed onto your land at night. But Harold wasn't in dire need of silk or swords. It doesn't make sense."

"You didn't answer my question." Her voice was quiet, yet seething. "Have you been tracking my spoils of war?"

Matthew's ribs were so stiff he could scarcely breathe. "Fine. I have been watching that chest, but only because I want the black matter controlled as much as you do. I think there is some in that chest."

"Why do you say that?" Reiya's lips curled back into a snarl. "I ordered it all destroyed. My grandmother picked open that chest last evening just to make sure it contained nothing dangerous, and she told me she only found swords and silk inside." Her cheeks turned red. "You accuse her of lying."

"I don't want to accuse. I only want the truth. If your tribe does have the black matter, one day, one of your villagers will use it, and the truth will come to light. Then our people may fight over—"

Reiya spun away and tightened her arms around her torso. Blood pounded in Matthew's ears as his face burned. So far, the villagers had preoccupied themselves with feeding their fire and pouring water into a cauldron. No one looked their way, but Reiya could easily stand up, make a scene about his prodding, and throw him out of her village.

"I'm not here to accuse you either," he said. "I hope you've seen enough of me to believe that. And I've seen enough of you to know..." He gripped his kneecaps to stop his shaking hands. "That you won't kill me for confronting you."

"Indeed. Very bold of you." She thinned her lips. "I believe my mother and grandmother told the truth, so I have nothing to hide. But I do want to know what the writing said. And to make you stop questioning my integrity."

Her last sentence caught Matthew off guard. Why would she equate her honesty with that of her elders? "I never questioned your integrity. Regardless, will you please take me to the grove?"

Reiya straightened, looked behind her, and played with the torque around her neck. Matthew took the hint and snapped his mouth shut. Two villagers carried Abithi toward the stone circle's exit, close to where he and Reiya sat. The two women exchanged a few words in Vasfian. Matthew pretended to take an interest in the feast preparations before him.

Once Abithi was carried out of earshot, Reiya turned back to him. "They're taking her to the private offering. I told her I'd join her soon."

Matthew tapped his toes. "And me?"

"You had better be good at climbing." She jutted her chin toward the mountain behind the chieftain's house. The waterfall, taller than any castle tower, cascaded down and threw mist into the air. Blood drained from Matthew's face. Why had he not realized that visiting the sacred grove meant going *up*?

"I'll change out of this robe, and then we'll go." Reiya waved her arm. "Yana! Galiden!"

Ahead of them, Yana and the man who had forced entry into Aliwyn's watermill stood from their logs. Reiya called out further instructions while pointing at Matthew. The two warriors hurried to the outskirts of the stone circle and picked up crossbows slung over a post.

Matthew eyed their weapons. "They're coming with us?"

"It's not proper for us to run off by ourselves." Reiya cocked her head. "Rumors will spread."

But there was no need for them to carry weapons when Matthew had none himself. He passed a hand over his face. "Fine. Let's go."

Why the Krakens did the sacred grove have to be on a mountain? Why did Abithi have to leave for the grove at the same time? But this was no time to be afraid. When Reiya stood, Matthew rose beside her and forced his stiff legs to move. Yana and Galiden followed.

CHAPTER 23
THE CHEST

Matthew

IT SURPRISED MATTHEW THAT Reiya was the slowest as they trudged uphill. To catch up with Abithi, their party climbed straight up instead of taking the easier northern path. Matthew followed Yana, while Galiden marched behind him. Each glance back at Reiya increased his unease.

The emerald tunic and leggings she wore appeared comfortable, but she braced her stomach as though in pain. The shadows cast a sickly hue over her usually vibrant complexion. Was she ill? Ignoring Galiden's scowl, Matthew strode downhill to meet her.

"Are you all right?" He spoke over the waterfall's roar and extended a hand. "I don't think you ate anything."

"It's not about food." She kept her eyes lowered. "My grandmother skipped the ceremony. She must be furious that I brought you to the *Anuin*. Now I'm taking you to the sacred grove, and that's even worse."

Matthew's mouth went dry. "Well...thanks for bringing me anyway."

"I'm doing it to ease your mind. Your thoughts will make us lose."

He stared at her. "What are you talking about?"

"You're dense, aren't you?" She walked up to his outstretched hand with a frown. "It's about the chest. If I don't reveal its contents, you won't trust me. How can we fight as allies without trust?"

With this, Reiya brushed past him. Matthew dropped his hand with a sinking feeling in his gut. He didn't trust Abithi or Namanti, but Reiya always spoke as if she and her family were inseparable.

They continued uphill. Matthew's panting made him cough. He sucked water from his costrel as Yana pointed at something below. When everyone paused and began muttering, he looked in the same direction.

The River Humber shimmered in the distance with nearly a dozen Norman longships dotting its surface. Each boasted blue-and-yellow striped sails with Jacques Verdun's half-black, half-red flags fluttering at the stern. The oars moved in perfect unison.

Matthew exhaled sharply. "Those are Jacques' ships. You don't need to send scouts anymore."

"I agree," Reiya turned to walk. "We'll sail east ourselves after we finish here. I have just as many galleys."

Matthew nodded and followed her. If not for the black matter investigation, he would've set sail immediately to find Aliwyn.

His gaze lingered on the ships, and he soon regretted it. The sheer drop below made his stomach lurch. Staggering back, he tripped over a tree root and landed on the ground. The impact sent a wave of pain up his spine. Matthew groaned and doubled over, but worse was knowing three Vasfians had seen him.

"What's wrong?" Reiya asked, kneeling beside him.

He couldn't answer. With his head pressed against his knees, Matthew struggled to swallow the metallic taste flooding his tongue. When Reiya's hand landed on his shoulder, he dared to look up.

Worry lined her features. She brushed back his hair and spread her cool fingers over his forehead. Matthew flinched.

"You're not feverish," she said. "I thought you were getting better."

"I am." He swallowed hard, watching her hand float back to his shoulder. "But I'm...afraid of heights."

He should not have told her that. His cousin Rufus always guffawed whenever Matthew stumbled off his pony. But Reiya didn't laugh.

"I didn't know that," she said quietly.

"My father thrashed me until I agreed to ride horses, but I can't stand anything higher."

Shame burned through him. Nothing triggered his father's anger like watching his son, a future knight, whimper while mounting his pony.

"Everyone fears something." Reiya kept her hand on his shoulder.

"This is different. Even climbing the stairs is difficult."

Reiya clapped him on the back. "But I've seen you climb stairs alone. All soldiers are afraid of something. The courageous ones fight all the same." She paused, meeting his gaze. "It's all right to be afraid."

She smiled, but Matthew only stared at her. His tutors had never spoken that way, and a blush crept up his neck. She was sitting too close.

"We should go," he said hoarsely.

This time, she offered her hand, and Matthew gripped it as he straightened to his full height.

"Look ahead and not back down," she said. "The ground is solid beneath you."

The sensation of her hand lingered as they resumed their climb. His pulse still raced, but he forced his mind elsewhere.

Her braided hair swept over her back. "You tend to look down and imagine yourself falling, don't you?"

"I... How did you know?"

"You draw maps from memory. That means you picture everything, the good and the bad."

She gave him a knowing smile, and Matthew nodded slowly. He had never made such a connection between his passion and his fear.

The slope steepened, forcing them to grab roots and rocks. Pebbles tumbled down close to his face. Matthew tried to conjure pleasant images, but his gaze kept drifting to Reiya.

He eventually hoisted himself up beside her as she sat panting on a tree root.

"You gave me good advice," he said. "Thank you."

Reiya grinned. "Some of what I said, my mother said first."

That sentence ruined everything. Matthew grunted and wiped his sweaty forehead.

"I should've asked you this earlier...what if your mother refuses to let me near the chest? What then?"

"I keep my word. You'll get to look inside."

Despite what she had said, uncertainty lingered in her gaze, and Matthew hardened his jaw. "You're an adult. Why are you afraid of opposing her?"

Reiya stood with sorrow creasing her forehead. "You don't understand. It's part of my upbringing—"

A woman's voice shouted in Vasfian above them. Reiya froze, and so did Yana and Galiden ahead of them. More shouting erupted beyond the trees, out of sight.

He and the Vasfians exchanged bewildered glances. No one appeared between the thick oak trunks along the steep slope.

"Unbelievable." Reiya knit her brows. "They're saying there's a thief in the sacred grove."

Matthew blinked. A thief, today?

"How did a thief get up there?" he asked.

"I don't know, but he's probably after grave goods." Her upper lip twitched. "He will pay. My grandmother just sent apprentices after him."

All the skulls lining the cavern in Blaithin surfaced in Matthew's memories, and he shuddered. "How did your grandmother get up there so fast?"

"She didn't attend the ceremony, remember? I don't know what she was doing."

Namanti's sudden appearance in the grove, along with a thief, filled Matthew with inexplicable unease. Who was this bandit?

"Why are we standing here?" he asked. "Let's help catch him."

"The druids don't need help." Reiya eyed him up and down. "For your sake, we wait here until they finish their head harvest."

A slow, twisting dread wound up Matthew's windpipe. He had a reflexive urge to stop the killing. A dead thief couldn't give answers, and there was something too strange about this situation. "No. Let's go."

When Matthew bolted ahead, Reiya groaned and followed. They ran beneath sun-dappled evergreens, and Matthew's pounding boots made his teeth clatter. He and the Vasfians began scaling another steep section of the mountain. Unlike before, *kubozi* balls and other objects now littered the ground.

"Can you order everyone not to kill the thief?" Matthew shouted as he grabbed onto a protruding rock.

"Why? Robbing a sacred site is a serious offense!" Reiya pointed at a dirty *kubozi* ball lodged between tree roots. "And he's knocking over our displays!"

"But who sent him? He can't talk if he's dead."

Before he finished speaking, crossbows thwacked from above. Matthew ducked on instinct, but no bolts rained down. Instead, more *kubozi* balls and other objects tumbled down the slope. Cheering erupted above Matthew; this time, he recognized Namanti's triumphant shouts.

Matthew hung his head. "Did they shoot the thief?"

His chest heaved with exhaustion. Galiden and Yana climbed ahead of him, but Matthew's sore hand barely gripped the next root.

"No. Caught alive." Reiya knelt on the dirt path above Matthew. She gripped his arm and helped pull him up.

He scrambled onto the road beside her, panting. "Don't kill him. Not before you question him. You're the chief."

Stars popped in and out of his vision, and he could hardly talk while on his hands and knees.

Reiya nibbled on her lip. "All right."

She withdrew the whistle from behind her collar and blew a series of bird-like calls. Matthew exhaled with relief and sat beside her. He pulled on his mantle to cool himself as he surveyed the slope up ahead. Above, where the path traversed the mountain again, a beige stretcher caught his eye. He stiffened.

"I told everyone to halt until I get there," Reiya said, lowering her whistle. Her face was flushed. Was it from exertion or from ordering her grandmother to stop in her tracks?

"Good." Matthew nodded. He wished he could give her some reassurance. "I just saw—"

"Reiya." Abithi's voice rang out from between the trees. "Why did you bring a Norman onto Mount Jethran?"

Matthew had never seen Reiya's eyes so wide and bloodshot, her forehead glistening with sweat.

"Greetings, *Amah*." She performed the circular gesture around her head, even though Abithi was above her and couldn't see.

With a flick of her finger, Reiya motioned for Yana and Galiden to climb the final distance to Abithi. Matthew pushed to his feet, his legs burning. He and Reiya exchanged a tense glance before plodding uphill.

Abithi lay on a stretcher with one stretcher-bearer standing beside her. Next to her was the black chest, so close and yet so unreachable. The stretcher-bearer's stoic face, along with his crossbow, curdled Matthew's stomach. He shouldn't have removed his gambeson.

Abithi's eyes were fixed on Reiya.

"I send help for grandmother to catch robber." She sounded more hurt than angry. "Now not enough people to carry me. Why you order everyone to stop moving? Why you bring Mattoo?"

"He saw writing on the chest that he wanted to read." Reiya stepped forward. "And I want to question the thief."

"You go see thief, but Mattoo go away."

"No. Matthew can read. He gave us important information before. I told him he can look and I keep my word, as you have taught me to."

There was a pause. Abithi's ringed fingers clenched the stretcher posts. "You fool. Mattoo is spy for Jacques! He need go away!"

Matthew froze, and the world turned white for a moment. Reiya shouted back in Vasfian. They argued. Everything was too loud, swelling in his ears, filling his chest with more emotions than he could name. He *was* a spy, but one who wanted to twist his mission around. Who would Reiya side with?

Her face was so red. Was she winning or losing? Just as Matthew wanted to burst with impatience, she turned to Yana and Galiden and muttered something. The two warriors exchanged uneasy glances, then moved to lift Abithi's stretcher.

To Matthew's surprise, Abithi fell silent. Only her seashell necklaces clinked as Yana and Galiden carried her farther uphill. The remaining stretcher-bearer, bewildered, lowered her crossbow and trailed after them.

"Now go look at the chest," Reiya mumbled, her arms braced around her stomach.

Abithi disappeared around a bend. *Good riddance.* Cold sweat prickled Matthew's back.

"Come with me," he said, marching toward the chest.

Her footsteps shuffled after him. Only the two of them remained in the heavy silence. No one opposed him now, but an odd sorrow crept in. He hadn't meant to tear Reiya and her mother apart. He could only reveal the truth and hope she could make amends later.

As he touched the chest, its waxy black surface warmed his fingers and grounded him in his task. Flipping open the latch, he lifted the lid and tilted it back.

The scent of pine tar drifted over him. Columns of symbols adorned the inner lid. Lines, squares, and diagonal brushstrokes formed each complex yet elegant symbol. Some were repeated, giving the writing a sense of rhythm. This must be a language, but one Matthew had never seen before.

What began as awe collapsed into a crushing defeat. He understood nothing. Who wrote this? What would he do now?

Bird calls rang out from the mountaintop, and Reiya groaned. "My mother is calling my grandmother down with the thief. What a mess. Can you hurry?"

Matthew hardly heard her. The symbols blurred in and out of focus with the thudding in his chest. This couldn't be a dead end.

"Can I remove the swords and silk?" he asked hoarsely.

"Why?"

"I don't understand this writing, but maybe there's something readable underneath."

Her forehead crinkled. "I'll take everything out. Then no one can blame you for touching our spoils."

She lifted the silk obscuring the swords. Setting the weapons on the ground, she began removing more silk covering the sides of the chest. Matthew's eyes fell on the swords' hilts. They were metal and embellished with animal heads. The first clue.

"These swords are made in the Danish style, but the writing isn't Danish," he said. "A mismatch."

A slight tremor began on Reiya's lower lip. Looking away, she began folding the silk.

Matthew peered into the empty chest. Its tarred sides were...dusty? He ran a finger along the edge and rubbed off a dark red pigment. Both he and

Reiya stared at his stained finger. Matthew tilted the chest so that sunlight brightened the inner surface at a tangential angle. Faint circular grooves, each the same size and barely touching, appeared carved into the sides.

The more he rubbed, the more writing appeared below the hinges.

His eyebrows shot up with excitement. "I see two languages. Latin and something else I don't understand. But the Latin says, *avoid flames*."

They were finally getting somewhere. On a whim, he sniffed the reddish pigment on his fingers. His mouth fell open.

"Smell this." He held his fingers under her nose, and she recoiled.

"You smelled the rotten eggs, too?" Matthew asked. "And there's the bitterness it leaves in your throat. This is black matter, just tinted red."

Too late, he wiped off his gloating grin. Reiya stared at the empty chest with her cheeks flushed. The fright on her face began to sink in as his own. She hadn't known that the chest contained black matter. She had unwittingly lied to Jacques Verdun. If Matthew reported this finding to his superiors, what would happen to her tribe? He blinked rapidly and tried to calm himself. Now was his chance; now he and Reiya would talk about what to do without her elders' meddling.

"So we know this chest once held black matter," he said. "Now we must find where it went."

But Reiya shot to her feet and spun away.

Matthew stiffened. "Reiya?"

She kept walking uphill with her arms wrapped around her torso. They must be near the sacred grove, as gray stone pillars appeared between the trees above. Footsteps and chanting echoed downhill, and Matthew's stomach knotted. Reiya was walking right back to the people who had lied to her.

He finally bolted and rounded on her.

"Let me help you," he said in Norman French. "I know you believed your relatives, and you're not at fault."

She backed away. "You've proven nothing. The chest could've contained perfume. So what if my mother wanted to keep perfume?"

Matthew barked a laugh. "You think it was a chest of perfume?"

"Why not? Perfume is also flammable. The fire pebbles are black, not maroon. And that stench on your finger could've been from humidity."

"Or your elders are hiding black matter!"

She bared her teeth. "Leave me alone."

She bypassed him again, and panic began quaking through his limbs. Had he misjudged her character? If she couldn't act rationally, then he was dead for pushing this far. It was already too late to run from the Vasfians parading downhill. Wiping his sweaty brow, he hurried after Reiya, who had covered her face with one hand.

His chest tightened. Now he understood. She mourned over a family who had let her down. He understood that all too well.

Forcing himself to run, Matthew blocked her way and dared to reach for her shoulders.

"Let me help you." He rubbed her fur vest with his thumb. "There's still black matter somewhere in your tribe. I can help you find it and destroy it. Then no one can blame you for having it."

Did he mean that? If he destroyed all evidence of the black matter, he'd have nothing to show for his scouting when he faced His Excellency. But Reiya was shaking beneath his hold, her eyes red and tearful, and he didn't know what else to tell her.

"You're wrong," she finally said, her gaze hardening. "You hated your family and you're trying to ruin mine."

Her words sank in like fangs. "What? I don't hate—and I'm not trying to—"

Shouting intensified up on the mountainside. Namanti's voice rang in the clear. "Mattoo!"

With a jolt, Matthew released Reiya's shoulder. Abithi, her stretcher-carriers, and Namanti stood on the ledge above him. The former chief lay with her head turned so she could glower at him. Behind them, the sacred grove's wooden animal statues rose like pikes from the ground.

Reiya had turned her back to him, and Matthew closed his eyes for a moment. He shouldn't have trusted her to hear the truth. What should he do now? Run for his life? Yet, the pain in his stomach so gutted him that he couldn't move.

"Reiya!" Abithi called out. "Look what this Norman bring to our village!"

Namanti raised her arm and beckoned the followers behind her. Two men thrust into view a young man with matted red hair and a green mantle. He'd been gagged, and his flushed face was contorted with fear. Chills swept through Matthew.

"Kato!" he shouted.

With two warriors pinning down his arms, Kato looked like a flimsy scarecrow.

"My mother find lockpicks in his bag before he left," Abithi said. "He hide them in deer bone. He a thief, like his mother. My mother bring him to grove for sacrifice."

Matthew wanted to punch a wall.

"Don't hurt him!" he cried. "You gave me your word!"

"*My* word, yes. But my mother, no."

Matthew gnashed his teeth as Abithi continued in a cool voice, "This Kato should be headless by now, but he run away from my mother and destroy our grove."

"He's also an Englishman!" Matthew shouted. "He's subject to Norman law!"

In the silence that followed, Kato's whimpering reached his ears, and a grin spread on Abithi's face. The kind that made Matthew's skin crawl.

"I have idea," she said. "I ask my mother to give you Kato, but then you both leave my village. Now."

"I'll take him." Matthew said hoarsely. "I'll take him and leave."

Reiya remained silent, and something within Matthew crumbled. He'd been a fool for thinking she could take a stand.

Abithi barked an order in Vasfian, and the warriors restraining Kato let go. He staggered toward Matthew and lost his footing on the slope. With a muffled scream, he fell onto his back and began rolling downhill.

Matthew bolted up the incline toward the figure sliding and kicking through the undergrowth. Reaching out, he caught Kato as he bashed into Matthew's chest. Matthew dug his heels in to stop sliding down and wrapped his arms around the younger man.

"You all right?" Matthew pulled back and patted down Kato's upper arms. "No broken bones?"

Kato shook his head and coughed into the gag around his mouth. Matthew yanked it off. Kato gasped for air. The scratches on his face swelled, and blood pooled below his nose again. Rage surged within Matthew until his vision washed with stars. Abithi had won. She had exploited his concern for Kato and ousted him from her village just as he was about to unravel her plot.

Matthew looked down at Reiya, who stood with a stricken expression on the dirt path below. Uphill, numerous druids with studded clubs and crossbows watched him. Matthew shuddered in a cold sweat. Maybe the only reason they didn't shoot him was because they knew his 'disappearance' would give Jacques the perfect reason to attack their tribe.

Reiya's chest heaved. "Go, Matthew. Quickly."

Reiya. What a sore disappointment. Why had he wasted so much time with her?

Matthew gripped Kato by his upper arms. "Can you walk?"

"I think so," Kato whispered.

Matthew pulled Kato's arm over his shoulder and stood. At any moment, he expected a bolt to pierce the younger man from behind. None came.

The walk down the mountain was a blur. Matthew avoided looking at the village far below and forced himself to keep moving. All the same, his throat swelled with bursts of dread. The Vasfians shuffled behind him, and he kept Kato close by. By the time they walked on flat ground again, Matthew's legs were ready to collapse.

The scent of roasted game for the village feast stirred a hunger he didn't want. Colorful glass ornaments now sparkled from every tree, but Matthew wanted to see everything shattered and in flames and the druids scattering in terror. A string of curses sounded in his head as he imagined the wretched Abithi and Namanti being rolled into their graves.

"Matthew!" Domilo cried.

Matthew's breath hitched. Not now. Not when he was drowning in the blackness of his imagination.

Domilo, Nissa, and two other girls stood by the stable's fence. The boy carried a wooden chess set, a board that could fold in half like a flat box to contain the pieces. The children appeared stunned, and the lump in Matthew's throat grew. He knew who had carved that chess set.

"Are you all right?" Domilo asked. "What happened to Kato?"

Matthew felt Kato shrink against him. Warriors had surrounded them, and Reiya stood nearby. He tightened his arm around Kato and looked away.

"Matthew, take the wagon in the stable," Reiya said. "Hitch it to Porei."

Her expression was emotionless again, the way she had appeared before Jacques. Matthew gritted his teeth and looked toward the feeding troughs, where Porei and Mils grazed by a well and swung their tails in blissful ignorance.

"You're leaving?" Domilo cried in disbelief.

Matthew hardly registered the boy's voice. A stone's throw away but ever-present, Abithi watched from her stretcher with Namanti standing beside her. A dozen druids stood by with their staves. They were a venomous lot. All of them.

"Are you leaving?" Domilo repeated.

The sorrow in his voice tore through Matthew, and he wanted to sink into the ground. Jerking his head toward the feeding troughs, he motioned for Kato to fetch their pack animals.

Reiya walked to Domilo's side and murmured something to him, but Domilo shouted back, "That's not true! I *am* old enough to understand!"

Matthew cringed. Domilo and Reiya continued arguing in Vasfian. By the time he turned toward Domilo with Porei's tether in hand, the boy was gone. Only Reiya stared back at him with bloodshot eyes.

"These two warriors will escort you out," she said.

Matthew glowered at her. He hitched Porei to the cart and motioned for Kato to get on first. With a wary look at Abithi and Namanti, Matthew pressed his hands on the floorboards to climb on board himself.

His nails felt swollen. Painful. Matthew's brows twitched. He hadn't realized how much red pigment remained under his nails, which he hadn't trimmed in weeks. Throwing himself onto the driver's cushion, he rubbed his nose. That signature rotten smell was there.

A grin stretched across his chapped lips. Fate could twist in the most curious of ways. As soon as he was out of this village, he'd collect that pigment in Jacques' horn. It should be enough for Jacques and his hunting dogs to recognize.

He set the wagon into motion. The wheels trundled noisily through the village streets, and the two mounted Vasfians soon passed him to lead.

CHAPTER 24
FROM THE SHADOWS

October 3, Toby

THE MORNING AFTER THE Norman longships sank, Toby swung back the privy door and stiffened. Aliwyn appeared dead. Hazy sunlight entered through the vent hole and illuminated her pale features and sunken eyes as she lay within the hudfat. Only when he knelt did her breathing become noticeable beneath the thick layer of sheepskin and wool.

Relief tingled down his scalp.

"Aliwyn," he murmured.

She remained asleep. At least one of them had gotten some rest. Toby had spent the night reliving the battle against Vincent in his head, wondering if he could've used the thundercrashers' noise and smoke as a distraction while the *Fortuna* escaped. But could they have escaped? He'd never know.

Only one thing was certain. He and Aliwyn needed to separate.

Toby resisted nudging her with his foot. His arms sore from pulling the rigging, he lowered the knapsack he carried beside her and sat instead. Aliwyn looked the same now as when she'd collapsed by the Brocklesby ravine upon hearing of Aelfric's death. He had watched everything while suspended upside down. Although he had pitied her back then, he should've realized her reaction to Aelfric's demise meant the man was not just a co-apprentice. Why had Aelfric lied about Aliwyn being his sister? It didn't matter. The two of them were still close.

Had Matthew ever told Aliwyn who had killed Aelfric? No. Otherwise, she would've delighted in watching Aelfric's murderer get clubbed by lepers days ago. Toby's relationship with her had been doomed from the start, but he had been willfully blind.

With his throat tight, he finally patted her shoulder.

Aliwyn stirred. He couldn't resist running his hand along the length of her forearm. Against all reason, he had longed to feel her delicate frame melt into his arms last night as he'd deliberated over how he'd explain her disappearance to Edward. He had found no suitable solution.

Aliwyn sat up, her hair matted to her forehead and cheeks, and kept her head lowered.

"Get up," he said, standing.

Thankfully, all the shouting last night had rendered his voice gravelly and emotionless.

Aliwyn pushed herself up to stand beside him, the top of her head barely reaching his shoulders.

Toby turned to exit the privy, but she said, "I just wanted to tell you...I hope you end the revolt quickly."

He halted, his jaw hardened. What did she say? Part of him wanted to turn around and chuckle.

"I'm sorry again," she continued. "Even if that doesn't mean anything now."

Heat rose to his face. Did she want forgiveness? The permission to stay? She needed to leave before the winds carrying *Lady Fortuna* toward Driftmere picked up again. Everything she said now only distracted him from the meeting with Prince Cnut that Edward had arranged.

With a jolt, he recalled something he'd forgotten last night.

"Give me Odrianna's cloak," he said.

Aliwyn nodded and pulled the violet cloth off her shoulders. He tried not to inhale the scent of mint and woodsmoke wafting forth, no longer of Odrianna but of *her*. The tunic Aliwyn wore underneath was threadbare over the shoulders. How did someone this delicate manage all she'd done? With a bitter taste in his mouth, Toby picked up the knapsack he'd brought and offered it to her.

"What's this?" she asked.

A water costrel and biscuits and a tunic. Fire striker and kindling. Toby opened his mouth to speak but couldn't inhale through his stiff ribs. The sooner she left, the better.

He exited the privy and hung the cloak on a fishing spear affixed to a pillar. Aliwyn shuffled out after him, her arms wrapped around her stomach.

What if it rained again? What if no one found her within a few days? But he couldn't afford to care anymore.

Aliwyn was walking too slowly. Bracing himself, Toby gripped her bony shoulder and marched her forward.

"Is Cilebi still out there?" she asked.

Toby jutted his chin toward where the Norseman lay asleep in a hudfat, beside one of two pillars close to the staircase.

For all of last night, Toby, Zelrin, Emma, and Axlan had slept under the aftcastle and around the cauldron, which they had dragged underneath and filled with embers. They were still asleep. No one wanted to take shelter in the hull with Cilebi present. Toby sighed quietly. He and Cilebi weren't close, but the Norseman had listened to Toby years ago and given up a life of raiding. Toby should've tried to speak to him last night instead of leaving him to drink.

A rat scurried around the corner of a crate and broke his reverie. He had grown used to seeing them, but Aliwyn pressed against him. He stiffened at her closeness.

"Toby," she whispered. "I wanted to tell you I heard what sounded like two people down here last night."

"You heard rats," he muttered, pulling away. She was still making up lies, trying to stay longer, and he wanted none of it.

"I don't think it was rats—" Aliwyn gasped as another rat raced across the floorboards.

This time, Toby frowned. The longer he looked, the more rodents he saw. Why were they so active during the day? The storm last night shouldn't have flooded the bilge enough to drive them out. Aliwyn raised a sleeve over her nose. It struck him then that the hull smelled worse than the usual rat urine and rotten seaweed, as though someone had opened the door to the bilge. What had Cilebi been doing?

Another rat darted past him. Aliwyn tensed beneath his hold. Her skin was warm beneath her tunic, and it was unbearable. All worries about the bilge escaped his mind.

"Walk faster," he ordered, scowling.

Aliwyn took another tremulous step, and he clenched her elbow to pull her onward. Between the hull's two pillars, gray sunlight spilled from the stairwell's opening ahead and illuminated the rats scurrying around sacks and crates. Finally, a few crawled over the hudfat to the left, where Cilebi slept.

One rodent crawled up his black beard and sniffed his nose. The man didn't move. A bolt of panic pierced the exhaustion blanketing Toby's mind. He released Aliwyn to reach for his sword, but it was too late.

A shadow leaped from behind a stack of boxes and grabbed Aliwyn from behind. She flew back with a muffled scream.

Toby yanked out his weapon and spun around, his heart slamming against his ribs. But his weapon froze midair.

Aliwyn stood rigid with her back pressed against a filthy man's chest. His plump face and beady dark eyes glinted with glee, and seaweed clung to his thinning hair. Toby's stomach dropped. Rochefort. Norman Rochefort, who had attacked Ransley in the woods.

One of his arms locked across Aliwyn's ribs and pinned her arms to her sides. His other hand pressed a dagger just under her chin. A single twitch would slit her throat.

Norman's gaze met Toby's over Aliwyn's shoulder, and a mocking grin curled his lips. "Put down your sword."

He stank of mead and mold. Toby struggled to control his panting. A stowaway had survived for two days on board. It was too late to blame his crew or to hate himself for not searching every corner of the bilge. Aliwyn gasped in panicked bursts, whimpering, her eyes pleading. She had tried to warn him.

Toby stared at her. He couldn't move.

"Sword down," Norman snarled, pressing the dagger deeper. A thin line of red welled at the blade's edge.

Aliwyn squeezed her eyes shut, her legs twitching in vain.

Blood pounded in Toby's ears. He couldn't watch her die.

Crouching, he set his weapon on the planks with a purposeful tap. His gaze flicked upward. *Zel, Axlan, quick!* With trembling fingers, he straightened again. Aliwyn's feet hung above the ground as Norman held her up, slowly strangling her. A familiar axe hung from his waist—Ransley's axe. The one Toby had cleaned yesterday and left carelessly unguarded.

He wanted to strangle himself.

"What do you want?" Toby asked hoarsely. Backing toward the stairwell, he put up his hands. He needed to buy time.

A toothy grin split Norman's face. "The ship is mine. The bishop will love me and make me a knight again. But who needs him, because I'll be a god. Ha! A handsome little god! I can blow up anyone I want!"

The man was drunk, but he had heard everything about the potash compound and wanted it for himself. And Cilebi...Toby glanced at the pillar to the side, where the man's body lay within the hudfat. He was already dead.

Cilebi. Leaving him alone last night had proven fatal. Toby's throat throbbed, but he forced himself to focus. Two men, still alive, slept on deck. He needed to lure Norman upstairs before he killed Aliwyn. But she dangled in Norman's grip, her feet barely scraping the deck. The terror of watching Odrianna get stabbed, her body crumpling just out of his reach, flooded through him again.

Toby's voice cracked as he edged toward the stairs again. "Take what you want. But let her go."

"The cargo is all mine." Norman smirked. "And you all die." He halted beside the pillar opposite Cilebi and looked down at his dagger. "She dies first."

Toby's vision tunneled as he lunged forward; he'd never reach Aliwyn in time. Yet, the moment their gazes locked, her eyes flashed with something sharp. Not fear. *Intent.* She glanced at the pillar before her and to the side, raised both knees to her chest, and slammed her feet against the post.

The impact jolted through the hull. Norman staggered back, his grip loosening as he lost his balance. Aliwyn pulled her arms free and thrashed out of his grasp. She dropped to the floor.

Aliwyn

Aliwyn rolled aside, narrowly missing Norman's slimy boots as he staggered and roared. Her throat burned, and she fingered the fresh wound. The bloody scent of her collar sent a shock up her spine.

She had almost died. Her limbs weak, Aliwyn curled into a ball as footsteps quaked past her—Toby's. She opened her eyes just as he drove forward, locking his arms around Norman and sending him stumbling back onto a stack of crates. The drunk crashed down with a yelp. Wood cracked under his weight. Norman's dagger clattered to the ground and skidded across the floorboards until it stopped within Aliwyn's reach.

"Run!" Toby shouted.

The world seemed to tilt. Toby had no sword; how was he going to fight? Aliwyn had scarcely risen to her knees when Norman kicked Toby in the stomach. His cry of pain wrenched through her heart. She couldn't run. When Norman raised his axe with a manic yell, she grabbed the dagger within her reach and threw it. It flew without direction and fell onto the floorboards again, but Norman glanced at it. His mistake.

Toby surged up and twisted onto all fours. Pivoting on his palms, he swung his leg in a sweeping arc. His heel crashed into Norman's knee and sent him reeling.

Footsteps pounded down the stairs.

"Toby!" Zelrin cried, a knife in hand.

"No! You run!" Toby scrambled to pick up his sword.

Toby's shout had no effect. Zelrin bolted past where Aliwyn lay and into the mayhem. Norman laughed. He turned and swung his axe toward Zelrin, a youngster who would never be his match. Aliwyn screamed as the axe sailed down. It came within a hair of Zelrin as he rolled to the side.

Run. More voices rang from above—Emma's and Axlan's. Shadows shifted down the stairwell as they yelled for Aliwyn to go upstairs, but she was rooted to the floor. The men didn't carry shields. They were going to slaughter each other. She couldn't bear to look at the battle, and the shouting thundered in her ears.

Had Aelfric died in a battle like this while she sat at home wringing her hands?

She was useless again. Tears flooded her eyes, but Toby's pale face as he confronted Norman flashed in her mind's eye. He had been shaking. He had set down his sword for *her*. She couldn't leave him.

Her knees throbbing, she crawled toward Odrianna's cloak and the fishing spear that suspended it.

An arrow thwacked behind her, and Aliwyn covered her head. She dared to look behind her. Another arrow sailed down from the stairwell, then another. Axlan must have been trying to shoot Norman in the chaos, but his last arrow had only forced Toby to duck. As he stumbled back, Zelrin was suddenly exposed behind him.

Norman charged and raised his axe. With a powerful sweep, he hacked Zelrin across the chest and sent him flying. The boy cried out. He fell into a pile of crates, and Aliwyn's vision went white.

Zel! Sobs racked her body. All of her screamed Toby was next. She tore her eyes from the battle and forced herself to move, her knees scraping the floorboards, her heart lodged in her throat, until Odrianna's cloak brushed her cheek. The gentle touch steadied her. Aliwyn clutched the cloth, hauled herself upright, and seized the spear. The cloak fell silently as she spun back toward the battle and bolted.

Where the strength in her limbs came from, Aliwyn didn't know. She only ran, spear held close to her body, the black pebbles scattered from broken crates crunching beneath her feet. Norman had his back turned. Toby blocked all his blows, but each strike of the axe forced him backward. Finally, as her pattering footsteps drew close, Norman pivoted to the side. His eyes widened upon seeing her and the three-pronged tip of her spear. Aliwyn gritted her teeth. She swung the spear forward and thrust for his right hand, the hand wielding the axe.

At the last instant, Norman jerked aside, but Toby's sword swept under his chin. A terrifying howl erupted in the hull. Norman staggered backward. Chills raced down Aliwyn's back, but her eyes remained locked on his hand holding the axe. She spun the spear a quarter-circle and stabbed his hand again.

This time, Norman's weapon came tumbling down.

Blood flashed before Aliwyn. The resistance of someone's flesh against her weapon sent a wave of numbing horror up her arms. She stumbled back until her shoulder struck a post.

Norman was still alive. Toby swiped at his head, but the man ducked. For a moment, they both staggered, arms dangling from exhaustion, the sound of their panting rasping in the suffocating space.

Toby's free hand jerked to where the Vasfian had wounded him days ago, and Aliwyn's breath hitched. She was about to thrust her spear again when Norman grasped his bloody hand and bolted for the stairs.

Toby hobbled after him. A flurry of footsteps pounded up the stairs. In the dying sounds of battle, Aliwyn heard whimpering from the crates.

The spear slipped from her grasp. Zelrin was alive! She stumbled through the broken sacks and found him lying on the ground with a chest crushing one leg. Tears streaked his face.

"Zel!" Aliwyn stooped and tried to lift the chest, but she could hardly move it.

"Help!" she shouted. "Zelrin's trapped!"

Her voice was lost in the creaking floorboards and thundering foot-steps overhead, and sobs again rattled her chest.

"Zel…" She raised a shaky hand toward his face, and he grimaced with a fresh surge of tears. *Thank Heavens he's alive.*

The gambeson he wore day and night had saved him, but some of his ribs must be broken. Aliwyn hooked her hands beneath the chest and tried again to lift. The muscles of her back twinged. She held on to reduce the weight crushing him, but he was too weak to pull himself out, and she couldn't lift any higher. Her temples wanted to burst as she gasped for air.

"Help is coming," she managed to say.

Zelrin stared at her, his face relaxing with what looked like gratitude.

The corners of his lips jerked upward. "Good…aim."

Aliwyn mustered a smile.

More shouting echoed from upstairs. A cry of pain. The twang of arrows being released. Axlan and Toby must be trying to finish Norman, but the shout of victory she yearned for didn't come. Finally, someone kicked along the ship's side. What was going on?

Zelrin closed his eyes, his arms twitching, but all she could do was adjust her grip and hold on. After what felt like an eternity, uneven footsteps thudded down the stairs.

"Toby!" Aliwyn cried.

He rushed to her side, panting. "I lift, you pull him out."

He grabbed the chest's lower edges and lifted, bringing instant relief to Aliwyn's shoulders. This time, the object tilted back enough to clear Zelrin's legs. She crawled behind the youngster's upper body, gathered him into her arms, and gently drew him back. Zelrin squeezed his eyes shut but kept quiet. He was finally freed. Toby released the chest with a thud.

He crawled to Aliwyn's side. Circling an arm around Zelrin's head, he kissed the boy on his temple. "You fought well. I'll be back."

"Is Norman dead?" Aliwyn blurted out. That man was disgusting and ruthless. The fact that she'd thought him just an ordinary peasant back in Brocklesby now terrified her.

Toby bared his teeth as he rose to one knee. "He escaped by canoe. I'm hunting him down. Take care of Zel."

Aliwyn's eyes widened in the darkness. *Dear Heavens.* The thudding sound down the ship's side must've been Norman descending the rope ladder. If he paddled to a town along the Lincolnshire coast, he'd report the rebels' plans and ruin Toby's entire mission.

"Zel!" Emma cried from above.

The girl pattered down the stairs, and Axlan called down the stairwell, "Toby, quick! I lost sight of him!"

Toby planted a hand on a crate, struggling to stand. "I'm coming."

But despite what he said, he pulled the sobbing Emma into his arms as soon as she approached. A knot tightened in Aliwyn's throat. Everything he had worked for was tearing to pieces. Toby loosened Emma's arms from around his neck and turned her toward Aliwyn instead. Glancing at Cilebi's motionless body, his face contorted.

His grief intensified the ache in Aliwyn's chest. Cilebi was already dead. Strangled or smothered, maybe, when she'd heard the strange noises last night.

She reached for Toby's shoulder. "Go. I'll take care of the youngsters."

"The soporific sponge." He blinked rapidly. "There's one more for Zel. Look in my father's belt satchels."

She nodded. As Toby stood, he lifted her hand from his shoulder and squeezed her fingers. The gentleness she had so longed to see again had returned to his eyes, and Aliwyn smiled through her tears. The warmth of his palm shimmered through her as he pulled away and limped for the stairs. A moment later, he vanished onto deck.

The ship rocked to the side with a stuttering groan. A breeze from above chilled the sweat along Aliwyn's hairline.

Lord, please...

She couldn't focus on the next word in her prayer. Upstairs, the capstan creaked as the men reeled in the ship's anchor. They had yet to move the ship that morning, and with only two able-bodied men left, what were the chances *Lady Fortuna* could hunt down a nimble canoe?

Something within Aliwyn whispered that this was the beginning of the end, but she shoved the thought aside. Emma's shoulders, trembling against hers, drew her back to the present. Zelrin had closed his eyes with tension wrinkling his eyelids, and the girl hovered a hand above his head as though afraid to touch him.

Aliwyn pulled the girl close. "We'll take care of Zel. Let's look for that special sponge Toby talked about."

She stood and led the child by her hand. This was not the end.

CHAPTER 25
TO HAVE FAITH

Toby

ZELRIN TURNED HIS HEAD aside with a jerk. "I don't want to sleep."

He lay in a hudfat under the aftcastle, utterly helpless yet still bull-headed. Toby resisted squeezing the damp sponge over his face. "Just inhale. You won't feel the pain anymore."

"That sardin'...you kill him yet?"

Toby sighed. "No. He stole a shield and drifted out of range."

By the time Norman Rochefort had bobbed beyond reach, that stolen shield had been studded with arrows. Toby and Axlan had emptied their quivers, but the churl floated on toward the Lincolnshire coast, untouchable, then took up the canoe's paddles and urged it seaward. The Fortuna wasn't fast enough to chase him down.

I'll get you all whipped and hanged, you wait and see! Norman's taunts still echoed in Toby's mind, and chills rained down his back. Only a short prayer that Edward would know how to manage the situation tempered his surges of dread.

"Sorry I couldn't..." Zelrin flushed, his chest shuddering. "Don't leave me in Driftmere, please."

Toby swallowed as the sponge's sour vapors wafted around him. "I won't."

"P-promise?"

"Promise."

Toby lowered the sponge over Zelrin's nose. The younger man watched him with a trusting tranquility, and Toby blinked the haze from his eyes. With Norman escaped, the bishop's men would soon know that Zelrin was a rebel and not a victim kidnapped for the thrall trade. Even Driftmere's sanctuary was no longer safe for Zelrin to hide in, as it lasted only forty days. The Normans were known to wait outside sanctuaries to arrest asylum seekers.

Toby fought for composure. Without knowing why, he glanced at Aliwyn, who knelt on Zelrin's other side. She'd given the boy mashed herbs to further dull his pain, but blood glistened on her own throat. She, too, would be branded a rebel sympathizer for stabbing Norman.

His shoulders slumping, Toby brushed his hand through Emma's dark curls as she lay beside Zelrin in the hudfat. Her eyes were closed as though trying to shut out everything that had happened. He couldn't with good conscience leave her alone in Driftmere, either.

His arms shook. If he didn't win, he'd die watching everyone hang beside him on the gallows.

"I can hold the sponge for you," Aliwyn said.

Toby blinked back to his senses as Aliwyn reached for the object covering Zelrin's nose.

The boy turned his face aside again to talk. "Ali, you take care of him...and my brother's boots."

She smiled. "I will."

Zelrin's eyes grew glassy, then rolled back and closed. It looked like death, and a rock lodged in Toby's throat. He couldn't look away from the cut extending along Aliwyn's neck, either. Thank Heavens it appeared shallow.

"I'll tend to you soon," he croaked.

Her gaze lifted to his. "Don't worry about me."

Her smile, so out of place and yet so appreciated, washed him with emotions he couldn't name. He'd never seen a peasant woman fight the way she did. Perhaps she had truly aligned herself with his goals, but at a great cost to herself.

"You were very courageous below deck," he murmured. "Thank you."

"Sometimes we have to fight, like you said." Her voice was quiet, yet steady. "Please don't feel guilty about Zel or me. We fought because we wanted to."

Toby inhaled and let her words repeat in his mind.

"Did you mean what you told me this morning?" he whispered. "That you hope I end the revolt quickly?"

"Yes. Every word." Her brows drew as though she were grieved by regrets.

He wanted to believe her. Aliwyn had stayed to fight Norman instead of stealing a canoe for herself during the chaos. The tempest raging within Toby settled somewhat.

Placing a hand on her shoulder, he murmured, "Then you stay on board with me. I'll turn this ship back to Driftmere."

Her sorrow lifted.

He was about to stand when he noticed how her teeth chattered. She had carried the cauldron back onto the hearth to heat water for the sponge, and the aftcastle was no longer warm. Toby unlaced his gambeson. Pulling it off, he held it open to drape over her back.

"Take this for now," he said.

Aliwyn nodded, but as she leaned toward his gambeson, a flicker of wariness crossed her face. Toby lowered his padded armor over her shoulders. Touching her delicate chin, he waited for her eyes to rise to his.

"I won't let Ed hurt you," he said.

Her gaze lingered, clear as starlight on her dirty face. No words passed between them, but the certainty in her expression wove through him like a thread of warmth. He smiled and wished he could wipe away the violet bruise marring her lips.

Pushing himself up again, Toby braced his left side and hobbled toward the open deck. *Edward.* No matter how angry the man might be when he returned, he was still Toby's family. His only living relative. And now Toby had to fetch him.

He squinted in the gray sunlight to find Axlan watching the choppy gray waves by the steering oar. The barrier islands were but faint outlines behind the ship's stern, and the man's expression sagged as he clenched his shortbow.

"Axlan," Toby said. "We'll turn back to Driftmere."

The man glanced at him with bloodshot eyes. "So, you'll let the stowaway go?"

"Yes. It's pointless to pursue him now, but Ed will know what to do."

"Really?" Axlan asked hoarsely. "What makes you so sure?"

"I heard Ed tell my father he has a contingency plan, a smoke signal to change the meeting site. But only he knows the details."

Axlan grunted, still staring at the sea. "All he'll do is yell at you in a mighty big uproar."

Toby clenched his jaw to contain his frustration. Whose fault was it that a Norman had escaped notice for two days? Axlan and the others were supposed to search for stowaways. Yet, one had endured the bilge's squalid conditions, eavesdropped on all their plans, and attacked once the crew had been depleted.

Toby stepped beside Axlan and gripped the oar. "We turn around. *Now.*"

He plunged the wooden blade deep into the water. The ship lurched toward the side of the oar as the current pushed back against it. Toby's arms and upper back throbbed with the strain, but he held firm. Slowly, the *Fortuna* rotated.

Once the ship's bow pointed toward the barrier islands, Toby turned to tie the oar to a belaying pin, then paused. Aliwyn stood behind him, holding two bowls of water. He licked his lips; her role in the anchor's loss must not be repeated.

"Axlan," he said, clenching the rail. "Once Ed returns, we need unity on board. Please don't tell him what happened to the anchor. We simply lost it. I want to keep Aliwyn with me."

Axlan's gaze remained fixed on the distant horizon. "I won't tell. After all, what's the point?"

Toby narrowed his eyes. "What do you mean, what's the point?"

"This ship is cursed." The man's greasy face wrinkled in a frown. "How much more bad luck do you need before you abandon it?"

Unbelievable. Had both he and Zelrin been talking behind his back? Heat rose to Toby's face. "Why abandon it? We still have all our cargo."

"Who cares? We should save ourselves while we still breathe."

Toby shook his head and released the rail. "You're jesting."

"I... I am not." Axlan shifted his weight. "It's over. That stowaway will send the entire Norman army."

Toby wanted to grab the man's shoulders and shake him. "And how did he stay hidden for two days? Who was supposed to search the bilge?"

Axlan backed away. "Me and the others searched, but there were many distractions. We did our best."

"It wasn't good enough!" Toby shouted. He grabbed a belaying pin to control his fist. "And then when that man attacked, all you did was almost shoot *me*. Then you hid behind a post when he ran upstairs!"

He pointed at the aftcastle's four support beams. Emma lay on her side beneath the platform with one hand slapped over her ear. Aliwyn held both bowls close to her waist, her eyes darting anxiously between him and Axlan.

Toby's chest heaved. Refocusing on Axlan, who frowned at his boots, he hung his head.

"I apologize," Toby muttered. So much for asking for unity on board.

Axlan ran a hand over his face. "Toby, we have a rowboat left. Think this through. And Ed...he told me yesterday when you were sleepin' that you didn't exist. He won't be kind when he—"

"Stop," Toby said hoarsely. Unwanted anger again spiked within. "That's between Edward and me. You're dismissed."

The portly man trudged toward the stairs, and Toby closed his eyes for a moment. "I didn't tell you that Cilebi is..."

Axlan's face flushed. "I've guessed that by now."

With heavy footsteps, he descended the stairs. Beside the opening lay Ransley's axe, which Norman had discarded before scrambling down to a canoe. Scenes from the nearly fatal battle flashed in his mind, and Toby squeezed the closest belaying pin.

His legs stiff, he turned back to the sea. The remaining rowboat bobbed behind the vessel, almost out of sight, and the weight of Axlan's words pressed heavily on his shoulders. Both Axlan and Aliwyn distrusted Edward, and yet, Toby had seen a remnant of his goodness in the way he'd treated Ransley. Why couldn't Edward treat his nephew the same way?

The wind was in his favor now, and the closest barrier island rose as a dark shadow in the soot still hovering over the waters. Driftmere lay behind that island.

Edward would be on board soon with all his hired hands. Despite telling himself that help would soon be here, Toby's chest crawled with chills.

For the first time, he pictured himself stepping onto the rowboat with the youngsters, Aliwyn, and Axlan. Yet, all his cargo remained on board, and where would he go? He shook his head and dashed the fantasy from his mind.

A hand rubbed his back. Aliwyn stepped beside him and hooked her arm around his, resting her head against his shoulder. When she lifted the bowl of water toward his lips, Toby gulped it down. He didn't realize how thirsty he'd been. The warm water filling his stomach stirred his hunger, but he didn't want to eat.

"Thanks," he said, handing the bowl back to her. "I'll dress your wound now."

He didn't want to talk to anyone, but Aliwyn deserved better.

Toby ladled fresh water onto his hands to rinse them and purposely moistened his sleeve. He retrieved his orange tin with the mint ointment. His hold was so unsteady that Aliwyn needed to open it for him. With his sleeve, he dabbed the wound on her neck with a deep ache in his own throat. He had almost lost her. Now, without clean and dry linen strips, he couldn't even bandage her injury.

As he put away the tin, Aliwyn looked down at her belt and said, "I wanted to give this back to you."

She withdrew a recorder from her belt pouch and offered it to him. Toby stiffened. The familiar, worn fingerholes and the crucifix Miriam had etched onto its surface used to bring him comfort, but not today. Ransley had only told him last night who his mother was; Ransley had promised her not to tell while she still lived. And now, the recorder only reminded Toby of the one he'd killed, a boy Miriam helped raise and must've considered her other son.

Aelfric had shared a meal at his table almost every day. He listened patiently, had a dry sense of humor, and was in every way the reliable friend Toby had always wanted. That made it even more unbearable when Aelfric had backstabbed him to save someone as violent and senseless as Rufus—Matthew Marcotte.

"Toby?" Aliwyn whispered, her brows drawn with worry. "I didn't mean to upset you."

Toby cleared his throat, but he still sounded as though he were choking. "I don't want it anymore. You can keep it. It looks almost exactly like...like the one Zelrin threw away, doesn't it? Now you have another one."

A frown settled on her face. What felt like icy shards sank into Toby's scalp. There would be no replacement for the one she'd lost. He had conveniently forgotten, since this morning, that Aliwyn was never meant to be his.

"I'll keep it for now," she said, tucking the recorder away. "But I think you'll want it back one day."

Or perhaps not. Sorrow swelled in his chest. He had to tell her the truth about Aelfric's death if he were to court her. Perhaps that would be the last day she'd want to see him. Toby hobbled to the rigging and clenched the rope. They sailed in the right direction, though a thick fog still shrouded where Driftmere must be.

This was no time to tell her. She needed to be focused and strong for whatever lay ahead. So did he.

When Aliwyn tiptoed to his side, her expression anxious and questioning, he said softly, "When this war ends, there are some things I need to tell you."

She pinched her fingertips. "I-Is it because I did something wrong?"

Toby wanted to pull her into his arms, but he held back. "No. It's something I did."

"What? Why can't you tell me now?"

Sweat broke at his hairline, and he searched for anything that could distract her from the conversation. To his surprise, Axlan stood in the stairwell with his balding head protruding through the opening.

"Toby," he said in a small voice, "there's a puddle beside Cilebi."

Toby stepped toward him. "You mean a puddle of blood?"

"No. It's seawater. The hull is leaking."

Toby tensed, and a bitter chuckle shuddered through his ribs. Lightning might as well strike next. Maybe this mission *was* cursed. Only Aliwyn's steadfast hold on his forearm kept his dread at bay.

"What happened?" He hobbled toward the stairwell, taking Aliwyn with him.

"Splinters around the hole," Axlan stammered, his eyes wide with panic. "I think that axe man went too wild."

Toby shook his head. He and Axlan had searched the bilge after Norman's attack to ensure no other stowaways remained. No one had noticed a leak then. He brushed past Axlan and gripped the rail as he descended. Pain shot up his ankle with every step down. He had better be able to plug that leak; he dared not even think about how Edward would react to the news.

A moment later, Toby froze. Why wasn't Axlan following him below deck? Frowning, Toby called up at the older man, "Can you show me the leak?"

"Uh...you'll see it." Axlan ascended and stepped on deck. "I'll steer the ship."

The way he wanted to escape the disaster, again, made Toby bristle.

"No, Axlan," he said. "The steering oar is already fixed in place. Help me carry the crates upstairs so they won't get wet."

With his eyes downcast, Axlan descended the stairs and passed him and Aliwyn. Toby watched him carefully. At least he was obeying orders now.

Hobbling down the steps, Toby almost fell on the last few, but Aliwyn hooked her arm around his and stabilized him. Their creaky footfalls landed in the hull.

She pointed to their right. "It's there."

In the tangential lighting, a pool the length of a greyhound glistened from the hull's edge to Cilebi's body. A thin stream of water flowed down the wooden walls. Toby traced the source to a dent an armspan above the floor.

"The stowaway must've done this." He approached the breach with Aliwyn following.

They crouched by the hole, and Toby picked a splinter off the edge. It was fitting for the damage done by an axe's swing.

"It's small." He sighed as hesitant relief tingled down his arms. "I can plug it until Edward returns for a more permanent fix."

Aliwyn nodded. "Can I help?"

"My father has a hammer and oilcloth. Also some wooden wedges. We need to search through his belongings."

Standing again, he was struck by how calm Aliwyn looked. Was it because she trusted him? Believed he was a good person? Dread coiled in his gut at the fear of losing her once she heard the truth, but all that would have to wait. Right now, he needed her by his side. The icy water seeping through his soles anchored him to the present, and he stepped out of the pool.

Axlan continued to move crates upstairs as Toby and Aliwyn approached Ransley's now-empty straw mattress. His belt lay on top, and Toby drew a slow breath. It didn't feel right to sift through the man's belongings, even if he was dead. Yet, Ransley owned the only repair tools Toby knew of on the vessel.

He and Aliwyn reached the mattress and sat. While she struck flint against steel to light a rush lamp, Toby opened the pouches one by one. Out came a whetstone to sharpen swords, pieces of hard biscuits, and a small coin purse. A few tiny scrolls of parchment, already erased. Nothing useful.

Toby's pulse thrummed as he withdrew a loop of keys. "I'll have to look through his trunk as well."

It was disrespectful, something he never wanted to do. His lower back stiff, Toby knelt by Ransley's small chest of belongings and began trying the keys. The chest clicked open, and both he and Aliwyn resumed searching through the man's clothes.

Ransley's tunics, still scented by the sandalwood he brought from Asia, made Toby hold his breath. He'd give away all of these.

"Toby," Aliwyn said, opening a drawstring satchel from the trunk's corner. "What does oilcloth look like, exactly?"

"It's linen coated in wax to make it water-resistant. Usually dark, sometimes a bit stiff."

He glanced at her, then at the small scrolls she had collected in her hands.

"You're holding parchment letters," he said gently.

"O-oh." Aliwyn began slipping the rolls back into a satchel. But as the rolls turned in her hand, illuminated by the rush lamp, a piece of blue wax glistened from the parchment's surface.

"Wait," he said. *Blue wax?* He knew of only one person whose wax seals were blue.

Aliwyn retrieved the scrolls again and offered them with her thin hands. She smiled. "I think I see two roses. Is it from your friend?"

Toby scooted to her side, the loop of keys falling off his lap with a clatter. Ransley had no reason to keep anything with blue roses. He picked a roll from her hand and turned it in the firelight. The outline of blue roses joined at the stem appeared and faded; most of the wax had been torn off and only pieces remained, but the imprint itself was unmistakable.

This was Evelyn's rose seal. The one she always used.

Toby pinched the wax; it was still pliable. The letter was recent. Could this mean...that Ransley had been hiding her letters? He opened his mouth to breathe, the shock almost paralyzing him.

"Toby?" Aliwyn asked. The tips of her boots pointed toward each other.

"This is..." His fingers shook. "I thought she stopped sending letters after Odrianna died."

"Who?"

"Evelyn." The word burst from his mouth before he could think.

Aliwyn's eyes rounded, and he hung his head. Now she knew a part of his past he never wanted to talk about.

"Evelyn Marcotte?" Aliwyn shifted in her seat. "Matthew's cousin?"

His throat was too tight to speak. The urge to open the letters sent a ripple through his shoulders, but the ship was sinking. He had to fix her first. Toby laid the roll on the straw cot, and Aliwyn soon placed the two remaining ones beside it.

"I'll read them later," he mouthed. Maybe some text remained.

Even if the messages would now destroy him, he had to know.

Toby spun to the chest again and threw out Ransley's clothes. A hammer wrapped in oilcloth finally appeared at the bottom, and he grabbed both objects.

As Toby drove the wooden wedge, wrapped in oilcloth, into the hull's breach, Axlan asked for a break from moving the crates. Toby permitted him to go upstairs. The man ascended, and Toby stood back from the breach with his arms aching and his damp stockings clinging to his calves.

The wedge had reduced the leak to a slow drip. Toby prayed it would hold.

Back at Ransley's mattress, he and Aliwyn sat together. With unsteady hands, he reached for the nearest scroll and opened it. The ink had been hastily scrubbed away, leaving only faded brown Latin words at the bottom edge. It was the language he and Evelyn both knew how to read and write.

Why did you challenge Rufus to a duel? He'll send a thrall...

This was unmistakably her handwriting, and prickly heat crawled up his neck. Evelyn knew. She had known her half-brother would send an innocent man to die instead of fighting himself like an honorable knight should. And she had tried to warn him. *Good Heavens.* He had never received this letter.

Aliwyn shifted closer, but Toby hardly noticed. He grabbed another scroll and pulled it open. Smudged ink marred the second parchment, but a few sentences remained legible.

I spoke to Lord Seville, and he's willing...help you launch an inquest. Please write... I'll bring you to see him. I'm so sorry about Odrianna.

A dull ache began at the back of Toby's head. He had never seen this message, either. Aliwyn rubbed his shoulders until he turned to her.

"What are the letters about?" she whispered.

Worry tightened her expression, and he swallowed. He owed her an explanation.

"Evelyn tried to meet me," he answered. "She tried to help me after Odrianna died. Help me find justice. But Ransley hid her letters."

Aliwyn's forehead wrinkled with sorrow and surprise. "You two were that close?"

"Yes." Toby's whole body trembled. "She was my friend."

"How did she become your friend?"

"I met her at the Marcottes' manor. Ransley dragged me there to yell at Matthew's father after his son broke my arm." Toby sighed, the bittersweet memories making his throat swell. "Evie tried everything to make me smile."

For a moment, the ship's dim lighting blurred. A younger Evelyn darted from the darkness, grinning slyly and jabbing at his stomach. Toby had hated being tickled. Yet, if not for her boldness, he'd have stayed cowering in the Marcottes' church sanctuary while Ransley roared at Matthew's father. This all happened about eight years ago. So much had changed.

"I'm sorry," Aliwyn whispered.

Toby couldn't speak. One last letter remained on the mattress. Maybe there were more he'd never find. With a shaking hand, he picked it up and unfurled it.

Toby, I'm sailing on July...marriage. Can I see you one...

He read it again. And again.

Those were the only words left. But they were enough.

Ransley had intercepted these letters in secret. He had known Evelyn would be on that ship, that her whole family would be aboard. And yet, afterward, he had consoled Toby by saying it was an accident.

Toby's eyes roved the darkness, where every flickering shadow warped into another wounded man staggering onto the Marcottes' deck. Heat seared up his throat.

His instincts had been right. Ransley was a serpent whose fangs dripped with honey. And Edward—had he known about the wedding when he'd joined the slaughter?

The cold indifference Edward had shown the next day, just before sailing for Denmark, answered that well enough. Toby should never have welcomed him back after Aelfric's betrayal.

"Are you all right?" Aliwyn whispered.

Toby looked up at the hull's ceiling. The weight of the ocean seemed to crash over him, and he felt crushed by the need to confess.

"I attacked Rufus' ship to kill him." He turned to her. "I never knew Evelyn and her parents and sister would be on board. My household...my men were out of control. They killed everyone."

Aliwyn's cool hand touched his cheek. He flinched.

"Evelyn and Marie survived," she murmured.

She didn't mention Aelfric's escape. All the Marcotte soldiers had worn nasal-prong helmets. Toby hadn't recognized Aelfric amongst the dead, nor when the man had washed up beside the moat with a festering eye. If only Toby had driven away the Norman loyalist.

Aliwyn brushed his forehead. Her long eyelashes glistened as she stroked his face. Toby didn't deserve her care, and he almost pulled away.

The strangled words heaved from his chest. "Evelyn even convinced a Norman baron to help me. But she must believe I ignored her. She'll never forgive me."

The Normans, even a baron of high standing like Lord Seville, had been willing to help Toby incriminate Rufus Marcotte. To the world, Toby had ignored the Normans' invitation for dialogue. No wonder the Crown had so readily approved Rufus' petition to exile him.

Toby stared blankly at his knees. "If I had known…if I'd had an inquest for Odrianna months ago, I wouldn't be here."

He wouldn't have ingratiated himself with Ransley for funding. Wouldn't have agreed to kidnap Matthew for ransom from Lord Seville. Every poor decision traced back to that one failure.

A fresh surge of rage tightened around Toby's ribs. His family had taken advantage of Odrianna's death to stoke his hatred for those in power, to convince him they all deserved to be destroyed by a fiery new weapon. He had been a fool. Never had he truly questioned why Evelyn's letters had stopped after years of correspondence. He had only assumed she'd sided with her half-brother, Rufus. Now, she was alive, but the way she'd attacked him outside the leper colony left no doubt that she loathed him.

Toby couldn't apologize anymore. It was too late.

"What do you want to do now?" Aliwyn whispered.

What, indeed? Toby blinked, his head spinning. Two days before the meeting with Cnut, his world had shattered along with everything he thought he knew.

Thin fingers intertwined with his. He turned as Aliwyn leaned in and kissed him on the forehead. The warmth of her lips made his own twitch, and her breath cooled the tears flowing down his face. Aliwyn's gaze held his.

"I've tried to control you," she said. "That was wrong. Whatever you choose now, I'm with you."

A wry grin tugged at his mouth, and the salt stung his skin. "I don't know what to do. I only know I've made colossal mistakes." He screwed his eyes shut.

"What if I told you I've done the same?" She gripped his shoulder. "I nearly killed people with my bad medicine."

He raised his head. "What?"

"Before I met you, I'd given up on healing. I didn't know who I was anymore."

"But you're Miriam's successor."

"I was supposed to be, but I couldn't bear the pressure." Tears welled in her eyes. "I made mistake after mistake. Villagers stopped coming to see me. But then things happened…and there was one person in particular who believed in me."

"Who?"

She squeezed his fingers. "You, when I treated your hand."

Toby shook his head in disbelief, but she continued, "I told you I was out of practice, but you told me I was doing the right thing, that I was very skilled. Looking back, it made all the difference. Sometimes you just need one person who believes in you to push onward. For me, that person was you."

A fragile warmth bloomed in his chest, but his hand still trembled within hers. He had only two choices now—abandon the ship with nowhere safe to go, or stay with the same man involved in manipulating him. Neither stilled the tempest inside.

"You asked me to have faith in you, and I do." She placed a hand on his chest, over his heart, and drew closer until her forehead touched his. "Dear Lord, may You give Toby wisdom, even though the outcome of this battle is Yours."

He drew strength from the warmth of her hand. The world narrowed to the pulse beneath her fingertips and how his own breathing steadied to match hers.

He exhaled, leaning into that anchor. "Amen."

Aliwyn slipped her arms over his shoulders and rose to her knees. He followed and encircled his arms around her waist, pulling her flush against him. Time seemed to slow. There were no regrets about the past, no worries about the future. Only the present, with the steady rhythm of her heartbeat against his chest and a warmth that whispered against his skin. The scent of salt and wood smoke drifted from her hair. For a moment, he could forget everything but this closeness.

Yet, the ship's shuddering groans couldn't be ignored. The *Fortuna* would soon reach Driftmere. Toby had little time left to decide whether or not to take the rowboat. The urge for fresh air and clarity spurred the little energy he had left.

Toby pulled back and cupped Aliwyn's cheek with his hand. "Let's go upstairs."

CHAPTER 26
A MERCIFUL SOLDIER

October 2, Matthew

MATTHEW AND THE VASFIANS emerged from the maze of dirt walls around the Jethran hillfort just as the setting sun pierced his eyes. His tired limbs sank into the wagon's floorboards while hunger burned in his stomach. Despite his exhaustion, he kept a sharp glare on the two Vasfians leading him on horseback. He had abandoned his gambeson and cape in the roundhouse, and the terror of getting shot sent fire through his veins.

Kato sat huddled beside the wagon's rear opening and looked outside at Mils, who trotted behind the wagon. Matthew resisted speaking with him. Not until they'd left the Vasfians far behind and he could collect the precious black matter from under his fingernails.

Porei pulled the wagon in a sharp left turn. The view from the driver's seat swerved to an expanse of burned farmland. Vultures circled a sky blotted with thunderclouds in the distance. The two mounted warriors halted ahead of him, and Matthew stopped the wagon a short distance behind. His pulse quickened. He must have been riding through the Vasfian fields the Boltans had destroyed. A moldy stench cloaked the blackened stalks that stretched as far as he could see.

Both Vasfian warriors turned to face them with stark expressions. Matthew clenched his jaw. Reiya's stern face, both proud and condemning, seemed to float over both redheads. They began talking gibberish.

Matthew's gaze darted to Kato. "What are they saying?"

Kato wiped his face in the dimness, and Matthew's mouth filled with sand. He didn't know the younger man had been tearful. Maybe he should've spoken to Kato earlier to calm him down.

"Please interpret," Matthew said as gently as he could.

Kato's chest jerked with uneven breaths. "They told us to follow the River Humber to the closest Norman settlement."

"What is it called?"

Kato spoke to the warriors, who responded in Vasfian. The only word Matthew understood was "Marcottesville."

Matthew huffed, shaking his head. This had to be a cruel joke.

"You must know about Marcottesville," Kato said. "It's your father's manor."

"Yes, I know about it. But I don't want to go there."

Who governed it now that his father was dead? Was it full of people he hadn't seen in seven years? Matthew wasn't ready to see anyone from his past, not until he'd obtained a knight's signet ring and declared himself lord of the manor. Only then would anyone respect this runaway heir.

"What's the next settlement after that?" he grumbled.

Kato interpreted the warriors' response. "Humberston, but we can only get there after sunset."

"That's fine. Plenty of merchants travel on this main road. We'll go to Humberston."

"Uh...they say Reiya wants you to go to Marcottesville."

"Who cares?" he snapped.

Kato shuffled in his seat. "They say they used to trade with Marcottesville."

Matthew smirked, although the Vasfian warriors facing him remained stoic. What was Reiya trying to do by lying? Frederic Marcotte used to rant about how ugly the redheads were when he was drunk.

With a dismissive wave of his hand, Matthew said, "Tell those Vasfians to leave."

Kato spoke to the warriors again. One reached into her saddlebag and withdrew Kato's knapsack and leather sling. Another warrior pulled out Matthew's bulky gambeson, folded and flattened to fit, and tossed it on the ground. His dagger followed.

How dare they treat his belongings like that? As the redheads departed, maneuvering the bellies of their steeds around Matthew's wagon, he almost spat on their legs. The clopping hoofbeats of their mounts receded.

Matthew collected his belongings and set the wagon into motion.

Not much was left in his belt pouches other than a tinderbox, an eating knife, and his dagger. The Boltans had robbed him of his money long ago. His best hope was sheltering at a church with criminals and other unsavory personalities. Matthew growled and hunched over.

The perfectly sanded floorboards he sat upon came into focus. Reiya had sent him away on a solid oak wagon, but why? Something must be wrong with it. Matthew twisted around with a scowl, but there were no signs of rats chewing around the trapdoor. No black and moldy beams about to snap. Anger nonetheless smoldered in his chest. If Reiya had given him this wagon as an apology, it meant nothing to him.

Kato broke into his thoughts. "What are we going to do tomorrow?"

The younger man's haphazardly cut hair stuck up in all directions, and his wide eyes still carried the terror of his narrow escape.

"You can go wherever you want." Matthew tried to relax his frown. "You said Barton-upon-Humber, right?"

"Yes...and you?"

"I have to rejoin my troops at Ravenser's Point."

"You mean rejoin the knight I saw in Brocklesby?"

"Correct." Matthew's nose twitched. "It's the only way I can save Aliwyn and fight the Boltans. I have no troops to support me right now, and no one to lend me a double saddle, armor for Porei, a sword..."

He stopped himself. Naming all that he lacked made everything worse. The clopping hoofbeats and grinding wagon wheels filled the silence. Kato had never looked so melancholy. Matthew wanted to say something reassuring, but nothing came to mind. No one had comforted him when he used to snivel in the dark.

He refocused on driving. His wagon neared the edge of the charred fields, and canyons loomed ahead. Before long, the sunlight vanished behind steep dirt walls, and the wagon rolled into cool shadows. The narrow path they followed branched to the left, where a towering wooden dam stood buttressed by an equally massive pile of boulders. These canyons appeared to be a former ravine, now drained.

It was an excellent hiding place for robbers. Matthew shuddered and urged Porei into a trot.

Soon, plains of tall grass unfurled ahead of them. White-winged gulls swooped and dove over a line of trees, and their harsh cries echoed in his ears. An ox cart, driven by an Englishman, appeared as the path curved left.

Matthew heaved a sigh of relief. They must be drawing close to the River Humber.

"You all right?" Kato asked behind him.

"I'm fine." Matthew pulled gently on the reins so Porei wouldn't exert herself anymore.

"Thanks for getting me out of there."

Matthew said nothing. Looking back, Namanti had wanted Kato's head since he'd entered Jethran. She'd searched through Kato's knapsack for something to condemn him, found his old lockpicks, and dragged him up the mountain before he could leave. It was Matthew's fault for not escorting Kato out of the village before the *Anuin*.

The timid voice behind him spoke again. "I see smoke puffs rising from Jethran. A small puff, then a big long one, over and over. Is it a code?"

Matthew grunted. He settled back in his seat. "Ignore it."

Reiya had sent the signal unique to the two of them, but it was too late.

"What does the code mean?" Kato asked.

"Forget it!"

Matthew heaved a sigh. With Porei now walking at a comfortable pace, he was about to clean the powder from beneath his nails when he heard crying from behind.

He turned. Kato had pulled open his drawstring knapsack. In the dimness, he sat holding a wooden board with his shoulders slumped over.

Matthew swallowed. "What's wrong?"

Kato held up the board, snapped in two with only splinters holding it together. "Namanti must've broken this. It's my license to sell ale for Norman. The only work I've ever had. And if I don't find him at Barton, then..." He drew a sharp breath. "I'll be on the streets again."

Kato's face was drenched with tears, the emotions so raw that Matthew didn't know how to address them. No one in the army would cry this openly. He fought the urge to distance himself even as sympathy stirred within him.

"We don't know where Norman is," he said. "Until we find out, there's no use in fearing the worst." The thought of another person made him sigh. "It's the same for Aliwyn. I've stopped worrying whether she's dead or alive because it changes nothing. I still want to find her."

Kato nodded, but his gaze carried a haunted, vacant look. After what the Vasfians had done to him, it could be many days before he slept well again.

Matthew lowered his eyes. "Want to drive? It'll take your mind off things."

"Oh, yes. I can do that." Kato put his license away.

Matthew tossed him a pouch of walnuts, which he eagerly inverted into his mouth. As Kato scooted into the driver's seat, Matthew smirked at the sight of his bulging cheeks. Kato didn't complain and knew how to eat quickly, like a good soldier.

But Matthew's cheer faded as he put away his emptied walnut bag. The compacted powder under his nails resembled dried blood. Maybe this wasn't far from the truth. This condemning evidence still had to be collected somewhere.

He uncorked the empty cow horn. Steadying it on his thigh, he began scraping under his nails with the other hand. Curls of compact powder fell out. Matthew's stomach turned at the filth, but his plan was working. Soon, the horn held enough material for Jacques's dogs to sniff. He'd send his entire army to Jethran for a search.

Just an hour ago, the thought of Jethran in flames was so satisfying, but now his hands shook. He was going to spill everything.

"Stop the wagon," Matthew called out.

The wagon lurched to a halt. He gasped and grabbed the horn before it tumbled off his thigh.

Kato frowned over his shoulder. "What are you doing?"

"J-just cleaning my nails."

"They're bleeding!"

"They're not."

"Then why are they all red?"

Matthew struggled for a lie to give, but his mouth wouldn't open. Kato dropped the reins, his forehead wrinkled with worry, and crawled under the canopy.

Matthew leaned backward. "Go drive."

Kato ignored him and pulled on his hand for a closer look. Matthew jerked away, but the words burst from his mouth. "It's black matter."

"Black what?"

"Black matter. It's what the Boltans carried in their crates. Their chests carried it, too, but it's red because they mixed pigment into it. That's what I have here."

Kato sniffed Matthew's fingers before jerking back. "Heifers! I smell it. How come it's under your nails?"

Matthew passed a hand over his face. Part of him felt relieved to tell someone, while the other part screamed he was an idiot.

He told Kato what had happened on Mount Jethran, and how the powder was evidence the Mehi had possessed the black matter all along.

"They were hiding it, lying to Jacques Verdun and trying to get rid of me," Matthew muttered. "Well, I'm reporting them. This stuff is dangerous."

Kato shuffled in his seat. "Was this why you had lockpicks? To steal what you call 'black matter' from the Mehi?"

Drat. Kato sure made the connection quickly. Matthew shuffled in his seat, but there was no use in hiding his motivations now.

"Yes," he muttered. "Jacques ordered me to do it. He accused me of deserting the army, and I won't get my knighthood restored unless I bring him some black matter."

"So, this is why you want to see him again."

The judgment on his face was obvious. The last thing Matthew needed was someone challenging his decisions. Quelling a surge of irritation, he simply nodded.

Matthew finished scraping out his last nail, corked the horn, and turned his back to his passenger. He gritted his teeth when Kato spoke again.

"Can your teacher help you?"

"Lord Seville is probably still in Norwich because of the rebellion. And no, this is not something he can resolve."

"But you saw what Jacques did to Aliwyn's watermill. He's not a good knight. He robs the people he's supposed to protect. What'll he do to the Mehi tribe?"

"Why do you care?" Matthew growled. "The Mehi almost killed you."

There was a pause. Then Kato said softly, "The Vasfian children did nothing to deserve what's coming."

Matthew spun around. "Stop trying to make me feel guilty. If you don't have any better ideas, then shut your mouth."

Kato met his glare with a boldness that Matthew didn't want to acknowledge. He slung the horn back over one shoulder and crawled to the driver's seat, his fists pounding the floorboards.

"I looked at the chest with Reiya, but she sided with her family. She ignored everything I said. Now they'll all face the consequences."

The pain behind Matthew's ribs deepened. Fear for her tribe's welfare was one reason he'd dared to confront her in the first place. He had tried to connect with her in earnest. So much for that. A merciful soldier may not be a dead one, but he was an exhausted, hungry, and wretchedly stupid man.

Matthew threw himself onto the driver's cushion and grabbed the reins. Porei trotted onward with her mane whipping in the wind. In the distance, the gray River Humber flowed behind a thin strip of evergreens. The sun had disappeared behind a blanket of clouds. Wind carrying the odd mix of horse manure and evergreens plastered Matthew's sweaty tunic to his chest. Other wagons sped past in a flurry of clopping hooves and dirt clouds to escape the impending rain.

A storm. Matthew grinned wryly to himself. Nothing worked in his favor. Soon, the roads would become slick with mud.

The rocking wagon shook him out of slumber repeatedly, and sipping the last of his water didn't soothe his throat. Why did he have to deal with the black matter? Wasn't there someone else more competent?

As lightning flashed in the distance, the wooden ramparts of a manorial village peeked through the treetops ahead. It must be Marcottesville. It was bigger than he'd expected and probably full of people who'd known him as a boy. People he wasn't ready to see. Matthew's teeth chattered. Now, with this storm, could he still make it to Humberston?

The sky dimmed into a glowing, haunting shade of gray. The rain began as a drizzle, but soon intensified into a downpour that undulated with the wind. Droplets struck the canvas overhead in a deafening cacophony. Porei neighed, slowed down, and finally halted.

Matthew suppressed a flare of panic. He clicked his tongue to encourage her. "We're almost there."

Mils brayed behind the cart instead, and Porei only lowered her head with a sputtering sound. Matthew's stomach sank. He reached out and patted her on the flank. If only he could offer her a warm barn and some feed right now.

Kato sneezed several times behind him, and Matthew turned around. The younger man sat on the wagon's trapdoor and pulled on his mantle, which wasn't long enough to cover his knees. Dirt and blood streaked the linen strips of his stockings.

"Why are we stopped?" Kato squinted in the blustering wind.

"Porei needs to rest. Then we'll continue."

"You're still bent on reaching Humberston?"

"Yes. It's just a little rain." Matthew reached for his gambeson and threw it over his shoulders. Thunder rumbled overhead, and he chuckled bitterly. "Haven't you heard? Good fortune follows me everywhere."

A flash of lightning lit half of Kato's face. He appeared even more scrawny than he had that morning, and Matthew struggled to remain stoic. Had Kato not been embroiled in the Marcottes' problems, maybe he'd still be happily delivering ale somewhere.

The redhead scowled at the storm. Then he said something that made Matthew stiffen.

"Have you thought about asking the Heavens for guidance?"

"You mean pray?" Matthew laughed. "No."

He sat sideways, his jaw hardened. They stared at each other until the words surged from Matthew's chest. "I used to have a friend who encouraged me to pray. He died last week. I don't have much to say to God right now."

Kato tightened his arms around his knees. "I'm...I'm sorry about Aelfric."

There was no way to respond. Matthew turned back to the road and slouched.

Kato soon crawled forward to sit beside him. He offered Matthew an orange tin, saying it was ointment Evelyn had given him in Brocklesby. Matthew smeared the stuff on his hand without looking up. Would Kato ask more questions? Did he pester Norman this way, too? And still, Matthew didn't have the heart to send Kato away.

Kato's lingering smile made Matthew's windpipe twist. Soon after, the younger man retrieved a bucket from the canopy to catch rainwater dripping from the overhang. Too distraught to acknowledge his thirst, Matthew drank the entire offering with his gaze lowered.

Then Kato screamed behind him.

Matthew flailed his arms, and the bucket went flying. "What? What happened?"

CHAPTER 27
CLAY APPLES

Matthew

THE FLOORBOARDS QUAKED AS Kato scrambled to his feet. He pointed at the trapdoor. "There's noise! Down there!"

"A rat?"

"A *giant* rat!"

By the Devil's tail. Matthew sneezed into his sleeve and pulled Kato behind him. Something told him that there was no rat. If only he had a lamp! Withdrawing his dagger, Matthew tiptoed toward the trapdoor. The sound of rain drumming on the canopy filled the dark space.

Then there was a thump beneath the floorboards, and Matthew's chest squeezed. But was that...whimpering? Finally, he knelt, and a child's crying reached his ears.

"Domilo?" His jaw dropped.

"I can't get out! Let me out!"

Now he was certain it was Domilo. Matthew flipped back the metal latch securing the door and lifted it. Domilo lay on his side with his limbs folded in the rectangular compartment below. His tearful eyes darted between Matthew and Kato. The boy must've overheard everything they'd said.

Matthew's stomach twisted, and he could barely speak. "What are you doing here?"

"I saw the way you were looking at my sister. I knew something bad would happen." Domilo's chin quivered. "Please don't get Reiya in trouble."

This reckless prankster! Matthew shook his head, his chest heaving with flashes of chills and heat. But yelling at the boy would serve no good. "You... I'll help you get out."

He offered his hand. The boy gripped it as he sat up and scrambled onto the floorboards. At least the jostling wagon hadn't seemed to hurt him. Domilo crawled beside Kato, who watched the whole scene with bewilderment.

"Can I have water?" Domilo wiped his cheeks with the back of a hand.

Kato brought over the bucket and helped Domilo drink from it. As the boy finished, Kato tucked the object under his arm.

"Are you all right?" Kato asked.

Domilo nodded, then glanced at Matthew and shrank in his seat. "I...I was afraid to come out."

"Right you are," Matthew said between his teeth. "Your whole family must be looking for you. You're in dire trouble."

The boy hugged his knees, his brows jerking between a scowl and an expression of terror. "Maybe, but you're getting us all into bigger trouble."

Kato sighed. He scooted toward the driver's cushion. "I'll drive. You two talk."

A moment later, the wagon resumed its course.

Matthew sat glaring at his new problem. How could he take the boy home without seeing any of the loathsome Vasfians again? Matthew's jaw worked until fresh tears streaked down Domilo's face. The memory of sobbing in front of an adult who never reacted stole into Matthew's mind. A sliver of him acknowledged the grit in this boy.

"Your family is hiding something very dangerous," Matthew muttered. "That something can destroy villages and harbors in a few hours. The fact that your elders are hiding it makes me suspect they'll use it against my king. I can't let this go."

"Can you talk to my sister?"

"I already did. She wouldn't listen."

"But try again, *please.*"

Matthew opened his mouth to respond, only to suck in the scent of wild roses wafting from Domilo. Was it from hugging his sister? Was it because she washed his clothes? A grief he didn't understand sank into him.

"You didn't see how she behaved on Mount Jethran," Matthew mumbled. "Seeing her again won't make a difference."

"Yes, it will, because I'm here. I'll tell her you were right about the chests being emptied before the ceremony."

Matthew looked up. "What?"

"I saw my grandma open the chest last night, when she wasn't supposed to." The boy's eyes grew steely, almost scornful. "She took out some clay apples."

"Clay apples?"

"Yes. She emptied those apples into baskets we use for *kubozi* balls. She and one of her students carried them away."

Matthew scratched between his brows. A runaway Vasfian boy, and now clay apples. He searched Domilo's face for any signs of deceit, but the boy remained solemn.

"I don't believe this," Matthew said. "The Boltans would never haul around balls of clay."

"But it's what I saw. The balls were dark red, like old apples. And they had a cork that looked like an apple's stem."

A moment of clarity struck. Matthew had seen circular grooves on the chest's inner surface. Each groove had been the size of his fist, but at the time, they hadn't made sense. He rubbed the stubble on his chin. Now he had to reconcile Domilo's report with his absolute conviction that the chest held black matter, tinted red. Clay vessels often stored perfume, mead, or oil, and the ones Domilo had seen were corked...

"So those 'clay apples' could be containers for black matter," Matthew muttered.

Domilo sucked in his lower lip. Maybe he regretted saying so much.

Matthew's eyes slid to Kato. "Did you see anything of the sort before? Maybe when you sold ale to the Boltans?"

Kato shook his head.

"Tell me the truth, Kato."

"That *is* the truth," Kato answered, his expression blank.

The two of them frowned at each other, and Matthew looked away first. There was no use in trying to draw blood from a stone.

Domilo sniffled. "I wanted to tell my sister everything my grandmother did. I waited for Reiya outside your roundhouse last night, but she opened the door looking so angry to see me. I got scared."

Matthew remembered seeing the boy standing outside and looking anxious. "But even if you told on your grandmother, it would've made no difference. Reiya is blind to her faults."

"Please talk to her again. She didn't want to hide anything. She even had the crates of stinky stuff destroyed right after finding them and made *Amah* and my grandma mad. So mad that they made her move out."

Matthew chewed on his tongue, and the words didn't stick. The boy's eyes were identical to Reiya's, and all he could hear was her yelling at him, accusing him of making her hate her family...

"Grandmother's been trying everything to make *Amah* walk again," Domilo said. "Nothing's working, but she told her apprentice the clay apples are special. They'll finally make Lenus and the other gods happy so they won't be mad about the dirty springs anymore. Then they'll heal *Amah*."

Matthew jammed the side of his fist into his eye. The Vasfian rituals would never work. There was nothing magical about the Boltans or anything they produced. The rebels must've concealed black matter in airtight clay vessels. This way, they could infiltrate towns at night, ignite them in a flash, and escape. Maybe the crates of black matter were all destined to fill clay balls. His temples began to pulse.

The Danes were coming to meet the Boltans for trading, and Matthew could guess what they'd exchange. He couldn't manage this. He needed to notify his superiors.

"I can't trust your sister again," Matthew said, his breath scorching. "She's always surrounded by warriors. They'd shoot me. All I know is that you need to go home. I'll find someone else to take you."

Domilo's face crumpled, and Matthew looked away. "Kato, let me drive."

Kato had been sitting sideways and watching them. He crawled toward Domilo, and the sympathy in his eyes made Matthew bristle. What was wrong with him? Domilo's grandmother had almost killed him!

Matthew shoved past the younger man and grabbed the reins.

Forget what Kato thought. Matthew had a solution to his problems. The Marcottesville bailiff would surely recognize him and obey Matthew's orders. He'd ask the man to bring Domilo home first thing tomorrow morning. Matthew would then continue to Ravenser's and meet Jacques.

"We're going to Marcottesville!" he declared.

"Oh, so not Humberston?" Kato called back.

He shouldn't sound so hopeful. Matthew only chose Marcottesville because he'd find someone there to deal with Domilo.

Questions swirled in his mind. How would the peasants who once served his father receive him? Would they throw rocks because Matthew had been such a bad son?

Porei's hooves clopped onto hollow floorboards as the wagon rolled onto a series of wooden bridges leading to Marcottesville. The rain's raw scent reached his nostrils. This was it. He'd soon face people he'd avoided for seven years. Matthew tried to stop shivering.

Two guard towers of the Marcottesville ramparts loomed in the foreground of a darkening sky. Atop each tower, the bishop's blue and yellow flags flew alongside the Marcottes' heraldry. It was a relief to see his family's familiar white flag with a red lion, but uncertainty nonetheless gnawed within Matthew. So much hinged on his hope that the bailiff would recognize him at all.

Domilo spoke again, quietly. "Your Papa would be so sad at what you're doing."

"Don't talk about my father!" Matthew shouted.

But a part of him crumbled inside. Tomorrow, he'd turn in Jacques' horn with the evidence. Tomorrow, he'd ruin the boy's life.

The faces of all the Vasfian children paraded before his eyes, followed by visions of the children huddled outside Brocklesby, who couldn't go home. Their faces had been so small and tender, fearful when their future should've been certain. Like Kato had said, they couldn't be blamed for what their parents did.

What was Matthew going to do?

CHAPTER 28
CLARITY

October 3, Toby

AN OMINOUS STENCH ACCOSTED Toby's senses on the way back up the stairs. It was the first sign that something was wrong.

He had been below deck for longer than he'd intended to read Evelyn's letters. As Aliwyn stepped on deck beside him, he gave her a look of warning and pulled her behind him.

Powerful gusts blew soot past his watering eyes. Its ashen particles clung to his throat. The splashing sea was hardly visible beyond the ship's edge. Where was this smoke coming from? It couldn't have blown all the way here from Myton?

"Axlan!" he shouted. "Did you see another fire—"

But the steering oar lay limp within its wooden bracket. The Englishman was gone.

Toby tensed. He rushed to the aftcastle, where Emma and Zelrin lay within the same hudfat with their eyes closed. Kneeling, Toby touched their necks. Both were breathing and warm beneath his fingers. *Only sleeping.* He sighed with relief, then searched the deck again for Axlan.

Aliwyn crouched beside Toby and touched his elbow.

"Where is the rope ladder?" she asked, frowning.

Toby turned to where the object used to be folded between the hudfats. It had vanished. Realization then struck like a thunderbolt—Axlan had escaped. Shooting to his feet, Toby lunged for the back rail and looked over its edge.

The rope ladder dangled over the ship's outer side. Axlan stared up at him, his face rigid with terror as he clung to an upper rung of the ladder. Below, the rowboat lurched with each swelling wave and tossed too violently for anyone to board.

Toby reached down and grabbed the man's shoulders. "How could you do this?"

"P-Please don't hurt me!" Axlan cried. His thinning blonde hair whipped about his forehead. "You wouldn't listen. I didn't know what to do!"

Toby's vision blurred at the edges. Aelfric's equally frightened expression flashed in his memory. Another betrayal. Another surge of rage that threatened to blind him. This time, Toby gritted his teeth and forced it down.

"Come up," he said. "I won't hurt you."

A wave slammed the rowboat against the hull with a sickening thud, and Axlan yelped. Toby gripped the man's upper arms and pulled. Axlan finally relented. He heaved his weight up over the rail and onto the deck.

Landing in a sputtering heap, he rose to his knees and put up his hands. "I'm sorry. But Driftmere's burning, did you see?"

Toby blinked. He stumbled into Aliwyn, and she huddled close to him.

"Too much violence." Axlan's reddened face contorted. "Too much. I want out."

Toby turned toward the ship's bow, his body feeling strangely foreign. For what seemed like an eternity, smoke drifted in thick torrents in the distance, but an opening revealed the familiar rocky cliffs he used to stand upon as a boy, eager for Uncle Ed to arrive. Numerous canoes and sailboats dotted the water's surface as they fled the island.

An icy pain began in the pit of Toby's stomach. Edward had reverted to his days as a Norseman.

"He promised he wouldn't do this," Toby murmured.

Axlan rubbed his head. "I was afraid to tell ya, but I saw the hired hands opening a thundercrasher chest downstairs and reaching inside."

Toby swallowed, his throat raw, as the faces of Driftmere haunted him. Brother Dunstan, smelling of tallow and parchment, hummed over the bylaws he copied. Brother Claude, the gruff Norman, passed blankets to shivering boys and drilled them in French. The other brothers collected alms at daybreak while fishermen mended nets by the docks. Who had survived?

"Edward means a lot to you," Axlan said, his brows drawn. "How could I tell you?"

Toby wiped his wet eyes. He could still see the stone chapel, the stable's weathered beams, and the cottage nearby with its crooked door. He could hear the laughter of village children as they chased wild seabirds on the beach. All of it was wreathed in fire.

But this was no time to collapse and mourn.

Beside him, Aliwyn said in a trembling voice, "I'm so sorry."

Toby ducked his head. He prayed for everyone's safety.

"It's not your fault," he said hoarsely.

"But I told Edward that Ransley could still be saved," Aliwyn murmured. "He must've gotten so angry when he found out—"

"It's not your fault. Ed is responsible for his actions."

Anger seared in Toby's chest. Edward must've accessed Ransley's loop of keys. He must've told his men to steal what Toby had worked for months to recreate.

"Ali," Toby said, "can you bring me that loop of keys I used earlier?"

She squeezed his upper arm for a moment before darting for the stairwell.

Toby shifted back to Axlan, who was still kneeling before him, and croaked, "Where were you planning to take the rowboat?"

"Well...Saltfleet. I still have friends there, and they send trading ships to Scotland every week. Figured I'd board one."

Scotland. It was a country not embroiled in war with England, at least not right now. Toby's gaze refocused on Aliwyn, who had stopped just before descending the stairs. The mention of Scotland made her eyes widen, and a smile tugged at her lips. Perhaps she wanted to go.

As she pattered down the steps, Toby lowered himself beside Axlan. The possibility of escaping to Scotland cast a numbing and comforting spell, even over him.

"You're sure you can make it?" he asked.

"Oh, yes. Yes, Toby." Axlan shifted closer, his breaths quickening. He clapped his hands over Toby's shoulders. "Come with me, won't you? And bring the other three. Together, we look like a family. A refugee family! It would be much easier to escape and settle in Scotland."

Toby couldn't resist a smile. Indeed, they'd resemble a household traveling together, with Axlan as his father, Aliwyn as his wife, and Zelrin and Emma as his siblings.

The longing was visceral, and his throat tightened until he could hardly speak. "But that will leave Ed with all the cargo," he whispered.

"Oh, to blazes with the cargo." Axlan waved a hand. "You have nothing to do with it anymore."

But that wasn't true. Toby had smuggled a sample into England, painstakingly tested it, and unlocked the means to reproduce it. Yet, he'd never stopped to consider how something so powerful would warp the people who wielded it. He had felt that addictive rush of superiority himself when he attacked Vincent. Now, his uncle had used the substance on innocent people Toby once visited, ate with, and slept beside.

I'll be a god...a handsome little god! I can blow up anyone I want!

The words of the drunken stowaway rang in Toby's mind. Ranting or not, Norman Rochefort's words had reflected the truth. Absolute power corrupted without fail.

The compound wouldn't be forgotten after this rebellion. It would spread. Its production would grow. War would follow, then another, then another, because killing was now easier than ever. Each generation would give birth to more ruthless tyrants.

And in England, Toby would be the one who had set it all in motion, unless he found a way to destroy what he'd started.

Aliwyn returned with the loop of keys and dropped it into his hand.

"Were you talking about Scotland?" she asked eagerly.

Axlan grinned. "Yes. About going to Scotland!"

"Really?"

The two continued talking in excited voices, but Toby only flipped through the keys and scrutinized each one.

He had not noticed it earlier, but Ransley's master key to unlock the thundercrasher chests was missing. Only Edward could've identified it amongst the two dozen keys Ransley owned. Toby checked his own key ring strapped to his belt. His master key also was gone. Stolen, perhaps overnight.

Edward wanted absolute control.

The Uncle Ed Toby had known was dead. It didn't matter if Toby had loved him. Standing, Toby pocketed the keys, hoping Aliwyn and Axlan wouldn't notice how he could barely control his hands. He limped toward the ship's bow with the smoke's vile stench blowing past him and fluttering his sleeves.

His mission had been cursed from the beginning, built upon his household's deception and his pride. For a few months, replicating the potash compound had been his sole distraction from Odrianna's death. It had made him feel he was more than an unwanted son. But what began as a plan to save Earl Ralph de Gael's estate and rescue his wife had slid into something much darker. Something unbelievably destructive.

All this because he'd wanted to prove his worth to the world, to his Uncle Ed and, strangely, even to a father he didn't love. It had never been about improving England's future. Why else had he ignored the foreboding tales of wars overseas, fueled by the potash compound? Why else had he planned to live in Denmark even after he 'liberated' England?

Toby blinked the mist from his eyes. He had been lying to himself.

Aliwyn's voice rang out from behind. "Are you all right?"

She had caught up with him. He turned around and tried not to shudder at the way she looked at him, her pale blue eyes full of concern and so trusting.

"I just realized…" He coughed. "Edward stole all the keys to unlock the thundercrasher chests. They're watertight. If I throw unopened chests overboard, they'll just float until someone finds them." He grinned wryly at her. "But individual thundercrashers will sink if I get them out."

Her brows drawn, Aliwyn pulled his gambeson tighter around herself. "How *will* you get them out?"

"I have a plan. Axlan mentioned going to Scotland, correct?"

"Yes." She smiled faintly. "But how is that part of your plan?"

"I'll explain later."

Toby drew a slow breath and gazed out at the waters, where canoes and sailboats drifted in and out of view in the haze. "First, we need to leave this ship. Our rowboat will blend in with those other boats, and Ed will never know which one is ours."

A smile of expectation brightened her face. Behind her, Axlan's eyebrows shot up with enthusiasm. Toby smiled back at them, battling the grief that threatened to smother him. He had found a family all along that he hadn't acknowledged. God willing, they'd live on. No words could express how much he wanted to leave with them, but he couldn't.

Aliwyn would detest his plan, but she had prayed for him to have wisdom. He'd also made a promise to Heaven to do as much good as he could if he survived hanging upside down. Now, Toby saw his next steps with clarity.

It was only a matter of time before every country knew of the potash compound, but he still had a chance to delay its impact on England. He would end what he'd begun.

"Axlan," Toby said. "Help me throw out the anchor. We're moving the cargo upstairs."

CHAPTER 29
TO SAVE ONE

Aliwyn

ALIWYN WIDENED HER STANCE on the ship's deck and felt along the thick fishing net Zelrin now lay within. The youngster opened his eyes occasionally, still drowsy, while Emma sat beside him with an eager smile and watched the ropes and pulleys.

The crew had anchored the ship within a semi-circle of islands that sheltered it from waves. Everyone had helped carry the remaining crates and chests onto deck and set them against the stern. This would help stabilize the ship, Toby had said. Every slight rocking made it challenging to lower Zelrin onto the rowboat.

Despite the strenuous labor of lifting cargo, the four of them had worked with zeal and efficiency. Aliwyn's now damp tunic clung to her back.

Toby knelt by Zelrin and checked the knots he'd tied to secure the youngster in a makeshift hammock. He leaned close to Zelrin's ear, cupped the side of his face, and whispered something. Zelrin's eyes only rolled back and closed again.

Aliwyn pinched her thumbnail until its edges throbbed. It was hard to believe they were all boarding the rowboat, but Toby seemed certain. He left Zelrin's side, his brows knit, and gripped the pulley's rope.

"Ready, Axlan?" he called down.

"Aye!" the man answered. Far below, he sat on the rowboat tethered to the *Lady Fortuna*. Zelrin's lute, bags of provisions, and multiple round shields already cluttered the small vessel.

Toby had rolled back his sleeves, muscles tensing as he worked the pulley to lift Zelrin from the deck. The makeshift harness creaked under the strain. A gust of salty wind whipped the boy's sandy hair about his temples, but he remained limp. If he weren't so drowsy, perhaps he'd be celebrating their departure.

Should Aliwyn celebrate, too? She knew a family that had moved to Scotland five years ago, two parents and a toddler, and she'd love to see them again. Yet, Toby had never explained what he'd do with the cargo. After they left the ship, would Toby alert the Normans to the compound's presence or simply let Edward seize it? She'd told Toby she trusted him, but the question gnawed at her ceaselessly.

He nodded at Aliwyn. "Move Zel over the side."

Her body tense, she guided a suspended Zelrin over the ship's side. Toby lowered the youngster slowly toward the rowboat below. As he disappeared below the deck's level, Emma stood and peered over the rail.

"Oh, Toby, can I go down the same way?" she asked. "This looks so fun."

"No." He smirked, but he didn't look at her. "You're alert and you have legs. Go use them."

His expression became stern again as he strained to keep the pulley's movement steady. Below, Axlan reached up to position Zelrin's body as the youngster touched down. Aliwyn exhaled. That part was done.

Axlan stood behind Zelrin and braced him beneath the arms.

"The lad is safe with me!" he called out, pulling Zelrin free from the netting.

"Emma, it's time to go," Toby said as he pulled on the ropes to raise the netting again. But as the girl darted for the rope ladder, his breath hitched.

He approached Emma, lowered himself, and embraced her. "Be safe, all right?"

She grinned. "Oh, you know I love to climb things. I'll be fine."

Toby smiled, but it didn't reach his eyes. It was as though he mourned something. Aliwyn frowned as Toby picked up Emma and helped her climb over the rail. The girl descended the rope ladder within heartbeats.

"You're next," Toby said. He kept looking toward the ship's bow, and Aliwyn's unease grew. Maybe he was having doubts about leaving.

"Are you sure about this?" she asked softly. "You still didn't tell me what your plan—"

"I'll explain once you board the rowboat." He finally looked at her.

The steely glint in his eyes reassured her, and Aliwyn nodded. She turned to the rail and was about to climb when Toby placed his hand on her back.

"You'll be all right going down?" he asked.

"Yes. I had to climb a ladder to clean my chicken coop." Turning, she was surprised to see Toby flushing a deep red. Had she said something upsetting?

Toby had ordered his chest of books carried upstairs, but the full collection remained abandoned behind him. They were not safe to bring. Everyone would question why simple peasant refugees would own so many.

"It must be so hard to leave everything behind," she said.

He nodded. His red-rimmed eyes locked with hers for longer than seemed necessary, and she quivered. A deep and unspoken pain seemed to roil within him. What was it that he couldn't tell her?

"Get romantic later, will you?" Axlan hollered from the rowboat.

His voice forced Aliwyn back to the present. She stiffened as he continued, "I just heard a woman yellin' for help! Says her canoe is leaking."

"Where?" Toby's head snapped up.

"That way!" Emma pointed past the rowboat's stern. "I heard her, too, and a baby crying!"

Aliwyn gripped the rail. A canoe bobbing in the haze held a woman with a gray hair covering and two children. They had landed on one of the rocky islands nearby to bail out their boat. As she and her older child heaved buckets overboard, her toddler's thin cry carried over the waves.

Aliwyn's stomach dropped. "Toby, can we take them on our rowboat?"

But he was already calling out to the woman, "We'll take you! But what happened to Driftmere?"

"Raiders burned the monastery!" came her reply. "Then the fire spread!"

Toby's frown deepened, and he ducked his head at this confirmation. Aliwyn squinted at the newcomers with her pulse in her throat. A loaded crossbow rested on the bench beside the woman. She must not have seen Edward disembark from this very ship or known that Toby was his nephew. Otherwise, she would've shot them instead of asking for help.

"Go, Ali," Toby said behind her. "I'll help you over the rail."

Before she could speak, Toby clasped her waist and lifted. Aliwyn gasped as the pressure released from her aching feet, and she clambered over the edge. Despite everything, heat rose to her cheeks. The motion felt so natural for him, as though he were helping her onto his horse. Maybe one day.

She glanced at Toby again, but he was adjusting his filthy right glove. The bandages underneath needed to be changed. Aliwyn made a point to remember and descended the rope ladder. The twine bit into her palms as the waves below sprayed icy water on her face. Finally, as she neared the rowboat, Axlan and Emma reached for her arms and pulled her safely on board.

Zelrin slept curled at their feet. The shields salvaged from the *Lady Fortuna* leaned against the rowboat's sides. Aliwyn adjusted the knapsack containing Odrianna's cloak beneath Zelrin's head and looked behind her, expecting Toby to be halfway down the ladder.

But he had disappeared.

She and the rowboat's other passengers exchanged puzzled glances as the waves lapped about them. Farther out on the waters, the same baby wailed again. What was Toby waiting for?

"Toby?" Aliwyn called out.

"Sit down!" he shouted.

She scowled at his strange command, but Axlan shrugged and sat on one of the rowboat's two benches. Emma sat also and patted the space beside her. Aliwyn sighed. As she lowered herself beside the girl, an oar extended from the *Lady Fortuna's* stern high above and thrust toward them. It slammed into the rowboat's bow and shoved it toward the open sea. Aliwyn shrieked as her body lurched from the momentum. The rowboat spun, and the twine tethering it to *Lady Fortuna* fell limp into the water.

"Toby?" Emma cried.

"What are you doing?" Aliwyn shouted.

The rope ladder began to withdraw back onto deck, and Toby finally appeared over the rail.

"Go on, all of you." His voice shook. "I'll dump as much of the cargo as I can before Ed reaches me."

"What?" Aliwyn stood, tipping toward the edge before Axlan grabbed her arm. "You said you were coming!"

"Someone must destroy the compound!" Toby shouted in Vasfian.

This was his plan? To stay behind and do it himself? Aliwyn wanted to slap him even as tears stung her eyes.

"The Normans," she sputtered, barely having the sense to switch to Vasfian herself. "Tell the Normans about this ship and they'll—"

"No! No one can be trusted with the cargo. Not the Normans, not me, nobody!" He threw the tangled rope ladder on the deck. His voice breaking, he staggered back from the rail. "Go help that woman and her children. I just ruined their lives. So many people's lives."

He'd gone mad! Stumbling back to her seat, Aliwyn grabbed an oar and splashed it into the water. They must go back for him.

Axlan only watched her row with a resigned expression. "You won't change his mind."

She wanted to whack him with the oar as she doubled her efforts. The resistance of the water strained her whole body. Beside her, a stricken Emma took an oar but only managed to flail it up and down. Waves beat back the rowboat, farther and farther.

"Toby!" Aliwyn screamed until her throat was raw.

"Stop." He appeared at the rail one more time. "I'm not the person you think I am. Miriam had two apprentices." Passing his hand over his face, he continued. "I killed one. The other one must live on."

Aliwyn opened her mouth to speak, but the weight of his words crashed into her.

The oars slipped in her sweaty palms. An eerie silence, punctuated by Emma's gasping sobs, settled over the rowboat. Zelrin's huddled figure twitched as he opened his eyes a slit.

"Why so much yelling?" he drawled.

"It was his choice to stay, Miss," Axlan said. "You can't change him. Now, we need to fetch that mum and her young'uns."

He rowed toward the canoe and left Aliwyn staring but seeing nothing. Toby's last words echoed in her mind. He killed the other apprentice. He killed Aelfric.

Had she ever wondered, in the recesses of her mind, if Toby had dealt the final blow? Maybe she had, but she'd been afraid to know. The truth had been lurking in the shadows all along, and now it had seized her completely.

She had spent days falling for Aelfric's killer. Aliwyn couldn't breathe. Her throat pulsed with pain as though hands were strangling her, and her face split into a grimace.

"Aelfie," she finally sobbed.

"Aelf-what?" Zelrin tried to sit up, but he winced and slumped back down. His gaze sharpened with panic. "Where's Toby?"

Emma tried to explain. Zelrin's breathing grew erratic, and Aliwyn buried her face in her hands. Time seemed to slow to a crawl.

"Leof, go first!"

The woman's voice snapped Aliwyn to the present. She looked up, her face icy with tears.

With the canoe and rowboat now side by side, a stench of rotten eggs emanated from the newcomers' clothes. A boy, no older than Emma and sporting a shock of black hair, poured one last bucket of seawater overboard before climbing onto Axlan's rowboat. His mother passed him the toddler and threw over several knapsacks. Finally, she grabbed her crossbow and climbed over herself. Her heavy-set frame rocked the vessel.

Aliwyn's throat was too tight to speak. For a moment, the only sound was that of the woman panting. Her gray eyes settled on Aliwyn, Zelrin, and Emma, and her forehead wrinkled with concern.

"I'm Yersa." The woman spoke with a Danish accent. "Difficult morning it has been."

Her toddler whimpered on her son's lap. Murmuring something to both children, Yersa embraced them and kissed their foreheads. Something about the sight was unbearable. Aliwyn hugged herself, her skin tingling as the memory of Toby's warmth flooded her mind. The scent of woodsmoke in his clothes. The comforting murmur of his voice in her ear. To yearn for his presence, even now, twisted her stomach with disbelief and sorrow.

Behind her, the rhythmic striking and shattering of wood rang forth. She turned around. The *Lady Fortuna* was now the size of her hand held at arm's length. Toby stood at the ship's side, his blond hair blowing in the wind as he emptied a crate of compound into the sea. Then he tossed out the empty crate like a dark pebble.

Aliwyn's chin trembled. He was finally doing what she had hoped he'd do. Alone.

"What's going on over there?" Yersa asked, her face flushed. "And why'd you all leave that big ship?"

"'Cause it's sinking," Axlan said emotionlessly. "And that man smashing things up there just went mad." He sighed and took the oars. "All right. Enough time wasted."

Emma grabbed his hand. "No! No!"

He glared at her and shook free from her hold. Meanwhile, Yersa dipped her own oars into the water and said, "Agree that we cannot waste more time. The men who attacked us were trying to steal a longship. Maybe they'll sail this way. Let's hurry."

But Aliwyn couldn't budge. Aelfric's smile the last time they'd seen each other surfaced in her memory, followed by Toby's wistful gaze last night in the hudfat. Even then, she had sensed a sorrow twisting within him. He must've finally confessed the secret he couldn't tell her, one he believed she could never forgive.

And could she? Aliwyn squeezed her eyes shut. She didn't know what to think. Zelrin and Emma spoke in broken, incoherent voices to each other. Oars trailing water trickled on either side as the sound of shattering wood echoed once more.

Another crate of the potash compound splashed into the waves. The sound thundered in Aliwyn's ears, but it was not until Zelrin spoke that she stirred to her senses.

"He's gone completely flipped," he croaked. "Sards, he's goin' to get killed."

She blinked as a chill ran through her. Zelrin was right.

Yersa had said that Edward and his men had taken a longship. They'd soon reach the *Lady Fortuna*. More compound splattered into the water, and the sound intensified the fear rippling through Aliwyn. The mercenaries would be furious to see their precious cargo missing. They'd slaughter Toby.

The pain behind her ribs felt as sharp as when she'd heard Aelfric had died, except Toby was not dead. Not yet.

He was both Aelfric's killer and the young man she'd bared her heart to. He could not be split in two. Although he might try to make amends, he'd never bring Aelfric back. To bind him to such an expectation would only cause her a lifetime of bitterness.

"Do something," Zelrin said, his eyes pleading. "Ali…do something."

The same youngster had cursed Aelfric's name and thrown out his recorder, but it was because his side of the story had been so different. Toby had reasons to retaliate. And Aelfric, no matter how dear he'd been to her, wasn't blameless.

Toby's confession still pounded in her consciousness, but the urge to go back pulsed stronger still. Aliwyn didn't want to question it, and there was no time. With the rowboat gaining momentum, she seized the only choice that eased the knots in her throat. She wouldn't leave Toby.

Yersa's canoe still floated within reach. Aliwyn could return, help Toby finish dumping the cargo, and then pull him off the ship. The idea gripped her and pulled her from her grief.

She thrust out her oar and caught the side of the second vessel.

Axlan frowned. "What are you doing?"

Aliwyn glanced at Emma, who was sobbing against Zelrin's shoulder. She swallowed hard. "Emma, don't cry. I'm going back."

Both the girl and Zelrin looked up.

"You're going…" the child whispered.

"Back." Aliwyn steadied her voice. "I'll go back in this canoe and help Toby throw everything out. Then we'll paddle away and hide on an island."

Emma's eyes grew still, but sobs shook her small body. Who knew when they'd see each other again? Aliwyn scooted close and kissed her forehead. She nodded at Zelrin's stricken expression but forced herself to look away. Extending her oar again toward the second canoe, she drew it closer but not close enough.

"You've also gone mad!" Axlan raised his voice.

Aliwyn lifted her chin. "I already lost another man to this madness."

Yersa's son, who braced his brother in his lap, spoke for the first time. "Ma! Don't let her steal Da's canoe!"

Aliwyn tensed. She hadn't thought about asking for permission, but the woman didn't seem angry. She reached with her own oar and helped Aliwyn tug the canoe closer.

"Go," she said. "I would save my husband too if I still could."

The waterlogged canoe floated within reach. Aliwyn turned to Yersa and said softly, "Thank you."

The woman smiled back. "Now, you be careful. She's got no small leak. Pause on an island if you need rest."

"Right, careful," Zelrin croaked.

She glanced at him. The fresh tears streaking his face spoke louder than words, and she mustered a smile back. Aliwyn grabbed her bag of provisions with a water costrel and five biscuits. Forcing her legs to straighten, she prepared for her step of faith. This was unreal, but it was happening.

Maybe, finally, she understood what Aelfric had felt when he'd left home for the last time, that reckless determination to save one person.

Maybe it was called love.

CHAPTER 30
THE HEIR

October 2, Matthew

As THE RAIN LIGHTENED to a drizzle, the wagon clattered onto the Marcottesville drawbridge. It rolled toward the massive gatehouse of the town ramparts and the archway running below it, which was protected by a metal gate.

Matthew clenched his jaw to stop his teeth from chattering. He still hadn't decided if he'd hand Domilo over to the Norman bailiff of Marcottesville.

Three bearded soldiers stood before the massive, closed gate. They approached the wagon with their conical helmets and spear tips glinting in the torchlight.

"Halt! State your name and purpose."

The blond-bearded one spoke French with a thick English accent. At least he made the effort. Matthew forced a disarming smile and responded in English, "I'm Matthew Marcotte, son of Frederic Marcotte. This is Marcottesville, correct?"

No one smiled back at him. "Correct."

"Then let me in."

He faced a wall of stoic stares. Did they not recognize him? Matthew's teeth chattered, and both Porei and Mils shuffled restlessly.

"I'm here to see your bailiff. Please let me in."

A guard with a blond beard shook his head. He responded in English. "We cannot simply allow anyone inside. Are you a merchant?"

Matthew grunted. "Yes. I sell hay, ale, and an endless supply of bad luck."

The soldiers appeared unamused, and Matthew sighed. No one in his family had found him funny, either.

"Look," he said. "I just told you my name and who my father is. I'm here to see your bailiff with two—"

"Vasfians." One of the guards peered into the wagon and raised an eyebrow. "Why are they with you?"

Matthew blinked. For some reason, the guard didn't seem alarmed by the redheads, and Matthew glanced behind him. Kato had taken off his mantle and wrapped it around Domilo. Their frightened eyes fastened on him, and Matthew's hands curled over his kneecaps.

Somehow, he couldn't hand Domilo over to these men. Not yet.

Finally, he responded. "They...they're my travel companions."

"From the Mehi?"

The question was so precise that Matthew didn't know what to make of it.

"Correct," he muttered.

The guards glanced at each other, and one with a trimmed black beard said, "Show me your identification."

"The rebels stole my signet ring." Matthew's chest heaved with impatience. "If you don't recognize me, your bailiff will. Please fetch him."

"But we heard all the Marcotte men are dead."

Matthew threw up his hand. "Do I look dead?"

Silence. His jaw clenched. False rumors must've spread following his family's shipwreck. May the Boltans choke on their murderous blood!

A timid voice rose from the passenger compartment. "I have a merchant's plate. I used to deliver ale along the east coast."

Matthew tensed as Kato reached over his shoulder, holding out a wooden plaque marked with an ale barrel. The guards leaned in.

"You speak English?" one asked, his eyes widening.

"Yes. My father was English, and I grew up in a church. I sold ale for Norman Rochefort of Wynthorpe."

Recognition flickered in the blond guard's gaze. "I know him...and your face looks familiar."

Kato grinned. "You've probably seen me before. I usually wear a hat. Anyway, Matthew's telling the truth about himself." He jabbed Matthew's shoulder. "And he's very much alive."

Matthew jerked away with a scowl.

"See?" Kato said. "Solid as a tree stump and twice as stubborn. Definitely not dead. Can we go in?"

Domilo wiggled to the front and stood by Kato's shoulder. "Hello. I also speak English."

Now the guards seemed more curious than defensive. Matthew wanted to melt into a pile of mud. Outdone...by two illiterate redheads.

The blond guard turned to Matthew, and his gaze softened.

"You do resemble Sir Frederic Marcotte," he admitted. "I don't know what to believe, but you can drive your wagon under the archway. Someone will fetch the bailiff."

He waved to other guards standing watch over the town gate, and the wooden doors began creaking open from the inside. Already, the scent of fire from within ushered forth a delicate warmth.

Relief shimmered down Matthew's back, but he couldn't bring himself to thank his passengers. One day, he *would* be recognized like the knight he was meant to be. Matthew jiggled the reins, and the wagon jerked forward.

The smoke in the air intensified. In addition to a dozen foot soldiers standing on guard, peasant families huddled around fires in their woolen cloaks. What were they doing here? And those fires looked so pleasant... Matthew blinked hard, snapping himself back to alertness.

A man wearing a hooded cloak stood from a nearby hearth and approached the wagon. He was bald and only reached Matthew's shoulders in height, but his gait carried confidence. A short sword hung from his belt. Was he the constable?

To Matthew's amazement, the newcomer threw up his arms with a bright smile. He cried in Norman French, "Heavens rejoice! You're alive!"

Matthew grew rigid. "Have we met?"

"Yes, when you were a boy." The man quickened his pace, his grin broadening. "I often traveled to Sicily with my friend Frederic, and you look just like him, but with hair!"

He had an unusual accent, and Matthew forced a smile back. Although he loathed how he resembled his father, today it was convenient. More emotions flooded his mind than he could make sense of. Shouldn't his father's friend resent his disappearance from their lives? Resent how he'd stolen from his parents to fund his escape?

Without thinking, Matthew scooted back in the wagon until his shoulder bumped into Kato's.

"My name is Gabriel." The man stopped beside Porei and stroked her neck. "Please tell your Vasfian friends to get off so we can search them for weapons. It's routine for anyone who enters except for the heir himself, of course." His eyes twinkled. "Matthew, stand up so I can see how much you've grown."

Matthew squirmed under his dirty clothes. His stiff legs almost buckled as he landed on the ground. Behind him, footsteps thudded as Kato and Domilo also stepped off the wagon. This man was too...enthusiastic. Who was going to fetch the bailiff?

Before he could ask, Gabriel clapped Matthew's shoulder. "I'll send messengers to Norwich first thing tomorrow morning. Lord Seville will be relieved to know you're alive."

Matthew sighed. "Yes, thank you. He's probably worried sick by now."

His tutor had kindly dismissed him after Ransley's letter arrived, claiming the Marcotte family had been shipwrecked and injured in Wynthorpe. But it had all been a trap, and Matthew had fallen so easily for it. He hung his head.

Gabriel's voice snapped him back to the present. "Let's welcome the heir of Mar—"

"No! Not so loud!" Matthew hissed.

"Why? Everyone must know!"

Matthew stumbled out of Gabriel's reach. Now that the man had spoken in English, a chorus of voices rose from the peasants nearby, and Matthew grimaced. No one would respect a Norman who looked like a drowned vagabond with two redheads in tow!

"Oswine!" Gabriel waved at someone back by the gates. "You didn't even recognize Matthew. Come here."

The blond guard hurried over with a worried expression, and Gabriel turned to Matthew. "Oswine is a former mercenary whom your father hired as a soldier and stablemaster. And he was your father's courier."

Matthew swallowed. So Oswine was the hapless messenger he'd sent away without even a glance. He was probably a decade older than Matthew, with a gaunt face and a crooked nose from a previous fracture.

Oswine pulled off his helmet, and wavy blond hair tumbled down to his shoulders. "Your father wanted me to serve you if you ever came to Marcottesville, my lord. I just didn't expect..." He cast an uneasy glance at the Vasfians, then lowered his chin. "My apologies for not recognizing you."

"Don't apologize." Matthew massaged his sore throat and the itchy stubble on his neck. "And I'm not your lord yet. Just call me Matthew."

What an awful first impression he was making on a subordinate.

Twitchy all over, he changed the subject. "Why are these peasants under the gatehouse?"

Gabriel's grin finally disappeared. "Their villages caught on fire, and they had to evacuate. The churches are full, but Marcottesville's gatehouse arch offers some shelter. So here they are."

Matthew sighed. At least these peasants weren't his vassals, the ones he'd govern one day, watching him trail in like a wet mop. Yet, it felt wrong to be glad about it.

Behind him, both redheads had raised their shaky arms to be searched. Oswine and the other guards began patting down their sides, and Gabriel pointed a finger here and there to direct the men. A thought stole Matthew's breath.

"Gabriel, are you the bailiff?"

"Yes. Did I forget to say that?" The man grinned and puffed out his small chest. "His Excellency appointed me here to be a temporary bailiff, and these mercenaries are under my leadership. All except Oswine, of course."

Matthew snapped his jaw shut before he could gawk for too long. Unbelievable. His Excellency had hired an entire company of mercenaries to protect Marcottesville. Were they trustworthy?

"For how long are you in Marcottesville?" Matthew muttered.

"For as long as His Excellency wants me here." Gabriel placed his hand on the stone wall beside him. "I heard the Danes will arrive by water in three days. The town is preparing for a siege."

At least the bailiff had been warned. "Who told you about the attack?"

"A knight named Jacques Verdun." Gabriel smiled. "He's in the gatehouse. Want to see him?"

Matthew almost choked on his own spit. "He—what? What is he doing there?"

"Well, it's raining. People take shelter."

Flying Krakens.

Matthew's gaze darted to Domilo as foot soldiers circled him and Kato. His arms raised and shaking, the boy stared pleadingly back at Matthew. Kato had turned gray.

One of the soldiers turned to Gabriel and said, "We've found nothing dangerous on these Vasfians, Master Bailiff."

Matthew's hand hovered over Jacques' cow horn. To end up in the same manor as the knight he'd sped out to see...shouldn't he be glad for the convenience? Yet, he wanted to scream. When the faint barking of dogs reached his ears, echoing from either side of the gatehouse archway, Matthew's scalp prickled.

He couldn't do it in front of Domilo.

"Gabriel." He struggled to sound calm. "I'm too tired to see Jacques right now. Please show me where I can get changed. My horse and this donkey also need to eat."

"Certainly. Drive your wagon after me. I'll take you to the barn, then Oswine will show you the cottage where you can sleep."

Matthew's pulse roared in his ears as he trudged toward his wagon. Maybe after Domilo was out of sight, maybe after a change of clothes, he'd feel ready to show the horn full of incriminating evidence.

"Do the two Vasfians stay here?" Oswine asked.

Matthew turned around. Domilo and Kato stood pressed against one another, and one of them sniffled. Neither dared approach the wagon again to climb aboard.

"They come with me to the barn." Matthew heaved himself onto the driver's seat. "And they sleep there."

He needed to find someone to take Domilo home. But what was the point of sending the boy home if it was going to be attacked?

With a ball lodged in his throat, he set the cart into motion.

Porei's breath puffed in the cool air as she pulled the wagon after Oswine and Gabriel. They passed between shuttered stalls and workshops, where the air hung heavy with the muskiness of rain. All the peasants had gone home. Torches from the town ramparts' towers cast a haunting glow over the maze of buildings.

Oswine excused himself to fetch bread at the bakery. Matthew kept a wary gaze around him for Jacques, but all he saw were numerous branching side streets.

Shortly after Oswine caught up to them with a basket of food, a cry rang out from behind the wagon.

"Domilo!"

It was Kato's voice, and he sounded worried. Matthew reined Porei to a halt. The two redheads had been walking behind him. Was something wrong?

CHAPTER 31
OF SILK AND PIG PENS

Matthew

"Hold!" A deep voice shouted behind the wagon.

It was Jacques. Matthew sucked in his breath.

"Good evening, Sir Verdun," Gabriel said, dipping his chin.

Domilo sprinted into view on the side of the street. Kato finally grabbed the boy to stop him from running. They turned around with their eyes wide.

Matthew gripped the reins. Domilo must've fled because of Jacques, and Matthew himself was seized by a strange urge to run.

A moment later, Jacques walked into view in his linen nightshirt and a simple woolen cape. Whatever anticipation had lit his face soured into boredom.

"Matthew Marcotte," he muttered. "What a surprise. Have you heard from Vincent?"

"No," Matthew said sharply. "Why would I?"

Jacques grunted. "He was supposed to return before sunset." His gaze flicked to the two redheads cowering by the street. A bemused smile crossed his face. "Interesting. Why are two Vasfians here?"

Matthew heaved several breaths before answering, "They...followed me."

"Oh?" Jacques raised an eyebrow. "And why did you leave the Mehi tribe?"

Matthew only stared back at him.

Jacques smirked, his missing front teeth dark like a pit. "You are impossible to work with, you know that?" Narrowing his eyes, he switched to French. "Did you get what I wanted?"

The ache in Matthew's stomach rose to his throat. He had it. But handing it over in front of Domilo...

If only Reiya had been there to throw a sleep sack over Jacques' greasy head. But how dare he wish for her help?

Jacques chuckled. "Never mind. It's all written on your face. Got rejected by another woman, didn't you? My poor boy, you don't have what I want. Let me walk you to the barn."

Turning to the bailiff, he said, "Gabriel, return to your position at the gatehouse."

Gabriel glanced warily between Matthew and Jacques.

After a beat of hesitation, he nodded. "We'll talk tomorrow morning about how long our Vasfian guests will stay. Rest well."

With that, Gabriel departed down a side street, leaving Matthew covered in cold sweat.

Jacques whistled as he led the way to the barn. When they entered the spacious building, three stablehands in simple brown tunics greeted them. The men brought water for Porei and Mils, and the mare nuzzled against one stablehand's neck. He greeted her by name, and Matthew's eyes rounded. How could he possibly know her name?

"You can leave the wagon over here," the man said.

He pointed farther down the barn, musky with the scent of rain and lit by numerous rush lamps. The meager lighting revealed many other wagons. They looked identical to Matthew's, with high-arching beams, solid construction, and thick-set wheels built with more spokes than usual.

Matthew gawked. "Was I driving my father's wagon?"

The stablehand only nodded and busied himself with unfastening the straps that secured Porei to the wagon.

Jacques walked into view. "Ol' Fred traded with the redheads. He even gave them free food when their farms burned and began an alliance with them. Unfortunately..." He cocked his head. "That ensured the Boltans hated them."

Matthew curled his toes. He vaguely remembered Reiya telling him how two knights had brought her tribe food in their time of need. Why hadn't she told him they were his relatives?

"How do you know all this?" Matthew rasped.

Jacques smiled. "Your father and I were business partners. But alas...he began favoring the pagans instead." He shrugged, already turning toward the barn door. "Good night."

Matthew's own father and uncle had begun the Vasfian-Norman Alliance. He struggled to breathe. He had never felt so abandoned. So useless.

"Sir," he called out.

"Yes?"

"How long are you staying in Marcottesville?"

"Until tomorrow. Then I leave for the Lincolnshire coast."

He meant Ravenser's Point, specifically. Matthew also needed to go there, but he wouldn't survive the battle alone. He needed help.

He squeezed the cow horn strapped to his shoulder. Stiff with exhaustion, his knees almost buckled as he stepped off the cart. Jacques was nearly through the gap in the barn's main door.

"Sir—" Matthew tried again.

Jacques let out a sharp sigh and turned. "What now?"

Matthew opened his mouth. In the dim barn light, Oswine passed linen sheets to Domilo and Kato. The boys clutched them around their shoulders and stared back at him.

Matthew couldn't move.

"Are you begging me to take you back?" Jacques suppressed a yawn. "No one wants you, boy."

He exited the barn and disappeared into the night.

Domilo rubbed his eyes. "My sister said there was no point in telling you about Sir Fred and Henri. You wouldn't have believed us, anyway."

A wrenching pain coiled in Matthew's gut. Maybe Reiya had been right, but it still felt like betrayal. Had he known his father died because he supported the Vasfians, maybe Matthew would've...what?

He pushed aside the emotions roiling within him. Before Jacques left tomorrow morning, he would need to decide what to do with the horn. But right now, he wanted to be alone.

Kato gripped his blanket, his knuckles white. "Who's taking Domilo home?"

Blood pounded in Matthew's ears. He shook his head.

When Porei nickered, he had the sense to rub her neck but wanted to throw his arms around her instead.

Turning to Oswine, he asked, "Where's the cottage?"

MATTHEW FELT DOMILO'S AND Kato's stares on his back as he left the barn.

He followed Oswine down an empty street with misty rain blowing on his face. Marcottesville's stone castle was built on a slope, where it rose over everything like a silent headstone. Two towers behind the keep remained unfinished, and wooden scaffolds melted into the darkness.

The dull clang of the blacksmith's hammer echoed in the distance. Almost every forge they passed glowed despite the late hour. Gabriel must be pushing for a rapid production of weapons, and Matthew passed a hand over his swordless belt.

He called after Oswine, "I want armor, a shield, a spear, and a sword. My father must have left spares behind?"

"Yes, in his armory." Oswine kept several paces ahead. "Do you need them for something?"

"Yes. I'm leaving for the Lincolnshire coast tomorrow. Show me the armory after I get changed."

Maybe if he armed himself for battle, he'd feel more decisive.

With time, his empty stomach burned. Soon, all he could think of was the fragrance of butter and dill drifting from Oswine's basket.

"Give me something to eat." He quickened his steps.

Oswine turned around with a guarded smile. He pulled back the dark green blanket covering the basket. Two small buns lay at the bottom along with one pie with a cracked crust. Diced carrots and oats seeped from the opening, and Matthew almost tripped.

"Baked pottage?" His eyes fastened on Oswine.

"Yes, because of the...trade."

Matthew's forearms crawled with chills.

He grabbed the two buns and shoved one into his mouth. "That's all I want. Let's go."

The smell of that basket brought back *her* face, and her voice, and copper tresses that caught the sunlight like molten gold. But it also brought back the yelling and rejection on Mount Jethran that hurt more than all the times his father had slapped him combined.

Matthew tried to outpace Oswine, but he didn't know where to go. Finally, he resigned himself to trail behind his guide, who led him down several different streets. The castle loomed higher and higher until its double-door gates stood straight ahead.

Oswine introduced Matthew to the guards stationed outside. Matthew only ducked his head and strode through the gate.

The two of them passed through the castle courtyard, where the four stone walls enclosed the stench of horse manure and damp straw rotting in the corners. Where was the cottage he could finally shut himself in? Yet, the smell of baked pottage wouldn't leave him alone. The question finally tore its way out.

"Oswine, why did my father begin trading with the Vasfians?"

They passed dozens of open barrels collecting rainwater for the possible siege, and Oswine answered, "From what he told me, he turned yellow from drinking last year and was bedridden. Bloodletting only made him worse, and he became desperate. He sent messengers everywhere—"

"How does this answer my question?" Matthew snapped.

The other man stumbled to the side, and Matthew clamped his jaw shut. "Sorry. Please continue."

Oswine deformed the basket's wickerwork with his grip and murmured, "The nuns in Saltfleet heard of Sir Frederic's illness and told him about a healer in Brocklesby. Sir Frederic eventually visited her and was taken to the Mehi hot springs. He gave them a warhorse in exchange for visiting rights. That saved him. And he stopped drinking."

Matthew's eyes stung. He wanted to laugh, but what came out sounded deranged. "Was the warhorse brown like mine? With a white star on the forehead?"

"I don't know. I was still a mercenary at the time."

Could Porei be one of the fillies he used to feed in his father's household? Was this why she'd been comfortable with Matthew since he received her? But he already knew more than he wanted to know. Matthew buried the other questions in his mind.

Oswine stopped at the entrance of a spacious house with limewashed walls. An empty animal pen extended from the left side of the building, and a thatched roof stretched over Matthew's head.

"Welcome," Oswine said quietly. "This is your family home."

"It's just a guesthouse for anyone."

"No, sir. Your father built it for the family."

Matthew drew a slow breath. His and his parents' bed chambers had always been in horribly high rooms, never on the ground. But nothing should surprise him anymore.

Oswine withdrew a loop of keys and opened the door with an easy click. "There's a back door leading to an old Roman bathhouse if you wish to bathe tonight. Rest well, sir."

That was unlikely to happen. Already, Matthew shuddered at the utter blackness of the cottage and the damp air clinging to his skin.

"Don't go yet," he said hoarsely. "I need you for something."

Oswine gave him a questioning look, but Matthew couldn't think of another order. The empty cottage he had so desired now enveloped him like a sudden frost. Matthew forced himself forward until he was in the middle of a substantial room, where the furniture lurking in the darkness seemed asleep but alive. Oswine followed to just within the doorframe. It was so quiet.

"Is there a lamp?" Matthew whispered.

"Yes." Oswine reached to his left and picked up a flattened clay vessel with a rushlight. He reached for his belt pouches and withdrew a tinderbox. As he struck the flint, Matthew stood in the darkness with his pulse pounding behind his ribs.

It was unreal, escaping with a substance carrying immense consequences, only to dive into the cobwebs of his past on the same day. But there was no turning back.

Light flickered in the room, illuminating an elaborate wooden bedframe with a mattress big enough for two people. A chest stood in one corner. The sight of the twin lions carved onto its surface made Matthew's breath hitch. His parents had received that chest for their wedding. The beeswax candlesticks and two silver goblets sitting on a round table were also gifts from their wedding, but they'd never displayed these gifts. Their marriage had only ever been a superficial arrangement.

Memories of his father flooded his mind—the thick and punishing arms Matthew always fled from, the bloodshot eyes with a hint of madness, and the stink of soured poiré on his breath. Matthew never blamed his mother for avoiding her husband, even if it meant he hardly saw her. Even if it meant growing up wretchedly lonely and without siblings.

But something had changed.

Matthew walked to the side of the bed and placed his hand on the sheet. It was made of silk and was cool to the touch.

"They...slept here?"

"Yes."

"Both of them, on the same bed?"

Oswine stared at his feet. "They retired here in the evenings, but I never stayed overnight."

Matthew smirked. "No. I suppose you didn't."

Oswine's face remained ashen. He hadn't looked Matthew in the eyes since they'd left the gatehouse, and Matthew's smile faded. This unfortunate man remained only because he was afraid to leave. And Matthew was now afraid of being alone.

He tried to distract himself with the unusual embroidery on the silk sheet, a pair of ducks with bright turquoise and red plumage and tiny stitched symbols he didn't recognize. His mother loved birds, and it seemed as though his father had made the effort to get her something she'd enjoy. The knot in his throat worsened. Why?

His fingers clawed into the silk. Neither could tell him now.

"Your bedchamber is down the hall this way." Oswine pointed to a door at the opposite end of the room.

With a weight on his chest, Matthew followed his servant through that door.

They entered another room where Oswine's flickering rush light revealed an imposing bed frame and mattress large enough for five adults. Matthew gulped. The implications were clear; his parents had prepared for him to get married and have plenty of children, as young children often shared a bed with their parents. His parents had developed a sense of humor, and Matthew smirked. Where had they expected him to find a wife?

Oswine clutched his hands. "I'm sorry you don't have bedding. Your father wanted you to choose your own once you returned."

Matthew's smile faded. "That's fine."

"There's a chest of your old clothes and sheets for tonight."

Matthew's eyes roved the room. A chest he recognized from his boyhood stood by the bedframe, but he tensed at the thought of opening it. Why hadn't his parents gotten rid of these clothes he'd never fit into again? As he stood there, fighting the urge to barrel out the door, Oswine busied himself with lighting more rush lamps. One by one, the new flames illuminated the corners of the room. There was a large desk heaped with blank wooden boards of all sizes, a setup Matthew didn't understand. He staggered to a small enclosure with a low fence in one corner and peered inside. It was empty.

"What is this for?" he asked.

"For your favorite pigs to overwinter."

Matthew turned around with a start. His eyes refocused on the cluttered table behind Oswine. It struck him then that the boards were for him to paint on.

"I don't understand this." His voice faltered.

"What don't you understand?"

Matthew's throat closed. No more drawing in pigpen mud, only to see his drawings trampled by the next wandering sow. No more befriending piglets only to hear them screaming before they were butchered for Christmas dinner. He shook his head, silent.

Oswine watched him with a sympathetic gaze. "If you're wondering why the bedchambers are outside the castle, your father told me...that you prefer being on the ground."

Matthew swallowed. He flung open the chest from his past and dug into tunics and cloaks he had forgotten existed. He pulled out many embroidered clothes his parents had bought to show him off at important dinners. But what he had wanted most from them was something they'd never given him.

"What else did my father say about me?"

"That you were an artist. Very loyal to those you loved. And that you'd be back one day."

Matthew froze with his face pressed between a smile and a grimace. He finally yanked out yellowed sheets and a wool blanket and threw them onto his pallet. He was going to lose control, but he was now a squire and not a spoiled rich boy who could scream at his servants with impunity.

Oswine should leave. Matthew couldn't keep him just because he was afraid of himself. He stuffed all his clothes back into the chest.

"These things no longer fit me. You can have them." Matthew lifted the entire chest, the width of his shoulders, and dropped it at Oswine's feet.

The man jumped. He stammered something about the tunics being worth too much, but Matthew interrupted, "I don't want them. And if you don't want them, then give them to someone in need."

Oswine's face reddened. "I...will. That's very generous of you."

"You're dismissed. Your family must be waiting. Do you have a wife and children?" Matthew sank into his huge and vacant mattress. Why was he even asking?

"I have twins, a boy and a girl. They're with my mum right now."

"Twins? That's lucky. Good for you." That didn't sound sincere because it wasn't. "I wager you retired from mercenary work because you wanted to be with them."

"Yes..."

"I see. Then go home."

Something within Matthew had shattered. He had missed something pivotal within his family, and he had no one to blame but himself.

Matthew picked at the dirty bandages on his hand. Thinking of his future was no better than dwelling on his past. He had no energy to even draw water for a bath. With his vision dimming, he saw Reiya's face dancing before his mind's eye. The way she had cheerfully brought him water and firewood again after he'd made a mess in Aelfric's roundhouse. Her encouragement for him to continue climbing when she realized he was terrified of heights. He had appreciated her until the moment she'd refused to acknowledge her family could do wrong.

Something pulled behind his ribs. He had no right to judge her. She believed her elders were irreproachable; he believed his parents were irredeemable.

For all his supposed pursuit of the truth, he had let his presumptions blind his judgment. Matthew clenched his hands and strained his bite wound until it burned. What was she doing now? Could she have calmed down after their argument and realized there was truth to what he'd said? Unlike his parents, she wasn't dead, and there was a possibility of making amends. But if he went back, he risked getting shot by her elders before he even reached her.

Chills racked his body as indecision threatened to tear him in two.

"Sir," Oswine said.

Matthew flinched. He thought Oswine had left, but the man stood scowling at the ground.

The chest remained at his feet, and he continued. "I have something you may want to see."

Squatting, he opened the chest and reached deep into its contents.

To Matthew's amazement, Oswine withdrew a parchment still sealed with a red wax seal of twin lions. "This is your father's last letter from this summer."

Matthew stared at the scroll. "You kept it? In my bedchamber?"

"Yes. Of course, you don't have to read it."

Parchments were usually erased and reused, but his father's last message had survived. Matthew's chest shuddered with emotions he couldn't name. Would reading the letter bring relief or more pain?

But the need for closure was overwhelming. He finally extended his bandaged hand. Oswine placed the letter onto his palm.

CHAPTER 32
THE LAST LETTER

Matthew

THE LIGHT OF THE rush lamp flickered over the letter's seal, and Matthew traced the intricate relief of the wax with his thumb. After avoiding such letters for years, he never thought he'd want to read one so badly.

He broke the seal with shaky hands and unfurled the parchment. The French words penned in familiar cursive seemed to leap off the page.

Matthew,

You hate reading, so I'll keep this short.

Matthew grinned despite himself. The letter continued.

You must have heard about Evelyn's wedding in Normandy. In truth, there is no wedding. We are meeting Venetian traders there instead. Only two people within the family knew this, your uncle and me. As my heir, you are now the third.

Matthew's smile disappeared. The wedding had been a lie? His father's deep voice resonated in his mind, as loud as though he stood in the room, and Matthew looked up with a jolt. But only Oswine stood there holding a tinderbox. He looked worried.

"I-I'll light the hearth, sir." He fumbled open the tinderbox lid.

Matthew gave a stiff nod. The mention of Venetian traders intrigued him, and he returned to the letter.

Another revolt is descending upon us and the wedding is our excuse to leave until peace returns to England. His Excellency approves of our departure. The wedding pretense was his idea.

Join me before July ends if you wish to sail with us. We are departing from Marcottesville, and Oswine will take you there.

Matthew's vision swam. If only he had read this message in time. Could he have been the one extra soldier the Marcottes needed to survive? And poor Evelyn. Her elders had planned such an elaborate hoax without her knowledge so that they could meet Venetian traders for...what, exactly?

Oswine struck a flintstone while voices began to multiply outside the cottage, but Matthew hardly noticed as he continued reading.

If you believe your training is too important to interrupt, I'll tell you two things. One, that unusual weapons from Asia may render all our current defenses and offenses in England obsolete. It's only a matter of time. Don't stop training, but understand that your weapons won't save you. Only alliances with the right people can. Therefore, do not see this journey to Normandy as an interruption, but as an opportunity. We'll meet merchants who are key to our survival, for they've visited and learned from warlords in Asia. There, they've concocted a new substance. They know how to fight with fire.

Matthew stopped breathing. *Fight with fire.* Had his father written about the black matter even months ago? If so, the substance originated in Asia. The strange symbols embroidered on his parents' silk sheets passed through his mind. He had seen something of the sort before, like a peculiar style of art. Standing, Matthew reached for the closest rush lamp left on a wooden table.

Oswine remained squatting by the dead hearth, blowing strenuously on the straw cupped between his hands. Fire should be this difficult to start, and yet, a foreign country had discovered a way to summon it in battle. Matthew clenched his jaw as he picked up the rush lamp. If only his father were still alive to answer questions.

He strode to his parents' bedchamber and set the lamp aside. Touching the embroidered silk again, he remembered where he'd seen similar symbols before. They'd been engraved within the chest on Mount Jethran. That chest could've been from Asia. The watertight chest had contained silk, which he couldn't imagine the Vasfians procuring on their own. The Boltans, however, were merchants with access.

Matthew's temples throbbed. His father had been aware of something momentous developing in Asia. His Excellency had even sent him to meet informants, but he'd been killed before going far. The Boltans had murdered him. Was it because they wanted the black matter for themselves?

The realization sank in. Matthew's family was murdered not only because of the Vasfian Alliance, but also because the Boltans sought to acquire the black matter before the Marcottes.

Fury surged within Matthew's chest. There would be revenge. There would be justice. But he had to wait until it was time.

What else had his father written? Anything to explain away the clay apples? Grabbing the letter, Matthew struggled to refocus on the words in the dim rush light, but his vision wouldn't clear, no matter how fast he blinked. Loud rapping came on the cottage door. A flurry of voices reached his ears, mostly women and children.

They sounded anxious, although he couldn't discern their words. What was wrong? Oswine appeared through the darkness of the doorway and shuffled to Matthew's side.

"I hear my wife outside," the man murmured. "May I open the door?"

Chills crawled down Matthew's arms. He was in no condition to see anyone, but the concern in Oswine's eyes was genuine. It felt cruel to keep the door shut. His father's letter would have to wait.

"Open it," Matthew said hoarsely.

Oswine swung open the door, and the pungent smell of ashes and smoke blew inside. Over a dozen people stood by the door, several of them carrying torches. Matthew instinctively cringed. Had he not known better, he'd think they were insurgents wanting to kill him. The fear lingered nonetheless. As the only Norman in the room, he'd been cornered by the English.

"Oswine!" A woman with a beige hair covering stepped in. "Are you all right?"

"Yes. Why wouldn't I be?"

"You need to sleep before your shift tonight! What does that Norman want from you?"

"Nothing. And he's right there, you know. Why are you all here?" Oswine gave Matthew an apologetic glance. "Th-this is my wife, Twyla."

Twyla peered over her husband's shoulder, and her eyes widened. Maybe she realized then that *this* Norman understood English. The terror on her face and the firelight flooding the room reminded Matthew of what his father had done to her people. He looked away. He should address that fear, tell her he hadn't been one of those soldiers, but he couldn't speak.

Finally, an older woman spoke from behind Twyla. "We wanted to know if Sir Marcotte the younger brought any survivors with him."

"He's busy right now." Oswine held up his hands and tried to usher the crowd back.

Matthew's throat swelled some more. Of course, these women and children wanted answers. Years ago, he'd told Aelfric to correct all his English mistakes and pronunciations so he could speak to his vassals one day. One day like this.

"Oswine," he said. "Let me talk to them."

Oswine stepped aside. One by one, women with children clinging to the folds of their gowns walked through the door. Nearly a dozen people entered. More remained outside with their torches casting sharp shadows on their faces. The older men outside the door peered at Matthew with their somber, leathery faces. Perhaps they already knew the truth.

Memories stirred in the depths of Matthew's mind. He knew these people. They were the people he'd known as a boy, including the servants he used to thrash and scream at. Yet, the male servants in their prime were missing. They were dead. Matthew almost crumpled his father's letter.

"Good evening." He tried to stop shaking. "Unfortunately, I...I came back alone, other than the two redheads I entered with."

They stared at him. A few of the women grimaced, then collected themselves. Between the restrained angst on their faces and the empty gazes of the children, Matthew could hardly keep his composure.

"No survivors?" one of the women murmured.

"My cousins Evelyn and Marie survived. They're in Barton-upon-Humber right now, but they said no one else survived." Matthew's chin quivered as one face resurfaced in his memories. "I mean...they did escape the ship with one man, Aelfric of Brocklesby, but a rebel killed him soon after."

Anxious and mournful murmurs swept over the crowd as the women turned to each other. The men outside bowed their heads.

"That be over half the Marcottesville men passin' in one day," one of them said.

A deafening thrum filled Matthew's head. The entire Boltan household must die, starting with Tobias for what he'd done to Aelfric. Matthew clenched his fists as though he were gripping the rebel's throat.

He raised his voice. "Let me be clear. My family didn't die in an accident. Evelyn saw the men who attacked our ships, and they were from the Boltan household."

Twyla gasped. "The Boltans from the neighboring Humberston?"

Matthew stared at her. "I didn't know they lived there."

"One of them did. Edward Boltan was the lord of Humberston before His Grace evicted him."

Maybe that was how the Boltans knew exactly when Matthew's family was sailing and could plan the perfect ambush. Hindsight could be so clear, and yet so useless. The irony made Matthew smile.

"I won't rest until the earth is cleared of their scum," he said through his teeth.

He sounded so sure, but who was he going to fight with? The mournful faces of the gathering didn't encourage him, either. Was his speech not inspiring enough?

Matthew sighed. "Any questions?"

"Yes, sir," Twyla whispered. "My brother died on that ship." She sniffled, and Matthew held his breath. "Will you take Oswine with you to fight the rebels?"

Matthew shook his head. That was one fear he could address. "No. I've never trained with Oswine, and it wouldn't be fair to take him into battle."

Twyla gave a hesitant smile.

The crowd in his cottage finally began to leave. The unnerving silence of their children, who dragged their feet instead of skipping through the fields like they usually did, kept Matthew's relief at bay.

"My condolences to all of you," he said.

A few people glanced at him before stepping out the door, their expressions still miserable, and Matthew flushed. He still wasn't good enough, somehow. Fidgeting in his seat, he loosened his hold on his father's letter, which he risked smearing with his sweaty hands.

Matthew pretended to read again. Yet, his mind was consumed by the image of Domilo's agonizing trek through the burning village, where most Vasfians lay dead. Dead in one day, like what had happened to many within Matthew's household. Reiya would die, too. She'd defend her people until the end. His teeth began to chatter.

"Matthew," Oswine said. "Do you still need to access the armory?"

Matthew looked up. Oswine had finally taken a torch to light the central hearth. A much-needed warmth began to fill the room.

Unable to think, Matthew nodded stiffly.

Twyla pulled on Oswine's arm, but he stood his ground. "Your father carried the armory key with him, but one of us must have a spare." He frowned as though in thought. "Wait a moment. I'll be back."

He stepped outside with his wife. The door shut before Matthew could remind Oswine he'd forgotten the chest of clothes. As the echoing thud died away, all of Matthew's problems came crashing back. He returned to the letter as though his father's words held the power to keep his demons away.

The second thing I must tell you is difficult for me. I never told you why I began drinking. It was not because of you or your mother, but because of the people I've killed and the things I have seen which I cannot unsee. I haven't slept well since the horrors nine years ago, and then again, during the last rebellion. Drinking was an escape. A dangerous one.

Matthew hung his head. Had it not been for these chaotic few days, the one Dane he'd killed in the forest would have plagued his mind. The girl he'd knocked into the ravine would've kept him awake again. He didn't want to know what it was like to massacre a village full of peasants or burn a starving town under siege. Perhaps he had inherited his father's burden of vivid, crippling memories. His eyes filled.

You are training hard, but learn from my mistakes. Don't resort to violence unless you have exhausted all means of peaceful negotiation.

Matthew smiled, but he didn't know why.

Lastly, Lord Seville and Aelfric both tell me you've never been drunk, and for this I am proud of you. I'm sure you've been tempted, and I'm sorry for the example I gave.

Come to Marcottesville and tell me why you read this letter to the end. I want us to start over in a new home. One day, maybe you'll be proud of me.

Cordially,

Frederic

Matthew read the letter again, but there was nothing else he could glean. It was still just a letter, unable to accept apologies or offer a reassuring hand. Matthew gasped through a suffocating ache that found no release. And yet, the ache itself seemed to hone his thoughts.

Why had he trusted Jacques to keep his promise? The man had never proven himself trustworthy. Maybe because Jacques was Norman, the wealthy lord of Barton-upon-Humber, and everything Matthew had been raised to respect, while Reiya was not.

Yet, she carried one of His Excellency's rings and a promise that she could seek his audience. Matthew hadn't granted her the esteem she deserved.

If he saw her again, they could talk about turning in the chest for investigation without incriminating the Vasfians as traitors. She had access to His Excellency that even he didn't have. He must decide if he was willing to trust her more than Jacques.

Reiya had sent him a smoke signal when he left Jethran. She had wanted to see him again. Now, he appreciated her decision to invent a pattern unique to the two of them.

When footsteps sounded outside the door, Matthew stood and set the parchment down on the mattress. His fingers lingered over his father's signature. The weight of the man's many regrets, long hidden, stirred sympathy within him for the first time.

Papa. It felt good to say that, if only in his mind. *I'm back. I'll uphold the alliance you began with the Vasfians. And I read your letter to the end because I...I'm sorry.*

Matthew held his breath, and the relief he longed to feel didn't come. The lump in his throat still burned.

Once his parents, his uncle, his aunt, and the fallen of Marcottesville were avenged, peace would come to him. It had to.

Matthew's father might have believed that alliances could save lives, but weapons were equally important. For the Boltans, all possibilities of peaceful negotiation had been exhausted.

By the time Matthew opened the door, he was shaking with rage. Oswine's smile under the torch he held made no sense.

"I found a spare." The Englishman lifted an iron loop with one key. He gestured to a drawstring sack on the ground. "Also, Twyla and I did some searching, and the laundress gave us your father's clothes. We also packed you bread and cheese for tomorrow."

Matthew suppressed a cough. It was good to see Oswine look him in the eyes again. "I appreciate everything. Please take me to the armory now."

"I could, but perhaps you'd like to sleep first."

"I can't sleep until I see the weapons," Matthew said. "Also, I won't go to the Lincolnshire coast tomorrow morning. I'll take the Vasfian boy home."

Oswine's eyebrows shot up, and Matthew scratched his growing beard. "So, can you send smoke signals in the morning? I want the Mehi to see them. Alternating short and long puffs."

"Oh? I've never heard of that pattern."

"Reiya knows what it means. She should leave Jethran to meet me here."

By now, the tribe must be in great distress over Domilo's disappearance. They'd come rushing to Marcottesville.

Oswine nodded. "Then I'll send the signal at dawn."

"Thank you. I'll also need to stop by the barn." Matthew lowered his eyes. "Domilo should know I changed my mind."

Oswine raised an arm to his right. "I thought you noticed them. Both redheads are here."

Matthew blinked. He leaned outside the doorframe and looked left; Kato and Domilo stood beside each other, sharing one woolen mantle between them. Bewilderment marked their faces.

Kato tightened his arm around Domilo's shoulders. "We followed Oswine here because we were worried about you."

"About me?" Matthew asked.

"Yes. We saw that big crowd come here with torches and... A-anyway, we didn't mean to eavesdrop."

"Don't worry. You heard everything you were supposed to hear."

"You meant what you said?" Domilo asked softly.

"Every word."

"What made you change your mind?"

"I read a letter from my father," Matthew murmured. He had no strength left to explain.

Domilo smiled and straightened. "When we go back, I'll blow my whistle often and let them know I'm with a friend. I won't let anyone hurt you."

The child was hardly the size to defend anyone, but Matthew nodded in appreciation. He needed any help he could get.

The heat from the cottage's hearth warmed his back. All the same, the building remained hollow and lifeless. A thought sparked within his mind. "Kato, Domilo, you can both sleep on my bed tonight. *After* a bath," he added with a sheepish grin. "Oswine told me the door in the hallway leads to an old Roman bathhouse."

The Englishman smiled. "That's correct, sir. I'll leave the chest with your old clothes inside so they can change."

Matthew nodded, wishing Domilo and Kato would stop staring at him like two startled deer.

Kato chewed on his lip. "You're sure we can sleep on your bed?"

"Yes. It's the bigger one inside." Matthew's voice sounded like his own again, but his ribs remained stiff. His father should be the one to show him his swords and armor, not anyone else. "I'll be back. I must visit the armory."

He gestured for Oswine to lead the way, then turned back to his two guests.

"Please go in," he said.

Domilo's eyes were bright with tears, but he smiled at Matthew. His face resembled Reiya's even more at that moment, and Matthew grinned back before he strode after Oswine. Worries and emotions continued to swirl in his mind, but he latched onto one reassuring thought. His cottage wouldn't be empty when he returned.

HE RETURNED LATE FROM the armory with a clean gambeson, a helmet, a dagger, and a new sword, although he couldn't find any chainmail that fit. Back in his bedchamber, both Kato and Domilo had cleaned themselves and had changed into Matthew's old tunics. They lay asleep on Matthew's bed. Yet, while Domilo was sprawled out and snoring, Kato had curled into a ball as though his stomach hurt.

Or was he cold? Matthew found an extra sheet and spread it over the younger man. He could almost pretend he had brothers, and something warm spurred up his chest.

With a drying cloth and rush lamp in hand, he stepped outside, where the trickling of water and a gust of warm mist greeted him. The smooth marble of the Roman ruins cooled his bare feet as he walked in time with the rhythmic chirping of crickets. He cast aside his belt and dipped into the pool fully clothed. His garments needed washing anyway.

Soothing warmth enveloped his limbs. Hot water cascaded in from cracks in the bathhouse walls. This was a remarkable place. He splashed his face and melted into the warm embrace despite the stinging of various cuts on his body.

What a relief to admit he needed cleaning, just like anyone else.

Matthew sat back with his legs partially floating. Patchy clouds drifted past a dark canvas dotted by countless stars. He'd almost forgotten what Twyla had said, that Humberston was once controlled by Edward Boltan. All of him trembled despite the heat. Had he sped there tonight, he would've faced Edward's former peasants. The rainstorm and the two redheads in his wagon, all infuriating at the time, had kept him from charging into another possible threat.

Marcottesville had exceeded all his expectations. The buoyancy of gratitude countered the grief within him. So many faithful and considerate people had died on that ship, while one insolent son had been spared. Why?

It appeared Providence had something planned, but Matthew only wanted to hide.

He still carried the Dane's cross in his belt pouch. Matthew thought about releasing it in the water and watching it float away, but it didn't feel right. There was something, however, he wanted to let go of.

Reaching across the cold stone, he dragged over his belt.

Your weapons won't save you. Only alliances with the right people can.

The memory of his father's voice made his eyes throb. There was one alliance he still wanted to honor.

Matthew pulled out the cow horn, opened it, and inverted its contents. Dark specks fell into the swirling waters and vanished. Matthew plunged the horn into the currents to purge it completely, then let it go. The object soon floated out of sight.

He smiled. The hot water tugging against his collar finally soothed his aching throat.

His limbs heavy with fatigue, Matthew swam under the remaining roof of the Roman bathhouse and sat leaning against a moss-covered rock. This spring was a brilliant addition to any manor. One day, Marcottesville would be his, God willing.

Before he knew it, Matthew had fallen asleep in the pool.

CHAPTER 33
EDWARD'S RETURN

October 3, Toby

The longship Toby had seen shortly before he sent everyone away drew ever closer. It carried a massive log stretching from bow to stern—the replacement yard. The passengers on board could only be the thieving Ed and his hired hands. Terror had nearly paralyzed Toby when he'd first spotted the vessel, but he hadn't wanted to alarm Aliwyn or the others.

Little time remained to destroy what he'd created.

Sweat trickled down his neck as he swung Ransley's axe into another chest. The wood splintered, but the blade wedged deep in the crack. His shoulders burned as he yanked it free for another strike. It was his fault for ordering these chests to be fortified with iron bolts and secured with locks too complex for him to pick. He never imagined he'd be the one breaking them.

Gritting his teeth, Toby turned to the more fragile crates. Each shattering blow sent shards flying. Each crack of wood echoed in his mind like the cries of those he'd disappointed. His grip ached and his hands grew slick with sweat, but fury drove him onward.

Aliwyn's tear-streaked face haunted him. She must loathe him now. May that anger give her the strength to care for Emma and Zelrin on their long voyage north.

By the time the longship drew close enough for him to count the men aboard, Toby had emptied all the crates on the side hidden from the longship. Two chests of thundercrashers had also splashed into the ocean, but twenty-two remained.

Twenty-two chests too many.

Edward had moved too quickly. Without a crew to raise the anchor, Toby couldn't sail away. Panic flared in his chest. He had failed. Worse still, in his desperation to reverse what he'd done, he had forgotten about the chest the Vasfians had stolen. He'd also forgotten about the potash production base he'd entrusted Zelrin to flood if ever he perished. Now, Zelrin was on his way to Scotland.

It was only a matter of time before the Normans or Vasfians discovered how the thundercrashers worked. Toby would die with that guilt hanging over his head.

"Toby!" boomed Edward's voice. He stood at the longship's prow, the sea foaming around its hull as the rowing of its many oars slowed. "What the blazes are you doing?"

Toby tightened his grip on the axe. The *Fortuna* rose much higher in elevation, and he'd been hurling the crates overboard on the ship's hidden side. Yet, the new arrivals must've seen the manic swings of his weapon over the rail.

"She has a leak," he rasped between pants. "I'm...making some amends."

He was reducing the load, after all.

"What happened?" Edward sounded genuinely concerned, but his gaze flicked past Toby. "Is the compound safe?"

Of course, that's what mattered to him.

Stiff all over, Toby forced himself to call back, "I'll explain later."

Edward pointed to his left. "Dock on that island behind you so we can board."

"Can't. A Norman longship attacked me. Got no crew left."

A wave of shock and dismay swept across the faces of the hired hands. Amongst them were Svein and Blakke, the two mercenary captains with long and braided beards. The potash compound's stench blew from the longship, and Ransley lay at the stern with his ashen face upturned. Toby twisted the hem of his tunic. The man was dead, but Edward hadn't disposed of his corpse.

Edward appeared unfazed. He paced the ship's length, picking up a grappling hook. "We'll board the *Fortuna* now and help her dock."

Another grappling hook. Memories of Vincent's attack flooded Toby, and he staggered back from the rail. There was no way to defend himself now. The hired hands rallied each other and began shifting their vessel parallel to the *Fortuna*.

A metallic tang wafted to Toby's nose. He touched his torso, and his fingers smeared away a warm, blood-tinged liquid. His wound had reopened. He'd soon die at the hands of these men, but so be it. This was the consequence of his foolishness.

But as he again pressed his burning right hand to the wound, a shadow of what looked like Aliwyn's hand passed over his. He looked up. The sight of her mournful face disappeared as soon as he blinked. Aliwyn…did she still care? Even if he was hallucinating, the sight made his jaw tremble. Her anxious voice filled his mind, followed by Emma's and Zelrin's. None of them sounded angry, just devastated. Toby pressed his fist into one eye, then the other.

Maybe one day, years later, Aliwyn would forgive him. And so would the others.

Toby turned, his vision blurring, and bumped into the ship's cauldron. He recoiled from the searing iron as the scent of boiled salted cod filled the air. Emma and Aliwyn had prepared one last meal that morning to sustain the crew through the cargo transfer. In their haste to leave, they'd left the cauldron unchained to the rail, and a third of the cod pottage remained.

The forms of everyone gathered around the hearth passed before his mind's eye. A hollow ache spread behind his ribs. His loved ones wouldn't want him to destroy himself, even if death loomed near.

He raised a ladle of hot pottage, blew on it, and took a sip. The heat spread through his chest and down his arms. His hands steadied.

Below him, the longship was now in a parallel position, and the crew prepared to raise a boarding plank. This could not be how his story ended, with Edward taking the remaining thundercrashers and wreaking havoc with Prince Cnut.

What, then, could Toby still do?

He studied the men's faces. A few couldn't open their eyes because of redness and swelling. Others moved with their expressions grim, their faces bearing a splatter of crimson puncture wounds. They were the telltale signs of thundercrashers exploding too close to an inexperienced wielder.

Toby's jaw worked. Power didn't come without a cost.

"Why did you attack Driftmere?" he called out.

The longship dropped its anchor, and Edward glared up at him. "Normans attacked first. I had to retaliate."

The ladle slipped out of Toby's hand and sank back into the pottage. "Normans?"

"Scouts looking for Jacques Verdun's squire." Edward exhaled slowly. "They found me instead. I had to eliminate them."

Toby's eyes bulged. Verdun had acted surprisingly fast for his missing squire. Edward had not ransacked the monastery out of spite when the brothers couldn't save Ransley. Yet, what was the truth? Edward could be lying, even if sorrow laced his voice.

"No one could save your father," Edward continued, his despondent face turned aside. "At least the Driftmere fire will distract the Normans from Ravenser's."

Edward, now closer and directly below Toby, looked as though he hadn't slept all night. Sympathy and condemnation tangled within Toby until he noticed sacks stuffed beneath the longship's benches. Candlesticks protruded from between the drawstring and scattered pennies lay between the men's feet.

The Normans might have attacked first, but what really happened was not so simple. Edward had raided Driftmere after taking an oath to never do it again.

Toby's chest heaved. "Are the brothers still alive?"

"How should I know?" Edward raised an eyebrow. "Am I their keeper?"

Sparks flew before Toby's vision before the older man simply looked away again. Edward could justify every broken promise and excuse himself from every misdeed. He was a tyrant and one who couldn't be trusted with the thundercrashers remaining on deck.

No one could be trusted to have them.

With his pulse lodged in his throat, Toby counted the dejected hired hands. The third mercenary captain was missing, and so were several other men. Probably dead. Those returning blinded and burned seemed to understand that their loot was not worth the cost.

Toby's gaze drifted toward his chest of books, and an idea took hold. It was a desperate gamble, but one that might let him live beyond this day. Maybe he could still flood the production base before anyone in England unraveled the compound's formula.

"Hang back!" Svein hollered from the longship, grappling hook swinging from his hand.

Toby withdrew from the rail as the sharp object flew upward. It latched onto the *Fortuna* with an earsplitting thwack, and many others followed.

As casually as he could, Toby limped to the aftcastle and slid his axe behind the rolls of hudfats. Pulling on his gambeson again, he whispered a prayer for guidance. Then he returned to the deck and swung aside the entry rail to allow for the gangplank.

He'd only win against these men if he didn't use weapons.

Aliwyn

ALIWYN CROUCHED BEHIND A boulder and gripped the edge of Yersa's canoe. She had beached the leaky vessel on a rocky island to let it drain while she recovered her strength, but her aching arms were the least of her worries now. On the opposite shoreline, a longship bearing a fallen log inched toward the *Lady Fortuna*. It could only be Edward and his men returning with a replacement crossbeam.

White waterfowl circled overhead, their sharp cries fraying her nerves. She had been too slow. It was too late to see Toby alone and take him back.

Aliwyn massaged a fist against the tightness of her ribs. No. It wasn't over yet. The men hadn't seen her behind this boulder, and they weren't looking for her. She could still get closer by running and hiding behind rocky outcroppings littering the island. Maybe she could still do something.

Wind cut across the island and whipped her damp hair against her face. The wound on her neck stung like fresh fire from the seawater's salty sprays, but none of that mattered. She scrambled behind another boulder and peered over its edge.

Mercenaries walked over a makeshift plank to board the *Lady Fortuna*. The larger vessel's anchor began to lift. Gusts filled the sails of both ships as they turned toward the nearest island, which was the one she stood on.

Aliwyn exhaled slowly. Perhaps it was a sign that her choice to remain there had been correct. For now, the only sounds were the calls of the sailors handling the rigging and the groan of wood against the waves. No one was attacking anyone yet.

The ships began to align themselves parallel to the rocky shoreline, too jagged for the ships to beach. With plenty of boulders to shield her progress, Aliwyn crept toward the beach as gulls scattered before her. What if she reached the *Lady Fortuna* only to watch them cut Toby down? What could she do against so many men? Yet, she had come too far just to sail back out on a canoe she could hardly control alone.

Aliwyn slipped toward another outcropping and left the canoe behind the rocks.

As she neared, more gulls took flight with raucous cries. She glared at them; they'd give away her position. Clam shells lay scattered beside her knees, and the stench of decaying fish turned her stomach. Crouching behind a boulder, she dared not move closer.

Forty paces away, anchors plunged from both ships and splashed into the churning waves. Two gangplanks thudded onto the rocky shore. Men from the *Lady Fortuna* hurried onto land while those on the longship wrestled with the weight of the new crossbeam.

A dozen men carried the log toward the larger ship, and Aliwyn watched its rail for any glimpse of Toby.

Finally, a flash of blond hair caught her eye.

His face appeared for only a moment over the rail, and her breath caught with longing. He was still strong and standing, within sight, but out of her reach.

Her fingers dug into her kneecaps. It wouldn't be long before Edward discovered what happened to the cargo and attacked Toby. She wanted to do something, anything. But what?

The memory of Toby's face over the rail flashed through her mind. He had appeared calm, as composed as he'd been when he'd hung upside down in Brocklesby. Everything back then had seemed hopeless to her, but Toby had formulated a plan. Aliwyn closed her eyes for a moment. She had to believe he could untangle himself again. And once he did, she'd be waiting for him with a canoe.

By now, the men had carried the new crossbeam on board and were lowering the snapped one. All moved in eerie silence until a scream erupted from the *Lady Fortuna*.

Aliwyn gasped. The voice didn't belong to Toby, but that didn't make it any less terrifying. What was happening on deck?

Her eyes swept to the side of the ship. Fishing nets still dangled over the Fortuna's railing and hung close to the shallow waters lapping the beach. No one was watching the ship's side.

An idea gripped her with the force of a riptide. But she'd only do it as a last resort.

She crept closer. The wind shifted, swirling more smoke across the shore and mixing the scent of burning wood with brine. Sand stuck to the sweat on her palms as she crouched behind another outcropping.

Now she was close enough to hear the men speaking.

CHAPTER 34
THE RECKONING

Toby

"Cilebi is dead!"

The hired hand who had gone below deck continued to yell.

Toby steadied himself against the broken yard, now lowered, with the slick sailcloth crumpled and covering a quarter of the deck. Its moldy stench worsened the turning of his stomach. Soon, the men would discover everything else.

Edward barely blinked as he wrapped rope around the new yard. "Dying is a normal part of combat."

The man who had cried out appeared in the stairwell with his bearded face flushed. On deck, the crew abandoned their efforts to untangle the knots tethering the sail to the old yard. Their frowns deepened as they clamored to the stairs. Only a few dared to descend to see for themselves.

Toby dragged his ankle as he limped toward the staircase.

"Cilebi passed away because of an unexpected attack." He met the gaze of each man with a look of apology before turning to Blakke, the captain of Cilebi's mercenary company. "My condolences."

Toby held back any mention of the murderous stowaway. Now wasn't the time.

Another voice from below deck, hoarse with panic, rang through the ship. "All the crates are gone!"

This time, Edward turned to Toby and scowled.

Toby forced himself to sound calm. "Are you sure?"

"Of course I am!" the mercenary barked.

"Look harder," Toby shouted down the stairs. "I had to move everything around."

Leveling his gaze at Edward, he continued. "I tried to patch the small leak below deck the best I could. Can you check on it?"

Edward's fingers hovered over the hilt of his sword. After a beat of hesitation, he abandoned the new yard and descended below deck. Meanwhile, the handful of men who had been downstairs pounded back onto deck and breathlessly reported their findings to Svein and Blakke, their mercenary captains.

Toby forced himself to stand tall. The two captains approached him with their fists clenched, watching Toby like wolves scenting blood.

"What in Thor's name—" Svein began.

"You are correct," Toby said quietly. "The crates are gone. I threw them out because the potash compound is a curse to anyone who possesses it."

"Curse?" Svein muttered.

"Yes. And my father's passing was an ill omen, as you had called it."

The mercenaries glanced at each other, and Toby licked his lips. They didn't share the same faith, but the concept of divine disapproval transcended that divide.

He gestured at the broken yardarm and the sandbox, forever blackened from Edward's carelessness with a thundercrasher. "The compound is a curse that will eventually strike down whoever carries it. But you've served my household well, and I'll pay you with my books. I trust you'll find them as valuable as gold."

Toby backed toward the aftcastle and his chest of books. The hired hands approached with calculated and creaking footsteps. The shadow of the raised platform fell over Toby's head. With a shaking hand, he grasped the journal he'd shown Aliwyn and withdrew it from the chest. It was the only one he couldn't let go.

The mercenaries crowded around the chest. They rifled through the books, their thick fingers skimming the jeweled leather covers. No one asked Toby about the prayers, hymns, and medicinal formulas he had meticulously copied inside from his predecessors. These men only saw wealth. Toby hung his head, but what others did with his books was beyond his control.

He forced himself to speak. "You have the longship, so sail back to Denmark. Your lives mean more to your loved ones than anything you bring back."

From below deck, Edward's cries of despair echoed through the ship. He must have seen the truth. Despite everything the man had done, he was still one of the closest people in Toby's life. The sting in Toby's eyes deepened.

Blakke shifted his weight and narrowed his hooded eyes. "You're a dead man, Tobias. We will never work for another Boltan."

Toby swallowed. Did Blakke mean Edward would kill him? Or that the mercenaries would take all the books and slay him anyway?

The sword hanging from his belt seemed to double in weight, but Toby resisted reaching for it. All around him, men he barely knew held the books he'd copied in Driftmere's sunbathed scriptorium. Many of the prayers and hymns were engraved in his mind. No one, and nothing, could separate him from the promises written within. A warm reassurance flowed down his shoulders.

He lifted his chin and looked each man in the eye. "You have your reward. Go in peace."

Low muttering rippled through the group. Some said that Odin had turned his face from them, while others feared vengeance from the dead. Others murmured that the stinky black rocks were curses indeed. A few men adjusted the bandages Toby had wrapped around their arms two nights ago. They looked at him thoughtfully, as though acknowledging his care.

Toby held his breath. The leather of his journal grew hot beneath his fingers.

Svein was the first to jerk his head toward the gangplank. One by one, the men turned and began to exit for the beach and the longship anchored nearby. Blakke grunted and shifted the book in his hands, testing its weight. His ringed fingers tightened before he finally turned away.

"Be gone with your cursed ship," he muttered.

Toby watched the mercenaries disembark but dared not feel relief. The first part of his plan had worked. Now came the harder part.

He lifted his journal and flipped through it. Edward had gifted it to him when he'd turned six, soon after Ransley acknowledged him. During that first visit to Driftmere, a younger Edward had been delighted to meet his nephew. Half the pressed plants inside were ones they'd collected together across the island. Toby's hands trembled as the memories rose like a tide.

Only five years later, Edward's family would burn in Dover. Toby had assumed grief destroyed him, but perhaps there'd been more. He should've asked, should've pried open the past, no matter how painful it was. Now, Toby feared it was too late.

With the mercenaries gone, he had one last hope that Edward would return the stolen keys before they went their separate ways. Alive.

He tilted back his head as white-winged birds glided overhead. May they be angels witnessing everything at play.

"Ed," he called at last.

A choked sob answered, followed by a string of curses in Danish.

"Why?" Edward cried. "What happened?"

Toby blinked rapidly. "This mission was never meant to be. There was a stowaway, and he sabotaged the ship."

"Where is he?" Edward demanded.

"Escaped. He'll tell the Normans everything." The weight of it all threatened to crush Toby once more. "And now that Driftmere burns, even more Normans will be after us. Come upstairs. We need to talk."

Light footsteps creaked the deck beside him, and Toby flinched. Blakke and Svein deposited the hudfat containing Ransley beside the gangplank. With the braids of their beards swinging, they departed without a second glance. Edward was sobbing below deck. Toby hardened his jaw, his tears slipping free. He should grieve his father's death, but he only mourned for Edward's devastation.

"I threw out the crates," he said hoarsely. "It's over. And I need the keys back for the thundercrasher chests."

A guttural laugh rang out from below. "You promised your father you'd let me lead this mission!"

"But I found Evelyn's letters," Toby said. The pain cut as deeply as when he'd first read them. "She offered to find me justice for Odrianna. You had a hand in hiding the messages, didn't you?"

Silence.

A wave of raw fury heated Toby's face, but it was useless to argue over those letters now.

"This mission was never supposed to happen," he said, his voice stronger. "Now it's evident God had cursed it from the start."

"Cursed!"

Manic laughter echoed from the hull. Footfalls thrashed up the steps. Toby stumbled back as Edward lurched onto the deck, disheveled and wild-eyed.

"You know what's cursed?" The man stepped forward, jabbing his finger in the air. "*You*. The wretch who was never supposed to exist. Who stole my inheritance!"

Stole. The accusation struck like a slap. Toby mouthed the word, but no sound came. Without thinking, he pressed the journal against his chest. Edward didn't even glance at it.

"Fiskerton was supposed to be mine!" Edward's voice cracked. "But Rans had the bishop change the grant in your favor!"

Toby's tongue stuck to his dry mouth. So, the divide between them had been about Ransley's inheritance. He should've known.

"You disappeared after I left Driftmere," Toby said. "Ransley said you wanted mercenary work after losing your wife, so he gave me Fiskerton."

Edward shook his head, and his shoulders shuddered. "You don't know the truth. I left because I couldn't bear what was happening." His gaze darkened, his voice thick with something ugly. "Rans began pursuing your wench of a mother again...he began to love *you* more."

Toby took a shaky step back. Ransley never told him he and Miriam had begun...what?

Edward dropped to his knees beside the corpse and gripped Ransley's ashen hand. "He gave you what should've been mine. Wasted so much on you, and yet you never loved him back. Neither did that woman." His jaw worked. "Rans was blind, but I was not."

Toby struggled to keep his balance. There was so much he longed to apologize for, though none of it was his fault. So much he couldn't undo, yet he still yearned for forgiveness. But even as he wanted to throw his arms around Edward, terror churned in the pit of his stomach. There would be no peaceful resolution. Edward would not return the keys without a battle. Toby's pulse hammered, his hand jerking to the sword hanging from his belt.

But something kept him from gripping the hilt.

Edward's head snapped up. "Where are the men?"

"They left." Toby exhaled, barely above a whisper. "I paid them with my books."

Edward stood, a smirk stretching his dirty face. He staggered toward the starboard rail. A few paces away, the mercenaries silently pushed the longship out to sea. Snarling, Edward pivoted around. He lunged for a spare shortbow lying beside the mast.

The deck seemed to shift beneath Toby's feet.

"Ed—" He reached to stop him, but his gaze snagged on something over the rail.

A wisp of fine brown hair. Blowing, long strands, clinging to the side of the ship.

Toby's limbs locked. *No.*

The mercenaries on the shore saw it too. Their heads were turned, their eyes narrowed as they stared at the fishing nets.

Toby's arms went numb. The moment seemed to stretch in time. He'd never save her now.

Pain exploded across his face. He staggered and dropped his journal, his vision going white. Edward had struck him across the cheek with the bow. Before he could recover, the man bolted toward the mercenaries' ship with the arrow already nocked.

Toby wheeled toward the rail, his heart hammering.

Ali, run!

Aliwyn

ALIWYN CROUCHED JUST BELOW the level of the rail. When the mercenaries swarmed off the ship, one of them had broken away while muttering Danish curses. He had taken a blade to the anchor's rope and severed it. What cruelty! What had Toby ever done to deserve this?

Without an anchor, the ship began pulling out with the tide. Aliwyn had finally jumped and latched onto the fishing nets. She couldn't let Toby disappear forever.

But his cry of pain still rang in her ears and shuddered through her limbs. If he couldn't overcome a man consumed by hatred, what could she still do? Clinging to the net, she felt the ship carry her further and further from safety, but she couldn't let go.

The floorboards above quaked and vibrated through her arms. Aliwyn almost screamed when an arrow sailed over her head and toward the mercenaries. Shouts thundered on deck, Toby's and Edward's, and understanding dawned. Edward was shooting at the very men he had hired because they'd abandoned him.

Aliwyn couldn't turn to see what was happening below, but the longship erupted with screams of pain. Edward released again, then again, the bowstring snapping like a toy in his hands. Arrows thudded into wood and, no doubt, into flesh. Aliwyn gritted her teeth.

He was ruthless. Blaming Toby for Ransley's sins. Cutting down men who had every reason to desert him. A sudden urge to pounce and stab Edward with a spear flooded her, and chills swarmed her back. Where had that bravado come from? If Edward so much as glanced down—

"Enough!" Toby cried.

Scuffling feet and muffled cries reached her ears. Aliwyn gripped the fishing net, torn between fear for herself and fear for Toby. She held on.

Edward's bloodshot gaze slid downward. His eyes widened upon seeing her, and ice filled her veins. He barked a laugh.

"Prostitute's apprentice!" he shouted.

His hand shot out to seize a fistful of her hair. Aliwyn screamed as he yanked and sent agony rippling through her scalp.

"Stop!" Toby shouted.

The two men struggled, their pounding feet quaking through the deck. Desperate to relieve the pain, Aliwyn scrambled up the fishing net. Edward swung her aside like a rag doll toward the heated cauldron.

She slammed into it face-first. Sparks exploded around her. Heat seared her cheek as she recoiled and collapsed onto the floor. The unfettered cauldron wobbled on the sandbox and nearly toppled.

Aliwyn trembled at the lingering burn, but worse was the word Edward had spat at her. Had spat at Miriam.

Toby's boots planted before her as he widened his stance. Aliwyn could scarcely breathe. Both he and Edward had drawn their weapons, and it was sword versus sword. Neither carried a shield nor wore a helmet.

Miriam's memory would have to wait.

"Get off," Toby muttered, glancing behind him with a scowl.

His boot nudged against Aliwyn's side, urging her to move, but her fingers felt fused with the floorboards.

"Ed, I don't want to fight you," he said hoarsely. "Just give me back my keys."

Edward smiled, but his eyes remained vicious, smoldering. "Why should I? You owe me everything that's left."

Aliwyn's open mouth quivered. Toby smelled of blood, even though she couldn't see where it was coming from. Everywhere she looked, his clothing was either torn or filthy. Her instincts screamed that he was about to be slaughtered. He needed to fight. And yet, he lowered his sword.

"Toby, no!" she cried.

No one seemed to hear her.

"Ed, we've both lost so much," Toby said, his voice taut. "It's enough."

Edward scratched his stubbled chin. "Correct." His tone was deceptively calm. "It's enough."

Aliwyn barely had time to register the words before the man lunged.

She screamed as he swung for Toby's head. Toby ducked to the side and swiped his sword in the same motion. Their weapons clashed, metal shrieking against metal. Edward struck again, and Toby parried the blow. For a breathless instant, their blades locked before Toby shoved back and widened the distance between them.

"Run!" Toby shouted.

Aliwyn shot to her feet and bolted, veering toward the back platform as Edward's sword slashed down.

"I've had enough!" he roared.

Her heart tearing, Aliwyn glanced behind her. Toby barely parried Edward's blow, but the force drove him backward. Another strike, then another. The two men trampled the lowered yard and the crumpled sailcloth. A relentless rhythm of steel clashing with steel filled the air and swallowed her whole.

"You're the curse!" Edward bellowed.

"Jump!" Toby cried.

Their shouting swelled in her ears. Unable to think, she yanked a fishing spear from behind the hudfat rolls, but feeling its weight only deepened her dread.

This fight was beyond her. If she moved closer, she'd only be a liability. Or worse, a casualty. She had been a fool for coming this far.

Aliwyn stumbled until her back hit the railing. The raw scent of fish wafted to her nose, and the rhythmic lap of water against the hull seemed to envelop her. Memories pulled her elsewhere, somewhere impossibly distant. For an instant, she stood by the stream powering the Brocklesby watermill, cleaning her spears beside a loving woman who sang with her. Miriam.

Edward's sneer echoed in her head. Prostitute's apprentice.

Aliwyn's numbed hand almost dropped the spear. Instinct had always told her Miriam was hiding something shameful about her past. Perhaps Edward had spoken the truth.

Aliwyn never knew someone so beloved and cheerful could hide such a dark secret. Maybe Aliwyn's self-righteous attitude toward the Vasfians had prevented Miriam from ever confiding in her.

Despite the chaos, many things fell into place. Now she understood why Miriam never talked about her youth. Why she'd never told Aliwyn about a boy with a broken arm. And finally, why traces of Miriam's smile kept appearing on Toby's face.

The realization struck hard, and the world around her blurred into white-hot pinpricks.

Miriam had a son. Not all remnants of her had been lost.

An inexplicable, trembling joy bloomed within Aliwyn's chest. Yet, the warmth withered away just as quickly. That son, Miriam's legacy, was in grave danger.

She shook with cold sweat. The open water just over the railing glistened with the pristine promise of freedom. If she leaped, she could escape. She could live. But what was worse—dying here or living with a lifetime of regret?

Miriam had once saved her from a fatal illness. Her son had stolen her heart. The least she could do was stay until every possibility of saving him was gone.

She had for so long avoided battles for fear of dying, for fear of taking a life. But there existed evil that must be faced.

Aliwyn's fingers tightened around the spear. When Edward bellowed out in anger behind her, she snapped to her senses and whirled around.

Toby stood with his back turned close to the stairwell. With one ankle crooked, he couldn't straighten as he parried Edward's strikes. Aliwyn gripped the spear and forced her feet to move even as fear choked her. The weapons clashed as furiously as before, but Toby's faltering movements made it clear he was at his limit. Edward, by contrast, seemed unharmed. When he slashed at Toby's lower legs, the younger man leaped and kicked him in the stomach. Yet, Edward's padded armor dulled the impact. He recovered quickly and retaliated with a sweeping side strike.

Toby blocked the blow. This time, Edward lunged forward and seized Toby's left wrist. In one swift movement, he twisted Toby's arm behind him and wrenched it upward.

A sickening pop split the air.

Toby screamed, and so did Aliwyn. He gripped his shoulder, his arm dangling uselessly at his side. But as soon as Edward let go, Toby bolted and rammed his forehead into Edward's face.

The impact cracked against Edward's nose. Both men cried out in pain and staggered apart. Toby's sword slipped from his grip and clattered onto the floorboards.

Aliwyn couldn't breathe. She dashed for him just as Edward, his face twisted in fury, swept his blade toward Toby's neck.

Toby lunged sideways to avoid the strike, but he lost balance and tumbled toward the staircase. His leg landed on the first step.

Edward barked a laugh. He reached down, grabbed Toby by his collar and hair, and hurled him down the stairs.

A series of thuds reverberated through the floorboards as Toby rolled downward. He gasped and wheezed as though he had no strength left to cry.

Aliwyn went rigid as devastation rooted her in place. Her spear slipped from her hands. It struck the floorboards with a sharp clack, and Edward glanced behind him.

He smirked at her. Adjusting the grip on his sword, he turned his back again and began walking down the stairs.

Fury surged within Aliwyn until her head spun. Her face still throbbed from where that monster had thrown her against the cauldron. There it stood at the other end of the ship, black and imposing on its sandbox with scalding pottage inside.

Now Edward would pay.

Aliwyn darted to the hearth. Pulling her sleeves over her hand, she grabbed the cauldron's handles, ignoring how its weight pulled her already sore shoulders. She spun back for the stairs, her light footsteps hardly audible.

The back of Edward's head had just disappeared down the staircase when she drew near. With the perfect aim of having poured cooking water for years, she inverted the cauldron over his head.

Edward's tormented wails burst forth from within that fiery confinement.

The air filled with the briny tang of salt and sweat. Aliwyn jerked back as he struggled to yank off the cauldron, only to burn his hands. Scorching pottage splashed down his collar rand arms. Losing balance, Edward toppled down the steps. His demonic howls echoed into the darkness.

Aliwyn could scarcely breathe. Toby lay at the bottom of the stairwell, narrowly missed by Edward's body as it crashed down. The danger wasn't over. Turning around, she ran and swooped down to snatch the fishing spear she had dropped. The grip of Zelrin's gifted boots sustained all her movements.

Back down the staircase, Edward had staggered out of sight, but his screams echoed into one with his thunderous footsteps. Dank air seeped under Aliwyn's clothes as she descended with her weapon. Screaming reverberated from all sides. Her dread deepened as the sunlight faded, but the sight of Toby facedown, twitching, quickened her footsteps.

She was almost halfway down when a blood-curdling cry boomed forth.

Edward appeared in the dimness as he threw off the cauldron. It crashed with a thud to reveal his swollen and beefy red face. He pulled a dagger from his belt. With a barbaric shout, he charged at Toby with his blade angled down and ready to stab.

Rage nearly blinded Aliwyn. She bolted down another three steps and leveled her spear for Edward's neck. As he lunged close, his gaze snapped up to meet her three-pronged weapon. Too late.

With a wild cry, she stabbed his neck.

CHAPTER 35
SHACKLES AND KEYS

Aliwyn

HER SPEAR PIERCED THE major vessels of his neck, as she'd intended.

The resistance sent a wave of shock up her arms, but she had the sense to withdraw her weapon. The three barbed prongs did even more damage on the way out. Edward staggered backward and clutched at his throat before collapsing. Aliwyn's stomach lurched. She dropped the spear. It clattered down the steps as she slapped her hands over her ears to block his gurgling gasps.

She had just killed someone.

The sights and sounds bound her in a spiral of terror. Edward was not dead yet. What if he rose with his last breath and finished his nephew? Toby lay on the floor, still vulnerable.

Shaking, Aliwyn stumbled down the steps and fell to her knees beside Toby.

"Ali." He rolled to his side so that he faced her. Grimacing, he braced his injured arm.

She tried to pull him up, desperate to move him away, but he was too heavy. Her tugs only made him stiffen with pain. She wrapped her arm around his shoulder and stared behind his back at the doomed man, still kicking, sliding in spilled pottage, until he finally rolled away from her and grew still.

Aliwyn couldn't speak. She lowered her head until her ear rested against Toby. He was shaking, but he'd be all right. *He'll be all right.* Aliwyn squeezed her eyes shut as Edward's heinous snarl flashed in her memories.

"He...dead?" Toby whispered.

With pins sinking into her scalp, Aliwyn retrieved the spear she'd dropped and prodded Edward on the nape. Hard. He didn't move. She stabbed him again to the same effect. As much as she hated him, striking his inanimate body made her shudder with sobs.

"He's dead." Aliwyn lay aside her spear.

She pulled back and wiped a strand of hair from Toby's forehead. Blood welled under his nose, and she blinked only to have tears flood her eyes again.

"You all right?" Toby mouthed.

Aliwyn managed a nod. They had never been this close, their noses almost touching. His ragged breaths cooled her damp cheeks, and her gaze dipped to his lips. An urge to kiss him made her own lips quiver, but he was in too much pain.

She reached for his gambeson. "I need to see your arm."

"Must be broken," Toby rasped.

Aliwyn swallowed hard. There was no use in pulling off his gambeson now; she had nothing to dress his wounds or sling his arm with.

"I'll cut a piece of sailcloth to brace your arm," she said. "And find salve somewhere."

He licked his lips. "Take...Ransley's dagger."

Aliwyn nodded. Leaning close, she kissed him lightly on his cheek. A slant of light fell across his face and caught the streaks of gold in his hazel eyes. It was a light she prayed she'd see for a long time.

"I'll do it," she whispered. "Wait for me."

But his mournful gaze had grown distant, and he said nothing.

Unease gnawed at her as she pulled Ransley's dagger from its sheath and scrambled up the stairs. Could Toby be upset that she'd killed Edward so ruthlessly? No. She was overreacting.

Aliwyn stepped onto the deck with the salty ocean breeze tugging at her damp clothes. The sight of Ransley's corpse made her flinch. Another body now lay below, and a sorrow she didn't understand swelled within her. She forced herself to focus. She could still do something for Toby.

She approached the crumpled sailcloth as waterfowl circled overhead. Pinching the cleanest edge she could find, she began cutting a long strip with her blade. Yet, her mind remained on Toby's silence. Was it because of his confession about Aelfric? Because she now knew the truth about Miriam? Both were painful subjects, and he had just lost his father and uncle. She'd have to talk to him later...hopefully, there would be time.

The Normans would inevitably come this way to investigate the flames in Driftmere. They'd find this ship. And then...

Her pulse spiked. She scanned the deck, taking in the debris, the slackened ropes, and the replacement crossbeam that would never be raised. If she could still save one thing from this decaying ship, it would be Toby.

But how? Even if they escaped on the leaking canoe, and it didn't sink, Toby would still be arrested when they reached land.

Restless, Aliwyn left the sailcloth behind and paced the cluttered deck. She finally ducked beneath the back platform and found a small jar of mashed herbs she had prepared for Zelrin's pain. It still contained some medicine.

The jar had been one stolen from the leper cabin, and Aliwyn sighed. She remembered Evelyn's skirmish with Toby just outside its doors, and how the noblewoman had hesitated to kill him. Now Aliwyn knew why; the two had been friends.

And to think she'd been jealous of Evelyn, suspecting a romance between her and Aelfric! Aliwyn shook her head, her face warm. In truth, Evelyn had been engaged to another man overseas.

Garrett the leper had told her the Boltans would certainly be sentenced to death following an inquest, but was it so certain? If Toby could enlist the help of a few Normans, like Evelyn, could he be exiled instead?

A daring plan took shape in Aliwyn's mind, though she doubted Toby would accept it. Perhaps she'd have to argue with him now, after everything they'd been through. A knot of unease tightened in her stomach as she returned to the sailcloth. She finished cutting the piece she needed.

The waves beat against the hull more violently than before, and Yersa's canoe was long out of sight. She and Toby were never meant to escape on her small boat. Aliwyn lowered Ransley's dagger onto the floorboards and clasped her hands.

Emma, Zelrin, everyone else. Godspeed to Scotland.

Maybe missing all of them had made Toby so silent.

She descended again and found him lying sideways beside his uncle. Tears drenched his face, and she dipped her chin. Aliwyn started toward him, intending to comfort him, until she saw the objects clutched in his right hand.

A loop of keys, but also shackles. They were the ones that once bound her wrists. A cold mist seeped beneath her skin.

"What...what are the cuffs for?" she whispered.

Toby

TOBY FUMBLED WITH THE handcuffs as his vision swam with stars. It was still hard to believe the Aliwyn before him was the same young woman from the Brocklesby mill. She had done the impossible in fighting Edward. Yet, at the sight of the shackles, her expression faltered.

"I'll explain," he murmured. "They aren't for you."

As he mustered the strength to speak again, sorrow and uncertainty flickered across her face.

"I'll check your arm first," she said. "Where does it hurt most?"

"Shoulder..."

Aliwyn was still a skilled healer by trade. He managed a smile as she drew near.

Yet, he hadn't planned to see her again. His last words to her before pushing her away on the rowboat must've wounded her deeply and left many things unsaid, things he'd never meant to revisit. Discomfort twisted within him as her hands found their way to his shoulder and arm, guiding him onto his back with practiced care. He trembled at her touch. She knew exactly how to move him without causing more harm.

Relief warred with the frustration within him. She had returned, but at what cost? She was supposed to travel to Scotland with the two young ones and care for them.

Toby closed his eyes as Aliwyn unlaced his gambeson and reached underneath, feeling along his left shoulder and arm. Agony pulsed through him. He willed himself to think of something else. Anything...

Uncle Ed appeared to him over a decade younger. His face was lined with laughter and still unscathed by the hardships he'd face. Toby shook with another surge of tears. Edward was gone, but it didn't feel real. They'd see each other again, one day. His eyes closed, Toby whispered a prayer for Edward to reach Heaven.

"Toby," Aliwyn said just then. "I don't think anything is broken, but your shoulder's out of its socket. I need to push it back in."

Was she sure nothing was broken? Toby hesitated for a beat, but decided to trust her.

"All right," he whispered.

Her brows knit, Aliwyn held his forearm and gently pulled it outward while rotating it. Nothing happened. She did it again.

Toby gritted his teeth. He hadn't hurt this much since Matthew Marcotte shattered his arm because Toby had become the new chess champion. If Toby could survive that, he could survive this.

It was only pain, after all. Not the gallows.

But the noose loomed closer. The *Fortuna's* rolling movements confirmed its aimless drifting, and he could neither swim nor run. Vincent had vanished, the stowaway had escaped, and the fires from Driftmere would send every Norman soldier within leagues swarming in this direction. Maybe they'd arrive by sunset. Maybe before.

Toby struggled against the guilt of leaving the production base and the lost chest of thundercrashers behind. It was Heaven's will that his battle would end on this ship.

Finally, there was a pop in his left shoulder, followed by a tingling numbness that radiated to his fingertips. Toby gasped for air.

"It's back in place," Aliwyn said, a small smile on her face.

He nodded in thanks, still mesmerized by the tingling sensation and the overwhelming sense of relief.

Aliwyn's eyes glistened as she stared at his battered torso. Reaching for her jar of medicine, she asked in a quiet voice if she could lift his tunic. All her care was for naught, but Toby held his tongue and nodded.

She unbuckled his belt and peeled back the tunic adhering to his wound. With careful fingers, she smoothed the salve over his torso, then took off his right glove and did the same for his hand's arrow wound. She smoothed the last of the salve over his cracked lips. It was a tenderness he didn't deserve. Toby quivered. Fighting the ache of his shoulder, he grasped her fingers and kissed them.

Aliwyn smiled at him, half of her face reddened from the cauldron's burn. For a moment, he forgot about the ship, forgot about Aelfric's death and his deeply buried regret of killing him. He focused just on the warmth of her hand.

A pang of something raw surged within his chest, filling him with affection, longing, and the unbearable weight of knowing he wouldn't live long enough to court her, to build her a watermill in Denmark...

She laced him up again and looped his belt back into place. Toby let out a slow breath as he tried to move his left arm again. His shoulder was sore, but the excruciating pain was gone.

"Ali," he whispered. "Thank you."

To his dismay, she grimaced in response. "I can't...I don't have all the herbs to—"

"You've done everything for me. I just have a few last requests."

It sounded final because it was. His time was running out.

Aliwyn blinked rapidly. "What?"

He forced himself to speak. "Help me open the chests and dump the thundercrashers. When the Normans come, and they will come, tell them you killed Edward. Say you tied me up. It's the only chance you have at a pardon."

Aliwyn's arm twitched under his hold. Her eyes widened briefly before a frown knit her brows.

"No," she said. "I'll throw away the thundercrashers, but I'll never tie you up and turn you in."

The defiance in her voice stunned him. Toby inhaled slowly. "It's the only chance for you to walk free—"

"I don't care. I didn't come back just to betray you."

Aliwyn snatched the shackles beside him and tossed them out of sight. The clatter of metal rings reverberated in the hull, and he clenched his jaw. The same impulsive nature that had brought her back now turned against him.

"Don't you know how the Normans torture their prisoners?" he muttered.

Aliwyn met his gaze with sorrow glinting in her eyes.

"I'll take you upstairs. I'll open the chests." She paused, and her lower lip trembled. "Then I'll tell you what I think."

Before he could argue, she reached behind his back to help him up.

CHAPTER 36
THE PURGE

Toby

THE *FORTUNA* HAD ALREADY drifted thirty paces from shore, but Aliwyn hadn't spoken. Toby leaned against the rail, wary of both her and the mouth of the River Humber to the northwest. There were no Normans yet, but it wouldn't be long.

As Aliwyn knelt before the last chest to unlock it, Toby hobbled toward her. Every rollicking motion of the ship threatened to throw him off balance.

"Your plan?" he asked hoarsely.

Aliwyn glanced at him, still kneeling, and folded her arms as though caught stealing.

"The Normans know the potash compound exists," she murmured. "They'll want to know more about it. If you talk to them...negotiate, I believe they'll let you live."

Dread twisted Toby's stomach. Unbelievable. After all she had seen this weapon do, all the people it could kill, she wanted to leverage his knowledge of its secrets?

"No," he said sharply. "I already said no one gets this compound."

Aliwyn held his gaze. "You said you lost a chest. The Vasfians and Normans *already* have it."

"They only have one. I won't tell them how to make more."

Aliwyn looked away with a huff, but her fingers trembled as she opened the lid. Dozens of reddish-brown thundercrashers lay inside within grooved trays stacked several layers high. The powdery residue covering each one released a faint stench, but Aliwyn didn't seem to mind. She turned one over as though it were a precious stone.

"Throw it out," he snapped.

Still, she hesitated. After what felt like eternity, she finally stood and hurled it overboard. She grabbed another one and threw. Then another. The swings of her arm were wild, angry movements.

"Keep going," Toby croaked. "Please."

She didn't look at him as she continued.

With his right hand, Toby wrenched a thundercrasher from the chest himself and heaved it into the sea. His entire body ached as he pressed himself against the rail for balance. A spray of seawater sent chills up his back.

Aliwyn must understand how he had long ago exhausted the Normans' patience, but she didn't act like it. What was wrong with her? Whichever army discovered the *Fortuna* first could beat her to death if they didn't find her standing over his shackled body.

He wasn't worth her sacrifice. Wasn't worth her life being spilled out in the gallows alongside him...

"Did you not understand what I said when I set the rowboat sailing?" He swallowed. "About Aelfric."

Aliwyn squeezed one more thundercrasher, her knuckles white. Her glare dared him to continue, and he did.

"For months, I trusted him." Toby clenched and unclenched his hands. "Aelfric was excellent at chess. We watched the spice ships sail in at dawn. We had..." his voice cracked. "We had every midday meal together at my table, with Zel and Emma."

Aliwyn lost her balance from her squatting position. Sitting back, she wrapped her arms around her stomach.

"What I never told anyone..." Toby closed his eyes briefly. "Is that Aelfric helped me escape the Vasfians the night they ambushed my father's manor. He lured me outside the town ramparts, alone. He lowered his sword. He tried to talk to me." Toby's shoulders shook. "I still killed him."

The words hung between them like a blade. Aliwyn stared at the rail behind him, her eyes brimming with tears. It was working, his wicked plan to drive them apart.

Memories clawed their way back. Aelfric had opened Wynthorpe's side gate at night so dozens of Mehi warriors could flood inside. They torched Ransley's manor and killed the remnant of Toby's foot soldiers, already dwindling in number after his expulsion from Fiskerton. All this to free a senseless brute named Matthew Marcotte.

Rage within Toby spiraled with a yearning to change the past. Now Aliwyn knew. Now she'd make an informed decision.

He waited. She turned away. Silent, she picked up another thundercrasher and flung it out to sea. Toby picked up a few himself. Whatever medication she had given him dulled the pain of his bruises, but his limbs still throbbed.

A long time passed. They hurled destruction overboard. Thundercrashers struck the water with a heavy splash while the opened chests with their telltale, powdery residue sank more slowly. Progress was steady, but neither joy nor relief coursed through Toby. The rift between himself and Aliwyn couldn't be undone.

Sunshine broke through the haze engulfing the ship. Sweat stung the scrapes on Toby's forehead as his arms burned from the repetitive movements. What was she waiting for? He wanted to yell at her for not already grabbing the shackles from the hull, but he had no strength left.

Finally, while they emptied the last chest, his unsteady hands dropped a thundercrasher. It struck the deck with a thud, and Aliwyn whirled around. Toby's eyes widened as the round object rolled over the floorboards with a hollow, grating sound toward the stern.

Aliwyn turned to him, her lips pinched. The ship was tilting.

The leak below deck! Toby's mouth fell open. After all that had happened between him and Edward, he'd forgotten about it. The wedge he'd hammered into the breach was never meant to hold against these waves.

Toby stumbled toward the stairwell, but Aliwyn shot to her feet and raced there first. Without a word, she disappeared below deck.

A sudden urge to run shot through him, but there was no escape. All the same, Toby spun to the open water. Waves sparkled in the sun and almost lulled him into believing he was free. Gulls swooped in and out of the haze. The wind stung his face and left the sea's salty taste on his lips. In the distance, ships still escaped Driftmere as smoke rose in a gray pillar over the island.

He squinted at them, sending all the regrets he couldn't voice. Would the refugees on board be satisfied to know he'd soon meet his reckoning?

Toby finally tore his eyes away from his childhood home that was no more.

He hobbled to the last chest, already half empty. Grabbing a clay sphere with his remaining arm, he threw it overboard. Then another. Finally, he grasped the last one. The object weighed heavily in his hands with all the blood it had claimed. He hurled it into the water with all his might.

And it was gone.

His chest heaved with relief and yet sorrow. He had done what he could, but it wasn't enough.

Turning toward the mouth of the River Humber, Toby caught sight of longships streaming down the river. They bore stripped blue and yellow sails, like that of Vincent's vessel the day before, but these ships also flew a red and black flag at the stern.

Black and red. Those were the colors of Jacques Verdun's heraldry. Those were *his* ships, and Toby's stomach dropped. Which was deadlier—the sinking *Fortuna* or the arrival of a knight who'd be furious about his squire's disappearance?

For now, Jacques' ships sailed toward Driftmere. He didn't seem to notice the *Fortuna,* but there was always a chance he'd veer south.

Too numb to feel, Toby limped back to the chest with his journal inside. He traced the chest's edge with his right hand, remembering the brothers who'd made it for him. They'd waterproofed the chest to safeguard Toby's most treasured possessions.

Now that the ship was doomed, maybe he could use it to keep something else safe. Maybe he could still finish this battle knowing he'd convinced Aliwyn to move on.

She soon returned upstairs, barefoot and carrying her shoes and stockings.

"The leak is worse," she said breathlessly. "Water covers my ankles at the stairs. And I can't find the wedge you drove into the hole."

She sat to pull on her stockings.

Toby clutched his journal as he sat slumped against the rail. His head spun from a thirst he was too tired to quench.

"The fix was only ever temporary," he murmured. "There was nothing else in Ransley's chest to plug the leak."

She frowned at him as she wrapped twine around her stockings. Even now, she seemed more worried about him than resentful.

"I'm sorry I dragged you into this," Toby said hoarsely.

Aliwyn pinched her fingertips one after another in a moment of silence. Then, looking around, she said, "I'll get a bucket."

"You can't bail her out by yourself."

She grew still, her expression somber. "But we can slow down the sinking. And won't you help me bail her out?"

"Forget about me," he said. "You take my watertight chest and use it as a small boat. Also, take one of the *Fortuna's* oars. I hope one of those ships escaping Driftmere will take you in." He turned the journal in his hands, bracing himself for what he'd say next. "Tear off this cover. Sell it when you reach shore."

A look of horror came over her face. "What about you?"

"I stay here."

She pursed her lips. "Then I'll also stay. Your chest won't keep me afloat for long, anyway."

Toby was just about to protest when her eyebrows shot up.

"What if we sent a smoke signal?" she cried. "That'll tell the Normans we need rescue."

Toby grinned, then burst out laughing. He sounded so much like Edward, but he couldn't stop.

"Rescue? You think they'll rescue us? I saw Jacques Verdun's longships. He'll kill me, and it's exactly what I deserve. Stop arguing and do what I say for once!"

They locked eyes, the tension thick between them. Aliwyn's face was unreadable. Had she finally accepted that he was right?

But Aliwyn walked to his side and knelt. She pulled the journal, the weight of all his regrets and triumphs, out of his grasp. A tremor ran through him. He'd been willing to give it to her, but to have it taken was too much. Yet, before he could snatch it back, she took his hand and threaded her fingers through his.

"Why do you say you deserve death?" she asked.

He wanted to jerk away, but her light blue eyes held his.

"After all I've told you about Aelfric," he stuttered.

Aliwyn swallowed a few times. "Aelfric wasn't perfect, but you treated his eye and saved his life. You gave him a home for a few months. I never…" She blinked quickly. "I never thanked you for doing that. It's how I got to see him one more time."

Toby couldn't breathe as she continued. "What I didn't know…is that he tried to save you, too."

"But then I…" His voice broke.

"I lost a friend that day, but so did you." She wiped her eyes. "Everyone loses in a war, but I still have you. Please don't push me away."

Toby's hands shook in her grasp. "I'm scared of what they'll do to you."

"I feel the same about you. Whatever happens, let me make my own decisions. I don't want to turn against you when the Normans arrive." She gave a quivering smile. "Didn't you say there was a baron who wanted to help you when Odrianna died?"

"Yes, Lord Seville. But I doubt he'd want to help me now."

"I've heard good things about him from A—" She clamped her mouth shut and changed the subject. "What about Evelyn?"

Toby shook his head. "She tried to kill me outside the leper colony."

"I saw the opposite. She could've cut your neck, but let you recover instead."

Narrowing his eyes, Toby struggled to remember, but the details of the battle now escaped him. He only remembered Evelyn wielding the sword and having the advantage. Could it be…that she'd spared him?

The thought opened possibilities he no longer wanted to consider and wounds he'd tried to forget.

His scalp prickling, Toby said, "I'm still not telling anyone anything about the compound."

"Fine. Don't tell them." She nibbled on her lower lip. "But can we agree… Can you tell me you don't want to sink with this ship? There's still an inquest ahead. If we find Normans who will defend you, maybe you'll be exiled instead of killed."

"But if you try to find me help, everyone will know that you're—"

"That I'm a rebel sympathizer. But Norman already escaped with the truth, and soon everyone will know anyway. I'm willing to be exiled with you." Her brows drew with longing. "Then we can both go to Scotland and look for Zel and Emma."

The two names made his ribs shudder. Aliwyn had thought this through, and her words sparked the faintest hope within him. And yet, what didn't make sense was why she so adamantly refused to leave him.

His pulse throbbing behind his eyes, he said, "But what if we're both hanged instead? You deserve better than me. You can still escape to Scotland by yourself, find men who aren't guilty of treason. Men born to families who actually wanted them."

Aliwyn leaned in until her face hovered close. She brushed her lips over his. "But you're the one I want."

A tingling sensation ran over Toby's back and down his chest. His eyes stung as he fought against the flood of emotions threatening to break him.

Aliwyn continued softly, "We all have something about our past we wish we could change. I wish I could've told Miriam I love her, even if she'd made mistakes." She smiled tenderly. "She is your mother, right?"

By now, thanks to Edward's yelling, Aliwyn knew Miriam's secret.

Toby's voice was barely a whisper. "Yes."

"In her new life, she saved so many people."

"But I'm not her. I'm just...her mistake."

"You are not. Someone greater than your parents wanted you here." Aliwyn glanced at the sky, her face brightening, then reached up and stroked his cheek. "You've cared about so many people. Emma, Zel, me. Even the mercenaries. Will you let us love you back?"

He didn't know how to answer.

Aliwyn tilted her forehead to touch his. "You told me sometimes we need to fight. And I found someone worth fighting for."

Toby closed his eyes, his throat burning. After all she'd done, he had no reason to doubt her loyalty. Aliwyn's presence grounded him against the taunts from the boys at training school, against Edward's claim before the hired hands that Toby never deserved to live. In the end, the jeers and beatings he'd endured over his birth were just memories, only as powerful as he allowed them to be.

He wouldn't give them so much power. He could let go. With this, the tempest within him began to settle.

Aliwyn's decision to stay seeped like a balm through the longstanding cracks of shame and bitterness. He would respect her choice.

Dear Lord, there must be a reason you brought us both here.

He opened his eyes. Aliwyn's hand still cupped his face. Reaching behind her shoulders, Toby pulled her closer and stared into her eyes, those two lucid pools of blue he could gaze at forever. The thought of kissing her raced through his mind. Yet, the ship's tilting floorboards filled him with the urgency to move.

"I'll help you send the smoke signal," he whispered.

CHAPTER 37
UNFINISHED MATTERS

October 3, Matthew

Matthew wouldn't meet Reiya again under the circumstances he'd hoped for.

Sometime during the night, Kato poked him awake in the hot spring and helped him back inside. That was a good thing, as by then Matthew had been a wrinkled prune.

Matthew slept on his parents' bed until a hushed voice called his name. He stirred, still sluggish, and squinted at Kato and Domilo standing before him. Shafts of sunlight entered through the narrow window beside them and illuminated their expectant faces. Domilo, now wearing one of Matthew's old woolen mantles, clutched a jar and a cloth.

"Good morning," Kato said. "Oswine and Master Bailiff are at the door."

"Oh, good," Matthew drawled. He hadn't slept so well in a long time, but the day's ambitious plans soon rushed back to him. "Did Oswine say he sent the smoke signal?"

"No." The younger man blinked rapidly. "He just told me to get you. It's almost midday."

Matthew gulped. "All right, I'm up."

He sat up and flexed his right hand. It looked clean and felt less stiff after a thorough soak in the hot spring. His throat wasn't sore anymore, either. What a relief.

"This is for you." Domilo smiled and handed Matthew a warm wash-cloth and the jar of water.

Matthew smiled back and thanked him. He washed his face, drank the minty water, and stood to leave the room. To his surprise, Kato raised an arm to stop him.

"Wait. I have salve for your hand." He pressed an orange tin into Matthew's palm. "Evelyn said my antidote is good for dressing wounds, too."

He sounded tense. Matthew caught the shadows beneath Kato's eyes, signs of a restless night, but he didn't know what to make of them.

"Good. Thank you." Matthew flipped open the orange tin and spread the dark paste over his wound.

Kato accepted the tin again with a shaking hand. "I need to tell you something before you go."

"What?"

Kato glanced at Domilo, who took it as his cue to leave and exited the room.

Folding his arms across his stomach, Kato said, "You asked if I've seen anything like the clay apples before, and...and I didn't tell the truth."

Matthew squeezed the empty jar. "Then what's the truth?"

"I saw them once in Ransley's manor, then again on Mount Jethran when I knocked over some displays. Food balls fell out, but there were also clay spheres."

Matthew looked aside, his jaw working. "Why didn't you say anything?"

"I thought... I thought they were just corked perfume jars. Toby called them perfume. Everyone knew that's what he sold." Kato blinked rapidly. "I didn't think the containers mattered, not until I heard Domilo talk about Namanti emptying a chest...and you talking about black matter."

Matthew stared at Kato's trembling frame, but his thoughts had already spiraled elsewhere. Tobias had been transporting black matter in broad daylight, hidden in those clay spheres, and what Matthew sought had rolled under his nose on Mount Jethran. He had seen the *kubozi* balls tumbling downhill alongside other items he hadn't deemed important.

Namanti and Abithi must be laughing at him now.

"So you..." he began. "When Abithi questioned you yesterday, did you tell her that Tobias traded those clay spheres? That he called them perfume and kept them away from fire?"

Kato flushed a deep red. "Yes. She kept asking what I saw. I just told her the truth."

"But you lied to *me*." Matthew's voice cracked.

"Y-you were so mad last night. I was scared you'd send soldiers to Jethran and get everyone killed. I know what the Normans can do."

And so did Matthew. Yet, to be looked in the eyes and lied to… His ribs spasmed as grief compounded his indignation. He stepped past Kato and out the door.

"I didn't want people to die," Kato called after him. "I'm sorry."

Matthew trudged down the hallway. If only he'd had more time on Mount Jethran. If only he'd cracked open one of those spheres, proving to Reiya beyond a doubt that her family had betrayed her. Then maybe all of this would've been resolved yesterday.

Abithi and Namanti must've realized what the clay spheres contained without opening any and releasing their alarming stench. According to Domilo, they had also opposed Reiya's decision to destroy the Boltans' crates. Did the two older women want the black matter for their rituals, or was that just an excuse? Perhaps they also wanted to fight with fire. What if Jacques ever provoked a vengeful Abithi into using the fiery weapons?

Matthew's chest tightened. He couldn't save the Norman-Vasfian alliance unless Reiya finally confronted her elders and forced them to produce what they'd hidden. And he would stand with her.

Matthew turned. Kato trailed behind with his head lowered, but he wasn't the problem.

"Kato," Matthew said, waiting for the younger man to look up. "Don't apologize."

Kato halted. "You're…not mad at me?"

"No. Now I can tell Reiya where the chest's true contents have gone. We'll need to put everything back in."

Thankfully, the chest had grooves inside to account for every clay ball.

Kato heaved a sigh. The tension lifted from his face.

Matthew stared at the light streaming into the hallway as another thought set in. The Vasfians had a chest full of black matter. If they chose to fight with fire, they could use most of the clay *kubozi* against the enemy and reduce their Danish longships to cinders. His Excellency would surely recognize the Vasfians' achievement. Matthew and Reiya would both be praised when they presented the bishop with the remaining clay *kubozi*.

His pulse kicked against his throat. What justice could be sweeter than turning the enemy's own fire against them? The Danes would be frantic to save their precious vessels while Matthew escaped with Aliwyn.

This tactic could be his redemption and a turning point in warfare. Yet, something told him Reiya wouldn't agree to it. Matthew's scowl deepened as he entered his bedchamber. He'd better focus on finding her first.

In his room, Domilo sat at his drawing desk and ate bread and cheese. The main door was ajar. From outside rang the metallic rasping sound of soldiers sharpening weapons on whetstones.

"Oswine, Gabriel." Matthew strode toward the door. "I'm here now."

He swung the door open. Outside, the cloudy daylight cast the stone walls of the castle courtyard in gray, and the sooty smell of blacksmith forges filled the air.

Oswine stood with a nervous twitch to his lips. Beside him, Gabriel's bushy gray eyebrows knit as one line. Matthew swallowed. What was wrong?

"Good morning," the blond soldier said. "I sent your smoke signal as instructed, but now three Mehi war galleys loaded with warriors are sailing toward us."

Matthew stared at him. He had hoped Reiya would ride out with only a few followers. "Did they give a reason?"

Gabriel fingered the hilt of his sword. "The first galley sent a smoke signal of peace, but I find it hard to believe when so many warriors are arriving. I have ordered all the farmhands to return home."

Matthew's tongue stuck to his dry mouth. "How far are the ships?"

"Quite close," Gabriel answered. "The fog made them hard to see from afar. Now, Matthew, I need to ask you." He cocked his head. "Did you leave the Mehi on good terms?"

Judging by the scowl on the two men's faces, they already knew the answer.

Matthew leaned against the doorframe. "There...was an argument."

"About what?"

"Religious practices."

Gabriel rubbed his bald head. "The worst kind of argument. Could the Mehi be here to retaliate?"

"They..." A chill crept down Matthew's back.

What if Abithi and Namanti were arriving on those ships? Could Matthew have angered them so much yesterday that they wanted to break the Norman-Vasfian alliance once and for all?

As these fears surged within him, Domilo walked to his side and said, "I'll explain everything to my family." He looked up at Matthew. "My sister was supposed to sail toward Ravenser's Point, remember? That's why her ships are passing by."

Matthew frowned at him, then at Gabriel. Who was he going to believe?

The bailiff stroked his shaved chin. "Domilo, I didn't know you were the chief's brother. Why are you here with Matthew?"

The boy pressed himself against Matthew's arm. "I ran away to follow him."

A growl rumbled in Gabriel's throat, and he muttered, "I should've clarified everything with you last night."

He nodded at Oswine. The man grabbed a few logs of firewood from the stack beside the door before approaching the stone staircase rising along the inner castle wall. The clack of his boots rang in the courtyard as he ascended.

"Come with me, Matthew." Gabriel turned toward the stairs himself. "The Vasfians probably believe you kidnapped the chief's brother. For safety's sake, my soldiers will stay within these walls. Oswine will send a smoke signal to call back Sir Verdun."

"What?" Matthew cried. "He'll make everything worse!"

"Worse?" Gabriel raised an eyebrow. "How so? Sir Verdun will be our reinforcement. He just departed, and we should call him back before he sails too—"

But Matthew interrupted him and shouted, "Oswine, stop! Don't send anything!"

With a puzzled look on his face, the blond soldier halted on the steps.

Gabriel's hand landed hard on Matthew's shoulder.

"Matthew," he said, his voice charged. "I am still responsible for Marcottesville until the deed is passed to you. Do not contradict my orders. I simply came to ask why the Mehi may be upset, and now I know."

All the man's cheer from seeing Matthew yesterday had vanished. Matthew's pulse hammered, but a glance back at Domilo and Kato, who watched the exchange with rounded eyes, convinced Matthew to stand his ground.

"The Mehi tribe is our ally," he said. "I was supposed to help them fight at Ravenser's. Let me ride to the gate to clarify the Mehi's intentions."

Gabriel shook his head. "Why risk yourself? Sir Verdun can face her outside the castle walls while we watch from the ramparts."

Before Matthew could respond, the older man marched past him for the stairs. He motioned for Oswine to continue, and the young man resumed his climb.

Matthew strode after them with his chest heaving. Gabriel did have authority over Marcottesville, but Jacques must not return. His near pillaging of the Mehi outside Brocklesby could become outright slaughter outside Marcottesville.

Should Matthew speak the truth about Jacques? The man was a decorated knight. Gabriel could choose to label Matthew a slanderer of the royal army. Matthew would lose rapport with the Normans when he'd already been accused of desertion.

By the time he looked up again, Gabriel and Oswine had reached the top of the steps.

Matthew raised a hand. "Wait!"

His cry prompted the two to halt. Matthew struggled up the steps with his knees wobbling. Why had no one installed handrails on these blasted stairs? The full courtyard came into view with Gabriel's soldiers sharpening their weapons on the benches. Everyone seemed to stare at Matthew, and his stomach heaved toward his mouth.

"Can we come with you?" Kato called out.

Matthew had forgotten Domilo and Kato were behind him. He pressed a clammy hand against the stone wall and croaked, "Yes."

Footsteps rushed behind him. A hand gripped Matthew's shoulder. It was Kato's. The sensation grounded Matthew and quelled the anxious burn in his throat. When he resumed walking, his boots no longer thudded alone.

Reiya had advised him to look ahead and not back down. Matthew locked gazes with the bald bailiff, who was scowling down at him. The truth about Jacques needed to come out. What other reason could Matthew give for refusing the knight's return?

"Gabriel," he said. "The Mehi won't be reckless enough to attack us in front of our fortifications. Reiya's here for her brother and for me, but if you call Jacques back, *then* you'll have bloodshed. He almost robbed the Mehi tribe outside Brocklesby. He sent soldiers straight toward their young and elderly."

Gabriel exhaled sharply. His fingers tapped against his belt. "Sir Verdun? Do such a thing?"

"I was there." Matthew's feet climbed the stairs on their own. "I stopped the fight from happening."

Domilo called from behind him, "Matthew's telling the truth. I was one of the children Jacques tried to attack."

A low muttering swept over the English soldiers in the courtyard. Sweat broke at Matthew's hairline. Maybe he should've spoken in French so only Gabriel could understand. Yet, he couldn't take back the truth.

The bailiff's darkened face was unreadable. Fear of retaliation stormed in the back of Matthew's mind, but he shoved it aside. If Jacques were ever to be stopped, his actions needed to be revealed.

Matthew strode to Gabriel's side and said, "Thank you for considering my complaint against Sir Verdun."

Jacques might evade His Excellency's justice today, but let enough grievances pile up, and even a rat finds its trap.

Gabriel squinted at the flags fluttering nearby, decorated with the Marcottes' red lion heraldry, and muttered, "We can't afford to lose the Mehi's support in this war. If you say Sir Verdun has been a threat to our alliance..."

"He still is." Matthew hardened his jaw. "And let me suggest something. Please repeat my smoke signal, the alternating short and long puffs. I wager Reiya would ride out to see me."

Gabriel drew a slow breath. He strode onto the wall-walk of the Marcottesville ramparts with the wind blowing back his cape. "Fine. But if she does not appear by the time Oswine's firewood runs out, I'll switch the signal to puffs of three to alert Sir Verdun."

He nodded at Oswine, who carried his firewood toward the far end of the parapet. There, a massive brass basin cradled the signal hearth.

Now they'd have to wait. Matthew could scarcely breathe as he, Domilo, and Kato stepped onto the parapet. Gabriel and other soldiers had gathered behind the row of arrow slits to peer at the rolling farmlands and the River Humber in the distance.

As Matthew walked between the other men, a wind carrying the river's scent lifted his hair with a revitalizing chill. A dense fog hung over the River Humber. To the west, Vasfian galleys with half red and green sails and dark crimson hulls sailed in a startling contrast to the river's gray waters. Each ship featured oars on either side and could probably seat forty warriors each, plenty to strike fear into any peasant. Indeed, farmhands and pack animals hurried home like dark beetles between the vast strips of gold and brown farmland.

Matthew clenched his hands to stop them from trembling. There was no going back. He'd trust Reiya more than Jacques. Soon, puffs of smoke in the pattern he'd requested rose from the brass basin.

The signal had repeated less than a dozen times when Domilo jumped with a wave of his arms.

"Reiya!" he cried.

In the distance, a lone horse sped from the forest's edge. The rider was a woman with red hair and a vest.

Matthew's breath caught. "You're sure? I can't see her face."

"Yes! I recognize her horse and the way she rides. And I'll prove it's her." Domilo withdrew the whistle from behind his tunic and blew. A shrill and melodious sound rang forth. Moments later, the rider responded with one of her own.

Domilo grabbed Matthew's forearm. "That's my sister's whistling pattern. She says she comes in peace!"

Relief began as a tingling sensation down Matthew's back. "Good. Let's go see her."

Turning to Gabriel, he added, "Thank you for listening to me."

"It's for the sake of us all," Gabriel said. For some reason, he sounded like Matthew's father just then. Matthew stifled a rush of longing.

The bailiff placed a hand on Matthew's shoulder, his grip firm but not punishing like before. Concern shone in his gray eyes. "You seem to trust a Vasfian more than our own. I find that puzzling."

Matthew's mouth twitched into a smile. "It doesn't matter where Reiya's from. She's been kind to me."

Gabriel nodded. His expression softening, he lifted his hand. "You're not the person I remember. Go. My archers will cover you from these walls."

AFTER DONNING HIS GAMBESON and retrieving his sword, Matthew bolted through the courtyard and out the castle gates. He managed a nod at each peasant who greeted him while he hurried toward the barn.

There, he did a double-take. Porei was already saddled with a leather chamfron fitted over her face and a quilt draped over her flanks as makeshift armor.

"Who prepared—" he began, but stopped himself short when Kato and Domilo shuffled out from behind Porei's muscular neck. Kato held a teardrop shaped shield and a spear.

"Surprise!" he cried, grinning. "Domilo and I were busy while you slept this morning."

Matthew smiled and ran a hand over Porei's saddle. It was a double saddle, just like he had hoped for. Had he ever told Kato he needed one?

"Thanks for preparing this," he said.

"We didn't do everything," Domilo said. "Twyla knew where to find horse armor and the shield, and she packed your breakfast."

Matthew ran his hand down to the bulging saddlebag, which emanated the fragrance of cheese and bread. He'd enjoy that later. Hoisting himself onto the saddle, he searched until he found Twyla standing beside her husband, Oswine, with her hands folded before her flour-caked apron. Matthew nodded in appreciation, and she smiled back.

"So, are you leaving with Reiya?" Kato asked.

"If Reiya's here for the reason I think she is, then yes."

"Right. Good luck, then." Kato's cheer faded. "And I...I'll go to Barton-upon-Humber soon."

He passed Matthew the spear, then arched his back to lift the shield for Matthew to take. Matthew's throat knotted. After today, he wasn't sure when he'd see Kato again.

"Wait." Matthew pulled off his helmet and nestled it under his arm. "Thank you for what you said on my wagon yesterday."

"Thank?" Kato's eyes rounded, and he dropped the shield with a thud.

Matthew continued. "I wasn't prepared to face the truth last night. So, thank you for disrupting my plans."

"Oh, I...I'll try not to do that too often." The younger man smiled wryly.

Matthew turned back to Oswine and his wife. "Kato is a guest in my cottage until he wants to leave."

The couple answered in agreement, and Kato stammered, "Thank you. But in all seriousness, I wish I had the training to come with you." His forehead crinkled. "I have trouble even lifting this shield."

"But you can still help. Keep praying for me, for the court I need to attend in a few weeks. There's so much that..." Matthew's voice faltered. "So much I can't control."

A slew of things that could go wrong passed through his mind, but he refused to engage with them. "I want to be lord of Marcottesville next year, maybe even move Aliwyn here. But I need to be a knight first."

His ribs twinged with longing, but Kato's expression gave him hope.

"You can count on me." Kato hoisted the shield upward again and stood on his toes. "Godspeed, Matthew."

Matthew put his left arm through the strap. "Send my greetings to Evelyn and Marie in Barton. And Norman, if you see him."

Kato's smile broadened. "I will."

Matthew's chest heaved with the anticipation of seeing Reiya again. He fitted his helmet back over his head and picked up the reins.

THE REFUGEES BENEATH THE southern archway added to the congestion surrounding the town gates. Matthew kept a tight grip on Porei's reins. Tossing her head, she meandered into the throng of peasants and pack animals streaming back from the fields.

Small and agile, Domilo had already run ahead and disappeared into the crowd.

Matthew scanned the shifting sea of sackcloth hats and headscarves for a glimpse of Reiya. Nothing yet. Finally, the crowd funneled through the archway and cleared his line of sight. With a snort, Porei surged forward with hooves clopping against the cobblestones.

Copper-red hair flashed in the distance, and Matthew almost fell off his seat.

Reiya stood with her arms wrapped around her brother. At that distance, safe from crossbows, she was just a thumb-sized smudge of color. Her mare grazed on hay scattered on the ground.

She'd truly come alone, like he had hoped. Matthew was afraid to speed up, afraid that if he drew too close, she'd vanish like a puff of smoke. But she didn't disappear, and only stared at him with a pensive frown that he knew hid much more underneath.

Matthew pulled off his helmet so she could recognize him from afar. As he drew close, she straightened.

"Thank you for keeping Domilo safe," she said.

Matthew nodded, his throat too tight to speak.

Porei trotted onward, and a reddish mark covering half of Reiya's face suddenly leaped at him. Had someone attacked her? All thoughts of the black matter flew from his mind. How dare anyone strike her!

"Your face...what happened to you?" He jumped off his mount and lowered his spear to the ground.

Reiya was silent for a moment as she stared at his spear. "I'll tell you later."

She released her brother, and Domilo rubbed his own wet eyes.

"I knew I made a mistake as soon as you left," she said. His heart gave a great leap as she continued. "Domilo just told me that my grandmother emptied the chest before the *Anuin*. It confirms everything."

"I'm glad," Matthew managed to say.

Back in Marcottesville, men on the manor walls called out to each other, and her stoic face finally crumpled. "Did you already tell your people about the chest?"

"No. Only that we had an argument."

Her expression relaxed.

"Thank you," she mouthed. "Will you leave with me today? I need to talk to you."

"That was my plan. Thanks for answering my signal."

Her eyes glistened beneath the blowing strands of her hair, her face still restless with memories untold. Matthew raised his hand and almost touched the reddish mark on her face, but Gabriel's shout from behind reached his ears.

Matthew turned as the sound of pounding horse hooves filled the air. Gabriel was riding out with five other foot soldiers. Instinctively, Matthew widened his stance before Reiya and Domilo.

"You've met Gabriel the bailiff?" he called over his shoulder.

"Only once since your father's passing," she answered.

Matthew drew a pained breath. They'd need to talk more about his father after the revolt.

Gabriel reined his black warhorse to a stop before Matthew and the others. The chainmail layered over his gambeson clinked, and the nasal prong of his helmet masked his expression.

He and Reiya exchanged greetings.

The bailiff then said, "Honorable Reiya, please state your intent in sending your fleet."

Reiya straightened to her full height. "I wanted to fetch Matthew and my brother on my way to Ravenser's Point. I apologize if my ships frightened your people. I came to assure you we mean no harm...and because Matthew called for me."

Relief tingled down Matthew's scalp.

The bailiff nodded. "Expect to see Sir Verdun at your destination. He left Marcottesville earlier this morning."

Reiya's eyes widened, and she shot Matthew a worried glance. "Then we must be on our way."

Matthew nodded, but Gabriel shifted his weight with a frown. "Matthew, are you leaving with the Vasfian warband?"

"Yes, sir."

"Weigh this decision carefully. You're the last of your bloodline."

Matthew lowered his head for a moment. With the Danes arriving in two days, he'd need to convince Reiya to use the clay *kubozi* for the right reasons. And fast.

His fingers drifted to the belt pouch where his father's letter lay beside the crucifix he'd found. Just feeling the contours of both objects sent him a surge of strength.

The magnificent stone walls of Marcottesville stood in testimony of what his father had accomplished, and pride flared within Matthew for a moment. But his father couldn't hear him speak, and Matthew could never welcome his best friend inside those walls. His hands quivered, but he balled them into fists. There would be justice.

He pushed his helmet over his head and aligned the nasal prong to the center.

"I must go," he said. "I have unfinished matters with the Boltans."

CHAPTER 38
THE SELKIE

Matthew

Gabriel and his men retreated. The warhorse's hoofbeats sent broken stalks of wheat skittering around Matthew's feet.

Reiya stroked her mount with her face in a pensive frown. The sheen of sweat darkened the beast's neck and flanks.

"Let's go," she said, pressing on the saddle to mount. "Domilo can ride double with you. We can't let Jacques catch the Boltans first."

Matthew's tongue lay thick in his mouth. Tobias would die, under his hand or by hanging from the gallows, but Reiya didn't know that capturing him first wouldn't clear Matthew's name. The bet Jacques had made with her was nothing but a ploy to stir her sympathies and make her accept Matthew into her tribe. When could he tell her the truth? They should be returning to Jethran for the chest, not sailing to Ravenser's.

But Reiya had already mounted her steed. Matthew helped Domilo onto Porei's back, unable to look the boy in the eye. Resting his shield against Porei's side, he swung a leg over the saddle. He and Reiya soon took off, side-by-side through the bronze fields with the watchful walls of Marcottesville behind them.

He should let Reiya talk first.

"What happened after I left Jethran?" he asked.

A frown had molded into Reiya's ashen face. "The biggest fight I've ever had with my elders."

He expected her to continue, but she gazed into the distance with a nervous tick in her eyes. It was a look that he had never seen before. Maybe he was imagining things? Matthew surveyed his surroundings, but Domilo with his blowing red hair was the only person in sight. The farmland lacked cover for ambushers to hide, and the first Vasfian galley was moments away from the River Humber harbor. They should be safe on board.

"You all right?" Matthew asked.

"Just...unpleasant memories." She wrapped one arm around her stomach again. "I forced my way back to the chest after you left. Let's just say there was a scuffle." Gesturing at the red mark on her cheek, she grimaced. The rest of her face flushed the same color.

Matthew drew his brows. "Thank you for going back to see for yourself."

"I scraped off the powder you showed me and used it to light up some leaves." She kept her eyes ahead. "It burned so quickly I almost hurt myself, and there was that foul smell. My whole village then understood they had been deceived." She glanced at him. "And one Norman was probably speeding away to accuse us..."

Her bloodshot eyes met his. Matthew wanted to rub her shoulders, but she was out of his reach.

"I admit I came close," he said.

"Everyone was convinced you would send Jacques our way, except me." She gave a trembling smile. "You could've given that man rabbit droppings, told him it was black matter, and he would've come to raid us."

Matthew's back stiffened. He had never seen the situation that way.

"Domilo and Kato helped change my mind," he murmured. "Now it's up to us. The chest still needs to be—"

"It's on my ship," she interrupted, her gaze fixed ahead.

"Really?" Matthew's eyebrows shot up.

"Yes. And I put everything back inside. All those things Domilo called 'clay apples.'"

This called for a celebration, but Reiya neither smiled nor looked at him. Matthew's grin faltered, and a dull ache began at his temples. He pulled out bread and cheese from his saddle pack, splitting it with Domilo, but Reiya refused any.

"Is something wrong?" he asked.

A faint smile curled her lips. "I'm just thinking of many things. Don't worry."

For the rest of the ride to the River Humber, she spoke little. Her silence weighed heavily on him. Matthew focused on Domilo instead, adjusting the boy's posture and showing him how to press with his legs gently to guide Porei.

With time, the rhythmic splashing of oars from the arriving Vasfian galley reached his ears. Its large red and green sails seemed to fly above the gray waters. Domilo turned his head and smiled, trying to catch Matthew's eye, but Matthew couldn't match the boy's expression. The rawness of brine and wet wood in the air made his stomach turn.

The oars ceased to splash. Redheaded sailors cast ropes to the mooring posts. Others greeted them from on board the ship, each tracing a circular shape over his head. Reiya greeted them back the same way. A pulley system lowered the gangplank to the quay, and she motioned for Matthew to approach.

"Welcome to my ship, the *Selkie*," she said.

Matthew tightened his grip on his shield. The number of Vasfians crowding the galley made the air grow thick around him. None of them looked at him, either. If they were his allies, why were his instincts screaming that something was wrong?

"Reiya," he said. "I can ride alongside your galley. And I'll look at the chest after your ships dock."

That seemed to strike fear into her. "Why? You don't trust me enough to get on?"

"Hello, Mattoo," said a woman on board the ship.

Abithi! Matthew sucked in his breath and reined Porei back.

"*Amah!*" Domilo cried.

He squirmed, and Matthew had the sense to help the boy jump off. Domilo scrambled toward the plank. Matthew caught sight of Namanti standing amidst the barrels and the shifting bodies of warriors. The skull staff stood erect in her hand.

Her other hand held a clay sphere. As Domilo's footsteps pattered up the plank, her stoic composure softened. She embraced her grandson, and Matthew lost sight of the sphere.

"Mattoo," continued Abithi's voice. "If you want to see chest, all full, I have it here."

"Please trust me," Reiya said. "I had to bring you far from the other Normans so you can talk to my mother and finally settle the matter. We don't mean you any harm."

Matthew's chest heaved with the urge to flee. "What does she want?"

"She wants to show you the chest and dump it in front of you. Then you know we don't have it anymore. It's the only way we'll have peace."

Matthew shook his head, unable to speak.

Two men solemnly lifted the chest in between them. This time, the lid was open; what looked like massive brown eggs filled the chest. They could indeed be what Kato had seen in the Boltans' manor. Matthew strained on Porei's back to see them better, but the ship's railing was too high.

"Don't dump the chest," he stammered.

"I prove to you I never want to destroy with those things. Reiya gift me the chest. I use clay *kubozi* to help me heal. It contain most precious thing the enemy own, a thing they die to protect. The best offering..." She rolled her eyes. "Even if it stink like bog pit. Now before full moon of Samhain month, I finish ritual. I throw."

"No!" Matthew cried. "I have a different proposal. Let me see them."

"Then you come on ship. I no bring to you."

But the thought of being trapped with Abithi and Namanti on the same ship racked Matthew's body with chills.

Porei took a step forward at the sight of people she'd lived with, but he jerked her back. If he ever set sail with the Vasfians, he was at their mercy. At Abithi's mercy.

"Matthew," Reiya said.

Her expression tense, she dismounted and tugged at the brass buckle securing her crossbow strap. She lowered her unloaded weapon onto a patch of weeds. Turning to the ship, she swiped her hand in the air as though slicing something in half.

To Matthew's amazement, the warriors on the galley all unstrapped their crossbows and lowered them. They began stacking them in a pile around the ship's mast.

"Why you do this?" Abithi called out.

"I trust him." Reiya approached Matthew and extended her hand. "Will you come with me? We can't waste any more time."

He curled his upper lip. "You didn't tell me *those two* would be here."

"You know why." She blinked rapidly, her eyes bloodshot. "I bet my mother I could bring you here alone and in peace. It was the only way she'd show you the chest."

Something about the way her fingers trembled to reach his hand cooled the indignation within him. At the end, seeing the despicable duo again was inevitable.

Fighting the stiffness of his limbs, Matthew slid off his saddle. He positioned his shield ahead of him, but Reiya extended her arm past that and placed her hand on his wrist. He flinched.

"Let me show you I brought all the clay *kubozi*," she said.

There was no malice in her face, only a quiet resolve. Matthew swallowed hard. With a curt nod, he followed her toward the waiting ship.

The *Selkie* was as long as his father's longship, but with a wider deck and shallower freeboard that made it sit lower in the water. Vasfian warriors led Porei and Reiya's horse toward the stern to be secured. The rush of the wind swallowed their excited snorts. With the anchor withdrawn, the deck rocked beneath Matthew's feet as the ship pulled away from the shore.

What had he gotten himself into?

Reiya led him to the vessel's center, where a large chest rested between two Vasfian warriors. She knelt beside it and lifted the lid. All the grooves were occupied with what appeared to be giant, brown eggs with a cork plugging each one. Matthew's hands grew sweaty within his gloves. These formidable weapons looked so...strange, and so dull.

A second Vasfian stepped in to help Reiya as she removed the trays one by one. The trays below were also filled.

"See?" she asked. "Every clay *kubozi* is accounted for. Smell them so you know they're authentic."

Reiya handed Matthew a sphere, and a mere whiff of the cork sent him reeling. They were authentic, all right.

"I'm glad you've brought them," he said, his voice tight. "But you must keep them."

Silence. As he'd feared, Reiya's lips pinched into a tight line. "Why? You agreed back in Jethran that no one in England should possess such a monstrosity."

"I'll tell you why." Matthew adjusted his grip on the sphere. "My father warned me that other countries already know how to fight with fire. Fight with the substance in these clay balls. If we don't investigate how this new weapon works, those other countries can attack us. We'd be at their mercy."

As he spoke, Domilo ran to his mother's side and curled up beside her. Abithi wrapped an arm around her son's back, her gaze contemplative.

"What your father say is true," she said. "But how he speak to you?"

Matthew exhaled. "I read his letter in Marcottesville." He reached into his belt and pulled out the parchment roll. Turning it, he displayed his father's red lion seal.

Abithi's brows lifted. "So, you finally go home and read. Good. Your father my friend. He be happy to know you change."

She smiled. It was the first time he'd seen her appear genuinely cheerful, but Matthew still watched her warily.

"So, you agree we cannot dump the chest?" he asked.

"No. We do not agree." Reiya stepped forward. "If His Excellency wants to understand the clay *kubozi*, he confiscates them from the Boltans."

"But how easy will they be to attack?" Matthew widened his stance even as her scowl hovered close. "Why not use the rebels' own weapon against them?" He rubbed the sphere's stopper, its texture oddly greasy. "Maybe there's a way to ignite these without opening them—"

"No! You've seen how uncontrollable the black matter is, and you still want to use it? You agreed we'd get rid of it. The chest gets dumped."

Reiya motioned for her followers to help lift the chest. Matthew's breath caught. Panic clawed at his throat. He moved to stop them, but she yanked him back by the arm and whirled him around.

"Who is chief?" Her eyes blazed into his. "Me or you?"

Matthew wanted to yell back at her, tell her she was making a stupid decision. Yet, facing her fury, something crumbled within him. She was taking a stand like he'd encouraged her to do, even if it meant clashing with him.

And he'd been lying to her about why they'd partnered in the first place. It wasn't right. The only way forward in their alliance was to admit the truth.

"Reiya," he stammered in French. "I need to bring these to His Excellency if I want to redeem my knighthood."

She clenched her jaw. "Jacques said we need to capture Tobias Boltan first. Then he'd revoke the charges."

"No, that was a lie." The truth hovered on Matthew's tongue, both terrifying and inevitable. "Jacques told me in private he'd revoke the charges *only* if I stole a sample of the black matter from your tribe."

Reiya's lips parted, and her frown lifted.

"But I didn't give him what he wanted," Matthew continued, his face burning. "So he won't revoke his charge of my desertion. The accusation will reach His Excellency. I'll be called to court in Norwich. Then I'll need to prove myself still worthy of service..." His pulse hammered, and it was all he could do to keep speaking. "This is why I need to bring this chest to court. With you."

Her upper lip twitched with a flicker of emotion. Whether it was disappointment or anger, Matthew couldn't tell.

"Stop speaking French," Abithi demanded. "What he say?"

Reiya turned to her mother and interpreted Matthew's words into English. His mouth fell open. What felt like a blade of ice slid down to his stomach as he backed against the rail. When Reiya next spoke in Vasfian, all her followers, from the oarsmen to the worker forking hay for the horses, turned to stare at him.

What would they do to him now?

He finally locked eyes with Reiya again, unable to hide the terror swirling within him. Domilo sat up beside his mother. His eyes were wide with alarm, but Reiya spoke first.

"So you did plan to rob me," she choked out.

Abithi grunted. "You see? *Amah* be right. But you decide what to do now, Reirei."

"I'm sorry," Matthew murmured. "I aborted my plan, though. It would've ruined the Norman-Vasfian alliance. I didn't want that."

Domilo stood. "Matthew told Gabriel the bailiff about all the bad things Jacques did to us outside Brocklesby. Don't punish Matthew. He told the truth to help us."

The boy shot Matthew a worried glance, then stared pleadingly at his sister. This time, what looked like sympathy softened her features.

"Jacques left Marcottesville this morning," she said. "And you didn't tell him we had these clay *kubozi*?"

Matthew shook his head, and Domilo said, "That's right, he didn't say anything."

When Reiya turned to converse with her family again, Domilo walked to Matthew's side and pressed his shoulder against Matthew's arm. Neither spoke.

To his surprise, Abithi dug her elbows into her stretcher and tried to sit up. Both her son and mother rushed to her side to help. She finally sat slumped against Namanti. With great effort, she plucked one clay *kubozi* from the chest.

"I have idea. We save one." Her green eyes fastened on Matthew. "We make trade. You bring me dead Boltan for my healing *Anuin* on Samhain. I give you clay *kubozi* for your knighthood. I wait three days. If you no come, I throw down waterfall. Then no one can say, Vasfians hide something."

A faint smile lit the face of this woman who looked almost identical to Reiya but was decades older. Matthew's chest heaved as her words sank in. Her proposal sounded reasonable. Never did he imagine Abithi would align with him.

Reiya dipped her chin. "Fine. We'll throw everything but one."

She turned to her warriors and called out orders. Namanti raised her hands toward the sky, rattled her staff with the skulls, and began to chant. Two men lifted the chest over the railing and inverted it. Each plunk and splash of a sphere hitting the waves intensified his dread.

Could he still save Aliwyn without the help of those weapons? And save his knighthood with just one? It was not even his yet, not unless he brought back the enemy's corpse.

Finally, the Vasfians hefted the empty chest overboard.

"Now I leave," Abithi said as Domilo helped her lie back down. "I wait in Jethran."

She motioned to her followers, who reached over the rail to unfasten the anchor secured to the bow. The anchor splashed into the river, and the ship creaked as it settled. Matthew inhaled slowly. A raw breeze swept across the deck and lifted the scent of damp wood. He tried to stop shaking in a cold sweat.

The truth had come out, finally. And he was still alive.

Abithi and her household exchanged a few words before two followers lifted her off the ship. She clutched the last clay *kubozi* to her chest.

Domilo ran to Reiya and threw his arms around her in a fierce embrace. When he pulled away, his red-rimmed eyes sought Matthew.

"Thanks for everything," the boy said. "Even the horse ride at the end."

Matthew held his breath as the boy embraced him around the torso.

"Come back soon." Domilo's cheek pressed against his gambeson. "I still want to play chess with you."

A lump formed in Matthew's throat. He gave Domilo's checkered headscarf a tug over his red hair. When the boy stepped back, Matthew remembered the only word he'd learned in Vasfian.

"Sankei," he said.

Domilo beamed.

Reiya's family and several warriors disembarked one by one. Their figures shrank into the woodland along the shore as the galley's oars dipped into the water once more. The ship groaned as it eased away from shore.

Once the oars were rising and falling as before, Reiya stepped before Matthew. What if she still wanted to yell at him for his deceit, now that Domilo was gone? Matthew's back stiffened against the mast.

But Reiya's gaze remained calm as she said, "Come with me."

His pulse beat a double rhythm. Words tumbled in his mind, but none formed a coherent thought. When he didn't move, she grasped his forearm and pulled him toward the bow. He stumbled after her.

There was no shelter from the elements on the galley. Matthew squinted in the sunlight filtering through the overcast sky. Being alone with Reiya now felt different, somehow. She sat on a crate and leaned back against the rail.

"Sit." She jerked a thumb at the crate beside her.

Matthew did as he was told, grateful for her curt orders even as his pulse continued to race.

Reiya hunched over on her seat and raked her hands through her hair. "Do you really need clay *kubozi* to prove yourself? I find it ridiculous how much you need to perform to become a knight."

She truly didn't sound angry anymore, and Matthew sighed. "The strongest win. I can't change the rules."

"What if you prove yourself exemplary in battle?"

"That *is* another way. But I need to be in the right place at the right time. Most who try being 'exemplary' end up dead. We just don't hear about..."

His voice faltered. Aelfric's face as he told jokes and played recorders over the years passed through his mind. If he had survived Ransley's manor, he would've been—

"Matthew?" Reiya cut into his thoughts.

Blinking back to attention, he faced her concerned frown and forced himself to speak. "I was just thinking, that if Aelfric was still alive, I would've made sure he was knighted. What he did for me was exemplary."

Her brows drew with sorrow. "Never mind. Don't *you* try to do anything exemplary."

A low chuckle escaped Matthew, and he lowered his chin. What a relief not to have any more lies festering between them.

"I can also challenge Jacques to a duel," he said. "But Jacques will send a champion, while I don't have anyone to send in my place. Again, I'd risk my life while he risks nothing."

For a moment, Reiya fell silent as the ship rolled and creaked with the waves.

She drummed her fingers on her thigh and murmured, "I didn't know it was so difficult to become a knight. And stay one."

"Seems like being a chief is also difficult."

Strands of wavy hair blew across her earnest gaze. "Thank you for standing with my people. I didn't know Jacques leveraged your knighthood. That was terribly cruel."

Matthew grinned wryly. "Some people deserve to shovel manure for the rest of their lives."

Reiya huffed a light laugh, but it faded quickly. "Do you understand why I don't want anything more to do with that substance? It's too destructive." Her voice dropped, and the wind nearly carried her words away. "I know its use will spread, but I don't want to see it in battle during my lifetime. Or my children's lifetime, and even after that…"

Matthew thought of his father, who used to mumble to himself as he paced with a drink in hand. Now he knew the man had been haunted by the ghosts of old wars. A dark part of Matthew still longed to see the black matter's power unleashed on the battlefield, but it would come at a cost. Would he end up just as tormented?

He finally wrestled away the grim curiosity tangled within him. Torches were far less efficient, but they'd have to do.

"One *kubozi* is enough," he said. "Easier to carry, too."

She nodded. "I'm glad we agree. And I'll go to Norwich with you and ask to see His Excellency *before* your trial." She rubbed her gloved finger where the signet ring hid underneath. "Maybe he'll cancel the trial.

"G-good idea," Matthew said. Just imagining his accusations annulled lifted a weight from his shoulders, and the flicker of warmth spreading through him caught him off guard. "Thanks."

"You're…welcome."

As she spoke, a grimace descended over Reiya's face. Her fingers crinkled the fabric of her tunic as she pressed against her stomach. Matthew frowned. She had also braced her stomach while climbing up Mount Jethran.

"You all right?" he asked.

"I…I've been more tired than usual."

He shifted closer. "You can rest your head on my shoulder, if you want."

Reiya grew still, then lowered her gaze as a grin curled her lips.

Before Matthew could take stock of what he'd offered, she leaned in and settled her head on his shoulder. The softness of her hair sent a tingling sensation down his back, and the brush of their legs made heat rise to his face. What was happening?

But he'd already offered his shoulder; he couldn't take it back. Matthew swallowed and glanced at his other side. The rowing Vasfians faced the ship's stern, oblivious, and only Porei watched him contemplatively as she chewed on a mouthful of hay. Matthew forced his legs to stop quivering. No one here would tell anyone back home. A lady beside him didn't feel well, and any proper knight would offer a shoulder to rest on.

Reiya grew limp against him as she drifted asleep. The cold wind nipped at them, but the warmth between them held steady.

One thought weighed heavily on his mind. Courting someone outside his faith would anger the bishop and further jeopardize his knighthood. After the war, he and Reiya could only remain allies.

They sat in silence as the *Selkie's* bow cut through choppy waters. Sailboats emerged from the hazy horizon and glided toward them. The rhythmic sound of the oars barely broke the quiet. Matthew appreciated the silence that served to honor his fallen friend and family. In two days, all the scores would be settled.

The rotten egg stench of his gloves began to bother him. He should've taken them off before sitting beside Reiya. Trying not to wake her, he removed one glove, then the other.

Reiya stirred. As she blinked the sleep from her eyes, Matthew murmured, "I'm sorry for the smell."

Her gaze sharpened quickly. "No. It's not you."

Pulling back from his shoulder, she scanned the horizon and pointed. "Look. There's a column of smoke."

Matthew squinted into the distant fog before he saw what she meant. A gray plume rose from an entity he couldn't see. It was far too thick to be a smoke signal.

His body tensed. Something large was burning.

Reiya turned and called to her followers, and one woman began to climb the rope ladder leading to the crow's nest.

The rotten egg smell now enveloped the *Selkie,* and a deep unease settled in Matthew's gut. "Could the Danes be here early?"

"I was afraid of that." Reiya squinted at the fishing boats in the distance. "Maybe those ships are escaping the attack. We can ask them what is happening."

Matthew's pulse lodged in his throat. Two days. He was supposed to have another two days to prepare himself and Porei by practicing maneuvers and drills. Gripping his scabbard, he tested the strength of his right hand. It was strong enough, but he wasn't sure about Reiya.

Just then, the woman in the crow's nest shouted down her findings.

Reiya pushed to her feet, and her worried gaze met Matthew's. "She says the smoke comes from one island off the eastern coast, but I'm not familiar with that area."

Matthew stood as well. "It's probably from what my uncle called the Sinking Shoals." His jaw tightened. "The English call them the barrier islands. Some of those islands have fishing villages. They're isolated and vulnerable. Maybe they were attacked."

"We won't know until we go." She adjusted the crossbow and studded club strapped to her waist. "I'll prepare my crew."

She began to pass him, but Matthew called out, "Wait. You'll be all right?"

"I had a little nap." Reaching for his hand, she pulled it between the two of them where no one could see and squeezed his fingers. "Thank you."

Matthew's stomach flipped. He mustered a smile back just before she let go.

The galley sped on. It became clear that the fishing boats approaching them from the opposite direction had suffered through a fire, and their soot-stained sails emanated the telltale stench. Yet, they also veered away from the galley and its vibrant Vasfian colors. Matthew called to them in English and French, asking them questions, but he heard no response.

Only one sailboat with an empty canoe tethered behind it kept its course straight toward the *Selkie.* Nearly a dozen peasants in simple tunics and robes sat on board. They all stared blankly at the Vasfian galley, but one man with a black greyhound curled beside him waved a dirty, bandaged hand.

"Matthew! Reiya!" he called. "We meet again!"

Matthew scowled as he squinted at the filthy man. His voice had been familiar yet distant, as if pulled from another life.

Then it struck him. The man was Norman. And he was not well.

After his greeting, Norman's arm dropped as he slumped back in his seat. His bald spot was sunburned, and his damp tunic clung to his hefty frame. The dog curled beside him flicked an ear at the voices but didn't rise.

"Tell me Marcottesville is still takin' refugees?" Norman asked, his voice scraping like gravel.

Matthew stared at him and the dog, afraid they'd both disappear if he blinked. At least Norman hadn't died in the fire that consumed Myton. Now Kato would finally see Norman back, alive, and a ripple of relief coursed through Matthew.

"Yes, it should accept more refugees," he answered. "Are you all right? What happened to you?"

The man smirked. "I was hiding on the Boltans' ship. Eavesdroppin' on all their plans. I saw Sir Verdun pass this way earlier, and I told him everything..." He let out a rough breath. "Including how his squire is dead."

"What?" Matthew gripped the rail. "Vincent is dead?"

"Aye. Tobias killed him. He was a good man." His face despondent, Norman placed a hand on the dog's back. "I found poor Garrick here barkin' like mad on that little boat." He pointed behind him.

Matthew strained to see within the canoe trailing behind the sailboat. Clay shards littered the space between the benches, and its wooden frame was black.

He and Reiya exchanged tense glances. Were those remnants of clay *kubozi*? Could Tobias have used them in battle by...shattering them?

But then another thought struck Matthew like a fist. "Did you see Aliwyn?"

Norman's expression darkened. As his ship sailed past the *Selkie*, he lifted his wounded hand. "I saw her, all right, and she stabbed me. Tried to save Tobias."

Without thinking, Matthew scoffed. He couldn't have heard that right. "She what?"

"I said she stabbed me, that wench."

"*Stabbed?* The Aliwyn of Brocklesby?"

"What other Aliwyn can I be talking about?"

The deck seemed to tilt beneath Matthew. The Aliwyn he knew flinched at the sight of drawn steel. He stared at the blood seeping through Norman's bandages as the man cradled his hand. This former knight, dismissed from service because of his wanton drinking, must be exaggerating his tale.

"No," Matthew called out. "That's not possible."

"She made it possible!" Norman shouted back. The sailboat he sat on began to glide out of speaking range, and he twisted around with his teeth bared. "Go find the Boltans' ship! It's got a snapped yard and is probably sinking by now, 'cause I took an axe to the hull." He chuckled, a proud grin splitting his face. "And if you find Aliwyn alive, you'll need to arrest her. Sorry, Matthew, but she's in love with Tobias."

Now he had gone too far.

"That's ridiculous!" Matthew shouted.

A firm weight landed on his shoulder and tugged him back.

"We won't know until we find them," Reiya said. "But I had warned you..."

Matthew couldn't hide the grimace on his face.

Her lips pressed into a thin line, Reiya turned to her oarsmen and barked an order. The Selkie's strokes intensified, and the Vasfians repositioned the sails to maximize the galley's speed.

Matthew staggered to the bow as the rest of Norman's message crashed over him. The Boltans' ship was also sinking. What if he never found Aliwyn in time to discover the truth behind Norman's claims? Fingers curled around his upper arm from behind, steadying him, and Matthew turned.

Reiya's eyes were filled with sympathy. "You're imagining the worst again?"

"I..."

"You did everything you could to save her. Remember that."

The strength of her hand offered some comfort, but Matthew ducked his head. What if everything Norman had said was true?

CHAPTER 39
MIRIAM AND AELFIE

October 3, Aliwyn

Toby and Aliwyn stretched the hudfat taut between them over the sandbox fire. At his signal, she raised and lowered the fabric to control the bursts of smoke curling into the sky.

Her pulse thrummed as she watched Norman longships with sails of all colors glide toward Driftmere. Of course, the Normans' priority would be investigating the fire. The refugee ships fleeing Driftmere were only dark specks on the horizon now, and most had sailed toward the River Humber. None had arrived to answer their call for help.

She didn't blame them for trying to survive.

The *Lady Fortuna* continued its slow, tortured tilt. With the smaller vessels once tethered to it now gone, Toby and Aliwyn had no means of escape. The ship had also drifted too far from the nearest island for them to reach by swimming. Aliwyn prayed that their signal would bring someone with good intentions.

Only the cries of distant gulls broke the fire's crackle. Earlier on, Toby had shed his gambeson because of the heat. They had shared a quick meal of biscuits, water, and raw ginger to stay alert. As Aliwyn watched him, affection soothed the edge of her anxiety. Thank goodness he was willing to take care of himself again.

Over and over, they repeated their signal of three short puffs followed by a pause. Finally, five longships with black and red banners snapping at their sterns departed from Driftmere and angled toward the *Lady Fortuna*.

Toby had said those colors belonged to Jacques Verdun. Aliwyn wrung her hands. Of all the longships that could've answered their call, why did it have to be Jacques'? Would he now recognize Toby as the one who had evaded him outside Myton? Dread twisted within her until Toby touched her arm.

"Look." His voice was quiet but urgent.

He pointed toward the River Humber.

Another fleet emerged from around the bend. Its half-red, half-green sails stretched taut against the wind, while its blood-red hulls glided through the waves.

They were Vasfian galleys, specifically ones belonging to the Mehi tribe. Aliwyn had seen them docked at the lake beside her garden. Instead of sailing toward Driftmere, these galleys aimed their bows directly at the *Lady Fortuna*.

"No..." Aliwyn shook her head, despair slashing through her.

She had forgotten about the redheads. They must've been in pursuit of Toby ever since he escaped from Brocklesby, and they wouldn't care about trial by inquest. They'd only want Toby dead, maybe take his head. And her head.

"The Mehi," she stammered. "Those ships belong to the Mehi. How did they know to come all the way here? And right behind Jacques' longships?"

Toby lowered the hudfat beside him. "Perhaps because of Matthew?"

Ice wrapped around Aliwyn's stomach. She had expected to see Matthew after she and Toby had been taken to town and were awaiting the inquest, not aboard the same ship where she had so blatantly betrayed Matthew's trust. What if he sensed something had developed between her and Toby? What if he lashed out the way he'd attacked Emma?

Toby wiped the soot from his knitted brows. "It's unclear right now whether Jacques or the Vasfians will arrive first. And between Jacques or any other knight, I would've preferred the other knight."

He sighed, and Aliwyn couldn't move as blood pulsed in her ears. Would *everyone* who wanted Toby dead soon step on board? How would she face so much hatred?

"We can stop sending the signal now," Toby said. "Come check on the hull with me. Then I have something to tell you."

Aliwyn found a sliver of relief in his calm tone. They grabbed buckets from under the front platform and carried them downstairs. Silently, they filled both with seawater, but their efforts were futile. The water had already reached the second rung of the staircase, and the privy door at the rear was a third submerged. Aliwyn hurried back upstairs to avoid seeing the two corpses, but Toby stalled.

"Give me a moment," he said quietly, turning back toward the darkness. "I want to see Edward and Cilebi one last time."

Aliwyn's stomach turned. She ascended, set her bucket aside with a thunk, and waited on the last step. Thankfully, Toby returned only a short while later, but his eyes were bloodshot again.

"Are you all right?" she whispered.

He nodded, his voice somber as he answered, "I got what I needed."

Before she could ask him what he meant, he continued. "The others should be here before the *Fortuna* sinks."

"We should still try to bail it out," Aliwyn insisted. The thought of Vasfians stomping aboard the ship made her shudder. Desperate to distract herself, she picked up the bucket again.

Back on deck, Toby emptied his bucket overboard. He took Aliwyn's from her rigid arms, dumped the water, and stepped close. As his warm hand settled on her shoulder, she forced herself to look up at his pleasant expression. How could she feel so lost after being so hopeful moments ago?

"I know you don't want to deny me," he began, his hand sliding down to her forearm. "But listen. When the others board, whether they're Vasfians or Normans, you must pretend to have no sympathy for me. We'll separate after this. If God wills it, Jacques will let me live long enough for an inquest. That's when you'll seek help from Evelyn or Lord Seville. But that's only possible if one of us isn't in prison."

Separate. The word struck her like a blow. "I..."

"Matthew Marcotte is likely on one of those ships," Toby continued, his voice low. "He has connections to people who might...might still help me. Help us."

Aliwyn scowled at the frayed hem of her sleeve. Evelyn was Matthew's cousin, and Lord Seville was his tutor. Yet, Matthew himself wanted Toby dead. How could she face him and convince him to spare Toby?

"I don't want to leave you," she whispered.

"I can't think of another way." Toby's gaze was steady. "The hardest battles are fought without weapons, but you've given me hope. I want to see Zel and Emma again."

"I do too," Aliwyn said, but her composure crumbled.

"Prince Cnut will still be here in two days," Toby added. "Driftmere's fire will alert him that something is wrong, but I doubt he'll give up so easily. If he attacks, I can't protect you. Only the Normans can."

"Where are Lord Seville and Evelyn?" Her whisper barely carried over the wind.

"I don't know about Evelyn, but Lord Seville probably stayed in Norwich after the siege on Ralph's estate. And when you see Lord Seville, give him this." Toby reached into his belt pouch and produced a silver ring. The griffin carved into its face seemed to snarl up at them, its wings etched so deeply that they cast shadows across the metal.

Aliwyn's eyes widened. "This is...?"

"Edward's signet. Go to Norwich Minster. Show the chancellor this ring as evidence of Edward's death and ask to see Lord Seville." Toby pressed the cold weight into her palm. "And when you see him, tell him you killed Edward. God willing, he'll lead the inquest and grant us mercy." Smiling gently, Toby withdrew four pennies and offered them to her. "I also found these on Edward. The money will help you, I'm sure."

Aliwyn nodded and tucked the ring and pennies beside Toby's recorder. Norwich Minster. Now she knew where to go, but her chin still quivered.

Toby pulled her into an embrace. "You'll know what to say when the time comes, Ali."

She grabbed a fistful of his tunic. Toby was supposed to stay with her through all of this. Not...

He stepped back, squeezed her shoulders one last time, then stooped to pick up the hudfat they'd used to send the smoke signal.

His determined expression had softened. "Come with me under the forecastle."

"Why?" She wrung her hands. "We should keep bailing out the ship."

"That can wait."

"No, it's urgent."

Toby bunched the hudfat under his arm. "There's something more important I want to do."

"What?"

A hint of amusement touched his lips. "Come with me."

She hesitated, her heart still racing, and wiped her itchy face with the back of one hand. Before she could lower it, Toby's fingers laced through hers. He had taken off his glove, and his hold was warm and insistent. Aliwyn finally relented and let herself be led toward one of the pillars supporting the front platform.

The walk was on an upward incline, and her legs ached. What if the ship tilted to a vertical position as it sank? It would be terrifying.

"We can sit behind one of those pillars," Toby said.

They reached the shelter beneath the front platform. As he spread the opened hudfat behind the post, she understood why he'd chosen this area. If the ship tilted drastically, they could huddle behind the pillar and avoid falling into the sea.

Toby sat with an almost casual grin on his face. What was he thinking? Aliwyn blinked rapidly as he spread out his right arm in invitation.

She tried to match his expression. With sunlight breaking overhead, the gulls crying out, and the scent of woodsmoke drifting from the hudfat, she could almost imagine they were on a beach. Toby's endearing smile reminded her of Miriam yet again. She couldn't leave him waiting.

Fighting the stiffness in her spine, she sat beside him and pulled her tired legs to her chest. How strange that he'd want to sit still when everything argued against being...content.

Toby wrapped his arm around her shoulder and murmured warmly in her ear, "Did you ever think about a different circumstance in which we could've met?"

Really? He wanted to talk about *that?*

"N-no," she answered.

The ship tilted so much to its left side that Aliwyn could see the ocean over the rail without standing. She shuddered and stared at her kneecaps.

"Can I tell you what I think?" Toby asked. He reached up with his free hand and brushed a damp strand of hair from her cheek.

His touch was grounding, sending warmth past her chilled skin and into the aching places within her. She nodded and offered a quivering smile.

His expression turned serious. "Well, for one, I won't crawl through your rubbish hole."

Aliwyn let out a surprised giggle, and his face melted into a grin.

Maybe she should try to enjoy this moment that felt so out of place because so much could go wrong.

She leaned against him and gazed up at his face. "It wasn't the most dignified entrance, but I don't..." She bit her lip. "I don't know how we would've spoken otherwise. You're a knight, and I'm..."

He raised an eyebrow. "Are knights not allowed to speak to attractive women?"

Her breath caught. Despite all that was happening, he could still make her blush.

"One sunny morning in September," he said gently, "I ride back to Brocklesby to visit Miriam, and I see a young maiden weeding her garden."

Her garden. Aliwyn could almost smell the thyme on a crisp summer morning, and she felt her spirits lifting.

His lips quirked as he studied her reaction. "She is holding her chickens on her lap and is so sweet to them. I'm curious about her, so I ask her for a drink of water and where the mill is...even though I know exactly where it is."

Aliwyn drew back and narrowed her eyes in mock offense. "You silly flirt."

Toby chuckled.

"I would've seen through that guise right away," she huffed. "My garden is next to a lake, and anyone can drink from it. I would've just pointed toward the mill and left you alone."

Her chest fluttered. In truth, such a tall, well-built knight with a kind face riding past her garden would've warranted a very, very long stare.

"Oh, but my steed is hungry." Toby's eyes twinkled with mischief. "So he starts pulling up your carrots. You'll do something about that, yes?"

"Charge you for the carrots, obviously." Aliwyn smirked, but her smile faded as she added, "And...and ask why you want to see my mentor."

"I tell you she once tended to my broken arm, and it was about time I came back to thank her." His expression grew pensive, and Aliwyn's throat tightened.

"Miriam is alive?" she whispered.

"Of course. It's why I'm back to visit her."

"Does she...does she welcome you as her son?"

Toby hesitated. There was a hint of a frown, of deeply rooted longing. "She does."

Aliwyn wrapped her arm around his. "That would've been wonderful. I always thought she was so good with children that she should've had some of her own."

Toby became silent. She never wanted this to hurt him, but working through what could've been meant talking about their past again. Snuggling against him, she continued. "Miriam and I ask you to stay for lunch. She says I make a very good turnip stew."

"I stay. Of course I stay," Toby murmured. "But then someone knocks on the door."

Aliwyn looked up at him in surprise. "Who is it?"

"The other person who lives there." His voice faltered, and sorrow returned to his eyes. "Aelfric. He's also home for a meal."

Aliwyn's eyes smarted with tears. "Can...Can he come in?"

"Of course. It's his home, too."

She quivered against Toby's shoulder.

"Then Aelfie comes in with firewood and eats with us," she said softly. "We'll pull out the extra stool and talk about your travels. And then Aelfie..." Her voice broke. "He plays his recorder. Will you play yours?"

"Certainly, if you want me to."

Aliwyn wiped her eyes. "Thank you for including Aelfie."

Looking back, Aelfric had many reasons not to be himself the last time they'd seen each other. He had been consumed by his plan to not only rescue

Matthew, but also Toby. And Aelfric had saved both but never returned himself. Aliwyn smiled despite the pain in her chest. Aelfric had been so courageous. He'd always be remembered as her closest friend.

Toby's throat bobbed as he swallowed several times.

"Don't thank me," he said. "And...can I ask you something?"

"Yes?"

His fingers twitched against his knee. "Who was Aelfric to you? A good friend, or..." His forehead wrinkled. "Was there a reason you would've been offended at a little flirting?"

Her chin trembled. She had never told anyone about what she'd really thought of Aelfric, but Toby deserved to know. "I wanted to marry Aelfie. I wanted to for years, but he didn't like me back in that way. He told other people I was his sister."

Toby frowned, and sympathy shone in his eyes.

She managed to smile. "But it's all right. We don't choose who we fall in love with. And love is so much better when it's reciprocated."

Without realizing it, her hand had drifted to Toby's collar, and her fingers rested over the warmth of his neck.

"Actually," she whispered, "if you had come to my garden, I would've stared at you and probably lost my voice. Such a handsome knight talking to...to me."

Toby leaned closer, his breath brushing her cheek. His smile was soft, teasing, but there was something raw beneath it.

"I'm still yours," he murmured.

Aliwyn's heart ached at the words and the certainty they carried. His hand found hers still curled against his collar. He held them there, pressing them lightly to his pulse.

How wonderful it was to have her affection reciprocated.

"And I'm yours," she whispered.

Toby's smile grew as he eased back and drew her against him. She let herself fall onto his good arm, sinking down onto the hudfat beside him. Their breath mingled in the dim light below the back platform. His chest rose and fell as he shifted onto his side, mirroring her as she lay beside him.

His left shoulder must still be uncomfortable, but it didn't stop him from pulling her close. She trembled from the heat of his body over the soft wool.

When his gaze dipped to her lips, she leaned toward him, breathless and waiting.

Toby kissed her.

His warm lips sank into hers, his kiss at once gentle and yet hungry for more. Aliwyn cupped his face. The scrape of his stubbled jaw made her shiver. His kiss deepened, sending wildfire down her chest and through her limbs. She threaded her fingers through his hair, basking in the heat of his closeness and the open palm that rose behind her back with the warmth of the sun.

He was still strong. Her heart raced. With every breath she begged Heaven that he'd be allowed to live.

As they pulled back, their foreheads touched, and Aliwyn opened her eyes. Her face was wet. With whose tears, she didn't know. Gulls cried in the background, the wind was sweeping and harsh as before, and the doomed ship groaned from the water it carried. Fear returned to the depths of Toby's gaze as he looked around. The world around her whirled back with its full intensity.

Beyond the ship's rail, she knew the Vasfian warships and the Norman longships were approaching.

Still, she tried for a smile.

"If something happens to us," she whispered, "know that I forgive you."

Toby grew still. Even the sound of his panting ceased, and tears welled in his eyes before he closed them. He grimaced, but he didn't have to. She gathered him close again and kissed him tenderly over both eyelids.

"Thank you, Ali," he whispered. "One day we are all supposed to meet in Heaven. How the first conversation would go between us..." he drew a slow breath, "I don't know. But there are supposed to be no more tears up there, and I believe it."

He drew an arm around her waist, and she rested her head against his shoulder. She closed her eyes as the rough weave of his tunic graced her temples. When the time came to see all her loved ones again, she'd know what to say.

But before then, there would be another confrontation. She'd enter the struggle without regrets. Lacing her fingers between Toby's, she held them tight.

CHAPTER 40
TRAITOR'S HEART

Toby

It was late afternoon by the time Jacques' longships clustered beside the port side of the *Fortuna*.

Her stern had sunk dangerously close to sea level, but even more dangerous was the tilt toward the port side that threatened to slide Toby into the water. He widened his stance under the shadow of the forecastle to maintain balance.

One last time, he reached over the starboard rail, where Aliwyn clung to the fishing nets once more. Jacques and his men wouldn't find her on this side, at least not immediately. Now she had to follow through with the plan they'd discussed.

Aliwyn's slender fingers slid between his. He squeezed them, hard. *I know you can do this, Ali.*

Although grief and longing swirled within him, he dared not lean over to see her again.

The words he'd been waiting for rang over the rail. "The royal army commands you to show yourselves."

Toby could recognize Jacques Verdun's sonorous voice anywhere.

He hobbled behind a forecastle's pillar, the blazing orange sun slanting over his eyes, and braced himself for support. "Greetings, Sir Verdun."

The *Fortuna*'s sinking side dipped to the level of the longships. Foot soldiers grabbed the rail and climbed on board. One unlocked the entry rail and swung it aside, allowing a gangplank to slide in place. Jacques sauntered aboard with his plumed helmet, cape, and chainmail. His weight alone seemed to rock the ship.

More soldiers followed with spears upright and their expressions unreadable beneath their helmets. A few jolted when they saw Ransley's corpse, but none spoke.

Jacques' gaze swept the grimy deck, then settled on Toby. "Greetings, Sir Boltan. Your ship has seen better days."

"She has."

His gaunt face broke into a grin as he looked down. "And your father's dead! Saving him for the vultures, are you?"

He kicked Ransley's corpse, and Toby flinched. To see his father's body treated with such irreverence...was grief stirring within him at the worst moment?

"I wanted you to see that he was dead," Toby said coldly.

Jacques grunted. His helmet glinted under the scorching sky. "Where's your uncle? The dozens of mercenaries working for you?"

"Edward's dead in the hull. The other men evacuated ship."

Mocking laughter escaped Jacques' lips. "And what about that sweet woman and child you escorted outside Myton?"

Toby steeled himself against a wave of chills. Even with two of his relatives dead and available to him, Jacques still asked for Aliwyn and Emma.

"They also evacuated," he answered.

The wind shifted and carried the sea's briny scent through the *Fortuna's* crumpled sailcloth. She rocked again, and Jacques' soldiers exchanged uneasy glances as they shuffled their sliding boots.

Jacques arched a brow at Toby. "And yet you remain?"

"I knew there was no escape for me."

"Very good! I'm flattered that you have such faith in the royal army." The man paced the deck with deliberate steps, his boots thudding against the damp planks. "I believe you're in possession of a flammable substance. One that the Driftmere brothers are absolutely terrified of."

Toby blinked. "Th-they're alive?"

"It seemed like most of them survived."

And which ones did not? Toby looked away, his carefully rehearsed words escaping him.

Walking the length of the ship, Jacques frowned. His tone took on an anxious lilt. "Where are they, Tobias? The terracotta eggs I heard about? The black pebbles?"

"Gone. Thrown overboard to lighten the load."

Jacques' mouth twitched. "Unfortunate."

Toby glowered back at him.

Jacques ordered his men to scatter and search the ship. None approached where Aliwyn hid, but blood roared in Toby's ears. He crept down the incline and away from her.

"You're wasting your time," he called out. "Everything's gone."

"Hmm." Jacques' irritation was palpable. "And where can I find more?"

"Nowhere."

Jacques' face darkened. "Search the lower decks."

Toby licked his lips. It was now clear what Jacques wanted, and it was something Toby would never give him. His hands curled into fists. He already knew what Jacques would do next—extort his prisoner for information. And that involved torture.

He'd be dead soon unless Aliwyn... His vision tunneling, he forced himself to the present.

A soldier called from the bow's rail. "Vasfian galleys thirty paces away."

Toby inhaled sharply. Matthew Marcotte would be on board to rescue Aliwyn. He had to be.

Jacques massaged his temples. "Why must incompetence be so persistent?"

He turned toward the approaching galleys but paused when his soldiers pounded up the stairs.

"Sir," one called out. "I found no cargo. Just two dead men out of reach."

Jacques hesitated, and his forehead crinkled. "Vincent?"

"Not him, but one is Edward Boltan." The man's mouth twisted. "It looks like he vomited pottage before dying. Maybe...dysentery."

Jacques' face flushed red before smoothing back into icy indifference.

"Disgusting." He waved a hand. "Just leave the corpses there."

His hooded gaze narrowed on Toby. "I have a report that your ship was stocked with dozens of crates and chests. That you killed my squire in a battle of fire."

Who had given him that report? The stowaway who had escaped? Toby said nothing.

"Are you going to talk to me, Sir Boltan?"

"I have nothing to say before my inquest."

Jacques stepped closer. Toby edged backward, toward the sinking stern, and drew Jacques away from Aliwyn's hiding place. His boots slipped against the listing deck.

"Who says you'll have an inquest?" Jacques cocked his head.

"Convicted Englishmen have the right to inquest if they surrender peacefully—"

"Ahh, but I can change the rules during a revolt, you see? I already tortured and killed your Lord Yeaton and all four of his sons. They weren't very helpful, but you still have a chance. Want to see your monk friends? Or that little girl in the forest?"

Toby blinked. He reined in his grief for Lord Yeaton's family and his yearning for Emma. The wolf before him was finally baring his fangs.

"Then let's work together." Jacques leaned in, his breath stale, his voice like a blade. "If there is no more of what you called the potash compound, we will make some."

Toby stood his ground. "I don't know how."

"But you will remember." The man smirked. "When I find and torture your darling in front of you. Aliwyn of Brocklesby, yes?"

Aliwyn

WIND WHIPPED ALIWYN'S HAIR about her face as the rough netting bit into her hands. To her left, the Vasfian galleys cut through the water with their expansive red and green sails, but she was far from relieved. Jacques' threat to both her and Toby echoed in her ears. If Toby was shut away from the world to never receive a fair inquest, what could she still do?

A familiar man with cropped hair smiled and waved to her from the closest galley. Beside him stood a redhead who crossed her arms and did neither. Toby had been right. Both Matthew and Reiya would be here. Anticipation and dread churned within Aliwyn. She forced her stiff limbs to climb down until frigid seawater sprayed her boots.

Help was here, but tears stung her eyes. Who was going to rescue Toby?

"Aliwyn!" Matthew cried.

A wave of chills ran up her damp feet. Now Jacques would know she was here.

Reiya shouted orders to her followers to turn and anchor the galleys. Meanwhile, Matthew stood at the bow with his arms outstretched.

Her breath caught. She had never seen him smile so much. Did she deserve such a welcome?

Footsteps vibrated down from the deck of the *Lady Fortuna*. Aliwyn's pulse spiked. Someone was coming, but the galley was also bobbing within reach.

She had scarcely extended an arm toward Matthew when he grabbed her wrist. With a cry of triumph, he wrapped an arm around her waist and hoisted her off the netting. Her feet landed safely. She almost shrieked when Matthew pulled her to his chest in a tight embrace. His woolen cape was warm, and yet he was shaking.

"Thank God..." he whispered.

Aliwyn couldn't breathe. She had kissed Toby just hours before.

Reiya's boots thudded on the galley as she approached with her chin held high and her face flushed. There was something spiteful about the way her gaze traced Matthew's arms around her back. Aliwyn squirmed until he released her.

"Why did you stab Norman Rochefort?" Reiya demanded.

The redhead was as hostile as she'd feared, and Aliwyn struggled to calm herself. She gestured to the gash on her neck. "He almost killed me. I fought him in self-defense."

Reiya only narrowed her eyes.

Draping his cape over Aliwyn's shoulders, Matthew looked at her up and down. "What else happened to you?"

"I'll tell you later," Aliwyn stammered. She was afraid to look behind at the *Lady Fortuna*. "I just heard Jacques say he wants to torture me."

"What?" Matthew froze. "Why?"

The answer caught in her throat. If she admitted it was to coerce information out of Toby, Matthew would wonder why Toby would care at all. Aliwyn thought of a lie to give, but looking at Matthew, at the concern lining his face, she chose to tell the truth. "Because Jacques wants Toby to talk, to tell him how the cargo was made."

Matthew's upper lip curled. All the joy in seeing her vanished, and dread pooled in Aliwyn's stomach.

"No," Matthew muttered. "He won't get to. Tobias dies first."

"Oh, stop being a nuisance, will you?" A voice rang out from overhead. "I decide if he lives or dies."

Aliwyn sucked in her breath and looked up; Jacques leaned over the rail, his mouth moving as though he were chewing something repulsive.

"You'll let him *live*?" Matthew shouted.

"Useful men, I keep. Useless men..." Jacques flicked the back of his hand at Matthew. "I discard."

"No! Tobias dies now!"

Aliwyn squeezed her eyes shut.

Matthew's hand landed on her back. "Go hide in the stern. I'll never let Jacques take you."

Reaching down, he grabbed his shield leaning against the rail and pushed his helmet over his head.

"Let's go, Reiya!"

With a wave of his arm, he jumped to the adjacent galley. Two galleys and one longship were now anchored in such close proximity that he and Reiya could jump from one to the other until they reached the *Lady Fortuna*. Other longships and galleys floated within crossbow range around this dying, dark giant silhouetted in the tangential sunlight.

The battle Aliwyn had not dared to imagine was at hand. She stumbled after Matthew despite the Vasfian rowers calling her back. Her wobbly legs barely made the jump to the next galley.

She had agreed with Toby that she'd stay on the Vasfian ship, that she'd stay quiet and let him get arrested. But neither of them had expected things to spiral out of control.

"Jacques!" Matthew shouted as he jumped onto the closest longship. "I challenge Tobias to a duel, here and now!"

The sailors on board the longship recoiled as Matthew began stomping up the gangplank they had extended. Behind him, Reiya seemed to hesitate, but she soon hurried after him.

"On guard!" she shouted back at her warriors.

The redheads picked up their shields. They formed a defensive wall before Aliwyn, but she squeezed past them. Matthew's cape slipped from her shoulders.

No. She would not stay hidden and let one man kill the other.

Matthew

THERE WAS ONLY ONE way to kill Tobias now—provoke him into retaliating. Then he'd never get an inquest. He could be killed like any rebel on the battlefield.

Ever since Aelfric died, Matthew had been waiting for this moment.

He marched up the gangplank. The Boltan's ship was a disgusting mess. A broken yardarm lay across the deck while a replacement beam rested haphazardly beside it amongst heaps of sailcloth. Soot and wood chips coated everything. The reek of soot and sweat clung to the deck.

Matthew's target stood along the opposite rail, hair sticking out in all directions, and a look of indifference on his filthy face. Had he been this apathetic when he'd killed Matthew's parents, his uncle and aunt, his best friend? His hands clenched, Matthew stepped onto the slimy deck and marched forward. He almost tripped over Ransley's corpse.

He looked down; the old knave was dead. A rush of satisfaction surged through him. One Boltan dead. Another soon to die. He'd worry about Edward Boltan later.

Reiya fell into step beside him and raised her shield.

"Be careful." She gave Matthew a look of warning.

"Be careful of what?" he shot back.

Bandages covered Tobias' right hand while his left shoulder slumped at an odd angle. He had no shield and his gambeson was slit open in multiple places, the tramp. He looked like a man already defeated. Matthew chuckled to himself. Tobias would have no choice but to draw his weapon in self-defense.

"Accept that you've lost our little competition, will you?" Jacques straightened and adjusted his belt. "Tobias is my prisoner."

To Matthew's surprise, Reiya answered, "Let me have Ransley's body."

"Why? I got here first."

"I struck him on the head days ago." Reiya gestured at the bandages still around the man's temples. "I'm certain that's what killed him. We need his body for a ritual."

Jacques raised an eyebrow. "It doesn't matter. I got here first and he's my prize. But if you need a body…" He raised an upturned hand toward the staircase. "Go fish Edward's out of the hull. Tobias has kindly informed me he's already dead."

Reiya turned to Matthew, her brows knit with a concern he didn't understand.

"We already have the head we need," she said.

"But not the one we want!" He glared at her. What was this? Fear that he couldn't kill Tobias while everyone watched?

Matthew stepped forward, drawing his sword and spinning it with a flick of his wrist. "Tobias faces me in one-on-one combat. The loser dies."

Jacques rolled his eyes. "No. The sinking ship is too dangerous for any duel—"

"You have no authority to prevent one!" Matthew charged past him.

Tobias widened his stance, his gaze sharpening. When Matthew's blade came slicing down, he jerked to the side and ducked behind a heap of sailcloth. Matthew pursued him and leaped over the broken crossbeam. When he landed, his boot skidded sideways and sent him lurching in the opposite direction. His lower back twinged. Gritting his teeth, Matthew straightened just in time to see Tobias hobbling toward the stern. His sword remained hanging at his side.

Matthew's vision darkened at the edges. For his family. For Aelfric. He'd carve the indifference off that impassive face.

Jacques barked an order, but the words blurred into the blood pounding in Matthew's ears.

He charged again. Tobias sidestepped behind the mast as Matthew's blade whistled a thumbspan from his shoulder. Matthew swerved after him but slipped again on the planks. He caught himself on a crossbeam and accidentally shoved it aside. The heavy timber rolled toward Jacques and his men as they tried to intervene, sending them stumbling back.

Voices screamed all around him, but Matthew's world had narrowed to Tobias and the blade in his hand.

The wretch backed up the tilting deck, remaining close to the rail and always dragging one foot. Matthew's boots pounded over the groaning ship. When he swiped again, his blade snagged on ropes extending from the mast. He almost roared with rage. Finally, his eyes fell on the rebel's hearth. Matthew grabbed a fistful of hot sand and hurled it at Tobias' face.

The man shielded his eyes with his arms and stumbled back. When he struggled to regain balance, he grimaced and gripped his left side, where the Vasfians' arrow had struck him. Matthew's lips curled into a dark smile.

"Matthew, stop!" Aliwyn's voice from behind cut through the chaos.

He froze. Aliwyn? He'd told her to stay hidden!

Tobias hesitated too, his head snapping toward her voice. It was the opening Matthew needed. He lunged and swiped toward Tobias' face. His opponent jerked back, but Matthew's blade nicked his ear down to his chin. With a cry, Tobias spun aside and fell onto one knee.

Matthew raised his sword over the man's head. Yet, light footsteps pattered to his side, and small fingers clawed into his upper arm.

"Stop!" Aliwyn's cry rang in his ears. "Your commander told you to stop!"

He could've easily broken free of her grasp, but Matthew froze. Her tearful eyes pierced him through. To see her like this, blatantly disregarding his order to stay on the galley—

"All right, enough!" Jacques barked. He stomped to Matthew's side, grabbed his arm, and wrenched it behind him.

Something within Matthew crumpled. Aliwyn. Jacques. Both were supposed to want Tobias dead as much as he did. Clenching his jaw, Matthew glared at the blond churl whose mournful gaze remained locked on Aliwyn.

How dare he look at her like that!

Matthew let out a shout and kicked Tobias in the chest. The force sent him rolling toward the port side and straight toward Reiya, who doubled back with her eyes blazing.

Jacques locked Matthew's wrist in a vise-like grip. "If you don't stop, I'll add obstructing justice to your charges! Drop your sword!"

"You're already in enough trouble!" Aliwyn shouted.

His jaw tight, Matthew turned toward her. Why wasn't she proud of him for avenging Aelfric?

Jacques' soldiers stomped and slid toward Tobias, who lay writhing at Reiya's feet. She bared her teeth. As she looked up at Matthew, her gaze burned with the same fire that raged within him. Desperation. Sorrow. To know the man who had stolen their loved one would soon rise and walk away. The ache in Matthew's throat deepened.

He had failed everyone.

The soldiers grabbed Tobias and pulled him to his knees, pinning his arms behind him. Matthew could scarcely watch. Why had Aliwyn grabbed his arm at the last instant? Had Norman been right about her betrayal?

Jacques' death grip remained around his wrist. His face hot, Matthew looked up again. He should've looked earlier. Tobias was struggling to stand, his neck covered in blood from Matthew's sword, when Reiya released her club from its holster. She raised her weapon over Tobias' head in a blow that would surely crack his skull.

But Aliwyn pivoted in a whirl of brown hair and lunged toward her.

Matthew dropped his sword with a clatter.

He couldn't hear himself scream. Aliwyn drove her shoulder into Reiya's stomach. The young chief cried out in pain, and her club fell onto the floorboards.

Matthew threw Jacques' hand aside. He bolted toward the scene as Reiya shoved Aliwyn off. The smaller woman stumbled backward toward the water.

"No!" Matthew and Toby cried at once.

Aliwyn's head struck the edge of the rail's opening, and she shrieked. An instant later, she spun overboard and into the sea.

CHAPTER 41
BITTER CURRENTS

Aliwyn

THE ICY WATER STOLE Aliwyn's breath. Her head spun from striking the rail, and her flailing limbs did nothing against the waves pulling her under. The world around her blurred, the cold quickly sapping her strength. The shouts from the longship above grew distant.

Oars splashed close to her face, but her trembling fingers slipped when she reached for them. She gasped for air only to suck in a mouthful of saltwater.

Someone splashed into the water beside her.

"Hold on!" Matthew sputtered.

He hauled her arm over his shoulder and clasped her wrist against his chest.

Aliwyn coughed in agony as the salt stung her throat and nose, but she was breathing air again. Her head lolled against him as he fought the waves.

Scenes from the fight replayed endlessly in her mind, ending with her desperate move to stop Toby from suffering his father's fate. Even as Matthew held onto her, his torso heaving with the effort of keeping them both afloat, fear crept in.

Was he going to ask why she had done that?

With a grunt, Matthew caught onto an extended oar. Aliwyn felt the two of them being drawn in. The world tilted dangerously whenever she opened her eyes, but she forced herself to look up.

She could barely discern Toby on a longship with his hands bound behind him. Blood now stained the collar of his drab tunic, and none of the soldiers rowing around him seemed to care. When he turned to look at her, sobs racked her body.

Toby, wait for me.

And yet, she had no choice but to cling onto Matthew for now.

The oar pulled them both toward the galley. Vasfians reached down, pulled her off Matthew's back, and hauled her onto the deck. She collapsed onto the wooden planks, gasping for air, her wet hair plastered to her face. The wounds on her neck and elsewhere burned from the salt.

Blankets were thrown over her, but the cold still seeped into her bones. She curled herself into a ball and cradled her aching head. This, coupled with the blow to her head from tumbling off the donkey cart, meant days of headache.

"Aliwyn, are you all right?" Matthew's voice cut through the haze.

She opened her eyes a slit. He crouched beside her, propped up on one elbow with seawater trickling down his face. Even now, after she'd yelled at him and his Vasfian ally, Matthew's eyes were filled with concern. The guilt within her gnawed deeper than the cold.

"My head hurts," she whispered, "but it'll go away."

Matthew nodded, but his brow remained furrowed. He pulled his own blanket higher over his shoulders. "Why...why did you stop me from killing Tobias?"

Aliwyn's teeth chattered. Reiya stood behind him in the late afternoon sun and directed her warriors to board the *Lady Fortuna* and search for Edward's body. Her scowl kept flashing back to Matthew and the woman lying across from him. Aliwyn's toes curled; she had to choose her words carefully.

"I didn't want to see anyone die." She coughed, her throat tight. "And I was afraid you and Reiya would get into trouble with Jacques. I didn't want another battle like the one outside my mill."

That wasn't a lie, but she couldn't reveal the full truth.

Matthew's expression softened. When he ducked his head, Aliwyn's chest tightened with sympathy. He looked so different than when he'd rampaged on deck with his sword.

"I understand," Matthew said finally. "I probably...went too far. Tobias will most likely die in Jacques' custody, anyway."

Fresh tears surged from Aliwyn's eyes and mingled with the seawater stinging her cheeks. Her shaky fingers sought Toby's recorder in her belt pouch. It was all she had left of him since he decided to cast his journal into the sea. Now that he wanted to live, he wanted to break from his past. If only he had the chance.

"Matthew!" Jacques' voice boomed from the waters. "I want that peasant woman for questioning."

Aliwyn held her breath as Matthew straightened with a frown. All around the galley, Jacques' longships with their black and red flags circled like predators around their prey.

Reiya marched to the bow with her hand on her club.

"Why don't you talk to me?" she shouted at Jacques. "And no, you can't have her. My people found her first."

Tension between the two factions hung thick in the air. Aliwyn squeezed the wet strands falling to her fingers. She was grateful for Reiya's defiance, but the chief acted out of pride and not compassion.

Finally, Jacques grunted. "Expect unfortunate news later this month, Matthew."

The bridge of Matthew's nose wrinkled, but he said nothing.

"What news?" Aliwyn asked softly.

But he didn't seem to hear her, and Reiya shot her a glare that silenced further questions.

Her warriors erected shields around the galley and blocked Jacques from view. Above the makeshift wall, the longships' broad sails began to turn away in the evening sun. Finally, the garish black and red flags retreated.

Relief trickled through Aliwyn, but the worry for Toby's safety continued to choke her. What his captors wanted was information he refused to tell anyone. She prayed in silence that someone would tend to him until she could convince another Norman to extract him from Jacques' claws and grant him a fair inquest.

Whatever relief she'd felt at Jacques' receding sails vanished when Reiya marched toward her with her jaws set. The last time they'd met, in Brocklesby, Aliwyn had rudely dismissed the Vasfian's invitation to a sacred feast. Aliwyn had scoffed at Reiya's effort to form a partnership. Now, with Matthew thrown into the mix, Reiya seemed more irritable than ever.

The redhead picked up Matthew's cape and dusted it off.

"What are you going to do with her?" Her green eyes flashed to Aliwyn. "The battle is in two days, and Norwich is a long way from here."

Aliwyn drew a shaking breath. Norwich. Toby had mentioned it, too. It was a place she needed to go. Traveling with Matthew and Reiya might be her safest choice. She'd have to endure the redhead's scorn for Toby's sake.

"Matthew," she said quietly. "Do you have business in Norwich?"

He grinned wryly back at her. "Yes. Dealing with the unfortunate news Jacques talked about."

Reiya sat beside Matthew and spread his cape over his back. "Jacques accused Matthew of deserting the army because he returned to Brocklesby for you."

Aliwyn's fingers dug into her sides as she hugged her torso. She remembered Jacques mentioning this in the forest.

"I'm sorry—" she began.

"It's not your fault. I will clear my name after the battle." Matthew looked at Reiya. "And I won't be seeing His Excellency alone."

Reiya's smile back faded when Aliwyn sat up.

"Please take me with you," Aliwyn said, pushing past her fear. "I can cook. I can clean and—"

"So can any of my warriors," Reiya snapped. Then, in a calmer tone, she added, "I'll direct my galleys to land with the Ulai tribe at the mouth of the Humber. You're both too cold to last all the way to Jethran. The Ulai will give us shelter tonight." With a glance at Aliwyn, she continued. "I'll decide tomorrow if I allow this woman to come with us. She can always sleep in a church."

"Thank you," Aliwyn whispered.

The chief stood and walked away, leaving Aliwyn to nibble on her lip. Something had happened between Reiya and Matthew. Envy twisted the redhead's mouth whenever she spoke to Aliwyn, although he seemed oblivious to it. Yet another problem she didn't need.

Sighing, Aliwyn curled back onto the damp floorboards as Reiya instructed her warriors to carry hudfats, spears, and Edward's body onto another galley. Had they said they needed him for a ritual? Aliwyn dared not imagine what that was like.

The galley creaked with the waves as the steady drip of oars filled her ears. The blanket smelled of bitter herbs. Aliwyn's headache pulsed in time with the rocking ship, but when a Vasfian handed her a basin of fresh water, she forced herself to sit and clean her face and wounds. The thought of spending a night with the Vasfians made her heart race. Yet, their freckles no longer repulsed her. Maybe it was because of what Kato had done to protect her. Aliwyn remembered how he'd extended his freckled hand to help her stand inside the leper's chapel. Perhaps she'd see him again, too.

Those around her murmured in both English and Vasfian. Matthew and Reiya discussed how to have Edward's body examined by a Norman official to document his death. There was talk of Marcottesville and a strange mention of clay *kubozi*. Aliwyn grew still to listen. *Kubozi*s were sacred food balls the redheads made. But *clay kubozi*?

Then it struck her. They were talking about the thundercrashers.

The Vasfians had stolen one chest of thundercrashers. They must be wondering what those things were.

She rubbed Toby's recorder with her thumb. He hadn't asked her to remain silent about what his cargo could do. Maybe he knew she'd be questioned, and he didn't want her to carry that burden.

After what Matthew had done for her, she should tell him what she had seen on board. Perhaps that knowledge would help them fend off the Danes, who were still coming.

Next to her, Matthew stared at the wreckage of the *Lady Fortuna* with his face unreadable. Perhaps he still longed for a victory, but thank Heavens he had failed. If only she could make him see what she had seen in Toby.

"Matthew," she said. "I saw what the Boltans' cargo can do. And those clay balls are called thundercrashers."

He turned, his eyes widening.

"Wait until Reiya can hear this too," he said, glancing toward the chief, who stood at the prow with the sun blazing behind her. "And I'll make sure she lets you come with us."

Aliwyn nodded and forced a smile back. Everywhere she looked, she expected to see Toby rush toward her and pull her into his arms. But he wouldn't today.

The *Lady Fortuna*'s sinking, battered frame appeared to her for the last time as the galley turned for its destination. Remembering the battle between the two men crushed her as though she were grain caught between two millstones. Aelfric must have felt just as torn, just as pained. And the two he had died to save still wouldn't stop fighting.

"What's wrong?" Matthew asked, his voice softer now.

"So much has happened," she whispered.

"I know." He placed a hand on her shoulder, his teeth also chattering. "But you're safe now. I'm just surprised you'd want to come with me." He smirked. "I thought you'd want to go straight home."

"No. My mill's empty." Her lower lip trembled. "There's nothing for me there."

Matthew's hand tightened over her shoulder, and he smiled. "I saw your chickens pecking around a Vasfian hillfort like they own the place."

A startled laugh escaped her, and her breaths quivered with both joy and yearning. Toby had been right about the Vasfians taking them in, and Matthew still remembered her hens.

"We're going to that hillfort tomorrow," Matthew continued. "It's called Jethran. You'll see them."

"Thank you…"

The thought of seeing Clover and her other warm, feathery friends made her smile. Aliwyn's arms twitched with the longing to gather them close and to hear their familiar clucks.

"Try to rest," Matthew murmured. "I'm here."

She closed her eyes, though sleep felt impossible. As the waves lapped against the hull, Aliwyn prayed silently for Toby's safety, and for the strength to reach Norwich and plead not only for justice, but for mercy.

CHAPTER 42
AFIX

Matthew

MATTHEW AWAKENED AS THE anchor's splash shattered the evening silence. His fingers had turned to ice, and he couldn't feel his toes inside his salt-stiffened boots. The sunset's fading light revealed a crescent beach where redheads had gathered, their torches hovering like fireflies. The *Selkie* had reached a rugged stretch of coast where black cliffs rose in the distance. This must be Ulai territory.

Matthew suppressed a yawn and turned. Aliwyn lay curled nearby, her pale face slack with exhaustion. The dark smudges beneath her eyes made his chest tighten. He'd let her rest until the Vasfians finished hauling their oars ashore.

Would she get along with the redheads who helped rescue her?

Matthew stood and shook out his limbs. Reiya was at the stern beside Porei and her mare, their figures silhouetted against the darkening sky. Beyond her, the shadows of Jacques' longships sailed west toward the River Humber. Maybe they were sailing back to Barton-upon-Humber. Toby was still alive on board, and Matthew hardened his jaw. He had done his best to conceal his worries before Aliwyn, but now they came clawing to the forefront.

He approached Reiya with his eyes lowered. "I couldn't shut his mouth. I'm sorry."

She turned with the wind plucking at her braid. "Shut whose mouth?"

"Tobias." The name tasted foul. "And how he made the black matter formula. Now we may see it used in battle, after all."

It was as though he was standing at a cliff's edge, staring at the blackness below. Something harrowing lay just beyond, inevitable but unseen.

Reiya drew her brows. "We both did what we could. I'm starting to understand how no one can stop its use from spreading." She turned to squint at the horizon again. "To be frank with you, I was more terrified by watching you fight Tobias. I kept seeing Aelfric in my memories, fighting that same man. And dying."

When she turned back, the torchlight from the shore glimmered in her wet eyes.

Grief swelled in Matthew's throat. So that was why she had been reluctant to have him battle that English churl. He patted Porei's neck to distract himself. "If Jacques ever lets Tobias Boltan go, I'll hunt him down. Condemn him to death at an inquest."

"Good. Much less risky that way." A smile tugged at her lips, but Matthew didn't understand it. He had failed this time, and there was nothing worth cheering about.

Reiya extended her hand.

"Please give me your sword," she said quietly. "The Ulai will never let you stay otherwise."

It was not his sword, but his father's. And he was unworthy of it. His chest tight, Matthew unstrapped his blade and offered it. Reiya tethered it onto her own belt.

"Thank you for trusting me with your father's possession." Despite the grief lingering in her gaze, her smile was genuine.

So, Reiya had recognized his father's hilt and the lion carved onto it. He mustered a nod. Reiya retrieved a golden torque from her mare's saddle pack and slipped it around her neck.

"Let's go," she said, reaching for her horse's reins. "And I know you did your best today, Matthew."

He drew a deep breath. Her words brought some reassurance. Taking Porei's reins, he followed Reiya toward the ship's bow, which had been moored to a dock.

Aliwyn stirred beneath her blankets as he approached. Her glassy eyes opened when he knelt beside her.

"You strong enough to walk?" Matthew asked.

Aliwyn gave a hesitant nod, and Matthew smiled. At least she was with him now.

As she struggled upright, fear again tightened her features. Her hand emerged from the blanket clutching a wooden object, and Matthew's breath caught.

"You found Aelfric's recorder? How did you—"

"This isn't his." She quickly hid the object beneath the blanket.

Matthew blinked. Had she really hit her head that hard?

"You're confused right now," he said. "We'll talk later."

Aliwyn bit at her already chapped lips. She struggled to stand.

Matthew offered his hand, but she glanced at Reiya standing beside him and shrank away. Aliwyn rose on unsteady legs and dropped the recorder into her belt pouch.

He swallowed hard. Why was she so frightened? If they were to travel together, she had to trust him. And the Vasfians.

"You can ride Porei," he said.

But Aliwyn shook her head and stumbled toward the gangplank.

"I'll lead," Reiya said from behind.

Her brows knit, she squared her shoulders and strode past Matthew. He frowned after her back. What was wrong with *both* of them?

The Ulai tribesmen greeted Reiya with circular hand gestures that made their shell necklaces whisper. Reiya spoke to one elderly man who wore a torque around his neck, then turned to Matthew and said, "This is Fionn, the Ulai chief. His wife will take our mounts from here."

His teeth chattering, Matthew smiled at the unfamiliar faces and handed over Porei's reins. He copied their hand greeting, but Aliwyn only sneezed a few times. Fionn's face was an unreadable roadmap of wrinkles as he spoke to Reiya in their liquid tongue.

When Aliwyn sneezed again, Matthew put his arm around her shoulders.

Her stiffness beneath his touch made his stomach drop. Was it because watching him fight still scared her? Well, she had never seen Aelfric's lethal precision during their sparring matches.

The memory of so many afternoons spent together brought fresh sorrow. Somehow, in his last battle, Aelfric had fallen so readily to Tobias.

Finally, Fionn and Reiya stopped talking. She turned to Matthew with a stern look. "He says you can enter their village, but only if you agree to be blindfolded."

When Matthew pressed his lips together, Reiya added, "We don't have castles, only underground villages. I convinced Fionn to let you both in. I'll walk with you, so don't be afraid. Best you agree right away."

Matthew glanced at the redheads surrounding him. Just days ago, other Vasfians had thrown a bag over his head. Unease clamped his throat at the thought of losing sight again, but these people were his allies.

"Fine," he said. "Blindfold me and..."

He turned to Aliwyn, expecting her to agree, but her bloodshot eyes had rounded in terror. A Vasfian man approached and lowered a linen cloth over her eyes, and she gasped.

"I'm already dizzy," she stammered. "Please, I'll fall if I can't see."

She then said something in Vasfian, but the man tied the cloth behind her head anyway. Aliwyn's shoulders trembled under Matthew's arm. He remembered then how redheads had barged into her home and killed many soldiers outside. Of course she was frightened. He'd been an idiot for forgetting about her last experience with the Vasfians.

Matthew shifted to face her fully and rubbed her shoulders with his thumb. "Please trust me, Aliwyn. They're our allies. Let me carry you, and you won't fall."

Finally, her thin shoulders slumping, Aliwyn nodded.

Matthew pulled her arm over his shoulder and hoisted her onto his back. Reiya's expression remained somber as another man approached Matthew with a linen cloth.

The last thing he saw, before the blindfold descended over his eyes, was Reiya reaching for his upper arm.

"I'll guide you," she said.

He followed the steady push of her hand. The harrowing sense of blindness sent flashes of heat through the chill of his body. The tangling underbrush soon gave way to a dirt road beneath his feet.

Without sight, all his other senses sharpened. There was the clink of seashell pendants as the Vasfians walked. The distant call of gulls circling the beach behind them and the acrid, tallow smoke of the torches. He was led uphill, then downhill, before everyone paused for a break.

As the Ulai tribe whispered amongst themselves, Aliwyn asked, "Why are the people here talking about Aelfric?"

Matthew gulped. He hadn't understood anything the Ulai said, but Aliwyn did.

Reiya grunted. "Indeed, I wonder why?"

Aliwyn was in no condition to hear the truth about Aelfric's heritage. She'd get upset, probably make a scene, and then Reiya wouldn't let her go to Norwich with them.

Matthew couldn't see Reiya, but he turned toward her grip and whispered, "Later. Not tonight."

In a louder voice, he said, "Aliwyn, once we get changed, tell us about the clay *kubozi*."

She adjusted her arms around his neck. "I will."

Neither woman spoke about Aelfric again. *Good.* Matthew's panting roared in his ears as Aliwyn's weight reminded him of the responsibility he carried. Now that he'd rescued her, he wanted to keep her safe. He pressed onward.

The air turned damp and thick with the scent of wet stone and iron-rich soil. A grinding noise shook the ground as hidden stone dragged against stone. As though swallowed by the earth, the outside noises vanished. The mineral undercurrent of a hot spring nearby crept up Matthew's nose. Footsteps echoed differently now as they bounced off closed walls.

Her grip tightening, Reiya said, "Careful. Take a step up."

Matthew lifted his boot onto a ledge he couldn't see. As he set it down again, relieved to find footing, the entrance behind him sealed shut with an echoing thud.

His blindfold was finally pulled off. Matthew blinked as Reiya passed the cloth back to its owner. Warriors clad in padded vests stood guard at the entrance with spears in their hands, and they stared at Matthew. Was it the first time Outsiders had been here?

Beyond them, the tunnel split into three passages. The amber torchlight illuminated the intricate vines spiraling around their openings.

"Welcome to Ulai Gorem." Reiya gestured toward the leftmost tunnel where the walls bore handprints in red ochre. "I'll take you to the hot springs first. Men and women bathe separately."

Matthew shifted Aliwyn's weight on his back. "Who will watch Aliwyn?"

"Me," Reiya said, touching the bronze torque at her throat. "I promise you she won't be harmed, but do not wander anywhere without an escort." She pointed to a suspiciously smooth section of the floor. "The Gorem has traps everywhere for invaders."

Matthew raised an eyebrow. "Understood."

They moved deeper into the maze of tunnels. Clay figurines of stags with enormous antlers stood within recesses carved into the wall. The ceiling bore soot marks from past torches as well as ventilation shafts. Horses neighing and dogs barking echoed from somewhere out of sight, and the scent of roasting fish came and went. The entire village must've retreated within these caverns in preparation for the Danish assault.

Matthew stared at the veins of quartz that glittered like frozen starlight overhead. Was this how the Vasfians had survived the Norsemen raids for centuries? They had done well, and it was an honor to be granted entry.

The sound of rushing water grew louder as they descended. Heated air washed over them with the scent of minerals. Matthew passed between the shell garlands hanging from the entrance of the next chamber.

He and the Vasfians emerged onto the shores of an underground lake. Its steaming surface reflected dozens of oil lamps that hung from bronze hooks. Carvings of entwined serpents and oak leaves lined the walls, and Matthew fought the urge to gawk at everything.

His stomach now rumbled with hunger, but he had to wait.

Reiya gestured to a stack of folded blankets and clean tunics by the water. "Set Aliwyn down here."

Matthew eased her onto her feet. To his dismay, her brows were drawn in uncertainty as she clutched her blanket tighter. All around them, Vasfians murmured about Afix.

"Leave her now," Reiya said. "She needs to bathe, and so do you."

Aliwyn

It was maddening to hear the Vasfian pronunciation of Aelfric's name whispered everywhere. What were Matthew and Reiya trying to hide? All the same, Aliwyn smiled at the young Norman man who watched her with concern.

"Thank you, Matthew," she said. "I'll tell you about the clay *kubozi* soon."

Matthew glanced back at her as he followed two Vasfian men toward another pool in the massive cavern. Steam hung thick in the cave and muffled his footsteps.

Despite the heat, chills swarmed Aliwyn's scalp at being left with Reiya. She breathed again when the chief turned to two Ulai women and said, "Watch her."

Reiya strode behind a large rock protruding from the water, probably to bathe. Aliwyn shed her blanket and belt and waded into the pool fully clothed. Questions about Aelfric burned in her mind. As she emerged from the pool, the Ulai women presented her with a dark green dress and bandages. Aliwyn slid between rocky projections on land to change and dress her neck's injury.

She opened her belt pouch and fingered the recorder and Edward's signet ring, both safe inside. The instrument brought back both Aelfric's and Toby's faces, and she blinked back tears.

Aelfric had visited the Ulai tribe before. She could feel it. But why? As she emerged in her new clothes, she asked the two women, "How come you know Aelfric?"

"Not even a 'thank you' for the hospitality?" came Reiya's voice behind her.

Aliwyn whirled around. The chief stood in a blood-red dress with a thick torque encircling her neck.

"I'm sorry," Aliwyn said quietly. "I was just thinking of many things. I...I am grateful."

Reiya's eyes flashed to her belt pouch, still open, with Toby's recorder protruding from it. Aliwyn's heart fluttered in her throat. She pushed the recorder deeper down and pulled the drawstrings taut. This woman couldn't possibly know this instrument belonged to Toby, could she?

Matthew appeared around the stony path and drew Reiya's attention. *Thank Heavens.* Aliwyn needed to tell him and Reiya about the thundercrashers, and questions about Aelfric would have to wait.

Matthew looked thinner than she remembered. It was also odd to see him wear a Vasfian red and green checkered mantle, but his deep brown eyes remained the same, always carrying a hint of longing.

As he walked within earshot, Reiya crossed her arms and said, "Aliwyn, tell us about the Boltans' cargo."

Aliwyn laced her fingers. Whatever she said now, she must not reveal Toby's relationship with her. "The rebels carried clay spheres they called thundercrashers. They were filled with potash compound."

Matthew's brow furrowed. "*What* compound?"

Reiya answered first. "Potash. That must be what you called 'black matter.'"

Matthew nodded thoughtfully, and Aliwyn explained how the thundercrashers could be activated by lighting their cork stoppers. She recounted the battle Toby fought against Vincent, careful to leave out Toby's name and simply referring to "the crew."

Both Matthew and Reiya scowled at her.

"By the Devil's tail," Matthew muttered. "All the knights are useless against those clay...I mean, thundercrashers."

"Not just the knights." Reiya twisted the side of her dress. "The gods help us when those things enter the battlefield."

Aliwyn drew a slow breath. Matthew and Reiya seemed to want the black matter destroyed, just like Toby did. If only they'd stop tearing each other apart. If only she could make them see...

"You probably noticed there was no cargo on Tobias' ship," Aliwyn said. "It's because he threw it overboard. He said no one in England should have weapons so powerful."

Matthew and Reiya exchanged glances. Neither asked why Toby had done such an honorable thing, and Aliwyn wrung her hands.

Reiya tilted her head. "You must've spoken to Tobias. A lot."

"I eavesdropped," Aliwyn said, her shoulders stiff. "I wanted to gather information in case I came back."

Reiya raised an eyebrow. "So what exactly happened on that ship?"

Aliwyn hesitated, then began. She told them about sabotaging the rigging. About Ransley's injury and Edward dragging him to Driftmere for help. A Norman stowaway who axed a hole in the hull and almost killed her. The ship sinking.

Matthew's eyes widened. "Wait, you cut the ship's rigging?"

"Yes. I stole Ransley Boltan's knife to do it."

"You threw their surcoats overboard, too," Matthew said, grinning. "The Ahitan tribe found them and reported to Reiya."

Aliwyn sucked in a breath. "I...yes. I sewed those surcoats, and I cast them out." She flinched as she remembered an important detail. "I also killed Edward. I have his signet ring."

Reiya grunted. "*You* killed Edward?"

"Yes." Aliwyn calmly reached into her belt pouch, withdrew the ring, and displayed it.

Matthew only stared at her in bewilderment, and Reiya rolled her eyes. Aliwyn fought to keep her composure. They didn't believe her. What if the officials in Norwich didn't believe her, either? But she had no time to dwell on her dread, not with the redhead still questioning her.

"Anything else you care to share?" Reiya asked.

Aliwyn blinked as the memories returned. Toby's arm around her while they slept in the hudfat. The heat of his kiss still lingering on her lips...

"There's nothing," she whispered.

Reiya's mouth curved, but it wasn't a smile. She switched to Vasfian. "Then tell me why that recorder you're trying to hide isn't Aelfric's. His was carved from darker wood."

A wave of chills swept over Aliwyn. It was all she could do to stay calm.

Reiya twirled a strand of red hair on her finger. "Years ago, Miriam made a nearly identical recorder for a boy with a broken arm. Sound familiar?"

Aliwyn's face went numb. Reiya knew Toby from his stay in Brocklesby. She knew about his instrument.

Matthew only shuffled his feet as he listened to their exchange in Vasfian.

Reiya glanced at him, then said, "You think I didn't notice, Aliwyn? How you protected your lover on that ship, the look of longing between you two. You're not going to Norwich for us. You're going for that rebel. And the only reason I haven't exposed you—" Her voice caught. "Is because the truth would break the man beside you."

Matthew stepped forward with a scowl. "Reiya, Aliwyn found Aelfric's recorder first. Let her keep it."

Reiya gave a hollow laugh, then continued in Vasfian, "This squire is kind but blind. Painfully good at suffering for people, especially you. He promised Aelfric he'd protect you. That promise became his obsession, his way of staying sane." She dipped her chin, her gaze piercing. "But if you care about him at all, leave tomorrow and never return. Or I'll make sure you disappear."

Aliwyn's pulse pounded, but she met those green eyes with the same unyielding frost.

Reiya adjusted the torque around her neck and said in English, "Of course Aliwyn can keep the recorder. Let's go to your rooms."

Aliwyn could scarcely breathe. Her headache from being slammed against the ship's rail intensified as Reiya led her and Matthew through the tunnels, passing countless Vasfian guards.

The sounds of children laughing and a harp and recorder duet echoed around them. Despite the cheerful melody, Aliwyn fisted her hands. What would she do now? Without Matthew's protection, could she still reach Norwich?

Matthew glanced at the other two and cleared his throat. "This music...Is there a special occasion tonight?"

"For the couple playing, yes." Reiya remained somber. "Only married women play harp amongst my people. That couple is performing to announce they're expecting a child."

"Can we stop and listen a while?" Matthew asked.

"No, you need to eat." Reiya widened her stride, her damp hair swaying in time with her steps.

Matthew looked at Aliwyn and shrugged. She mustered a small grin in return. Thank goodness he was willfully blind. Yet, her stomach knotted with pity.

Two sleeping alcoves waited in a quiet side passage. Aliwyn's featured a wool blanket, dyed with spirals of red and green, that hung across the entrance. Matthew's opposite space held a simple pallet and a stone basin of water.

A man brought them a shallow straw basket with what looked like two glistening black bricks flecked with pale grains sitting on dried kelp. Beside it were wooden cups with shriveled purple berries and honey on the side.

"This is your supper," Reiya said. "Seal-blood pudding mixed with fermented oats and juniper." She pulled off a piece and ate it. "Boiled in its own gut, then seared on the stones. A warrior's meal."

She grinned, but all color drained from Matthew's face.

"Thank you," Aliwyn said. "I'll take my share and leave you two."

She reached in to grab a blood pudding. The food smelled strange, a mix of honey and rusty metal, but she didn't care.

"You're not staying to eat with us?" Matthew asked.

"No—"

Reiya tilted her head. "Don't you want to know why the Ulai know Aelfric?"

Aliwyn dropped the blood pudding back in the basket and backed away. "I..."

"Reiya, not now." Matthew frowned at her.

But Reiya ignored him. "Aelfric was a half-blood. Both his grandmothers were Vasfian."

Aliwyn gasped, and Reiya narrowed her eyes as she continued, "For years, you tormented him with your prejudices. So much that he confided in me. He lived with my people and visited every tribe for two months each winter."

Aliwyn began to shake, and she couldn't stop. The world seemed to darken for a moment. All those quiet afternoons when Aelfie withdrew now made sense. How he'd stopped holding her hand or dancing with her. And when he vanished into the Vasfian forest...was it to see Reiya?

Aelfie's final visit played again in Aliwyn's mind. No wonder he had so readily recruited Reiya's tribe to help rescue Matthew. Aelfie had carried so many secrets. And yet, after what she'd learned from Toby, nothing surprised her anymore.

Reiya smirked. "Aelfric wanted to court you but didn't dare reveal he was half-Vasfian. He finally left Brocklesby and called you his 'sister,' probably to survive the heartbreak."

Reiya's smile grew while the ache in Aliwyn's throat threatened to choke her. *That insufferable woman.*

With hot tears streaming, Aliwyn darted toward the hole that was her room. Matthew shouted her name, but she kept running. Sobs tore from her chest as she flung aside the cloth covering the entrance and ducked into her room.

The small space had nothing but a turnip lantern and a straw pallet. Aliwyn grasped at her hair and paced the room. It was her own fault that Aelfie had never asked for her hand. Her fault. If only she could tell him the Vasfians' freckles no longer disgusted her, that she'd change how she treated the tribes...

Aelfie, I'm sorry. I'm—

She almost shrieked when a figure appeared before her. Matthew.

"Hey," he murmured, holding out a kelp-wrapped pudding and a bowl of berries.

Aliwyn backed away and hugged herself. Now that he was alone with her, Reiya would be furious. Yet, before she could send him away, Matthew said, "You should eat. And...can I stay a while? I want to tell you something."

Aliwyn wiped her face. There was something about this towering Norman soldier, gazing at her with sincere sympathy, that made her quiver. He was no longer the obnoxious man pounding on her watermill's door and yelling to get in. She couldn't bear to make him leave.

Her legs weak, she staggered to the straw pallet and sat. Matthew set down the food and sat across from her on the ground. He scratched the scabs on his hand. "I felt the same when I found out Aelfric was half-Vasfian."

Aliwyn stifled a sob and couldn't speak.

Matthew continued. "I used to call the redheads only good for target practice. And other awful things."

It was as though they'd returned to the Brocklesby mill to talk about Aelfie again. Yet, for a long time, neither of them spoke as lights and shadows danced on the walls. Aelfric's recorder music drifted in Aliwyn's memories, and her eyes blurred between each blink.

Finally, Matthew cleared his throat. "Something that helped me..."

His voice faltered. She thought of reaching for his shoulder, but she couldn't move.

"Yes?" she whispered.

"I...I remember how Aelfric remained our friend till the end." The turnip light flickered in Matthew's damp eyes. Aliwyn braced her knees as he whispered, "I think that means he forgave us, even if he had to forgive us every day. And he wouldn't want us drowning in guilt."

Aliwyn drew a slow breath. Aelfie's arms seemed to wrap around her one more time. He spun her in a circle, even if it was just her headache making her dizzy. His laughter rang again in her ears.

She smiled despite her tears. Yes, Aelfie must've forgiven her a thousand times.

"And I know now you aren't his sister," Matthew murmured. "Sorry about ignoring you back in Brocklesby. But...but if you ever want an older brother, I'm here."

Aliwyn picked at the green Vasfian dress she wore, one that was too large for her. She could never become that close to him, but to reject him now would be heartless.

"Thank you, Matthew," she said softly.

"Call me Matt. That's what Aelfric called me."

He grinned, but the sorrow in his eyes remained. Dipping his chin, he scratched his hand again. Aliwyn remembered then how Emma had bitten him, and how anguished he'd been over her loss. That felt like so long ago.

"That was all I wanted to say," he said, sighing as he pushed himself to stand. "We have a long day tomorrow. Good night."

"Wait." She paused until he turned to her. "I have something to tell you, too. The child who bit you was on Tobias' ship. She was alive and well."

He blinked, then shuffled his boots. "Really? But I didn't see her."

"Tobias sent her away in a rowboat. To Scotland." Her voice trembled with the longing to embrace the girl again. "Emma survived the fall. You don't have to blame yourself anymore."

Matthew ran a hand over his face, and his smile brightened. "Thanks. Thanks for telling me that."

"No need to thank me. I should've thanked you earlier for rescuing me."

The calm joy in his eyes made her chest tighten. What had happened to him these past few days?

And the longer she stared at him, the deeper her grief gnawed at her. Although she might resent Reiya, the redhead had been right. Matthew would be devastated if Aliwyn's love for Toby ever came to light. It would bring out the terrifying side she'd seen of him on the *Lady Fortuna*.

She couldn't keep accepting his protection knowing she aimed to save the man he hated. Toby had given her four pennies, enough for boarding ferries and wagons to Norwich. Alone.

Tomorrow, she'd have to come up with an excuse not to travel with Matthew.

Clearing her throat, Aliwyn said, "Good night. And tell Reiya what you told me. That you want to be my brother."

"I'm sure she knows al—"

"No, she doesn't, and it's bothering her."

His eyes rounded. "Oh. Then I'll go make that clear."

Aliwyn hung her head as Matthew strode out of the room. He was a good person, but one who wanted Toby dead. Aelfric had perished caught in between them both, and she didn't want the same fate. The best thing she could do for Matthew, and for herself, was to disappear from his life.

Kneeling on her bed, she sought Toby's recorder again and hugged the delicate object to her chest. She couldn't save Aelfric, but she clung to hope she could save Toby.

Tomorrow, in whatever village Matthew and Reiya left her, she'd buy a fishing spear.

CHAPTER 43
"A" FOR ALLIANCE

Matthew

THE FOOD BASKET HAD been discarded by the time Matthew exited Aliwyn's room. Only a Vasfian guard, picking idly at her nails, stood beside it. Matthew's shoulders slumped.

"Reiya?" he called out. "I need to talk to you."

"I'm here," she called from his left.

Matthew spun around. She sat on a stool within a recess of the wall and held a bean bag compress against her stomach.

Matthew stepped toward her. "You all right?"

"I will be." She stood slowly and left the bean bag on the stool. "So, why should I know that Aliwyn's only a sister to you?"

She smiled, and Matthew's back stiffened. So, she had overheard. Aliwyn's alcove had no door.

Matthew shuffled his feet. "I just wanted to make everything clear..."

His voice faltered. Reiya was walking toward him, the scarlet of her form-fitting dress a vibrant splash against the dim cavern. Her copper tresses shimmered with gold in the fire's glow. Without warning, the tingly feeling Matthew had felt before the *Anuin* shot down his back again.

He was gawking like a fool. Matthew cleared his throat. "A-anyway, Aliwyn's like my adopted sister now. I want her to come with us to Norwich."

A frown tinged with sorrow descended over Reiya's face. *Now* what had he done wrong? Ducking his head, Matthew grabbed the basket.

By the time he looked up again, Reiya's expression had cooled to a calm indifference. "Let's see if Aliwyn still wants to go tomorrow." She gestured to the basket by his feet. "Enjoy your meal. I just stayed to say good night."

Reiya turned and walked away. Matthew stared at her back with his chest squeezing. Ending the day like this felt wrong. Reiya was already twenty paces ahead when he sprang after her, the basket swinging with each stride.

Finally, he caught onto her shoulder. "Wait. Please stay and eat with me."

They stood in the middle of a stone corridor with one brass lamp hanging from the ceiling and a beaten stool. Matthew's face burned. He might as well have asked Reiya to dine in a dungeon.

Yet, she smiled at him. "I wasn't hungry, but I'll finish whatever you can't."

"No, we split the pudding," he stammered, lowering the basket.

What was he trying to accomplish by having her stay? They could only remain friends.

With shaky fingers, he picked up the blood pudding, broke it in two, and passed Reiya the bigger half. Then he sat cross-legged on the ground and grimaced at the black brick he held. It smelled revolting, like urine on hot metal. Holding his breath, he took a bite. The outside was crumbly, while the inside was dense with fat and oats. It tasted better after chewing for a long time.

Reiya spread out her dress as she sat across from him.

"How do you like the blood pudding?" she asked.

Matthew swallowed. "It...looks bad, smells bad, but isn't so bad at the end."

She grinned as she nibbled on her food, then chuckled.

"Something funny?" he asked.

"Well." Her eyes sparkled beneath the firelight. "I recently met a man who matches that same description."

Matthew wanted to laugh, but his ribs were too stiff. He had been so obnoxious a few nights ago he didn't want to think about it. And that tingly feeling down his back was becoming worse. He shoved another bite into his mouth.

Music from the harp and recorder duet echoed faintly around them. Reiya picked up berries from the bowl. Cupping them in her hand, she said, "So, how do your people celebrate the birth of a child?"

Matthew uncorked his costrel and pretended to drink for a long time. It was a terrible idea to ask her to stay. He wanted to stare at her like an idiot.

"Well, there are parties." He struggled to sound casual. "Lots of food, honey wine, dancing."

"That sounds fun."

"For other people, yes. I found them too noisy, so I avoided them. Aelfric would sneak me honey cakes, and we'd eat by the lake or swim. If it rained, we played chess in the servants' quarters." Matthew grinned at the memories, then sighed. "Maybe I shouldn't have done that to Aelfric. Making him stay around me all the time probably kept him from finding someone to marry."

He looked back at Reiya and froze. Grief had tightened her face again, the opposite of what he'd hoped to do.

"Maybe we shouldn't talk about Aelfric," she whispered.

"Right, we..."

He reached for her shoulder. Tears also stung his eyes.

"How about..." he paused, grateful for the idea that came to him. "How about I teach you how to read and write in English?"

The hint of a smile returned to her face. "Really? It seems difficult."

"It doesn't have to be. I'll first teach you the words used in courier messages. I have a text in my belt—"

Then he froze. The Vasfian clothes had fit him so snugly that he hadn't worn his belt again.

Reiya leaned closer. "What text?"

Matthew couldn't answer. His belt. The soaked, forgotten belt was still hanging by the bathing pools.

"My father's letter," he whispered.

He could already see the ink bleeding across the parchment. *By the Devil's tail.* He hadn't taken it off when he dove after Aliwyn. Matthew dropped his unfinished food in the basket and pushed to his feet.

"I need to—" But even as he said it, he knew it was too late. The damage was done. His fingers curled into useless fists at his sides.

Reiya gathered up the basket and stood, her brows drawn with concern. Grasping his wrist, she said, "Let's go back to the pools."

A QUICK GLANCE AT the crumpled letter was all Matthew could stand. With a shaky hand, he passed the parchment to Reiya as she stood on the shoreline with guards flanking on either side.

"Gone," he croaked. "Sorry."

Around the bend, laughter and splashes echoed from another pool. The joyful noises rang sharp and jarring in his ears.

Reiya smoothed the wet parchment on her hand.

"I see a few words," she said softly. "Can you rewrite it from memory? I'll find you a quill and ink."

Matthew shook his head. First, there had been a humiliating battle, and now this. Just another loss in a trail of failures.

"I don't remember the message," he murmured.

She took his hand and placed the parchment on his palm. "When you wake up tomorrow, maybe you will."

Matthew couldn't answer. The soaked parchment trembled in his grasp. His bite wound had scabbed over, but pain lingered beneath the surface.

Reiya's fingers brushed his elbow. "Come with me. I know where we can hear the music better."

She lifted the basket of food and guided him up another winding path. The clamor of people bathing grew distant. They descended toward a circle of logs surrounding a large bonfire, whose glow bathed the cavern walls in amber. There, a smaller pool reflected the seashell garlands that hung from the domed ceiling.

The weathered log groaned as Matthew slumped onto it and set the parchment aside to dry. Reiya placed another piece of firewood into the flames. As sparks flew skyward, she bowed her head in what looked like prayer.

Matthew chewed on his tongue. Now he had nothing to help Reiya read. He'd better leave before he made another mistake.

But she turned to him and said, "Please stand up."

Her voice was kind, but Matthew looked up with a lump in his throat. "Why?" he whispered.

She smiled and extended her hand. "Just stand for a moment."

With a stiff arm, he reached for her hand. Reiya pulled him up, her eyes sparkling in the firelight. They held a gentleness that he couldn't look away from. Then she slipped her arms around his waist and embraced him.

"So I can do this," she whispered close to his ear.

Matthew sucked in his breath as her hands slid up his back and remained there. Her warmth seeped into his chest, and the scent of wild roses from her hair made him dizzy.

"I'm sorry about your father, about your family," she murmured. "I wanted to wait until after the war to tell you how he'd changed."

Her cheek was soft against his neck. He scarcely had the sense to respond, "Not your fault. It's my fault for not going back."

"Aelfric told me about the things he used to do. I don't blame you for not returning."

Matthew's jaw trembled. He dared to reach behind her back and return her embrace. Reiya's hair felt like silk, and her chest rose against his as she breathed. As firelight glinted off the iridescent shell garlands overhead, the harp and recorder's melody swelled and enveloped them. For the first time since Aelfric's death, the weight in his chest didn't feel like grief. It was something fiercer, something that made his hands shake as they traced the curls at the small of her back. But knowing he couldn't take her home after the revolt still clawed at him.

Reiya drew back and rested a hand on his forearm. "Forgiving yourself is often the hardest part, but tomorrow needs you more than yesterday."

Matthew managed a nod as she continued. "Thanks for being patient with me and my family. I know we haven't been easy."

Matthew smirked. He covered her hand with his own, but he wanted to do more. In the days to come, on the way to Norwich, this urge would only intensify.

He remained silent when Reiya beckoned him to sit down. She offered him the contents of the basket, and Matthew picked up his unfinished food with both fear and yearning wrangling within him.

Reiya watched the Samhain bonfire with her long eyelashes glowing in the amber light. When the revolt was over, would he still have a chance to see her like this? Finally, he resolved to do what he never thought he'd do.

He swallowed the last of his brick and asked hoarsely, "Do you like this music?"

She smiled. "Yes. It's called the Melody of Life, and I love it."

"Was the music at the convent also something you enjoyed? Because—" His breath caught as her knees angled toward him. "Because every Sunday there's music where I train. And in Marcottesville too, so if you..."

His stomach flipped, but Reiya murmured, "Go ahead."

"So if you come to mass with me sometime, I'd love that."

Heat flooded his face. Reiya's lips parted slightly before she turned to the fire.

"I doubt someone who looks like me is welcome," she whispered. "Even the convent was...well, not all the sisters wanted me there."

Matthew swallowed. "Then I'll stand beside you until they see you as I do. You'll be my guest."

"Th-thank you." A dimple appeared in her cheek as she smiled, but her fingers tugged at her torque like a prisoner testing a noose. Sweat prickled his temples.

Finally, she said, "Please...let me think about it."

"That's all I ask."

The longing in her eyes told him she understood what he'd tried to do. His pulse hammered against his ribs.

"Still want to learn reading tonight?" he asked.

"Absolutely." Her face lit up.

Matthew picked up his father's letter. Some words were indeed still discernible, but once he washed out the salt, everything might disappear. Reiya's presence kept his grief from overtaking him again.

Then one phrase emerged, clear as a blade's edge: *Your weapons won't save you. Only alliances with the right people can.*

Matthew blinked. It was the first sentence that had returned to him. A good start.

"Can I see your hand?" he asked.

With an amused smile, Reiya offered it to him. Her calloused but warm hand curled slightly against his fingers as he turned it upward.

"A for alliance," he said, tracing the capital letter on her palm. "Can you imagine it?"

"Yes," she whispered.

Matthew taught her all the vowels and the spelling of a few common words. Reiya learned quickly. Maybe by the end of their journey to Norwich, which could take a week, she'd know how to write a full sentence.

The flame's glow danced over her features as she bent over their joined hands, her focus so intense, he could almost forget tomorrow's uncertainties. When the fire grew dim, he helped Reiya feed it more firewood before following her back to his alcove.

Within the dark tunnels, the reality they both faced gnawed its way back. Would the Danes still land at Ravenser's Point after Norman longships had surrounded Driftmere?

"Thank you for this evening," Reiya said as they stopped before his chamber.

He smiled. "You're welcome." His lips twitching, Matthew continued, "But maybe I kept you awake for too long. Tomorrow we need to deliver Edward's body to Marcottesville for inspection, then to Jethran for your family. And the Danes...maybe they'll decide to land somewhere else."

Shadows pooled in the hollow of her throat as she turned toward him. "This is why tonight matters even more."

Her eyes carried the same fear as when he'd fought Tobias earlier that day. Now he understood why, but she had no reason to be afraid. Matthew reached around her shoulders and drew her close. "I'll be with you. I promise."

Reiya leaned against him, and her warmth added to his own. Somewhere beyond the caverns, war still waited. But here, with the rise of her breath against his, Matthew could imagine a different future. One where alliances outlasted weapons.

Epilogue: Hope

October 4, Toby

THE WORLD HAD NARROWED to the scrape of his boots against gravel, the burn of thirst in his throat, and Jacques' grip on the rope around his wrists. Toby stumbled forward, his eyes stinging from the sand Matthew had thrown. A night without water had turned his tongue to leather. It was now morning, but the sky above Barton remained a dusky gray. The scent of damp earth and woodsmoke clung to the wooden palisades of Barton-upon-Humber.

Toby was pushed through the open gates. A sharp pull yanked him forward, and the last of his strength gave out. His knees hit the dirt first, then his shoulder. Pain flared where Matthew had slashed his jawline.

Anguish roiled within him. He had surrendered without drawing a weapon. The law granted him a hearing, but he wouldn't last a week without water. If Aliwyn didn't find the right person to plead for him, and fast...

Jacques sighed. His figure loomed overhead, his hair unkempt and eyes bloodshot. "Remember, *you* are the one making both our lives difficult. Now, will you speak to me?"

Toby glowered at him. Silence was all he had left.

A boot slammed into his ribs. Pain exploded through his side, and this time, he couldn't swallow the cry that tore from him. Toby slumped onto his side. The next strike was coming. He could sense it, hear Jacques shifting his stance.

"Stop! Children are playing nearby!"

A familiar woman's voice cut through the haze. Toby tried to turn his head, but his body wouldn't obey. Then she stepped into view, her brown dress brushing over the mud. Behind her trailed a little girl who caught onto her hand. His breath hitched.

Evelyn.

She looked different with her dark hair bound neatly beneath a linen veil. Beside her stood her sister, Marie. His chest heaved. He hadn't seen her since the attack on the Marcottes' ship. The child shrank against Evelyn's robe, her small face pinched with fear.

Toby's lips moved soundlessly. Evelyn. Marie.

Evelyn's eyes rounded as shock flashed across her face. Yet, that expression shuttered quickly as Jacques straightened and patted down his hair.

"Miss Marcotte," he cleared his throat. "Please excuse this...unpleasantness."

Evelyn drew a slow breath. "Sir Verdun. Pardon me for not recognizing you, but please don't do this before our young ones."

"I'm simply enforcing justice," Jacques said as he stepped on Toby's fingers, making him flinch. "Since Tobias Boltan is now in my custody, Matthew has lost his chance to redeem himself. He remains a deserter."

Toby clenched his teeth as pain shot up his fingers. Evelyn...she didn't deserve this...

Evelyn spoke in a cool voice. "Nothing is settled until my cousin is heard in court."

"But how will he defend himself?" Jacques asked. "Matthew has done absolutely nothing of value. And when he is stripped of his knighthood, your father's and uncle's manors, and everything inside, will revert to His Excellency. He'll entrust it to someone worthy. Someone loyal."

Toby struggled to see through his tears. This scoundrel was lying. Only the land would get confiscated, not everything inside.

"Where is Matthew?" Evelyn asked.

"Off somewhere, indulging in Vasfian women," Jacques said. His heel finally lifted from Toby's fingers, and he gasped for air.

The knight strolled toward Evelyn, smiling, and clasped his hands behind his back. His voice had become a velvety purr. "As for you, have you thought about what I asked before we parted in Brocklesby? My marriage proposal?"

Jacques had proposed *what?* Toby's arms twitched, but he couldn't sit up.

Evelyn's voice faltered for the first time. "I'm already engaged to someone in Normandy."

"And yet here you are, alone," Jacques said, still smiling. "Your father cannot enforce that engagement anymore, so why not allow yourself a comfortable life in England? I can offer you stability, safety."

The churl, still dripping honey from his fangs! Indignation surged in Toby's chest.

"He's lying," he rasped. Jacques spun toward him, but Toby continued. "The furniture is still yours. The animals are also—"

Another kick landed on his chest. Toby groaned and turned his face toward the ground, shuddering.

"Found your voice again, Sir Boltan?" Jacques muttered.

Toby fought to breathe. Evelyn hadn't been taught the complicated laws of inheritance. A male relative was always supposed to guide her, but Matthew had been a wayward student, and now...

Jacques cleared his throat. "Miss Marcotte, I assure you that you and your sister will live a life of luxury with me." In a harsher tone, he said, "Take the prisoner inside."

Rough hands hauled Toby to his feet. As they dragged him down the road, he twisted to meet Evelyn's gaze one last time.

She didn't smile, but neither did she look away. Turning to another woman, she passed Marie into her care.

Then she began walking down the road, toward him.

Toby's eyes watered again. Perhaps she was only coming to argue with Jacques. But she was walking toward Toby, not away, and that stirred something fragile but fierce inside him.

Hope.

Would You Kindly Leave a Review?

Reviews are the lifeblood of indie authors. They encourage us to keep writing and help our books get discovered. Your review is unique and so greatly appreciated!

Please write a review for *Traitor's Heart* on <u>Amazon</u>, <u>Goodreads</u>, and/or <u>Bookbub</u>.

Thank you!

Medical Note

Ransley's Sporadic Breathing

Called Cheyne-Stokes respiration, this phenomenon is seen in patients with increased intracranial pressure and other serious conditions. In Ransley's case, a slow accumulation of blood within his skull (a subdural hemorrhage) would explain the symptoms he exhibited in *Healer's Blade* that culminated in his death.

I am grateful to my colleague, a medicolegal autopsy expert, who helped me expand the scene of Ransley's last breaths.

THE ADVENTURE CONTINUES...

ENEMY'S KEEPER BOOK THREE

Visit KyrieWang.com or subscribe to my newsletter for the latest updates on
Rogue's Rising (Enemy's Keeper Book 3).
All books/audiobooks of the Enemy's Keeper series can be found at <u>Books</u>
<u>.KyrieWang.com</u>
Thank you for reading!

About the Author

By day, Kyrie is a medical sleuth (also known as a pathologist, MD) in a small mining town in Quebec, Canada. By night, she scrawls story inspirations on various notebooks by her bed. These eventually become novels with medical intrigue sprinkled throughout!

She has been writing fiction since age nine and has always been fascinated by the tales of loyalty, redemption, and sacrifice from the Middle Ages. Few things excite her more than attending medieval fairs and cheering for jousting knights.

Her character-driven stories feature nuanced protagonists, rivetting adventure, forbidden romance, and ordinary people who discover extraordinary courage from within. When she's not writing, she enjoys Zumba dancing and cycling with her husband and daughter.

www.ingramcontent.com/pod-product-compliance
Lightning Source LLC
Chambersburg PA
CBHW030918120726
47906CB00002B/391